AMAZING

HEART

AMAZING

Heart

Broken Bottles Series: Book 4

Pamela Taeuffer

OPEN
HEART
PRESS

Published 2016
United States of America

This book is also available in print.

For more information e-mail: PamelaTaeuffer@gmail.com

Amazing Heart is dedicated to all the women in my family who, in their hearts were mustangs trying to run free, but were captive within their generational chains of dysfunction. May women and men everywhere shake their hair, stomp down their fences, and be unafraid with an open heart. I truly believe in order to walk out of our shadows, we have to take baby steps and eventually risk the hurt and reward of what could be. May you walk into the light of risk and transition into the joy of a life you could never imagine was possible.

To Dad and Denise, I have felt you guys each day through this process.
Claude, Aaron, I love you.
All the mustangs that have come before me—because of your life's twists, turns, bruises and rewards, you have freed me.
Thank you for your sacrifice.

WARNING:

Nicky here.

This book is part of an ongoing series with steep cliffs.

Hang in there!

There is a very good reason for them. When coming home to face my family's battle with alcoholism, I never knew what waited behind the front door—just turning the doorknob was an exercise in fear.

I know from living with my family's addiction that:

- Good things will end.
- My opinions don't matter.
- Peace never lasts.
- Those who love me will abandon me.

This is my family's saga and what we endured to break the chains of dysfunction and my love story: love of friends, parents, siblings, those relationships that give us life lessons and of lovers. This is about intimacy in all levels. Despite the lack of trust I have for others I'm desperate to have it. I'm only eighteen, but my entire life I've longed for the sweet touch of someone who wasn't afraid, raging, or drunk. I want joy.

Be patient, please. I formed years of bad habits, fears, and irrational behavior while trying to survive my dysfunctional family. This is my story.

Authors really need your review and I'm asking you to please leave one on Amazon and Goodreads.

Here are the links:

Amazon: bit.ly/AmazingHeart

Goodreads: bit.ly/GoodreadsAmazingHeart

The Story So Far

I am a woman who has just come of age.

I was raised in a family battling alcoholism.

It has affected me in ways I'm only beginning to discover.

The fears are horrible. They resonate inside me. They vibrate every minute, reminding me I am living my life being afraid . . . of abandonment, of the hammer dropping, of the next bad thing happening, that I'll never be good enough, my emotions will never be normal, I won't ever be empathetic to sorrow and hurt, and can't open myself to intimacy and vulnerability.

I want love. I want to be loved. I want deep, sensual, vibrant, jagged, raw and gorgeous love—the kind I'll never forget, the kind I'll never stop searching for.

Sometimes my father rages—and when he's drunk, he gets angry and sarcastic. When he's drunk, it can be physically abusive. When he's drunk, he's always mentally abusive.

My mother is the classic co-dependent in every way. She even rations Dad's whiskey shots to make sure he doesn't drive to the store or bar. Now that I am coming into adulthood, I can see how she used alcohol to keep him numb and under her control. An ally in alcoholism doesn't really want the addicted person to recover—that will change everything.

My name is Nicky Young.

I'm trying hard to break out of the dysfunctional cages in which generations of my family—especially women—have been trapped.

The result? Detachment. Running at the first sign of trouble. Cutting someone off without first listening to an explanation.

The chains around us are locked tight.

The beginnings of intimacy are knocking at my door. Ryan Tilton, a professional baseball player who has abandonment issues of his own from his father's early death, seems so right for me. When I'm with him I feel as if we've been joined on earth from some heavenly plane. I'm sure our hearts wait to beat lovingly together, as if connecting from a thousand years ago. His name whispers even in the misty hallways of my dreams. And yet, every fear I have inside of me is screaming, "his love is only pretend. He'll get tired of your fears and insecurities and leave you."

Challenges keep pulling us together and pushing us away.

We're both afraid.

He's afraid I'll never be able to open to sensual intimacy and fully love him—and he might be right. I'm afraid of the beautiful, experienced women in his past—and I might be right to fear them. One . . . Jesse Johnson—visits me in my nightmares.

I've just heard about Jesse during an evening when my sister and I double dated. According to Dana, a woman who used to socialize with Ryan and his ex, the two of them were like the king and queen of the city. She revealed that Jesse thought she'd found her prince.

At only eighteen, I can't understand what can I offer a soon to be twenty-six-year-old man. Am I a fool believing his promises? Even though I crave the stability of a mature man, shouldn't I choose people my own age and forget about relationships like this one? Is my only answer to focus on my education and career?

After spending an evening together, I've agreed to go to Ryan's baseball game and see him off on his long road trip. I can't stand to watch him—or anyone—leave. I'm afraid they'll never come back and the pain of being abandoned will fall down on me once again.

Unexpectedly, I find myself racing, running, desperate to tell Ryan the words and feelings I've withheld from the beginning—I love him.

I have to get to him before he boards the bus and leaves for ten days.

Leaving the stadium, I am almost to the player's lot where Ryan is boarding his bus. Jerry Stowe, a boy I grew up, texts me to announce he's waiting for me at the gift store. Recently he'd become more than a friend. Returning from a week of playing competitive league baseball, he was ready to discuss having sex and a serious relationship.

He is racing toward me. A big smile spreads across his face as he waves to me frantically.

He has no idea my feelings have changed toward him.

Or have they?

Ryan is also standing and waving at me from the player's lot. I'm standing in front of him—and in front of Jerry. There are only minutes to go before he and his baseball team, The San Francisco Goliaths, leave on their road trip for ten days.

I am split in half—one woman is ready to leap forward with a man ready to take me on a journey, and the other is ready to play with the childhood friend I've known all my life.

I stop as if I've run into a wall.

Suddenly, the right answer reveals itself.

I am ready to risk more and jump off my cliff, without the safety net I've held onto so tightly all my life.

I want to let go.

I let go.

Table of Contents

Prologue

"Nicky?" My Auntie Barbara is standing at my side.

"Hey Auntie," I answer her. "What do you need?"

Friends and family are helping my husband and me celebrate thirty-five years of marriage. I've stepped back to have a moment alone. I have always loved watching my loved ones when they have no idea I'm looking at them. Some of the sweetest scenes are when the raw emotions of life are all over their faces. I guess it was one of the twisted gifts my father gave me. Learning to survive in a family battling alcoholism, we had to stay in the shadows until we knew it was safe to come out. Now, it's a sweet respite, observing the special moments that too often fly by unnoticed.

"When do you want to get dinner going?" she leans into the hallway.

"Is everyone getting hungry?" I ask, knowing the answer.

"I'd say so. I just saw Darrell take the last radish off the vegetable tray," she laughed. "You know it's time when a man is cleaning off the greens. All the appetizers are just about gone."

"Can you ask my hubby to start the barbecue? I have the steaks and chicken marinating in the refrigerator with two big containers of vegetables and baked potatoes." I pointed to the kitchen. "They need to roast along with the meat and we need about twenty minutes to warm, right?"

"I'll tell that handsome devil," she kidded. "Why does having a man at the grill seem so right? Speaking of delicious men, remember when we were in the kitchen after you sang the national anthem? I asked if you'd ever slept with one of the ballplayers and that night you—"

"Yeah," I smiled at the memory. "I was just thinking about that guy."

As she walked away, I remembered the scene at the player's lot, when both Ryan Tilton and Jerry Stowe were focused on me, just outside of the ballpark.

THE ROAD TO HAPPINESS

I look to my mother
For the example of
What a loving woman should be
Her eyes are vacant
She has shut down
She's been left to find her own way
Her mother left her
Her father sought out another woman
My father chose alcohol instead of her
My father, a man who lost himself
A man who can't find
The way back to happiness

Where is that road
That golden highway promised in my youth
Why is that path so hard to find
Just when I think I've discovered it
The twists and turns begin again
It becomes unpaved
Gravel spews underneath my wheels
Rugged, deep ruts around me
Dangerous curves ahead

There are storms that threaten
I fear I'll be taken under the water, car and all
Floating down river
Bobbing and dipping under the raging current

My hand is barely above the water
I yell and scream for someone to help
Or notice
Or help
Or notice
Or

Chapter 1

Crashing into Love

A snap decision—that's how it came to me.

Clear.

Simple.

I knew what I had to do.

Tell him you love him. Don't wait. You can't expect him to hold on much longer. Isn't he about to leave you? Shout out your feelings now! He needs support and your reassurance that you love and want him.

I moved through the crowd, desperate to get to the one I wanted—the one I'd *always* wanted . . . from the very beginning.

* * * * *

Two nights ago, Ryan and I double dated with my sister and her boyfriend to the Waterfront Café Restaurant and nightclub. After he drove me home, we tucked into bed a very drunk Jenise, and on the living room couch, her inebriated boyfriend, Sean. Ryan had planned to be alone with me that evening and asked me to go home with him. I declined, too worried to leave my intoxicated sister without supervision. We'd come close to losing my dad a few years earlier when he'd nearly asphyxiated on his own vomit. When I explained, Ryan agreed to stay with me.

The next day, Ryan treated me to an evening at Pismo Beach. We rode on the sand in dune buggies and capped off the evening with a fresh abalone dinner cooked for us by a roaring fire. We finished our night watching the sunset.

Still afraid to be alone with him because of our disaster in Yountville earlier that week, I reluctantly agreed that in order to ascend to the next level of our relationship, it was necessary to spend the night with him. What a night! It was filled with sensual touch and the delicate web of intimacy.

When morning arrived, I promised I'd go to his last baseball game before he left on another road trip—this one ten days. In the midst of our new romance, it seemed like an eternity. As soon as the game ended, Ryan came to the railing for one final goodbye.

Cathy, an usherette, introduced herself and let me know she'd the sweet goodbye he'd whispered to me. The acknowledgment from another adult—not a friend, parent, or sibling, but an objective and grown woman—gave me a kind of unspoken permission that it was okay to have feelings for Ryan. Ridiculous or not, this simple gesture filled me with the confidence to move forward. In fact, joy filled me everywhere.

Wanting to be with Ryan wasn't a sin.

It was healthy.

A good decision.

Partially from Cathy's encouragement, some final checkmark had been made.

I needed to look Ryan in his eyes and tell him I loved him. That would be the completion of my decision and a step forward I needed to make—*now*.

But the time we had was dwindling—rapidly.

In only a few minutes the team bus would leave for the airport. Fumbling for my gate pass, I hurried toward the security guard, ready to spill my feelings. Happiness burst from my chest as Ryan waved, standing next to the team bus getting ready to board.

He was my love.

The moment revealed itself.

A full sprint to the gate.

I stopped suddenly.

My breathing became erratic.

My heart pounded with the beat of an unwelcome surprise.

Jerry, my childhood friend, ran toward me. He was certain I waited for *him*. A smile was plastered across his face. There was no doubt he was happy. I knew he'd be eager to discuss everything we'd shared before he'd left to play summer baseball—especially a relationship that included sex.

It was as if my body had ripped right down the middle and I became two women.

One was about to meet a lifelong friend. His goals matched mine. We stood ready to share new experiences with life, intimacy and our upcoming college adventure. Jerry and I were two young adults ready to take on the world. That relationship meant safety. I'd have control and that meant security. I longed for it. We'd shared a past and had a solid foundation. When life at home got rough, we covered each other's back. I knew I could say anything to him. He wouldn't judge or abandon me.

The second woman had fallen in love with a successful, professional baseball player, and soon to be twenty-six-year-old man. He'd gone to college and already accomplished many of his goals. Established social circle. A flourishing career. And the biggest challenge for me . . . was sexually experienced. Ryan Tilton seemed ready for a lifetime commitment and had positioned himself to have a partner, family, and all the things that would make his life complete.

* * * * *

Now, as I stood outside of the players' lot, I could almost feel Ryan's arms around me and taste the words I longed to tell him for many months. I knew our goodbye would be filled with big, bold, embraces and a flurry of kisses. I'd send him on his road trip after I proclaimed my love aloud, showing him I was no longer afraid.

My fingers touched my pass card.

A rush of relief washed over me.

I was settled.

Decided.

Ready.

I reached out, ready to hand my pass to gate security. Just as I'd made my way through the waiting crowd, I heard my name.

Jerry.

There was no escaping him.

As if frozen to the spot where I stood, my heart took a free fall into my stomach. Confusion seeped through my body.

Oh no. What do I do now? If I don't run to Ryan immediately, he'll be on that bus and then gone. But abandoning Jerry in front of all of these people with no explanation feels wrong.

My thoughts flipped, one to the next.

I spun around.

Jerry's eyes locked onto mine.

Run to Ryan! Don't stop.

I could feel Ryan behind me. It was as if he penetrated my very being. His love called out, clutching at my core.

My long time friend was almost at my side, waving and smiling. I could no longer run away. I only wanted my love and he had mere minutes before leaving for the airport.

Jerry had already reached me.

I had to face him.

He pulled me into a hug.

Each minute with him stole precious time from being with Ryan. Suddenly, minutes stretched into years.

"Jerry," I tried to disguise my nervousness. My neck was stiff. My head throbbed with the heaviness of anxiety. It rushed wildly through my body. "I said I'd meet you at the gift shop. I'm . . . not done with my business, and . . ." I was out of breath. Searched for something that made sense. I wanted to be honest, not abrupt. It was imperative I explained things right way.

He was my lifeline.

A tie to my childhood.

An anchor.

My safe place.

Just say it, Nicky: "I've fallen in love with Ryan."

"I couldn't wait! I had to see you." Jerry whirled me in a circle. "I knew you'd be coming this way. And here you are!" His eyes darted back and forth with excitement. "It's so good to see you." He kissed my cheeks several times. Without permission and once on my lips.

"It's great to see you, too, but I'll be another hour." I slipped from under his hug. Patted his back. Pulled away. The lie on the tip of my tongue tasted bitter. "I have to meet Jose and drop off the agenda for the next series, um—"

"Calm down," he interrupted. "I'm just letting you know I'm here." He hugged me again. "Can we step away from the crowd for a minute?"

"No, I have to—" *Let me be for now!*

"Just for a minute." He took my hand and pulled me with him, away from the players' lot and the gate . . . the gate that might have been the opening to everything.

I heard the engine of the Goliaths team bus start.

I knew Ryan had boarded.

I was too late.

Chapter 2

Three Ring Circus

*W*ould Ryan wait for me?

I dared to hope so even though I knew it wasn't realistic. How could he? The team was preparing to leave for the airport and their bus would soon clear the lot.

Regardless, I couldn't turn my back on Jerry. I knew how abandonment felt and refused to leave my childhood friend with the same sadness. Both of us had a big taste of being left behind from some of the rough times we'd gone through when we were kids—alone, confused, wondering what had happened.

Jerry took my hand.

We headed toward the pier.

I didn't want to make a scene.

I gave in.

"Look!" He reached into his pocket and pulled out a silver ring. "I couldn't wait to show you. Let me put it on your finger." He pushed the ring on. It was designed with two little hands that were linked together. When they opened, a heart was exposed.

Only a few weeks ago, I would have loved this. What have I done? Why wasn't I more decisive? Why didn't I take a stand?

I noticed a thicker, larger, duplicate ring on his finger. It was a perfect match with mine.

Oh, God. Do I take it off and tell him now? How can I, when his intentions were so lovely?

"Do you like it?" His whole body seemed to open with the certainty of a loving answer. "I know it's corny, but . . . will you be my steady girlfriend?"

If I didn't tell Jerry about Ryan immediately, it would be dishonest. If I did tell him, I knew what I'd face—the hurt in his eyes and the defeat on his body. I wasn't ready for that. Not here, the place where we'd rooted for the San Francisco Goliaths, sitting in the bleachers together. This was one of our special places. I didn't want to turn it into a nightmare.

"This is really sweet, Jerry. Can we talk about it later? I can't give you the full attention you deserve right now. I'm distracted and I have to go."

"*Distracted?*" His expression showed what he felt—frustration.

If you can't handle that one, I've got a doozey to lay on you.

"The ring is nice," I was on automatic. "Thank you."

"*Nice?*"

"More than nice. I'm just in a rush, so . . ."

"I'll wait for you at the Java House." He kissed my finger. Everything inside of me began twisting. "Try to hurry. I can't wait to begin our evening and spend time together. Finally." Once again, he embraced me full and tight. He kissed my lips hard and without my permission.

"I'll do my best." I squirmed to get out of his arms.

Jerry walked toward the Java House. I stood in place, afraid to move. Afraid he'd turn around. When out of sight, I took off the ring. Shoved it in my pocket. I should have told him. I reverted to the techniques I'd used when growing up to control the rage, the outbursts, and keep the peace and calm every situation.

I needed to risk the raw emotion and spontaneity of life. Even as one situation was under control, the other was slipping away.

What if Ryan rejected me after witnessing my embrace with Jerry? What if I had watched and waited for Ryan to say he loved me and as I stood and waited for him, he walked off with another woman? What would I have done?

When I said the words, would he believe me?

For once, I pushed the possible negatives aside rather than indulge in them.

I rushed to the gate.

The crowd had thinned.

Few people remained to cheer for the players as they prepared to leave for their road trip. I desperately clutched at the thick wire on the gate. Ryan wasn't there.

Oh no. Ryan won't understand—I want him, not Jerry. Will he ever believe anything I have to say if I don't get to him before he leaves? If we talk on the phone, will I hear the cold tones of his voice? Maybe this is the final act that pushes him to see other women. How could it not? Jerry kissed me. What a fool I am.

I had to believe that once he saw me, I could reach him. I had to try. It meant stepping up in front of others—his teammates, their girlfriends and wives, and the dreaded management.

This was my moment—*our* moment.

Maybe I was kidding myself. Would I look like a fool trying to get Ryan's attention? Worse—would I make Ryan look like a fool? Perhaps he thought he'd done all he could to encourage me to openly express my feelings and walking away with Jerry told him I unreachable. Maybe enough was enough.

A million doubts raced through my mind. I fought every urge to give into the hopelessness I'd always felt surrounding abandonment. My immediate reaction was to cut him off before he did the same to me. For once, I didn't run.

Didn't give up on what I wanted.

Had to get to him.

Anxiety surged.

My heart slammed in my chest.

My knees shook.

I felt as if I would crumble to the ground.

Forced myself to be brave.

One more goodbye.

I *had* to say it.

Ryan.

These were my baby steps—the first steps I needed to take in order to kick down the barriers that surrounded my whole family. Here was my beginning to a journey of learning to trust and opening the first link in the chain that held my family in paralysis, fear and dysfunction.

I took a stand to purposefully live my life the way I'd always dreamed I could rather than what I *thought* was best or how others *felt* was best for me. For once, I wanted to be selfish. I was even ready to cast aside the possible reprimand that might wait from the Goliaths' management. As soon as I stepped on the lot, my supervisors would know everything.

As little girls, Jenise and I had been desperate for Mom to read us bedtime stories. Tuck the blankets under our chins. Brush and lovingly caress our hair. We dreamed every day that she would come to us and make sure we were safe. I waited for her to peek in on me at night—just once.

It never happened.

I was tired of waiting for possibilities.

I needed to be my own storyteller and direct my life down the path I wanted. I was done leaving it to chance and always hoping for the best. This was my time to shower Ryan with love. No obstacle would stand in my way.

Not even myself—*especially myself.*

"Hi. I'm with the cheer team," I announced to security.

"I know." The guard smiled but was planted firmly inside of the gate. He obviously had orders not to let anyone inside.

"I need to speak with Ryan Tilton about a charity event." I pulled my pass card from my pocket. "Here's my ID."

"Mr. Tilton is already on the bus, honey." His reply was stoic and practiced. "I'm sorry, you're too late. I'm clearing this area now so they can roll out of here."

"You don't understand," I pleaded. "This is incredibly important. He needs this information immediately."

"Tell me and I'll give him the message," he offered.

"I'm not comfortable with that," I quickly countered.

"No one is allowed inside the gate." He crossed his arms. "Our insurance . . . it's too big a liability. I'm sorry."

"I have an important memo for him. I'm telling you . . . begging, please, he *needs* this information. Please, he's waiting and—"

"Okay," he put his hand on my shoulder. "I hear you. If you want him to get your message, give it to *me.* I'm only fifty-feet from the bus," he nodded toward it. "I promise that I'll walk it over right now. You can even watch me deliver it."

"Forget it." The tears flowed. "I worked so hard on this, and he needs—"

"I'm sorry. I can see this is important to you." Compassion surrounded his words. "If I let you pass it could mean my job."

"I understand." I turned to walk away.

There was nothing more I could say.

My head was down.

I felt the despair push through my body.

Why did I spend so much time listening to Jerry? I should have thrown his feelings aside.

Suddenly, the bus let out a huge "burp."

I spun around.

The door opened.

Ryan walked down the steps.

I hesitated.

He hesitated.

I waved.

He returned the wave.

He stepped onto the player's lot . . .

Chapter 3

Losing Control

"*L*et her pass!" Ryan shouted.

The security guard opened the gate.

I pushed through.

Rushed into his open arms without hesitation.

Our souls were new.

You and I became us.

The tips of his fingers connected. Lifted. Crawled. Danced on my back. I felt as if he had claimed me as his woman. Were sparks igniting around us? I closed my eyes and there they were—everywhere! I tucked my head into his chest. My hands grabbed his jacket, making fists with the brown suede material between my fingers.

"Kiss me, Nicky."

I lifted my head, my cheeks wet and my eyes teary. His head tilted. His eyes closed. I knew his kiss was mine. I wanted to watch everything he did before his lips took me into their tender kiss. His mouth opened, waiting for me to open with him. It seemed he sucked in a breath to prepare to love me. His body softened, letting mine fill every masculine valley.

This kiss.

His kiss. *My* kiss.

This was *our* kiss—and maybe our future.

When I closed my eyes, the sweetness of two came together. Our bodies melted into each other. Like some distant storm gathering, his soft moans grew louder. Stronger. My cheek felt the vibration of the low, deep, and sensual satisfaction of love.

His heart beat steadily.

Thumped.

With mine.

Against me.

He swallowed to catch his breath.

I gave myself over to his gravity.

A deep groan matched the passion of his kiss, igniting every tingle in my belly. Drowning, tumbling and twirling, immersed in our emotion, his hands were heavy, grasping for more, and yet lightly traced his design to some planned destination where love flourished.

I opened Ryan's jacket. Circled my arms around his waist. Squeezed as hard as I could. His masculine body was in my arms and my feminine body was his. I came alive. Played a lovely composition made from golden light.

"You saw me," I sighed in relief.

"I've seen you for over a year," he whispered.

Our souls burst with the brilliance of streaming light as we celebrated our new bond of love. I pushed my body against him. Compressed myself into each part of his body. For that moment, I was sure every pulse, every thought and every heartbeat were in tune and one love.

"Oh, Ryan." I looked up at him and quickly buried my head into his chest again. "I'll miss you . . . bad. So bad."

"What about management?" His arms tightened around me. "Earlier, you said—"

"I don't care anymore," I blurted. "I'm done hiding, pretending, waiting—I don't care! Cathy, you know the usherette? She was, she, she . . ." Scattered and sobbing, I tried focusing enough to tell him how my heart had overflowed with love for him.

"What are you trying to tell me, Nicky?"

"She said she could—" Tears trickled down my cheeks. I tugged on his jacket as if holding on for my life.

"What did she say?" His big hands caressed my hair.

"She could see we were more than friends. She's rooting for us. It felt . . . I felt validated. Of course I've known it. I know it's been tough being with me, but I'm ready to jump in with you now. Pull me in. Lead me. Let's float on the ocean together while we hold hands and then soar across a star-filled sky. Drown me in love! I'm in love with you, Ryan! I love you!"

All the emotions I'd kept inside had come unleashed.

"I'm in love!" I was in hyper-drive. "From the moment you kissed my hand. That kiss . . . I felt your thirst. Your invisible message went right through me. If management fires me, they do." I tried to reassure him—and myself—I knew exactly what I was doing. "I love you. Kiss me in front of everyone. I don't care."

He reached for my hands—the same hands I'd used to hold on to the edge of a cliff my entire life. Hands that tried to control when or if I'd let another person come close enough to make an intimate connection; hands that now rested gently around Ryan's thick neck.

His hands moved to the back of my head. He pulled me into his essence. Our lips were ready to touch.

The bus driver honked the horn.

Time was counting down.

Undeterred, our bodies used the unwelcome warning to accelerate our desperate urgency. Within the shattered air, his kiss wove together every hope I ever had about letting the silky softness of love in my heart.

All of the energy I'd used as a roadblock to stop the vulnerability of love, vanished. The steel walls of defense broke open. It felt glorious and amazing. I could almost hear the judgments and jaded views I'd stuffed down from my childhood smash together inside me. Tired of putting up a front to keep the peace, I let them break apart and radiate into a gorgeous rainbow of faith.

A permanent fog had lifted.

It was clear now.

I was clear.

"I'm sorry," I sniffed.

"For?"

"I know your teammates will tease you," I grabbed his shirt. "I needed to—had to—get to you. I had to tell you. Face to face."

"You're the woman I love. You've come to me to with an open heart. Do you really think I give a damn what my teammates say? You're all that matters." His hand cupped my cheek. "My sweet enchantress. I love when your green eyes sparkle so brightly when you look up at me." His eyes scanned mine. "We're breaking through all of our walls, taking them down brick by brick. Do you feel that, too?"

"Yes." I could barely speak.

"Soon you'll open to me in every way." His confidence flowed through me.

"I want to be in your life," I said hoarsely.

"It's been agonizing waiting to hear you say you love me." We broke our embrace. When he smiled, I could see hope reflected in his eyes. "You can't imagine how I feel right now. Please try to come to a few of our road games. Are you as desperate for me as I am for you?"

"You have such an intimate way about you. You have to know I am." I was suddenly aware of how I had started to relax. "That's why I'm here. The need to tell you came on so suddenly. When I let go, everything poured out of me and . . . I'm so sorry I waited this long to tell you."

He kissed me again. Every nerve seemed to jump in me. I could even sense the pulse from the tips of his fingers as they gently pulled at my hair, inviting me to come deeply into love. His other hand moved up and down my back reverently, as if our moment was precious.

"I want to come on this road trip with you," I trembled with renewed determination. "As soon as I get home, I'll ask Jenise if she can go with me. All I want is you."

The horn blared again.

We knew the bus driver and the team had lost their patience.

It was time for him to leave me.

"They can wait," he reassured. "Just let me know when you want to join me. I'll make the arrangements. Oh, my baby." His arms found their way around me once again. "I can't let go."

"Don't leave me yet, Ryan. Not yet." I looked at the bus as the enemy it was. The thought of somehow slashing the tires crossed my mind. "Just another minute; please."

It seemed all the parts of my body had something to let go of as I held onto his arms. My emotional dam was collapsing. My feelings rushed over the well-built walls that had once protected me. These barriers had been the only way I knew to survive my family's dysfunction. Struggling too long in the twisted waters of addiction, I was ready to break from their rip tide and was overcome. The sea was finally calming its harrowing waves.

I burst into tears and heavy sobs, grieving for all the wasted and lost moments that could have been precious with my father, my mother, and my sister.

None of us would ever get them back.

I mourned for lost intimacy and revelation that could have been shared between a child and parent; all of it traded for a whisky bottle, year after year. Instead of the parental love Jenise and I had hoped for and deserved, we saw and experienced rage.

Crying from my very core because of Jerry and all we had shared, the future we'd quietly planned when growing up was fading away. Neither of us had questioned it. We sat on doorsteps a block away from our houses, me escaping my father's drunken hugs and he fleeing his father's fists. Would the story of our friendship go unfinished?

I cried because of school friends that were soon to be lost. We'd already begun letting go. Now the speed seemed accelerated.

One stage of my life was ending.

Another was coming on fast.

The rush into my present and from my family's past was fresh, exhilarating and wild.

There was no turning back.

I had missed my childhood—almost all of it. Every day had been about survival—Ernie trying the bathroom doorknob, my father choking my sister; slamming my mother's head against the kitchen cabinet; praying we'd get home safely as Jenise and I rode in my father's truck while he was drunk at the wheel.

The tears I shed were memorials of a chapter in my life that had closed.

It closed in magnificence.

It felt . . . amazing.

Chapter 4

The Fallout

"Tell me what you're feeling." Ryan's voice was low. Quietly sensing his aura, I softened immediately when he held me to his chest. "Why are you crying so hard? What's the matter?"

"Closing . . . closing in." My eyes burned as new tears spilled onto my cheeks. "It's like dark and light thoughts spinning together."

He'd touched me intimately when I'd spent the night, but I'd never felt as close to him as I did that afternoon. Amidst the rush and noise around us, somehow we were able to feel the softness of each other's arms, wrapped in the protection of our love.

Our precious seconds together were almost over.

The equipment door on the bus slammed closed.

"I hate this," I protested.

"I know." He pulled back.

"You've waited for me to tell you I love you out loud. I've tried to say so many times to you over the phone." I patted his chest. "I've practiced saying them. I've waited for my courage to surface and finally, I have her in my grasp. I had to get to you before you left. Always face to face. I'm not hiding anymore. Are you ready for me? Will you be my boyfriend?"

"Oh, sweetheart." He pushed my hair behind my shoulders. "Take a breath, go home and tell your folks, pack and grab your sis and come with me. Be with your boyfriend." When he let go, I saw glistening tears in his eyes. He looked shaken; as if the love I'd just confessed to him was so powerful he was overcome in every way. The same emotional earthquake that had rocked me seemed to be doing the same to him.

A gentle whisper came from deep inside my spirit. Heard only by me. Blew quickly passed my ear.

Sometimes, it's just as overwhelming getting what we want as it is pursuing it.

"As soon as I get home, Ryan. I'll tell Mom. I promise," I declared with absolute commitment. I quickly visualized the scene. I was already in my room packing. "I wish I could leave with you right now. I can hardly stand it."

Enfolded in his arms, the furry wool collar of his jacket rubbed on my cheek; my arm gently hugged his thick neck; his eyelashes brushed my forehead; all of it a sendoff that would fill my mind's scrapbook forever. I drank in the sensations of touching him: the little twitches in his face when my fingertips traced his jaw, the movement of his lips as they quivered and the cushion of his cheek as it flattened against mine.

"You better wipe your eyes on my shirt so you don't get tortured by your teammates," I tried to lighten the moment. "Even *I* know men aren't comfortable showing emotion—*especially* jocks. They avoid it at any cost and make fun of others for doing it."

"I don't give a damn." His body spoke with urges that pressed on my soul. "Kiss me again." He brought his lips to mine.

Electricity snapped through me.

The blare of the horn jerked my body and brought me back into our present.

The bus driver honked three times.

His teammates yelled, whistled, mocked and cheered.

"You better go." I looked up at him, still sniffling. "I . . . I can't get my breath. I feel," I gasped for air. "I feel like—" I cried into his chest. "Why didn't I tell you sooner?"

"You said it," Ryan's voice cracked. "Even if you're not able to meet me, we'll be together again before you know it. I'll only be gone a week-and-a-half. You're so busy . . . all of your projects and volunteering . . . time will fly by. You'll be all right." He kissed my head. "This side you've shown me . . . what a tender woman you are. I've seen glimpses of her for a long time. I'm glad you finally let her step forward. I'm so happy."

"I hope we stay that way. Help me. I'm so lost. I don't know how to have a relationship."

"We'll help each other," he reassured. Several waves of tears came and went. Then, as if propelled, I moved into giddy joy and laughter. Girlfriends and wives were milling around the bus. They smiled with knowing looks. "I know how you hate goodbyes. You don't have to watch me get on the bus. I promise I won't pull you back or shout your name."

"Okay," I wiped my eyes.

"I'll call you tonight." His voice was calm and confident. "You know how I need to hear your voice."

"Yes, I need that . . . I want that." I tried to steady myself, preparing for his departure.

One more bear hug and his body said its farewell.

I felt as if I'd lost a limb.

Our fingertips lingered for the last precious seconds before they let go. I put all my strength to the test, fighting and holding back from yelling to Ryan and ask if he'd wait another minute.

I walked toward the gate.

Went through it.

In my mind it was a barrier to another world—a world that kept me from Ryan.

"That was some goodbye," a fan said as I exited the players' lot.

Suddenly his reputation raced to the forefront of my mind. Had I damaged it? Was the press lurking? They'd almost certainly question him—or worse yet—print a story.

"No." I tried to sound convincing. "Just friends who haven't seen each other in a long time."

"I've never seen anything like *that* between friends," a woman added.

I smiled without looking at any of them.

Hurrying to the streetcar stop, I was desperate to get home and pack my things.

Oh shit! Jerry!

Just as the trolley pulled up, I remembered he was waiting at the Java House. My heart drummed against my chest.

How am I going to pretend? I've been crying. I'm sure he'll be able to tell—what do I say?

As if I were committing adultery, I took the ring Jerry had given me from my pocket and slid it on my finger.

Why did I take this ring? Why did I let him embrace me? Am I cheating? There is no way to win this. I feel like such a bad girl— I'm a sinner.

Would postponing the inevitable make everything worse? Was the nausea washing through me from the fear of hurting both men and in the end I would be without anyone? Exactly *whom* was I betraying?

I began the long, tentative walk to the all night diner—the same diner that solidified a new friendship with Ethan and had also repaired a damaged relationship with Ryan.

On this late afternoon, what would it do for Jerry and me?

As soon as I walked in the door, he waved from one of the tables. I suddenly saw him like a pesky fly circling around me. If only he'd go away, find someone else, and leave me I could go home and write in my journal to sort through my emotions. Stuck and feeling cornered, I had to take care of my unfinished business.

Jerry stood up. Embraced me. Pulled me to his body. I did my best not to withdraw, even though I only wanted to get away.

"Let's get out of here," he urged me to follow, tugging my arm.

My head throbbed.

I clutched my backpack.

"First, I need to go home," I stated. "What did you want to do tonight?"

"Well . . ." His eyes had a mischievous glint. "We could go right up to my room—or your room. I read everything you wanted me to and researched the sites you suggested. I'm sure I can make you feel good. I'm ready to show you."

How do I do this? What do I say? He did what I asked and in a little over a week I'm rejecting him? What kind of person am *I?*

"Let's say hello first, okay?" I needed to slow things down.

"He said he was going to watch my college career." He talked loud and fast about what a baseball scout had told him while holding my hand. Traced his finger over the ring he gave me. His eyes sparkled with enthusiasm as he told me about a baseball scout who had approached him.

"That's great!" I feigned excitement. Jerry seemed to believe all the pieces of his life were falling into place. My pieces? They were tearing apart, melting down and being reshaped.

"I'll be over in a few hours. I have to unpack. Don't get impatient. I'll grab your curvy body soon enough, gorgeous."

"See ya." I fought an urge to cry and looked at the ground. When he grabbed and started to kiss me, I immediately protested. "No, let's, let's just . . . I'll see you a little later," I stammered.

"Something wrong?" He looked at me strangely.

"No, I'm fine." I wondered what thoughts ran through his mind. "See you in a little while."

As soon as he was out of site, the rush of my newly proclaimed love for Ryan flooded me. When I burst through my front door, I was out of breath. My cheeks felt flushed and my hair disheveled.

"Mom!" I yelled. "Where are you?"

"In the kitchen," she shouted.

I ran down the hall, threw my arms in the air and then planted them in front of her on the kitchen table.

"Ryan invited me to go on his road trip. I'm going upstairs to pack right now!"

I hurried out of the kitchen to head toward my room.

Chapter 5

Mom Gives Her Opinion

"*You're what?*" The skepticism in Mom's voice was obvious. Perhaps she'd hoped I hadn't announced what she heard me say only moments ago. "Nicky!"

Her chair scraped the floor.

She came out of the kitchen.

I froze at the bottom of the stairs.

"Ryan has tickets on hold for Jenise and me!" I stepped down to face her. "We're going to meet him in Denver!"

"Does your sister know about this?" Mom motioned for me to follow her back to the kitchen.

"Not yet. I was on my way upstairs to tell her." I followed Mom. "Even if she can't go, I am. I have to pack and call Ryan so he can . . ." My rambling began. "I'm telling you so you'll know why . . . I need some water." I grabbed a glass from the cupboard and poured from a pitcher we kept in the refrigerator. My tight throat seemed to have a heartbeat of its own. I gulped it down and then walked back to the table. I watched Mom circle the kitchen with a dishtowel, wiping the counter here and there. "The team is going to Denver. There's a farm he wants to show me. This little boy . . . he took a photo . . . his pictures . . . they're beautiful, and our connection is unique and unlike anything, and he's got these bunnies for sale, and . . ."

I slowed down just long enough to interpret the expression on Mom's face. It translated to; *my daughter is out of her mind.*

"Back up." Mom put down the dishtowel. Sat at the table. "Let's talk this over."

Talk it over? All of the sudden you care about the things I'm doing? Are you really interested? Aren't you giving me the same speech you gave the girls when you worked at the Juvenile?

"No." I was confident and certain of my decision. "I don't want to talk about this. I've already dragged my feet too long. Eighteen years, in fact. I've stayed in the gray areas of my life long enough. I should have jumped in with him weeks ago."

"What about your father? You don't care how this will upset him?" She threw guilt at me like Ryan threw his pitches—hard and focused. It was a part of her codependent habits—keeping the lasso around us without admitting her true feelings. "He's already dealt with a gun being held to his head at work. He doesn't need you holding it there again. What about us—your family? And what about college?"

"What are you *talking* about, Mom?" I yelled. "This is about *me* and has *nothing* to do with college or you guys."

"*Doesn't* it?" she challenged.

"Let me understand. Are you saying *I'm* holding a gun to Dad's head? You're kidding, right? After all the times he's driven me and Jenise home drunk and—"

"I agree Ryan is nice," she ignored my counter attack. "I'm not comfortable with you traveling across the country to meet someone you know so little about."

"You can't stop me," I retorted, feeling defiant. "I *know* him and I'm going to meet him."

"No, you don't know him," she insisted. "You've hardly spent any time together."

Here we go again. Her fear, my fear . . . all of us afraid. I've had enough of waiting for the next bad thing to come down on me. Nothing is ever resolved. I have to stop this twisted circle.

"I do know him. We have something special, and—"

"What if something happens?" Once again, she talked over me.

Damn it. Quit interrupting and let me tell you.

"Ryan is a part of a professional baseball team. Maybe he won't be available like you assume. Won't he have commitments every day? You're used to controlling everything in your world. On this trip, he'll come first, not you. There's no controlling him in *his* environment. What then? What if he can't give you the attention you're expecting?"

"I'll be okay." My chin lifted.

I don't need attention. I never got it here so why worry about my boyfriend giving it to me?

"Maybe you will. Maybe your fantasy world with Ryan Tilton will be amazing, but—"

"*Fantasy?*" I barely held myself together. "This isn't pretend!"

"No? He's not playing house with an innocent eighteen-year-old girl to see just how far he can push her?"

My old fear of Ryan playing an elaborate joke on me surfaced immediately. I shuddered. "He told me I can bring Jenise and—"

"What if she can't get away? You said you're packing . . . don't you think you should know if your sister is coming with you? When will you ask her?"

"I just got home, and—"

"What if someone's with him?"

"Are you accusing him of having another girlfriend?" Anger shot through me. Was I trying to reassure *myself* more than my mother? Obviously she made the statement on purpose, making me hesitate and reconsider going on the trip. Just as important as the intended pause, she'd made an accusation about the man I loved.

Why can't you ever be supportive?

"No." She poured herself a cup of coffee. "I don't mean another woman, although . . ." Mom seemed on the edge of confessing her worry about other women in his life. "I mean friends, business associates, family and social commitments. Will he expect you to step aside like a good girl and wait in your room while he's living a full life? Or be a bobble on his arm while he shows you off to his friends at some elegant dinner or club? Are you staying in his room, like a mistress would? Where will you meet him? How will you handle all the women he's been with who don't know he's in a committed relationship? They'll be in every city. You that strong?"

She wrung her hands.

"We support each other and that's how we'll deal with it." *I hope.* "As far as meeting him, I guess at the airport. I thought—" I tried to respond to each question thoughtfully and maturely. Each of her interruptions, however, elevated my frustration.

"How will you spend your time if he's busy? Do you have money of your own?" It was as if she'd been preparing for this moment for years. She didn't seem anywhere near the end of her questions. "Do you expect him to pay for everything? That makes you completely dependent on him—is that what you've envisioned for yourself? I thought you wanted a career and a first class education at Stanford? Instead, at only eighteen and at the beginning of your adult life, you're submissive to a man?"

"I'm not submissive or dependent, Mom. That's not how Ryan expects me to be with him. He likes how I speak my mind and that I have opinions and career goals."

"*Does* he?" She shook her head in disbelief. Pushed up from the table. Emptied her coffee in the sink and wiped the kitchen counter again. She started drying dishes that were already dry in the dish rack, waiting to be put away.

"Yes, he does." *What in the hell are you doing? Why are you so nervous? Look at me!*

"Will you go to his games and sit there like some pretty little decoration he can show off?" She rolled on.

"I'm not a decoration, and—"

"Even if you don't see yourself that way, you're a beautiful girl with a voluptuous body. Ryan sees you just. Like. That. What's your purpose going on his road trip? To feel important, like one of the other models he dated? You want to be his pretty little princess and when he snaps his fingers, you'll come running?"

"No, I won't—"

"If Jenise is with you, what does *she* do? Tag along like your little puppy dog while you and Ryan have fun?"

"Ryan wouldn't do that. Neither would I."

"No?" she challenged.

"No."

"Try reassuring me a little," she challenged.

"First of all, I love my sister and respect her way more than treating her like she's baggage. Second, the man I lo—the man I'm with is a good man. We'd never abandon her."

Like you *have.*

"Jenise is your older sister, not a security blanket." She waited a few seconds, almost starting again. I didn't let her.

"Yeah, she's my sister. Security is just what I expect from her." I straightened my back. "She's my hero and the *only* one in this family who ever took a risk. She—"

I was ready to spill it all. The things I'd held back for so many years had bubbled up. Why had Mom knowingly let my father sit on my bed at night when I was little, making me keep him company? Why did I have to tuck him in while she was at work or on the sofa reading her romance novel? Why did she refuse to participate in those parts of her marriage? Why couldn't she have a conversation with her daughters the night Dad had choked Jenise?

Why had she put so many things that were her responsibility on the shoulders of her children? Or wait years before she changed her shift at work, leaving her daughters alone at night with Dad— and sometimes his dangerous and drunk friends? All those things were magically left to resolve themselves. Wasn't this the perfect time to challenge her parenting decisions once and for all, the same way she was challenging me?

The time had come.

"Your barbs and sarcasm won't change the things I've asked you to consider, Nicky."

Really? Then why does this family use that technique so often?

"They're not barbs, Mom. They're facts. They happened."

Your move.

"Maybe Ryan won't want you at his game and would rather you wait at the hotel for him. Perhaps he has other connections to take care of while he's in town before he allows you in his world and he'll get you when *he's* ready." Her eyes slanted in judgment.

"It's not like that." *God, I hope it's not anyway.* "Ryan respects me. And I love baseball. I wouldn't go with him if I couldn't go to the games. We're like partners. He's done a lot for me—"

"Oh yeah?" Her hands slapped the counter. "*What* has he done for you besides made you cry? Awakened you sexually?"

Well for one thing, he's trying to save your husband's pension.

I thought about addressing her comment and elaborating about how I'd awakened sexually all on my own, but reconsidered it was too much. Bottom line, she was scared.

She didn't know . . . I was afraid, too. Our difference? I took one little step each day to overcome my fears in ways she hadn't.

"We have long conversations about life, Mom. He's helped me understand the things I've gone through in new ways. Plus, I've connected with him on a level I never thought I could with anyone. We've really gotten close."

"Close?" Her eyes darted around the room. "It was only a few days ago you came home sobbing because of something he did on your date. Now you're *close to him?*" She gave a mock laugh. "Yeah, I bet he wants you to be close. Without any clothes on."

"No, he doesn't—"

"Will he even *let* you stay with your sister?"

Let me? It's not as if I'll need his permission . . . or will I?

"Jenise and I—"

"You say you haven't had sex yet, but going with him will change all of that. How have you planned for it? Just *what* are you doing, Nicky?"

"I've thought about everything and—"

"You seem to be throwing everything to chance." Her voice swiped the air. "You need to stop and think this through."

That's the point—I'm tired of thinking everything through. For once, I just want to go. Let me go, please Mom. Let's stop this conversation so I can begin packing.

When Mom finally paused, I knew in many ways she was right. I was too eager. My emotions had overtaken me. I'd tried so hard to control everything in my life and yet it didn't change the fact that my father was still an alcoholic and my mother was a co-dependent spouse in denial. All of us except for Jenise, a rape survivor who somehow clawed her way back to life, had closed down and stayed away from new relationships.

I was hit with the sudden realization of what my sister had revealed to me weeks ago—when it came down to it, we have no control of anything except how we act and react, the choices we make, and how we treat other people. The randomness of the world can take us into its eye in a fraction of one moment. I understood those things in a new way.

I held my hand up and asked Mom to stop for a moment.

Chapter 6

A Pause

*T*o fully process the revelation, I had to sit down. The power of it had almost hit with the force of lightning.

Letting loose in a positive, loving way was all I had ever wanted. It was a part of the vision I'd written about—jumping off my cliff and taking a leap of faith with another person.

It knocked inside me.

Demanded my attention.

Now.

Jumping from the safety of my shadows, refusing to stand back or hide from people—all of them were risks. But I risked those things and more every day.

Presenting my plan for a high school cheer team to the Goliaths had been a creative and educational risk.

Sacrificing social time with friends, instead volunteering on most every weekend, being involved in committee work at school so I could pad my college resume, was a social risk.

Putting all of my hopes and dreams in attending Stanford was a risk for my future.

Going to prom was a risk in friendship.

Disagreeing with my father was a physical and mental risk.

Daring to be friends with a man like Ryan was a risk.

Saying yes to coffee with Ethan was a risk.

Just walking from my house to the streetcar was a risk.

My sister had been walking home from school when she was raped. Yet, she took that risk again and again, her fear put aside purposefully as she put each foot down on the sidewalk and stepped outside of our home. Each pound of her fist against her prison walls. Getting out of her bed to see her therapist. Making her way with new friends. The unfamiliar surroundings of college, planning a career—all because she dared to risk herself to the world once more.

My father was once an innocent boy who had a dark addiction that waited to take him over. He dared leave his mother and seek out a better life even while she struggled to survive after the gruesome demise of her husband to spinal meningitis. He and his brothers watched their father's skin darken each day, his spine bend, and his head pull backward toward his march of death. His mother made prescription pills a habit—even with three minor children still at home. He'd taken another risk, marrying Mom. He bet his every happiness on her. Had he lost that wager?

My mother had shut down after she quit her job because her children were unsafe with her husband. That took risk. She'd no longer have her own money. She loved her job and the friends she'd made at the juvenile hall.

I'd heard bits and pieces about Mom's past. Her mother drank. Her father drank. They had sex with other people, cheating on each other in more ways than physical. What were their problems? How did her parents change her life and dreams? Did they ever tell her they loved her or hold her in their arms and keep her safe?

Ryan had to deal with abandonment. He risked introducing me to his brother. He shared their story. He risked telling me he loved me. Every time he was on the pitcher's mound he took a risk the ball flying off the bat wouldn't hit him in the head. He'd risked bearing his soul at Java House when we were in turmoil after our Yountville trauma.

Changing things myself meant taking the baby steps that led out of the jagged twists and turns of fear. I had to put my whole heart on the edge. No one else could do it for me, even if they'd loved me in every way that was healthy. My life was my own, no longer under anyone else's control, including my parents.

My childhood was fading. The world of being an adult waited. It beckoned. I could hear it calling. I had to challenge myself. With challenge, risk was synonymous. To get ahead and realize my dreams would mean pushing myself in every way I could.

There was nothing sensible about what I was doing with Ryan.

What point was there in being sensible?

Where did it get my even-tempered, unemotional mother?

Where did sensible get *anyone* in my family, except bringing us more pain. Growing up, we chose to sit in the bazaar, twisted security of familiarity rather than take a chance.

We'd settled for shadows.

I wondered what might have happened if someone in our house took a risk so big, their lives might never be the same.

For better or worse.

None of us had imagined taking a risk like that.

Perhaps we really didn't want change.

Understanding how to maneuver through the dysfunction in every way was what we knew.

If we could only muster the courage, wouldn't *something* change?

If I took that risk, if I was that person who dared to meet Ryan on his road trip, would change happen for me?

It was about more than being with a man.

It was more than love.

It was about becoming and emerging from my frozen cocoon. It was embracing life and all of its terribleness and all of its beauty.

The vulnerability of opening my heart and taking a chance that another person would be gentle with it—in business, friendship, or the sweet intimacy of love—these were risks I needed to take. Life's dangers had dared to step in front of me. Could I reach out?

I'd had enough of checking in with people and moving only when I had their permission. The hell with making sure everyone knew where I was. It was time for Mom and Dad to help themselves. I'd never been in trouble. Even as my friends drank and experimented with drugs—I was the good girl.

I had to be ready and sober to handle the next disaster.

After all, Mom depended on me.

Dad depended on me.

How could they take care of their own weaknesses and emotional vacancies if I wasn't there for them? When had they ever done it? I was dependable. Home when expected—always, always, always. That was about to change.

I wanted to be with someone. That meant all the good and bad that came with him. We had a chance for something special. If Ryan and I didn't work out I would need time to mend. However I realized whether or not we stayed together wasn't the point. Most important was the chance to live life fully, because of *my* choices, *my* decisions and *my* actions.

Those stories and promises of first love—the bruises and happy balloons, the little hearts that fluttered, the heavy tears that fell—I was ready for them.

Everything seemed different with Ryan.

Maybe my mother reacted so severely at my declaration of independence because she saw I was stepping through a door from which I might never return. Had she understood I had fallen in love and had made a commitment to let my heart become vulnerable for the first time in my life?

"Are you all right?" Mom's voice suddenly brought me back into the moment.

"Yes, I—I was thinking, trying to figure out . . . trying to find the right way to tell you . . ." I was overwhelmed with my discovery and still in the midst of formulating my thoughts. I couldn't reveal them to her in a way that made sense just yet, so I veered in another direction. "I'm eighteen now, Mom. I'm not a baby anymore."

"I know you're not—"

Something clicked on.

I was ready.

And calm.

The words were coming to me in bits and pieces, trying to form whole, succinct thoughts I could discuss with her. I was ready to speak. No longer would I stop or be interrupted and allow my opinions and responses to be muffled.

"Mom, I've listened to everything you've had to say. It's my turn to speak. I'm asking you to listen to me. Can you?"

Her expression showed surprise. When she looked at her daughter, she seemed to recognize a new woman.

She nodded.

I hoped she was ready.

Perhaps for the first time ever, we were *both* ready to take each other for the flawed people we were. Maybe we could take the needed steps to develop our relationship.

"I'm going away in six months. I'll be making my own decisions every day. Some will work out. Others won't. You know that I've taken care of myself for years. I've never asked for much. I'm not blaming you or Dad for my choices or the things that have happened. I have the maturity to decide for myself. I'm going to meet Ryan in Denver."

Mom sighed.

Looked down at the table.

Was it that she didn't think I was ready for my cross-country adventure with Ryan or did she recognize her own shortcomings?

"I'll find out if Jenise can go and plan from there, okay?"

Mom nodded.

"Then I'll call Ryan to make sure I know where to meet him and ask about the money I'll need. After I have all the answers to your questions, I'll update you. Will that satisfy you?"

"There's more to it than that," she seemed refocused.

"Please be happy for me, Mom. I've never had a boyfriend or done anything like this my whole life. For once, I just want to do something without overanalyzing it. I need to let go and enjoy the freedom I have left before college starts. I'll be knee-deep into a four-year commitment soon enough."

It's been impossible for me to open up like this because of all the ways we've been shut down in this house. Please acknowledge that I'm changing and celebrate with me.

"That's my point." Her voice had lowered, talking from a more rational place. "You've never been with a guy and you're meeting a twenty-five-year-old man in a city thousands of miles from here? Your father and I haven't said anything about you spending time with Ryan. We've respected your decisions and your right to privacy. This is something else entirely. You're moving faster and faster. You need to slow down. Before you know it, he'll take you into his world and you'll have given up on your goals. You won't even know it's happening. You'll be too enamored and spellbound by his life and sensuality."

"I'll know. Our relationship didn't happen overnight." I planted my flag in the ground and claimed my territory. "We've gotten closer every day. We talk on a deep, intimate level. It's been since last year, really." I was done hiding the truth and decided to say it. "I'm in love. I feel sick when we're apart. I need to go."

"I know you're in love." Her voice trailed off followed by a long sigh. "I know. I've watched it happen over the last year. I know the kind of excitement and raw emotion you're feeling. I'm a woman. At one time I was where you are." Her voice held compassion, a quality I'd seldom heard from her. "I'm asking you to wait. Doesn't your father deserve to have a conversation with you like we're doing now?"

Since when do we talk about anything?

"I understand why you want Dad here but I have a good grasp of who Ryan is and where we're going." I couldn't resist. Sarcasm. I tried not to. Even counted to three. Swallowed the words. Lost the battle. "Dad didn't care about talking with me when he drove me home drunk from the bar, did he? In some ways I feel he's lost the right. Sorry. I have to be honest."

She sighed.

Sipped her coffee.

I felt as small as I ever had.

"I know you're concerned and what I'm doing obviously worries you. This is my choice and my life. I'm taking charge of it, Mom. I don't need to talk with Dad. I know he'd try and talk me out of it like you are. I won't change my mind."

"If in two days you still want to go, I promise I won't argue or interfere with your plans," Mom pleaded. "I know you hate to talk about it, but . . ."

"We're not going to have sex." My words were firm.

Just get off it, Mom.

"You don't think so?" she pushed.

"No!" I was emphatic.

"That's ridiculous. Yes, you will." She was stone-faced and serious. "Tell me the truth. *Are* you having it now? Promise me you're using protection if you are."

"I'm not having sex."

"You'll need to get birth control before you leave." Her stare never wavered.

"I'm not having sex," I repeated.

"And that's my point, Nicky. It's naive of you to expect that nothing will happen. You'll feel like you're in a different world, stepping into an adult life and you'll give in to him. You need to check into birth control before college starts. No time like the present. Don't you agree?"

"Maybe," I said stubbornly.

"Maybe?" Mom prodded.

"I'll think it over. I really—"

"You don't want to think about preparing for sex," she confirmed my thoughts. "I can see the look on your face. The time for indecision has passed. You need to take charge of your body and be smart about it."

"Yeah." I knew she was right. Still, thinking about a pill for sex every day was disturbing. I didn't like it. "I've been strong and firm in my resolve. I've held true to my moral and spiritual beliefs. I—" It was as if Mom waited for every pause to interject her opinions.

"Regardless, those beliefs disappear quickly when passion rises. You need to be ready for sex or you'll get pregnant. Condoms aren't enough," she said with startling finality. "There comes a time when you're carried away in desire. You'll both choose not to pause. He'll be too excited to wait. Since you haven't had sex before him, he'll know you're safe and he won't use protection. I know it, Nicky. I know how those times are. Condoms are fine for having sex occasionally. Entering into a relationship with someone like him? He'll want sex and lots of it."

I'll have it when I'm ready and Ryan's ready . . . maybe.

"You're so wide-eyed and innocent. I feel . . . please don't rush into a relationship with a mature man like Ryan. I wish you'd date boys your own age."

"I understand why you'd feel that way," I agreed. "The thing is, then what? Should I have sex with someone who doesn't know what the hell he's doing?"

"Or maybe not at all?"

"Mom," I gave her a look that conveyed ridiculousness. "I'm going to college. Come on."

"You'll let him do whatever he wants." She wrinkled her brow. "You need to be on the pill or get a monthly shot. Something that allows you to have sex spontaneously."

Damn, Mom. Where has this talk been before now? It's like I expect you to pull out some brochures!

"Well, like I said before, he invited Jenise. We'll have separate rooms and I'll stay with her. I don't think sex is on the table," I reasoned. "If it is, though . . . I'm just . . . well, I could've had sex with him a bunch of times already. I'll think about all the things we've discussed."

"You're being naive." She fidgeted. "Actually, you're being stupid."

"Mom, that's not nice."

Why does my family think it's okay to throw around insults like that?

"Maybe not, but sex is *always* on the table," she said bluntly. "I don't care how good of a man he is or how wonderful he treats you. Sex, with *any* man, let alone a man like him, is always in the forefront of their mind. It's all they think about at that age. Ryan is at the prime of his physical life and sexual peak. He's exposed to women who pull their skirts up or him every day. He competes with other men who have the same high testosterone levels. They talk about the intense, raw sex they get as a matter of routine." Mom gave me a pointed look before continuing. "Bet money. He's thinking of sex with you 24/7. Highly competitive alpha males like him push your boundaries. He's only waiting for the right moment. If you want your plans to be the way you see them now, you need to reconsider."

"You're wrong, Mom. We've already pushed each other that way. Our rational minds prevailed every time."

"What's rational about sex?" Her eyes narrowed.

"Uh . . ." Her frankness stunned me. I didn't have a comeback. She was right.

"Exactly." Victory seemed to fill her. "I'm only asking you to wait two days and go to the clinic and get birth control. If you don't have sex, fine. Being prepared is the smart thing to do."

"*I'm* the one who has the say so," I muttered.

Admittedly, it was a talk for the ages. She was level headed and overall calm and rational. As I left her and walked upstairs, I felt dejected. Even though I'd discussed every aspect of the conversation, ultimately, I'd given in to once again keep the peace in my house.

That peace was fragile, however.

It was a matter of time before it shattered.

Chapter 7

Checking in with Sis

*A*lthough I wouldn't admit it to Mom and Dad, as a general rule I listened to them. This time? I'd made up my mind—I was going to join Ryan on his road trip. Since his games in Denver were seven days away, the extra time would give me a chance to think about which form of birth control would work best for my busy lifestyle.

It bothered me to prepare for one of the most important moments of my life as if it were a purely clinical event. Getting pregnant—I understood Mom's concern about that. That was the last thing I wanted at this point in my life.

Was this trip really D-Day for my body?

I couldn't be with a man unless we were physically intimate?

So what if I decided to have sex?

Mom and Dad's virginal daughter—God, I was sick of that roll.

After Jenise was raped, it took Mom weeks to look my sister in the eye. She transferred to me all the dreams she had of seeing her daughter wear a white dress at her wedding—symbolizing all the antiquated meaning of past ideology. I knew behind her calm words encouraging me to get birth control was her hope of my sexual innocence. I wondered if having sex would free not only me, but my family as well.

Oddly enough, when Jenise began having sex after her trauma, Dad seemed to understand. For a brief period, they were close. As much as their relationship had suffered extreme turmoil, when it came to choosing physical intimacy, he never chastised her for her decision and instead confided that he understood her choices.

Still, neither of our parents had the mother/father-daughter talk with her they should have. She was left on her own to recover. Choices about her sexual life were her own.

Neither of our parents realized Jenise had transitioned into a magnificent, smart, and career-driven woman. It was unfortunate they couldn't celebrate their daughters' freedom from social stigma rather than disconnect—the same way they did to each other.

She's afraid. Honor the part of your mother that dared to speak up and challenge you. It wasn't easy, and maybe she's trying to reconnect with you.

I knelt at my bedside and said a prayer of thanks, asking for patience and understanding for both my mother and for me.

"Hey, you decent?" I knocked on my sister's door after I finished my prayer. "Hey."

"What are you up to?" She closed her book and focused on me.

Jenise and her boyfriend, Sean, had double dated with Ryan and me at The Waterfront nightclub and restaurant two nights before. They both drank heavily. Even though I'd never been hung over I knew my sister had paid the price. I wondered if she had gotten out of the house at all since I'd tucked her in her bed.

"How you feeling?"

"Fine now," she grabbed her hair and twisted it in a ponytail. "I had my milkshake yesterday."

"Milkshake?"

"A vanilla milkshake does the trick when you're hung over," she winked.

"Oh." *I have to ask. I hate to but* . . . "Do you drink a lot or . . ."

"Used to," she blew a bubble and then popped it. "I used to party a *lot,* especially in high school. Who doesn't, right? Oh." She shook her head. "I forgot who I'm talking to."

"Hey," I slapped her thigh. "I cut school once in a while."

"Drinking was like medication when I was going through therapy. Getting numb, escaping, feeling better for a little while . . . alcohol was a part of that. I wouldn't say I ever had an addiction, but then again, we all deny our bad habits until they're no longer invisible."

"Yeah, so your answer is . . ." I waited breathlessly, hoping I wouldn't hear that my beautiful sister had an alcohol problem.

"No." She looked into my eyes. Her stare was solid. "However, I know all the tricks from having done stuff."

"Did you ever take drugs?" I wanted to know everything.

"You understand alcohol is a drug?"

"I didn't mean—"

"Just making sure. I've done LSD, pot, of course, and shrooms."

"Wow!" my jaw dropped open. "I never knew!"

"It's not all that," she informed. "I only did it a half dozen times. Are you thinking of experimenting?"

"Sure I am." My voice dripped with sarcasm. "That's exactly why I came in here, to ask—"

"If you do, stay away from the mushrooms. They're dangerous. And weird. Well, at least for me. The high was I don't know. Different."

"How weird?"

"Like you're in a cartoon," she informed. "Should I go on, or are you satisfied your sister doesn't have a problem?"

"I'm satisfied." My anxiety deflated. "I'm sorry I asked. I worry."

"I know you do." She put her hand on mine. "You don't have to, okay? So you finally decided to come home after spending the weekend with Ryan?"

"Listen here, sissy." A grim note of warning laced my voice. "Ryan and I stayed here Saturday night to make sure you and Sean were okay. We could've gone to his apartment and left you guys all alone."

"Oh, now I feel bad." She put her book on the nightstand next to her bed. "I'm sorry."

"I was happy to do it. Well, not happy exactly. If you need me, I'm there no matter what. Anyway, now that I have all the information I need," I winked. "I told Ryan I love him!" I practically shouted the news.

"Oh, my God, you did? Where? When?"

"In the player's parking lot after the game!" I threw my arms in the air. The joy inside of me was just too big to hold onto.

"In front of everyone?" She looked as if she didn't believe me. "Even Kevin?"

I nodded.

"Matt and Darrell saw you, too?"

"They must have. They were on the bus." *It's overwhelming now that I'm talking about it. All of his teammates watching . . .* "They were only minutes from pulling out of the parking lot. I thought I'd missed my chance, but then Ryan stepped off the bus for me. We kissed, the driver honked, I cried; his eyes were teary—it was like a dream."

"Fuckin' great!" Jenise clapped her hands and bounced on her bed. "Have you told Jerry?"

"Oh damn," I slapped my cheek. "You won't believe it. He just got back in town and came to the stadium. I tried so hard to get away from him. I almost missed Ryan because Jerry had me cornered. I was about to make my move and I hear him calling my name. Mom told him I was there, the dirty rat. She did that on purpose."

"Of course she did." She clicked her tongue and then leaned forward, ready to hear every detail. "You scare Mom."

"Sure, I do."

"Yeah. You do. Dad's scared of you, too. They've never had control of you. You're slipping away to Stanford and now Ryan has entered into the equation. They've been pushed in ways they didn't expect."

"I never thought about it that way," I tucked a strand of hair behind my ear.

"Anyway, go on," Jenise encouraged.

"I had to lie so Jerry would leave me and I could get to Ryan. Oh, God, Sis. He's coming over and I don't even want to see him. What am I going to say? I've been rehearsing but can't seem to get the words right."

"What have you come up with?" Jenise leaned on her elbows, resting her chin in her hands.

"How about, *Jerry, I didn't plan this, but I've fallen in love?*"

"Hmm . . . I don't know," she frowned. "That will blindside him. You want calm. Saying it like that might bring out his anger. I'd try something like, *Jerry, you know I've always loved you and*

*your friendship means the world to me. Life is unpredictable, and .
. .* You can take it from there."

"So *do* you think we could still be friends?" I picked up her
Graphics Design book and absentmindedly thumbed through it.

"Why?" She changed positions and sat with her legs crossed
underneath her.

"I know this sounds like I'm using him . . . maybe when it
comes down to it I am. I don't mean to—"

"For fuck's sake, Nick. Just tell me why!"

"I'm afraid to tell him."

"Why?" she repeated.

"He's expecting me to be his girlfriend," I admitted. "Not just a
friend. That was the direction we were moving before he left. Now
it's all different."

"And Ryan says?" She waited for my response.

"Ryan doesn't think a man and a woman can be friends when
they've had sex."

She raised an eyebrow.

"Well, in my case, two friends who wanted more at one time
and are still attracted to each other. Well," I cleared my throat.
"One of them is attracted to the other. You know, I mean, he wants
more from me, not me from him but I was considering doing more
with him, or . . . something like that."

"Okay, so I get all that, but other than the friends issue, is there
more to it? I don't get why it's a problem telling Jerry. If you love
Ryan and want to be with him, that's all that needs to be said. Be
honest. It should feel great to say, *I've fallen in love and I hope
you're happy for me.* What's wrong with that?"

"I don't want to give him up because I'm afraid Ryan and I
won't last."

Nothing good ever stays around very long for our family and losing both would be terrible.

"Ah, now we're getting to the bottom of it." She adjusted her position.

"The other things is, I never told you this, but . . . I shouldn't tell you. Oh fuck it."

"Yes!" Jenise threw her hands up. "Good for you, you let a fuck out of your tightly wound body!"

"Yeah, well . . . sometimes there's no better word," I laughed half-heartedly. "So the thing is, Jerry's dad used to hit him. He and I were compadres even when we were only seven. So many times when Dad raged, his dad went off, too. We shared those dark family secrets . . . you know, what you and I went through, he went through fists and verbal abuse, too. Whenever it was bad here he'd listen to me and vice versa. I feel as if I'm abandoning him."

"Ouch. That's a tough one." She stroked her chin. "I can totally see why you're confused."

"And how do I, um . . . I just don't . . . well, look at this." I showed Jenise the friendship ring Jerry had given me.

"Oh, shit." Jenise's opinion of what I'd done was obvious. "Why'd you take it?"

"I don't know. Ryan was leaving and I knew if I took the time to explain myself I'd miss my chance to see him. I didn't want to wait any longer to tell him I loved him."

"So . . . yeah. I definitely side with Ryan on this one. The ring tells me you need to put a stop to this. Don't wait. Do it tonight. Promise me you won't beat around the bush and soft shoe it. Jerry wants you for more than a friend."

"I know." Remorse flooded me.

"You look sad," she stroked my arm. "You should be happy. You're in love!"

"I am happy." I pulled at my shirtsleeves. "It was only a few weeks ago Jerry and I had talked about an exclusive physical relationship through summer. I even made him search all these online sites and ask his pastor about sex. Am I a terrible person?"

"No!" Jenise exclaimed. "Get rid of that Catholic guilt from childhood. You can't help being attracted to someone. It's all those chemicals, endorphins, pheromones . . . it's animal."

"I feel like I've betrayed him," I admitted. "Actually, I feel like I've been dishonest to Jerry *and* Ryan."

"Attraction is what it is. Your body can't help it. Neither can Ryan's. You're a daughter of Aphrodite, Nick."

"What?" Her reference amused me. "Who's Aphrodite?"

"Greek Mythology." I looked at her with a blank stare. I hadn't studied anything about it. "The Goddess." Jenise punched me. "Her children are Shiva and Shakti. The goddess Aphrodite is talking to you. Your body is awakening. You can't help that you're attracted to someone. You have a big strapping man willing to be vulnerable with you. That's damn amazing. Jerry will get over it."

I blushed. Felt strangely drawn to the names she'd just said out loud. Feelings stirred in my belly. *Shiva.* He *is* Shiva—a marvelous, ancient, dominant and stirring power.

"So you could say to Jerry . . ."

My head rocked, suddenly drawn back into the moment.

"Where were you?" Her lip curled in amusement.

"Thinking about what it is to be Shakti." I smiled. "Tell me her story."

"Aphrodite stands on a seashell, a symbol of our vulva. The scene is magnificent as she rises from the ocean. Beautiful. Graceful. Her face glows with enchanting beauty. In her presence, everything is more radiant. Shiva and Shakti are the divine sensual beings of *The One*. It's like God dividing. Isn't it passionate?"

"Oh, wow! I feel like I've just had an orgasm!" I giggled. "I might want to study that in college. Maybe I'll be a Shakti major!"

"That would be some degree," she laughed. "Back to Jerry, you could also say *I really appreciate your friendship and hope we'll stay friends. Someone unexpectedly came into my life. I didn't search him out; it just happened.* You wouldn't be lying or abandoning him, and you put the choice right in his lap."

"Can you help me?" I begged.

"Help you *what,*" she teased.

"Rehearse what to say to Jerry."

We practiced the conversation a few times. Jenise ended by making the suggestion I ask Jerry to be happy for me and wish him the same success in finding love. It seemed short and too cold.

"And that's it?" I asked. "I don't know . . ."

"You think Jerry will be pissed?"

"Yeah, because he questioned me about Ryan's intentions when we were in the player's lot a few weeks ago."

"Why?"

"Well . . . remember that day when I wore those short shorts and your tight T-shirt to the ballpark? You were in the kitchen with mom and made fun of me for chasing two boys and how it wasn't fair? You called me a—"

"Cockteaser." She screamed in laughter. "Yeah, I remember!"

"Well, Ryan had the security guard give us passes after the game so Jerry could get some autographs and took the opportunity to give me his jacket. It was the day we had that talk on the beach and then went to Sammy's. He told me he loved me there."

"Oh, Nick. God, what a man you have."

"I know, he's so . . . he just takes care of my heart in every way. Because of the sneaky way my boyfriend got us into the player's lot, Jerry is already suspicious. At that time there was nothing going on, though."

"Oh no?"

"Well, yeah, there was. I didn't fully realize it," I grinned. "I admit I felt an attraction to Ryan *before* Jerry. If the situation were reversed, I don't know if I'd be so understanding."

"I think you would. You're very grounded like that. If Jerry's really a friend, he'll listen to you." She played with the heart pendant hanging from her necklace. "Friends support friends, no matter what."

"Hopefully our history together will be strong enough to keep the bond of our friendship. It's risky putting one friend aside and risking it all for someone I've only known for a year."

"You're right it is risky. Still, I think you're making the right decision. Ryan is so sweet on you. The two of you are like diamonds together."

"I do feel like I shine around him."

"Speaking of your honey, Sean and I were talking with him for quite a while at The Waterfront before we got toasted. By the way, I'm so sorry you had to help me into the car and up to bed. I let loose and it felt damn good to do it, but of all things, *you* taking take care of *me*." She put her head down. "Especially now, when you were worried I might have a problem, I'm sorry I got so drunk on our double date. What does Ryan think of me?"

"He—"

"More importantly, what do *you* think of me?" her face knotted.

"Well, Ryan seems to love you. Whenever I talk about you he gets a warm look in his eyes. You may not remember, but he's the one who carried you up to bed."

"*What*?" She appeared to be more than a little uncomfortable. "Oh, how embarrassing."

"I don't think he saw it that way. I wouldn't worry. Just so you know, I undressed you and tucked you in while he went down to take care of your sweetie. You know what?"

She shrugged her shoulders.

"Ryan stayed because I worried that you and Sean might get sick and choke. You know, that time with Dad . . . anyway, he asked me to go to his apartment. I told him we should watch you guys. He didn't even hesitate and stayed downstairs with your honey while I came up here to keep an eye on you."

"Oh, what a luvy you have there," Jenise said. "You guys are so sweet together."

"I do have a luvy." I wrapped my arms around myself, wishing they were Ryan's.

"So you're not angry with me? We're good?"

"We're good. I was just worried that . . . well, you answered my concern earlier."

We hugged each other. It was as if our embrace has released a little more of the hurt we'd pushed down from childhood—a little risk to open up to each other and a small step out of our shadows.

"Ryan admitted to Sean he's wanted you since last year." We let go of each other. "Did you know that?"

"Yeah."

"And you didn't tell me? What nerve!" She pushed me down on the bed.

"We weren't close then." I momentarily reflected on how my sister and I had drifted apart. "For the longest time I thought I was only a joke to him. He said he was making a move and then nothing for weeks." I closed her book where she had marked it and set it down. "What do you think about our age difference?"

"No big deal. In fact, I—" Her cell phone beeped. I saw Sean's picture on the screen. "Hang on." Her fingers busily texted something back to him and then she tossed the phone on her bed. "No problem with your age difference. Especially for you."

"Why for me?"

"No offense to Jerry, but you're too mature for guys your age. You'd scare them into the next county," she mocked.

"But eight years . . . I don't mean the gap in time, it's that he has so much experience." I flipped off my shoes. "He's gone to college and has his career. I haven't done anything yet."

"You've done plenty. Your whole life you've been working toward Stanford. You may not have the degree, but in many ways, you're already there. I don't mean this as an insult, so don't get pissed," Jenise warned. "I wish you *would* open up and party once in a while."

"I have no interest in getting sloppy drunk, or—"

"That's not what I meant. I mean going out more with friends. Go dance, experience college rallies, bonfires, big games and stuff like that. In my opinion? You won't go to any of them because that's not you. Oh sure you may attend a few events . . . we both know that's not how you roll. You went to one dance in high school—prom. You'd miss Ryan more than the typical college experience. Your personality is more about loyalty, friendship, and the importance of finding someone you can be close to. You need stability, not variety. I just don't see you having sex with a lot of guys. I see you with Ryan."

"Yeah," I paused to think about the things she'd just said. "I guess you're right."

"Hang on, I have to pee." She rushed off the bed and into the bathroom.

Chapter 8

A Recap

"*P*hew! What a relief." Jenise burst through the bathroom door fanning her face. "Back to your baby . . . ooh . . . I better close the door."

"And leave the fan on!" I cracked up. "You left a stinker!"

"One to be proud of." She opened her arms as if embracing the remnants of her bathroom break. "I think Ryan is the perfect man for you." She settled on her bed again. "I'm so jealous when I think about the great sex you'll have. All those women to practice with . . . lucky girl!"

"I don't feel lucky." My body felt as if it had deflated. "It bothers me."

My sister was comfortable and accepting of someone's past. I wanted to be like her. It was his *past*—over and done. My problem? I didn't trust it was over—not nearly over.

"Sorry. I know you have a tough time over sex." She paused for a few beats. "On another note, I talked with Ryan about getting my degree in architecture."

I was still thinking about her comments and the women he'd known. The frown I felt inside was visible on the outside.

"Hey!" she punched my arm playfully.

"What?"

"Come back here and stop dwelling on things you can't change," she reprimanded.

"You're right. Go on."

"You know that internship I was telling you about a few days ago? Ryan said he might have some sway. He knows the CEO of City Architecture. Figures you'd end up with someone like that. Damn, he's nice."

"*Figures*?"

"You're a big softie." Her eyes sparkled. "And he's a big softie. Regardless of how you both posture and try to put your chins up, it's obvious how much you care about each other."

"He embraces people, though. Sometimes he's aloof and protective when he thinks people are up to something, but generally he's pretty open. He seems so brave. I don't know if I'll ever get there." I gathered my thoughts. "When did you see him push people away? You were drunk."

"Not the whole night," she reminded. "He definitely took his turn shutting down with Dana, a few waitresses, women passing by . . . he's got his walls. I think they came down for *you*. You've softened him, you know."

"Thanks." My face heated. "I used to get so pissed about that word, *soft*. Now I've completely changed my mind."

"I know what you mean. I used to tell people to shove it when they tried to make me feel like the little woman, but the things I noticed the other night," she seemed to pull from a picture still fresh in her mind. "His eyes, his body language and his song! Holy God! I couldn't believe it when he took you up on stage. The whole club was stunned. The way he backed you up, held your waist, and then pounded the floor? Hot, hot, incredibly hot. How could you stand it? If it was me I would have collapsed!"

"Oh damn, Jenise, I almost did. My knees were shaking. He does that stuff all the time. He floors me."

"Sean and I could see it."

"See what?" I tapped my feet on the floor. "What do you mean? What could you see?"

"We saw how special you are to him. Tons of women in the club tried to get his attention and his eyes were only on you. You're his precious girl."

"He's overwhelming," I inhaled sharply. "Did you see that waitress kneeling down to take his order?" I stuck out my boobs, imitating her body language.

"Yeah!" she cracked up. "She was hot for your boy but he didn't even flinch. He knows some cool people. In fact, the whole table was cool."

"Yeah, cool cheaters." My dark, brooding twin tried to butt in.

"I think most of the guys and gals were just having fun."

"I guess," I protested. "A few of them sitting by me talked about my tight . . . you know, my thing? What the hell was I supposed to do with *that*?"

She cracked up.

"That's not funny, Jenise."

"I'm sorry." Her hand was on her mouth as she tried to stop laughing. "You're right; it's not. It's male intimidation bullshit and completely wrong. Why didn't you challenge them?"

"I could have. I was about to but then Kevin came back to the table and I didn't want to cause a problem that might ripple with consequences. Stirring up shit might get me banned from going out with him to places like that in the future."

"Yeah. That's smart, or . . . I guess . . . for the first time around his peers, you did the right thing. I don't know, I'm kind of . . . if it happens again, don't let them get away with it."

"I won't."

"Once you got up on stage all that stopped, didn't it? I saw you talking with Kevin. How was he?"

"He's nice. Oh! And Ryan's former girlfriend, well friend—or so he says—her name came up. Dana, the woman sitting across from me, was just getting into the juicy gossip when Kevin told her to shut the eff up."

"What was Ryan's reaction?" Her eyes widened. She put her hands on her thighs as if to brace herself.

"He was uncomfortable." I flashed back to the moment. "In fact, he got up and went to sit with you guys."

"Did you ask him about it?" she pressed.

"He said he didn't want to discuss someone from his past in front of me and it was no one's business."

"Ooh," she rubbed her hands together. "There *is* a hint of something juicy brewing there."

"When I was at his apartment, I brought her up again. I couldn't let it go because he keeps asking me to stop seeing Jerry, which, okay, I get that now, but I threw it back at him when I asked him if he's ever known a woman he didn't have sex with. Get this . . . he has women's clothes in his closet from former lovers. He actually suggested I grab something from the assortment!"

"Oh Sis, big deal."

"*Big deal?* Don't you think it's disrespectful?" I couldn't believe she wasn't bothered by it. "How would you feel if Sean had a collection? I felt like he was keeping trophies and I was a castoff. More than all that, I felt like he'd dismissed all those women as a piece of ass."

"Well, I mean . . . they were, right?"

"Maybe. They didn't need to be thrown away. Or—"

"If it was Sean," she gave me a stern look. "I'd be happy he had a healthy sex life before me and happy he was ready to be with me. You're too hung up about the women he's been with. In my opinion those clothes mean Ryan doesn't give a fuck about them. If he did, wouldn't they be hanging in his closet rather than carelessly tossed into a box?"

"I guess so." *Her analysis about the clothes does make me feel better.* "The thing is—women are everywhere; in front of him, behind him, to the side of him . . . when I was at the ballpark today, a few of them asked me to hook them up when he came to the railing to talk with me! How can he really stay away from them? One woman was spilling out of her top. You know all those underwear and swimsuit models on TV? He can call them, Jenise! He has the connections to do it."

"Ever look in the mirror?"

"Of course," I snorted.

"Really?"

"Yes. You're saying . . ." I was obviously irritated.

"I'm saying, look at yourself."

"What's wrong with me?"

"Take off your invisible shades and open your eyes," she taught. "You're a real person. Smart, on your way to stardom at Stanford, and of course, there's your tits and ass—dahyam."

"Not nice," I pouted.

"You understand the smarts you've been blessed with but you don't appreciate the dynamite you have loaded in your body. Your sweetie does, though." She started laughing. "In fact, I'll bet he holds that one-eyed lover in his hand at night and jerks off to a fantasy about your curvalicious bod."

"Oh, shit!" I wasn't sure I'd ever be as comfortable as she was talking about the body. Nothing seemed to faze her when it came to sex. "Now I've got a picture in my mind . . . thanks a lot. One-eyed lover. God, sis."

She's the female Ryan!

"Seriously, loosen up. Enjoy him and what you have together. You can't live life because of what *might* happen. You have to trust him. For God's sake, I was raped at fourteen. If that doesn't tell you something about what little control we really have, I don't know what will."

"I know." I put my hand on hers. "I was thinking about that downstairs."

"Bad things happen to good people," Jenise reminded. "I was given a hard and unexpected lesson about it and took years to get over the guilt. As if I should be guilty about *anything* from that day, right? I finally realized it wasn't my fault. I thought I could control my life and what happened to me. Reconciling with the notion I had encouraged the attack somehow . . . the questions the police asked me . . ." Her face knotted.

"I'm so sorry you went through that." I ran my hand down her arm. "I don't know how you come back so strong."

"Therapy. My psychologist helped me to understand trying to control other people is unrealistic. And now I have Sean!" Her eyes shined. "He loves all of me, including my past. In fact, he told me it's *because* of my past he was attracted to me."

"I'm proud of you." I put my arms around her and simply loved her. "I knew from when we were little girls you'd be a trailblazer. I like Sean. He's a gentleman. It's obvious he loves you."

"He *is* sweet," she agreed. For one of the first times ever, I saw my sister blush.

"Let's spend tomorrow together. We'll do whatever you want." I suggested. "That is if you're not doing anything with your baby."

"Beware . . . I'll put my little sister through the ringer."

"Looking forward to it. Why I came in here in the first place—Ryan left tickets for us to join him on his road trip. Mom doesn't want me to go unless you come with me. Would you?"

"So what if Mom doesn't agree," she challenged. "Just go."

"I should. I want them to like Ryan and not resent him."

"Valid point. When?"

"His road trip lasts for ten days. Any time during then next week-and-a-half would work. I was thinking Denver, which is about a week from now."

"Would you guys kick me out at night?" she winked.

"God, no, Jenise, come on, be serious."

"I *am*," she teased. "Let me check if I can skip any of my summer classes. I'll get back to you tomorrow."

"Okay, thanks." I kissed her and went back to my room to get ready for Jerry. I put on black jeans and a loose pink sweater with some black loafers. Just as I finished brushing my hair, my cell phone rang.

Ryan.

"Hi, Shiva." I was sure he had no clue of the meaning.

"My feminine, powerful, Shakti," he replied. "You made me . . . you move every part of me when we speak."

You know mythology? A jock knows about this stuff?

"How did you . . . ." I was stunned.

"I told you I have two degrees. That meant studying. You know the story about Aphrodite don't you? Rising from the wet ocean on a seashell . . . symbol of your—"

"I know," I interrupted before he got me hot and bothered. "My sister told me the story."

"God, I miss you. I wish we were lying next to each other kissing, hugging, kissing . . . mmm."

"Me, too. Don't say that stuff."

"We're about to take off," he chuckled. "I only have a few seconds. Did you check with your folks?"

"Yeah, I'm waiting on Jenise. She'll let me know if she can go with me tomorrow at the latest."

"Do you think you'll be able to meet me?"

"I want to come to you right now but I promised my mother I'd wait for my sister's decision." My body tensed even as I said it. "Mom's afraid, I guess. She keeps telling me to get birth control because you're thinking about sex 24/7." I laughed at my blatant honesty. After the prolonged silence, I got nervous and rolled on. "Maybe sex *is* on your mind all the time . . . hell, it's on mine, too. I still want to be with you. I'd love to see the farm out of Denver. I dream about that picture you took. You know the one of the little boy and his bunnies? I enjoyed looking at your pictures last night."

"Honey, we're going to Denver now." He laughed at my rambling. "If you want to meet me here you need to leave."

"Oh no." I felt like I was sinking through my bedroom floor. "How did I miss that?" Every breath seemed shallow as it fell from my body. "I thought Denver was at the end of the trip."

"We finish in Miami."

"I don't know about Miami. It's so far. I probably can't come after all." Even as I spoke, panic was rising. "I'll have to see if Jenise can get away with me. She's checking on her summer school schedule. I could go and my parents couldn't do about it . . . I feel sorry for Mom. I don't want to create problems or worry. They don't need me to add to their stress. Do you think I'm ridiculous?"

"No."

"I'm sorry." I could hear his disappointment.

"I understand. What your mother said makes sense. We need to respect her concerns."

"Ryan?"

"Yes?"

"Thank you for talking to Jenise about the internship and thanks for calling like you said you would. I love that you know who Shiva is. I just discovered him today. I should have guessed . . . you're so tuned in. How you could be so . . . well, I just love you and that's the story I have for you tonight."

I love you—it was so freeing to say those three powerful and intimate words to another person. Now that I'd said them, I wanted to keep saying them out loud and often. It was as if a lock on my heart had opened and my emotions were pouring everywhere.

"Peaceful dreams tonight, sweet Nicky."

"You too, my Ryan. Goodbye for now."

Shortly after I pushed end on my phone, the doorbell rang.

I knew it was Jerry.

I took several deep breaths.

I'd entered another world since making plans with him during the week. Still, I had to face whatever our relationship would be and talk with him about Ryan.

It would be one of the hardest things I'd ever done.

Chapter 9

Facing Off

*"H*ey you." I tried to be friendly.

Jerry leaned in to kiss me.

My gut reaction was to back away. I did the only thing I knew which might make him feel like my behavior was normal—I moved to the side, dodged his kiss, and hugged him. It was automatic and unplanned. I only wanted Ryan's lips on mine.

As I prepared for what I thought was our inevitable separation, I began to tremble. I could take anything that came my way, except the cold abandonment of a friend.

"Everything okay?" A crooked smile said hello. His eyes moved up and down my body.

"Yeah, it, um, it's been a strange day. I'm not feeling great and probably should have waited to do something with you tomorrow," I lied. "I even skipped cheering because I wasn't up to par."

I just told my good friend a lie. Is my relationship with Ryan healthy? This has nothing to do with Ryan. It's me.

"Let's see what your pal Jerry can do about that. Do you want to stay in your room and veg out? I can rub your back like you did to me at Point Reyes."

"I don't—"

"We can just lie together and listen to music," he interrupted. "We don't have to go anywhere."

No way in hell I'm hanging with you in my room. Mother Mary, help me through this.

"Let's do something different." I looked directly into Jerry's eyes. "I don't feel like doing anything normal anymore."

"What do you mean, different?"

"I don't know, but . . ." I shoved my hands in my pockets. "I don't know, Jerry. Maybe we could go to the acrobat show, or um, a soccer game? I think San Jose might be playing."

"Sounds good. Right now, I need your kiss, Nicky. I've been waiting to have it all week long." He started to pull me close. His head tilted. "Actually, all summer."

"No!" I abruptly jerked away.

"What's the matter?" he looked confused. "You're avoiding me."

"I might be contagious. I don't want to take the chance I'll be the reason you get sick and miss playing your baseball games. Let me make sure this is nothing, okay?"

"You sure?"

"Yes. No. I um, I actually have something, I—"

"I know where we can go!" he interrupted at the exact moment I was ready to begin the conversation I'd been dreading.

"Where?" I swayed back and forth nervously. *Stay away from anything romantic or a movie with make out scenes.*

"Cirque du Soleil." He brushed an insect away. "Damn it. Pesky bug." He waved frantically and I cracked up. "Think that's funny?"

"Yeah. It keeps circling. What did you do? Put on too much hair product?"

"I don't use that stuff."

"Oh yes you do you big liar."

"I do," he blushed. "They're performing at Pier 28. Wanna go?"

"Sure." *That's so thoughtful of him.* "Bye, Mom!" I yelled.

"Bye Mrs. Young!" Jerry shouted.

Mom returned our goodbye. As we closed the door, feelings of being just a girl and a boy rippled through me. Even as we hopped on the streetcar, in a way it felt as if we'd only gotten on our bikes and we were peddling to the beach. I looked at my friend when he wasn't watching and felt the threatening sadness of goodbye around the two of us.

Only a few feet from our stop and we already at the entrance to the tent that was home to the dazzling acrobats. After buying popcorn and a soda, we found our seats and for the next few hours sat amazed at their incredible moves. During the mesmerizing performance, I silently practiced the words I needed to say. Still I couldn't settle on the right way to say them.

Why was I unable to let him go?

I supposed it was that he was the first person I had let into my life of dark family secrets. He'd seen my fears. Shared the hurt from my childhood and adolescence. No one else knew me the same way. He had been the ground I needed; there for me like I'd been for him.

Who would he turn to now when his dad hit him?

Who would I turn to when my family spun out of control?

Were the days of needing each other in those ways over?

Was it time to bury our past?

Was that our only common thread?

"What now?" Jerry asked as we walked out among a crowd that buzzed about the show.

"How about some coffee?" I suggested. "And a little something to eat?"

Even after so many years of practicing good eating habits there were times I succumbed to the comfort of food. When I was little, if I wasn't being bribed with food to be quiet, I was rewarded with it. Just like alcohol was my father's vice, food was a friend that I knew would always be there for me, shielding me from the trauma and dysfunction of my family.

I was promised food in all forms—cookies, candy, chips, bowls of ice cream, pizza, and burgers—in any amount I wanted.

The message I heard consistently was: "here, eat this and watch TV," or "have some cookies while we wait for your dad to come home." While shopping with Mom it was, "pick out the snacks you want and put them in the cart."

Countless times, Dad came out from the bar with candy, nuts and soda to keep me quiet while he "talked" with his friends.

In our house these types of unspoken compromises were as common as a cup of coffee—or a shot of whiskey.

"Hey, I've got a better idea, gorgeous. You want a different evening? Let's go to the Top of the Mark for some appetizers."

"Coolio!"

We transferred to the cable car and took the slow trip to the top of California Street where the Mark Hopkins was located. The hotel restaurant offered a 360-degree view of the city. Day or night, it was spectacular to be seated there, whether to watch the fog roll in through the Golden Gate, or the skyline come alive with the lights of evening.

"Seems like yesterday we were across the street at prom," Jerry said after we'd ordered several appetizers of crab sliders, small green salads and spring rolls.

"Time goes by so fast." I took a sip of the delicious espresso. "Hey, I need to discuss—"

"I can't get over those stupid rangers at our bonfire." He interrupted and laughed hard. "I thought for sure their light was going to shine on my ass."

"Or something else," I giggled. "That *was* a close call." The window of courage I'd opened only moments ago, slammed shut. "That short one—the one with little man syndrome—what a dick. He sure loved yelling in his megaphone."

"Thank God no one got out of line." He dipped a spring roll in the sweet and sour sauce. "I had a feeling they were just waiting to pick a fight with one of us." He scooted his chair closer to me. Held my hand. "Can we continue where we were headed that night?"

The young couple at the next table smiled and the woman raised her glass to me.

I didn't think he'd start this early. Does that mean couples have sex even if they're sick?

"Oh, Jerry. I've been trying to tell you." *Take a deep breath.* "I know we've talked about exploring sex together when you got back. Not tonight. You uh, well, you don't want to begin that journey with me, because . . ."

Just then, his cell phone rang. I was sure I saw a picture of our classmate, Terrie, on his screen. He put it away so quickly, I couldn't be certain.

"Who was it?"

"No one." He avoided eye contact with me.

"You could have taken the call. Call her back if you want to."

"*Her?*"

"Whoever, I mean."

"It's not important." He tucked the phone back into his pants pocket. "Where were we?"

"Was that Terrie?"

"What?" His answer seemed defiant. "Why do you think so?"

"I thought I saw her picture on your phone. She doesn't care for me and the feeling is mutual," I laughed nervously. "If you're into her it's okay; I just wondered, that's all." My stomach clenched. She didn't deserve a good guy like Jerry. She'd toss him over quickly when she was through using him for her latest conquest. I didn't want to see that happen.

"It was just a teammate." He wouldn't look at me. I knew he was lying. "If it *was* Terrie, why would it be all right with you if I was into her? You wouldn't care?"

Join the club. Not easy to tell the truth about the person you've fallen for, is it?

"I would," I admitted. "She's got a reputation for using boys to hop up to the next level. I don't like her. If you do, though . . . well, it's your life, after all. So . . . I enjoyed our evening. Before we go, I need to tell you about—"

"It's my life?" He raised a suspicious eyebrow. "You're not included in any part of it?"

"That's not what I meant. I told you I'm a little upended."

"*Upended?*" he snorted. "Whatever, Nick."

"I'm trying to tell you something important—"

"Well, I know the world revolves around *you*." His words turned cold.

What does that *mean? Where did this come from? Because I challenged him about Terrie? I'm trying to have a serious talk and he's put off because I'm not jumping into bed with him. Screw it.*

"I don't know what you mean," I tossed out. "I think the world revolves around all of us, so . . ."

"I *mean* . . ." the veins in his neck stood out. "Nothing. Just forget it." He put his head down and then seemed to rise from the ashes in defiance. "Actually, no. I've done everything you've asked to begin a sexual relationship with you. I've pulled back. I've done the research online. Talked to my pastor and coach. You're still avoiding me. I'm fucked, I guess because . . ."

My face burned in anger. Without saying the words, he'd just told me he was fucked because I wouldn't.

"You're *fucked*?" I lashed out instead of keeping the peace. "Ha! That's a laugh. Because you fucked Terrie. Admit it, Jerry. What you just said is a bullshit statement. You've only been back a few hours and we're already here with your conversation? When you met me at the ballpark today I wasn't ready to see you—"

"Wait—let me get this straight—when you say you weren't ready at the ballpark, what you're really saying is you didn't want me there, right?" He crossed his arms.

"It wasn't that," I corrected. "I was finishing my business and I felt rushed with you waiting for me."

"Shit, let's just go home." His voice was filled with resignation.

"So just because you're back, I'm supposed to drop everything and everyone? What do I do, flip on a switch, Jerry?"

"No. Well, yeah. Yeah, flip your fuckin' switch," he lifted his chin in defiance.

"If you feel that way, let's go." I snapped back. "Fine with me."

"You think I haven't noticed?" he slapped at my hand.

"Noticed what?" I replied sarcastically.

"You've already taken off the friendship ring I gave you. I spent a lot of time picking it out for you and just . . . wow, Nicky, nice to see how much you appreciated that. Guess I know where I rank in your book."

"I've been trying to tell you—"

"I think you've said enough, *lady*."

Every time I started to tell him about Ryan, he cut me off. Because of Jerry's continuing sarcasm and insults, I took the coward's way out. I said nothing. We rode the streetcar home in silence. He at least had the decency to walk me to my door.

"I'll call you tomorrow," he mocked. "Maybe *then* you won't feel so *off*."

"You know what? Don't do me any favors," I opened the door and then turned around. "Thanks for walking me home. Oh, and say hello to Terrie for me."

I slammed the front door and went up to my bedroom fuming. It had begun so great between us. In the end Jerry's only mission seemed to have a discussion about the two of us having sex.

What did you expect? He doesn't understand what's happened with you. Just tell him!

I showered, put on my pajamas, opened the window and tucked myself under the covers. I was just getting comfortable, when I saw my cell phone light up.

Alex texted: *What are you up to?*

I responded: *???*

She texted: *Ryan?!!!*

I texted back: *I'll let you know when I see you.*

She replied: *Okay. Back late Friday.*

What could I say to her? I'd wanted to shout it to the world that I was in love with Ryan. Whether I was right or wrong in the way I felt, I had to be careful with Tara and Alex. They'd warned me about him and all but told me to stay away from him.

Beside my sister who was stuck with me forever, I'd never had friends older than myself. I wasn't sure what behavior I could get away with while being with them. These women were now better friends than those from my childhood.

But could I trust they wouldn't abandon me at the first sign of immaturity or trouble?

You either trust your friends or not. If they abandon you when you need them, you're better off without them.

Alex had already suspected I'd fallen for Ryan when we were together in LA a few weeks earlier. Matt had acknowledged he knew whom I was hanging with when he visited me at the railing before leaving for his road trip. Certainly Darrell and the rest of his teammates had seen me in the players' lot, throwing myself into Ryan's arms. Had he also heard about our date at The Waterfront? Did he tell Alex about it?

Of course he did.

It felt good to be in my bed alone, on my mattress, tucked in my sheets, in my house, surrounded by all my things. I could let my mind empty out and had nothing planned the next day except to be with my sister.

And that felt right.

Chapter 10

Golfing with Sis

"Wake up," Jenise rocked me back and forth. "Time to spoil your sister."

"What?" I mumbled.

"I've decided I want you to take me golfing." Her voice was annoyingly perky. "Hurry up before it gets too windy." She slapped my butt.

"Mmm . . ." I moaned, stretching myself awake.

"Come on, sleepyhead. Get ready." She stood at my bedside wearing an open robe that covered a little nightie.

"You sleep in that?" I raised an eyebrow.

"Sure. What do *you* wear? Oh, lemme guess, you sleep in the raw, huh?" She cracked up.

"Everyone's a comedian," I remarked.

"How did it go with Jerry, by the way?" She pulled on my arm.

"I chickened out."

She sighed in disgust.

"I tried, Sis. I really did. He kept interrupting. Then, because I wasn't all excited and ready for his sex he got angry. He brought me home and we ended up in a fight. Stupid, huh?"

"Fuck him and good for you, Sissy. I always thought he was such a sweet, innocent boy. Shows how much I know."

"Yeah, been trying to tell you how you don't know shit for years." I slapped her leg. "Actually, I'm still shocked about it. We were off to such a good start. After Cirque de Soleil, we went to the Top of the Mark. Then, just as I tried to tell him for like the third time, his cell phone rang. I'm sure I saw Terrie's picture come up on his screen."

"Who's that?"

"One of our classmates. She's been after him since our freshman year. She's . . ." I corrected myself and changed the words I had first thought to describe her with. A goal of mine had been to stop categorizing women as sluts and whores just because they enjoyed sex. "Let's just say she doesn't care who's going out with who. If she wants someone, she makes her move."

"Fuckin' testosterone," she said. "It takes away their conscience and all they think about is their stiff prick."

"That's what Ryan said about boys that age, too," I laughed. "Can you imagine he talks about Jerry that way with a reputation like the one he has?"

"Seems like someone is trying hard to turn you away from Jerry," my sister mused.

"That's already done—at least the sex part. What I'm trying to find out is if we can still have friendship. Jerry tried to pull me in for a kiss. I almost gagged. Isn't that terrible? He has no clue . . . my poor friend."

"Hell no. Fuck that. *Poor Jerry*," she imitated. "Too bad you chickened out, though."

"I was ready to grab his arm to get his attention, but then he pissed me off. I know it was wrong, but I gave up."

"He's a stupid boy whose dick is probably hard a dozen times a day." She rolled her eyes. "I'll bet he already feels awful—well, after he's jerked off about a hundred times."

"Maybe."

"You need to forget about all that. We already discussed being friends won't work. After he's had sex with Terrie he'll mellow out and you'll get another chance to tell him," she smirked.

"Yuck." I pushed myself out of bed, dressed in appropriate golf attire, and quietly slipped down the basement stairs and into the garage with Jenise.

"Here." She tossed me her keys. "Be my driver."

"Don't push your luck, *Sister*."

She looked so professional in her golf outfit—a vest and collared shirt, long socks and short pants that cut off at her knees. As we walked the fairways, I imagined her networking and socializing with her clients, discussing their projects, or having a strategy session with the higher-ups at City Architecture.

"You know why you can't golf well, don't you?" Jenise asked suddenly as we approached the tee on hole three.

"Why, oh why, golf genius?" I mocked her lovingly.

"Your huge boombas." She put her hands on her breasts and shook them.

I rolled my eyes.

"It's true," she giggled. "Every time you swing, those things get in the way. You'll never be any good unless you get a reduction. Of course, then you might lose Ryan. He's enamored with those girls."

"Shut up! No, he's not."

"Uh-huh, that's not why he got you those tight jeans the other night?" she reminded. "He didn't want to see your curvaceous ass; it was only a mistake with the size." She cracked up and then set herself, addressed the ball and took another swing.

Whenever I golfed with Jenise, I usually drove the golf cart and watched her play. I could only hit the ball forty yards at a time, and generally in a line drive. In no particular order I'd shank or slice it, roll it ahead a few feet, top it, pop it up, put it in the sand trap or in the water. Overall, I was a good athlete and even played on my school's volleyball and softball team. I could kick a ball far, and was even picked by the boys to be on their teams. But for some reason, I never could improve at golf.

"You want to know a secret, Nick?"

"Of course! I'm always up for a secret!"

"Golf helped me get out of the house after I was raped. It's a game you can play by yourself and I didn't want to be around people for a while. It's so serene out here . . . I used the time to meditate. You remember I was on the golf team in school?"

"No."

"God, Nick."

"Sorry . . . I didn't—"

"That's all right. I know you had your own shit goin' on. I got so good that my golf coach got the school to pay for my practices. I won most of my rounds, too—star of my team if I do say so myself. Volunteering and clubs at school were your way to get out of the house. I used golf to join the world again."

"No wonder you're so strong," I shook my head. "You're my amazing sister."

She smiled and then addressed the ball sporting a contented look. Our day on the golf links was the usual. Jenise was on her way to a solid eighteen holes having a score of just a few shots over par. I was down the two boxes of golf balls I'd just purchased: lost somewhere in the woods, under the pine needles, in the bushes, or deep in the water hazards.

My phone vibrated as we were coming off the eighteenth green.

"Who's that?" Jenise asked. "As if I didn't know by your smile."

Ryan wrote: *What's up?* ☺

I replied: *Golfing with Sis*

He responded: *Hi Sis! Have fun!*

"He says hi."

"Hi back," Jenise said.

I texted: ☺ *Sis sez hi. I miss u*

He texted: *Me, 2* ☹.

"He misses me!" I partially yelled. As he continued writing, my enthusiastic smile faded.

Next—Milwaukee, Miami, 2 far 4 u. talk 2 u 2nite. I luv u

NO! I wrote furiously. *WILL c u in Miami!*

He responded: *It's OK. No problem. Talk 2 u 2nite.*

"Huh." I was one hundred percent disgusted. A healthy anger rolled through me. Something felt wrong about what he'd just done. I felt small—like a little girl who'd been dismissed. He'd made the decision *for* me, assuming Miami was too far or too difficult, leaving me out of a decision that wasn't his to make. Just as I was getting close to the root of my upset, the wind whipped. The flag near the clubhouse snapped and caught my attention.

"What's up?" she noticed my troubled expression.

"Something Ryan did. I don't like it."

"Uh oh, trouble in Tiltonland?"

"He chose for me, Jenise. He told me to forget meeting him because it's too far. How would *you* feel if Sean did that to you?"

"Miami? I thought we talked about going to Denver?"

"We were, but last night Ryan told me they're in Denver now."

"I guess I'd feel the way you do, but after our date the other night? I can't believe Ryan meant it like that. Let's keep enjoying our day and you can call him later. Then you can have some good phone sex when you make up."

"Not the way I feel right now." My mood turned dark.

Chapter 11

Internet Girlfriends

"*T*he hell with all these men," Jenise announced. "Let's have some woman time."

We changed in the clubhouse and had a quick lunch at the golf course restaurant. While chatting over salads, Jenise's phone lit up. At first her face was bright and lovely. Then her mouth twisted, apparently over what she was viewing.

"What's going on?" From her expression I was concerned it was bad news at school or with her boyfriend. "Is Sean okay?"

"Yeah, it's um . . . it's not about me. Or Sean." Her entire body seemed to tighten.

"Tell me before I grab your phone, Jenise."

"It's about you and Ryan," she frowned. "There's a picture of you guys on someone's Instagram when he sang to you on stage."

"Oh well." I was ready to dismiss it.

"It shows when he had you pinned against the wall and he was leaning on one arm." She wrinkled her nose. "It's so obvious he's trying to make you weak. It's a great photo, but will you be in trouble with management?"

"Shit! Yeah, they could release our whole team. Oh, how reckless of me. Damn it."

"There's more, Nick."

"Is it bad?" I put my hand on my forehead.

"Kind of." She held out her phone. "Look at this."

It was a web site that featured athletes—mostly single—with an overwhelming majority of followers who were women. The comments weren't about the way he pitched on the field. Many of the posters seemed to be current and former girlfriends. There were haters, admirers, and apparently scorned lovers. Hundreds of pages were dedicated to male athletes of all sports. Each his own page on the web site. They were filled with photos and comments of all sorts, twenty to a page—and dozens of pages. Once again, I was faced with the reality of his public persona and this time, I was included—and not in a good way.

"Ew, look at these photos. Women hugging him, and oh, God, posing to make sure their breasts touch him . . . damn." I stopped as I saw the picture Sean texted. It was posted about two-and-a-half pages down, captioned: "Check out this curvy cutie with Tilton at The Waterfront in San Francisco this Saturday."

Among the few dozen comments that followed were these:

"She's so fat. *Really*, Ryan?"

"Aw, Tilton's in love."

"Tilton's taste has gone from blondes to brunettes?"

"Gawad, Tilton, you couldn't have picked someone more glamorous? Where did you find her . . . on a street corner?"

"What a big girl . . . it's obvious what part of a woman's body you like."

"After you had *my* body? Are you *kidding*, Ryan? You're dating *her*?"

"Give me a break. Guess I need to get plastic surgery on my boobs and ass to get you back. Those can't be real, can they ladies?"

"Rumor has it she's only seventeen."

"Ryan Tilton is a pervert and has always had a thing for underage girls. He's dated them younger than this. I've heard he ties them up, leaves, and comes back for more."

"After dating swimsuit models, you're with her?"

"She's so lucky—look at him singing to her—looks like love. Lay off of them."

"Another in a long line of soon-to-be castoffs for Tilton. Enjoy him now, lady. It won't be long until you're a memory."

When I finished reading the last one, I tried not to get emotional. It was so soon after he'd told to stay home . . . I couldn't hold them back. Tears filled my eyes. It was as if every mean girl in high school had grown up and posted their comments about me on the site.

"How mean." I gave Jenise her phone. Put my hands over my eyes. I couldn't stop sniffling.

"They *are* mean." She put her hand on my arm. "I know it's hard to look at it. I don't think those posts are real. Keep that in mind. They're only rude comments to make it seem like they know him. It's like they're phantom girlfriends playing make believe. I'll bet Ryan doesn't know any to this shit is even on here."

"He probably doesn't, or . . . knows but doesn't care. It's like . . . all those old comments and the names—those names I heard when I was eleven and twelve that reminded me every day that I was overweight have risen again. You never had to worry about that, Jenise, but I'll never get over hearing fat cow, heifer, fatso, hippo, tubs . . . the list was endless. I still think I'm too big and it puts me right back into those adolescent years."

"You're a beautiful woman, Nicky."

"Inside here?" I pointed to my heart. "I'm still a fat girl."

"Most of us are still insecure about *something*." She stabbed at a tomato. "Remember those awful glasses I used to wear before Dad and Mom got me contacts?"

I started laughing.

"Yeah, you know how awful they were. You can't stop laughing even now!"

"I'm sorry." Once again, she helped to lift my dark mood. "Those glasses were *so* bad."

"Yeah, when I'm not wearing my contacts, I still have those pings in my stomach when I go out in my glasses . . . even though I know I look good in the pair I have now. Talk about names! I heard crab eyes, goggle eyes, glass clown, Mrs. Harry Potter— childhood crap is tough. Kids are mean—especially girls on girls."

After my sister helped me to file away the ugliness of being called out for no good reason, we finished our lunch and then window-shopped downtown. Sak's had a display of their new arrivals. Jenise drooled over an Armani tunic top, which was paired with a tight pair of Burberry pants with ankle zippers.

"Ooh! I want to buy this outfit and wear it for Sean."

"Yeah, what happened to *the hell with men*?" I teased.

"I know." She clasped her hands together as if making a wish. "He makes me feel like I can fly." She sparkled. There wasn't any denying it; we couldn't stay quiet about our boyfriends for very long. Just being with Jenise made me feel better about Ryan's presumptuous text.

Mom and Dad beamed as they watched us come through the door laughing. I understood how precious those moments were. We sat down for a while and told them about our day before Jenise announced she was going over Sean's. When I went up to my room to write in my journal, I tucked our golf scorecard inside its pages.

Staying passive when I talked with Ryan, I stuffed down my feelings so I wouldn't cause him to seek out another woman. In order to maintain the peace between us, I withheld the conversation I wanted to have about our boundaries.

Peace at any price—it was what I'd done all my life.

Even though Ryan had told me to forget about the road trip, he sounded sad. Much of our conversation focused on how much he missed and loved me. I didn't want to cause a ripple of doubt with him. I was always mindful to protect myself from the resulting chance of being abandoned. Although I wondered if he already knew, I didn't even discuss the Internet site, photo of us, the rude comments or the "pretend" girlfriends.

Another upset swept under the carpet.

Chapter 12

Days with Tara

*A*fter leisurely sliding into the next day, I decided on a long walk. I stopped at West Portal Bakery for a scone and coffee. Finished and then made my way to Ocean Beach to sit and listen to the waves. I'd just gotten back and was ready to jump in the shower when Tara called.

"Nicky?" Her voice shook.

"Are you okay?" My heart felt as if it was in my throat.

"Can you come over? I know you're probably busy and you weren't expecting to come over until tomorrow . . . I need you." She sobbed. "Can you—"

"I'm on my way." I threw my phone on the bed. Quickly showered. I'd previously only heard stability and reassurance in her voice, never the fear-filled tones she'd just let go of. I left my house so off balance and worried I forgot my phone charger.

Tara lived in the Cow Hollow District in San Francisco. It was one of the nicest areas in the city and filled with beautiful homes, good schools, restaurants, boutique shopping—and all of it a ten-minute walk from most anywhere in the neighborhood.

Her townhome was on the second level of a modernized building with a brick façade. Big, stylish windows with black shutters adorned it. When she buzzed me in, I pushed open the glistening wrought iron gate and found her waiting at her front door. Immediately taking my hand, she led me inside.

She'd decorated the living room in light greens and pinks with lots of paisley and flower accents in the drapes and sofas. The room was classically romantic. A big fireplace with a large, cream-colored mantle was the focal piece. The dark Acacia wood floors were stunning. Her long and narrow kitchen had gorgeous black cabinets on each wall, polished black granite countertops, a six-burner Wolf range and stainless appliances. At the end of her kitchen was a greenhouse-style breakfast nook with a view out to her garden through floor to ceiling windows.

Wicker chairs with lush cushions surrounded a glass table. It was where Tara wanted to talk. Lines of worry crossed her face. Her eyebrows were taut. It was obvious she'd been crying. I squeezed her hand and sat with her quietly until she was ready.

"I," she wrung her hands. "I don't even know where to begin."

"When I was in pain last week, a friend told me to dive in." I put my hands together and pointed them as if diving into water.

"In some strange way, I don't want to say it out loud," she confessed. "I'm afraid I'll make what seems like a dream, real."

"What's wrong?" I didn't want to circle around the issue.

"Tell me about you first," she stalled. "What are your plans the rest of the summer?"

"Tara, you called me to come over and scared me half to death. Come on. Give."

"I'm being tested for uterine cancer." She looked out the window and back to me. Her eyes had welled up with tears. "I just finished the tests today. They told me it will be a few days and I couldn't stand to wait alone."

Not knowing what to say, I did the only thing I could—I listened.

"I knew there was a reason why I was having trouble getting pregnant. We've been trying for a year, you know. Recently, I've had some bleeding, so I went in for tests. I hope the results are back before Matt gets home."

"He already knows, doesn't he?" I prodded gently.

"He knows I'm getting tests, but not for cancer."

"I think he's guessed. The other day when we talked, he practically begged me to stay with you this road trip."

"Still, I want to know before he does. I need to prepare . . ." Her voice was shaky. "I knew. When I started bleeding, I knew." Her sobs were deep and she buried her head into my shoulder.

"You don't know anything yet." I played with her hair. "Don't go there."

"I can't stop thinking the worst." Her cheek rested against mine.

"It could be any number of things." I rubbed her back.

"I know I shouldn't be thinking this way," she agreed. Let's sit on the sofa where it's more comfortable."

After all, the next bad thing is bound to happen. It always does. And now it's going to happen to my girlfriend.

She talked for a few hours working through her emotions. Crumpled dozens of tissues. Threw them on the floor with all the others.

"I'm sorry you're here with me instead of having fun with friends." Finally it seemed she was able to let go for a little while and she changed the subject. "So what have you been up to?"

I told her about my date with Jerry. I couldn't let it go.

"That's surprising." Tara looked at me quizzically. "You two have been friends a long time and you've had nothing but good to say about him. Do you think his reaction is just because of sex? Something else bothering him?"

"Before he left to play in his summer league we talked about having sex. We agreed to consult with other adults and do some research online. As soon as he got back he gave me a friendship ring. I didn't want to embarrass him, so I took it even though I didn't want to. When we went out, I forgot to, no, actually I chose not to put it on. The thing is, as soon as he saw me, first thing he says? He's *ready* for me," I told her. "I get it. It was sweet he did everything I asked, but did we have to go right there?"

"Well, I agree it was rude. He was anxious. The thing is, boys his age have no tact. On the ring, has um, someone else caught your eye?" The inflection in her voice indicated she knew about Ryan. "You didn't want Jerry's ring and that's all there was to it?"

"Yeah, I've . . . I'm interested in someone else," I admitted.

"*My* girlfriend, Nicky, who swore off boys is interested in someone?" Her face blossomed from the wilted flower she was only moments before. "Spill the deets, girl! Were you *really* going to have Jerry as your first experience?"

"I thought so. I pulled back . . . and I've done that more than once. Crap, I've done if a half dozen times. I don't know if I'll ever by ready, Tara."

"Trust me, you'll know when you're there," she giggled. "If Jerry's turned some corner and he's comfortable with sex, I'm afraid that's how boys are in their late teens and early twenties. It comes up on them suddenly. Besides, you aren't the kind of woman a man can be friends with."

Why not? I still don't get it.

"You've got too much going on." She took a drink from her water bottle.

"I know." I took a long sip of water. "I'm busy all the time."

"No," she reached for me. Put her hand on my forearm. "I mean that you draw people to you in a way that's very deep."

"I don't believe I can't be friends with boys . . . well, guys, um . . . men. The thing about staying away from sex, I mean, Jerry and me—we've been friends all our lives. Whether it's him or the other man who's caught my attention, I always thought I'd stay a virgin until marriage. Parts of me want to remain untouched until then and other parts are screaming to hurry up and enter that world."

She put her hand over her face, laughing at my dilemma.

"I know it's not funny, Nick, it's just watching you debate over sex . . . are there spiritual beliefs complicating your decision?"

"My priest told me it's a mortal sin." I wove my fingers together.

"What does that mean?" she asked. "Sorry, I'm not familiar with that term."

"If I don't confess my sin before I die, I might go to hell." I knew my beliefs were conservative. The few people I'd shared them with . . . including my own family, seldom agreed with them. Jenise and I were baptized Catholic. My sister, always the one to find out the scoop, told me Mom had only agreed so their marriage would be "approved" by the church, which made my Grandma Young a happy woman.

"And how long ago was that, Nick?"

"It's been a while."

"I know your beliefs are important." Tara uncrossed her legs and sat on the edge of the couch facing me. "In my opinion? I think that piece of extreme guidance was for a young girl whose priest didn't want to see lose her innocence too early."

"You're probably right. I shouldn't feel this way, but I can't shake the feeling I'm doing something that's gravely wrong. That's what I mean by *sin*. It's a natural thing. My logical mind gets that. It seems dirty before being married; like it's just pleasure."

"And that's bad?" she raised an eyebrow.

"See there's the rub. I know sex isn't dirty, but—"

"Do you think Jenise is dirty?" she posed a great question.

"No."

"What about your high school friends? Your teammates?"

"No."

"How about Alex? Oh well . . . on the other hand, let's not use her as an example," Tara giggled.

"God, Tara!"

"Shh," she put her finger to her lips. "Don't tell her I said so."

"What the hell is happening to me?" I laughed off and on thinking about *Dirty Alex*. "I didn't want male relationships at all, especially before college. I was careful to stay away from guys."

"Life doesn't sit still very long, does it?" She leaned back and tucked her feet under her.

"Jerry even said we're too smart to let sex ruin our friendship. Yeah, sure. Guess we're as dumb as bricks."

"We're all dumb in the beginning, honey. I'm sorry to disagree with your priest, but I don't believe you'll go to hell for having sex. I understand spiritual values, but come on. Your creator is going to send you to a place of suffering for all of eternity because you had sex before marriage? And all because you didn't get a chance to confess you were sorry for acting on a powerful force that was given to us by the same creator that loves you? Why have hormones, a clitoris, wonderful orgasms and a penis if we're not expected to use them for pleasure?"

She paused to gauge my reaction.

"Isn't that part of what our sisters did for us in the sixties and seventies? Women's liberation pointed out how it was acceptable for men to have sex all the time and they were heralded as cool and suave, while women were tramps and whores. Those are stereotypes, honey. Give yourself time. You'll know when you're ready because it will feel right. As far as Jerry? He built an expectation that wasn't real. When he was rejected, he obviously didn't handle it well. If you check in with him when you get home, I'll bet he'd apologize that he reacted that way."

"Maybe you're right. I really don't want to check in with him so soon, though." I glanced toward her fabulous, gourmet kitchen. "Hey, how about I cook us something?"

"I could eat. Get what you want and I'll share with you."

"How's your tomato garden doing?" I thought back to a year ago when Matt and Tara asked me to housesit for them. They were impressed that I not only tended their garden the way they'd requested, I had also completed an entire checklist of items labeled "*if you have time*," and had dinner waiting for them on their first night back. "Are there any ready for a salad?"

"Yes! I'll go pick a few ripe beauties." She put on her garden gloves, which rested in a basket by the patio door. "Remind me to give you some before you go home."

I cooked grilled cheese sandwiches and made a salad of tomatoes, chopped apple and a few thinly sliced radishes.

"Olive oil and red wine vinegar okay for dressing?" I stood with the bottles in my hands when she came back into the room.

"Sounds perfect."

I drizzled both on the salad and served it with our sandwiches.

"Thanks for this; everything I mean. It's all delicious, Nicky. You obviously realize that simple meals are the best."

"That's good," I laughed. "Simple is all I can do."

We finished eating, cleaned the dishes, and returned to her family room. Two kidney-shaped, dark green sofas surrounded a second fireplace. Along with several unique lighting sconces, photos of friends and family decorated the walls.

"I have to use your bathroom." I excused myself after we'd talk another few hours. "I'll be right back."

"Would you mind if we went upstairs?" She yawned. "I'm ready to watch a movie in bed."

"Go on up and I'll join you in a bit." I turned off the lights and set the alarm, locked the bathroom door and reached in my backpack for my cell phone.

My heart thumped. My battery had died. I'd forgotten my charger. In my rush to get to Tara, I realized I'd left it at home.

Damn it! I can see it lying on my bed. What do I do? It's late and I can't ask her to take me home. Ryan's probably called already. Shit. I'm always doing something wrong with him.

My body was in misery.

I knew I wouldn't be able to relax.

For Tara's sake, I had to deal with it. She needed to be first.

Shake this off. Put your friend first. You can take care of the mistake when you go home. It's not the end of the world.

"What's wrong?" She'd noticed something wasn't right with me when I joined her in her bedroom.

"My phone died. I forgot the charger."

"Who do you need to call this time of night?" The inflection in her voice again hinted she knew things she was keeping to herself.

"I don't know . . . no one, I guess. I feel naked without it, that's all." I opened my backpack and pulled out my nightgown. "What if my sister or parents need to reach me, or—"

"If you're that worried, I'll drive you home." She turned as if she was going to get dressed. "It's no problem. Let me throw something on."

I wanted was to let her dress. The thing that stopped me—other than being a self-centered bitch—was that Mom might spill the beans about Ryan to Tara.

"No," I gave her arm a squeeze. "I want to be here for *you*. My needs aren't a priority right now. I'll make do. Besides, they have your number. Thanks anyway."

What if he calls, what if he calls, what if he calls . . .

I got into my nightgown and slipped under the blankets with her. Tara's big bedroom dripped with romance. I imagined it a lover's dream, surrounded by Michael Amini Chateau Beauvais luxury. Each piece was a hand-carved original, the ornate design an extension of the living room themes. The walls, draperies and bedspread were all compliments of light greens, pinks, soft reds, creams, and lavenders. Completing the room were oversized chairs, a dramatic chandelier, and a large Thomas Kinkaid painting that hung above the headboard.

"I love your bedroom. It's so romantic. Ooh, this comforter." I gathered it in my hands. "It's so thick and luscious . . . just begs for Matt to make love to you on it."

"For a young woman concerned with sex, you certainly have an active imagination," she giggled appreciatively.

"Yeah, well . . ."

What if he calls, what if he calls, what if he calls . . .

She started *You've Got Mail* and was asleep before the movie ended. When I heard her breathing heavily, I checked that her eyes were closed, turned off the TV, the light, and then went to dreamland with her.

Over breakfast the next morning, Tara told me she'd scheduled us to volunteer at Children's Hospital. We finished a simple breakfast of toast and fruit and headed to her favorite place. I realized as I watched her, the place was a key to her balance. She was at home cradling the children—some with cancer, severe burns, and others with incurable illness or debilitating disabilities. It was joyful to see her tenderness. She made an impact with those she touched—whether it was listening to a story she told or letting a child talk about her feelings, each little person seemed to love the gentle woman spending her day with them.

The anxiety I had felt from letting my phone battery drain lessoned and the heaviness regarding Ryan being dismissive of my decision to come on his road trip finally lifted.

Chapter 13

Tending Gardens

"*L*et's have a contest for the prettiest mud pie!" We had changed into our sweats as soon as we got back. I'd suggested the competition when weeding her garden, kneeling side-by-side.

"You're on!" her eyes sparkled at my proposition.

We scooped a few handfuls of the rich smelling earth, used her sprinkling can for the right amount of water, and carefully shaped the flat disc into a circle. Pulling the little yellow flowers from milkweed, the fluff from dandelions, and orange petals from a few poppies, we decorated them and declared our contest a tie.

"I wish we could save them." I always hoped I could preserve moments like those forever. I never believed another one that was just as sweet would come along for me.

"Let me take a picture and we can have it as a memory." Tara wiped the dirt off her hands and snapped a few photos with her cell phone. "I'm sending them to you now. When your phone charges they'll be there for you."

"Can't wait to take a look."

"You've got the rest of your summer ticking away," Tara wiped her forehead. It was as if she'd caught the worry in my response. "I really needed to see you last night but I'm okay now. As usual, being with you has made me feel better."

"I'm surprised you didn't call Alex." I pulled up a bundle of mustard grass and tossed it in the compost pile.

"She's not my sensitive girl; you are. Alex is my buddy, but when it comes to deep emotions, she has walls of her own. She can close down big time."

"Her mother, right?" I used a trowel to loosen the soil around some root-bound vegetables.

"Made her the tough, take-charge woman she is today," Tara nodded appreciatively. "Not unlike most of us when it comes to covering our hurt, I suppose. Look at how smart you are and you had family stuff. Maybe it's a kind of—"

"Twisted gifts," I answered without hesitation. "That's what I've always called them."

"See what I mean?" She placed her finger on the tip of my nose and then quickly took it away. "With Alex, she's the one I turn to her for hard-nosed objective advice. When I want softness . . . you're my go-to. You know how to listen."

"Thank you." It was as if a magical feather brushed across my face and another definition of *soft* had been shared with me. I knew the intimacy of that moment wouldn't come along often. What she'd said made me feel closer to her.

"Why don't you go ahead and take off, honey. You don't need to waste more of your free time on me." The look on her face was calm and her hopelessness no longer evident.

What if he calls, what if he calls, what if he calls . . .

"Time with you is never a waste. Even if I stayed with you the rest of the summer it wouldn't be a sacrifice at all; it would be a privilege. The things you did for the cheer team—the way you took us under your wing and made us feel like we belonged—the nervous knots in our stomach calmed down and our performances were better because of you."

"Oh, babe. It wasn't any trouble. You gave me a much needed project to focus on."

"Yeah I'll say you got a project. Me! Way more than you bargained for probably."

"So much trouble," she teased.

"Your friendship is like a rose that bloomed in the middle of my desert, Tara. You really don't understand what you've done for me." I took her hand in mine. "Partially it's because of your encouragement that I'm close with my sister again. You're my magnificent love. My second mom. While she wasn't capable of holding me, you've never hesitated."

"Oh, Nick." She kissed and gave me one of her *mom hugs,* then continued to dig in her garden in silence. Worry ate its way into our tranquility. "I just wish I could give Matt a child. It's on my mind all the time. What if it can't happen?"

"Maybe it'll happen when you stop trying." I thought I'd accidently pulled a flower from a patch of ground cover. "Is this a weed or should I put it back?"

"Morning glory," she huffed. "I made the mistake of planting some one year and now I can't get rid of 'em. They take over the whole damn yard. Pull as many as you can."

It had trumpet shaped flowers almost like petunias and she had them in pink and blue. It suddenly made me feel sentimental something so pretty was destined to be removed from the garden like a common weed.

"You know, these are just as pretty as some of the flowers you're keeping." I held up the little bouquet I'd collected. "Do you mind if I make an arrangement from them for our dinner tonight? There's a whole group of them, right here."

"Of course not," she smiled. "You know how lovely it is watching all your little wishes come to life? Sometimes I feel like you're my little girl."

I knew I'd blushed from her comment. After I'd picked all the flowers I wanted, I went into the kitchen and washed them. I found a large clear bowl, filled it with water and arranged a floating garden of flowers for the dinner table just as Tara came inside.

"If you can grow weeds this pretty, I think you have miracles coming that you're not even aware of, Tara."

"I hope you're right." She put her gloves in the basket by the door. "It's so beautiful outside. Let's freshen up and go for a walk before dinner, okay? We can grab a couple of sandwiches while we're out and bring them back to enjoy with your flowers."

We showered quickly and then began our walk. Several side streets and little alleys off Union Street had pocket gardens and Tara planned to copy some of them. Tucked away from the casual passerby, they were filled roses, camellias, flowers and herbs. Intent on redesigning her own yard, she jotted down several pages of her ideas and made drawings in a small notebook. When she was ready, we stopped at a little market a few blocks from her house. It had fruits and vegetables displayed in wooden boxes on stands in front of the store. We ordered our sandwiches and purchased nectarines, peaches and two bananas. Dinner seemed extra delicious, paired with our vase of pretty weeds and a warm fire burning in the fireplace.

Somewhere around ten she fell asleep on the sofa. The peaceful look on her face was so lovely I didn't want to wake her. I put a blanket over her and stretched out on the love seat until I fell asleep, too.

On the third afternoon I gathered my belongings to head home. Tara's mother was due to arrive in less than an hour. The two of them needed to be alone. I put my backpack over my shoulder and grabbed the bag of tomatoes she'd packed for me.

"You haven't said anything about the new man who's caught your attention."

My heart thudded.

"Oh, well . . . you don't know him."

"Don't I?" She folded her arms. "Ryan Tilton?" She'd come out with it so suddenly I was stunned.

"Yeah." I looked away from her. "I wasn't sure if you knew. I was trying to find the right way to tell you that, uh, I'm kind of seeing him." *Do I tell her that I'm in love? What will she think of me?* "I mean . . ." I tried to refocus my speech. "What do you think of me? Am I a cleat chaser?"

She cracked up.

I followed.

We both went into a laughing fit and finally calmed down.

"Far from that," she admonished. "Please reassure me you're using the brain God gave you and you're not being reckless. It's Ryan who took your attention from Jerry, right?"

I want to be reckless for a change. I'm tired of being careful.

I glanced at the ground and back to Tara.

"He must be a good man if you like him," she doubted.

"And?" I pushed gently.

"From what Matt tells me, he can be a handful," she reported like a dutiful girlfriend.

"Say what's on your mind." I put down my backpack and the bag of tomatoes.

"He's been with a lot of women. I don't know if he's the right one for your first experience. It might be nicer to be with a boy like Ethan Mathers. Matt told me you talked with him the other night. Do you like him?"

"Not like you mean. We're just friends."

If I had sex, maybe my friends would stop feeling like they need to protect me. It seems like a mountain on my horizon. I wonder how that would be if I just let go and had it. Would they still feel the same about me?

"Do you understand what it means to be with him?"

"I think so." *Who am I trying to reassure?*

"You'll be pushed in ways you can't imagine, honey. The level of stress and pressure if you choose to be with Ryan . . . I have trouble sometimes even with Matt and he's nowhere near as well known. It's tough."

"I've already experienced some of that. The other night we went out and women were all over him. Wherever we go, people want his autograph . . . my sister showed me this awful girlfriend site online her boyfriend found. A ton of athletes have pages on it. Of course Ryan is on there, and . . . have you seen it?"

"I hate that shit," she grimaced. It was the first time I'd witnessed real anger well up in her. "Women on those sites . . . God they're rude."

"Does Matt have one?"

"Oh, of course. Darrell, too. What nerve, putting something like that up for every groupie in the world to post their lusty desires." She shook her head. "I hate it."

Wow! My cool, cool girlfriend is pissed off!

110

"Someone posted a photo of Ryan singing to me the other night. The comments . . . they mostly ripped me apart. Other than a few nice comments, most of the posts were awful. When Jenise showed it to me, I felt like, I mean . . . does it ever stop?"

"No. That's why I'm upset he's dating you," she said protectively. "The lives of professional athletes are demanding, especially at the stage Ryan is in his career. He's the premiere closer on the team. Translation? The spotlight. All. The. Time."

"I get it."

"I don't think you do. You're too sensitive for that shit. I don't want to see you go through all that fucking social media crap. I'd rather see you in your jeans enjoying Stanford with your friends, free to be whatever and go wherever you want."

"I've thought a lot about what it means to be with Ryan. You wouldn't believe how many times I told him he should be with someone his own age, used to all the attention—like a model. I know he's dated them. I understand why it makes sense. They're used to the attention, too. He made me promise to stop talking about it, so I gave in."

"If I were you I'd keep that conversation open," she suggested.

"I don't get what he sees in me. Still, after all of my analysis, the bottom line?"

"You want him," she smiled.

"Yep. The only boy who ever came close—and that was a very distant second place—is Jerry. Even that was different. Ryan spins me around until I'm dizzy. Most of the time I look at him and shake my head in disbelief. It's like I'm stupefied."

"You're in deep!" Her face brightened. "He's got you going!"

"Going, coming, spinning and somersaulting." I hesitated a minute. Wondered if I should tell her the whole story. How would she judge me? Without another thought, it all poured out. "I was so worried about the way you and Alex might react." I blew out a breath. "I appreciate how calm you are. I don't know what I expected . . . I've thought it through. I'm giving us a try at least until I go to Stanford—if we last that long and if he can keep from screwing on the road. I don't know how I'd find that out, but . . ."

"What does your gut tell you? Do you trust him?"

"He's a good man and I trust that. On the other hand, his popularity, the way he's desired, and the other stuff . . ."

"What other stuff?"

"Like how wild he was. You and Alex have told me, but it doesn't take a genius to know about him. I've seen and heard things at the ballpark. Just the other day when I sat at the dugout, women were dressed in low-cut shirts flashing all the guys. And when we went out the other night, one tried to get a picture with him by sitting in his lap wearing nothing but a bikini top and shorts that showed her ass!"

"Oh shit, did he let her?" I could see by Tara's expression she assumed he had.

"No," I puffed proudly.

"Hmm . . . maybe Alex and I are wrong. At least promise me you'll take it slow," Tara warned. "Men easily confuse love with sex. They completely commit and they're so sure it's real—until it's not. Another pretty face draws them in and they realize it was only lust. You're pretty juicy after all."

"What?" I cracked up.

"Oh come on. Don't tell me you haven't a clue about the tasty little morsel you are. Most men would love to sink their um . . . teeth into you." Her eyes danced with mischief. "That's why men will have trouble being friends with you, Nick."

"Don't women do that, too?" I giggled from her ribald comment.

"True. I admit it's unfair to lump men together that way. However, in my opinion they mistake sex as love more often than women. Once a vagina becomes a part of the equation, well, they're enamored so easily with our bodies."

"I think Ryan's is pretty great, though," I clasped my hands in excitement. "I love his chest."

"It's pretty spectacular," she agreed. "Matt's butt is luscious! I wanted it as soon as I saw him." She motioned with her hands as if tracing his ass in the air. "Do you know Kevin Reynolds?"

"I met him on my date with Ryan the other night."

"Matt told me that he overheard Ryan talking to Kevin and admitted he's deeply in love with you. Maybe his intentions *are* honest."

"How long have you known?" I looked at her bashfully from under my eyelashes.

"A while," she grinned. "I hoped you were going to tell me."

"No way." I half-heartedly kidded her. "I didn't want to take the chance you'd think the worst about me."

"I'd never do that, Nick."

"I've wanted to tell you dozens of times. When I considered how you and Alex warned me, I didn't know what to say."

"Sounds like you've analyzed everything as much as can be expected by a lovesick little puppy," she eyed me. "I shouldn't be surprised the way you think everything through."

"I am sick, Tara." I put my arms around her. "If it lasts with Ryan, I'll need to talk to you often about how you handle it when Matt goes on the road."

"You and I have a standing date, then." She handed me the bag of tomatoes.

"You be sure to let me know your test results, young lady." I pretended to be stern, trying to keep her mood light. "I don't want to bother you with your mom visiting, but I will if I don't hear from you in a few days, understand?"

We hugged each other and then said good-bye. All I could think about was the missed calls from Ryan.

What was I supposed to do? Tara needed me and I couldn't inconvenience her.

When are you going to ask for what you want? My Evil Twin whispered.

When I got off the streetcar, I ran home and hurried up to my room. I immediately plugged the charger into my phone and when the first bit of the green battery icon appeared on the screen, I turned it on and played back the sad-sounding voice mails from my sweet boyfriend. I couldn't wait any longer. I had to call Ryan. I hoped he was alone or somewhere he could answer.

"Nicky! Oh, baby. I've called you so many times."

"I was—"

"At Tara's," he said. "I know. I called Jenise to make sure you were okay. Why didn't you call me back?"

"I'm so sorry. She hasn't been feeling well. When she called the other day she was scared, crying, and practically begged me to drop everything. I panicked and left without my phone charger. Then it died—"

"Take a breath," he reassured me. "Is Tara all right?"

"She doesn't—" I was getting ready to tell him more, but as I was scrolling through the missed texts in my phone, one caught my attention. "What the hell!"

It was as if my heart stopped.

I continued reading. Shook with anger.

When I finished, my fears had been validated.

Ryan needed a woman his own age after all. Apparently, he had one right next to him.

Chapter 14

I'm in Limbo, Going to Hell

𝒯he text read:

I'm Jesse. I'm sure you've heard of me—Ryan's girlfriend. I know he claims to have fallen in love with you. Don't be fooled. I'm with him now. We're having sex tonight like most nights when he's away. Honey, our sex is for adults only. His mouth is all over me and his big cock is inside me. So not fair, I know. He's too much for you—you're just a baby. Trust me, he'll rip your little body apart. He's duped you. I have a ring. We're engaged. I'm sorry, but you're only a fantasy—his joke. Live your life, don't waste time on him, he'll break your heart. So sorry, I'm sobbing and crying for you. Hugs and kisses, bye for now.

Jesse.

"What . . . what the hell is this text?"

"What does it say?" Ryan's voice shook.

"It's . . . I thought you didn't see Jesse anymore?"

"I don't," he denied. "You know I don't."

"Uh . . . apparently, you do." Panic, anxiety, fear—they coiled and then sprung through me. My belly twisted. A loud noise clanged in my head. "She says she's still your girlfriend. I guess while I was at Tara's taking care of a woman who's scared to death she might have cancer, you were having fun with the woman you really wanted with you. She says our relationship is a joke, by the way. Apparently I'm not woman enough for your sex because it's too rough and you'll destroy my body."

"What are you *talking* about?" Ryan's voice trembled.

"Your girlfriend, Jesse. She's with you right now, isn't she?"

"You know she's not—"

"She sent me . . . oh, yuck, it's . . ." I pursed my lips to blow long, deep breaths through them, trying to calm down. I couldn't. "It looks like, it . . . it came in last night. Oh God, it's . . . let me read it to you. You sure you're ready for this?"

"Yes."

"It's a doozy. Don't you already know what it says?"

"Forward it to me it that's easier for you."

"Nothing's easy about *this* message," I laughed nervously, and colored it in sarcasm and disgust. "Here goes . . ." I read the entire text out loud. "How did she get my cell number?"

"I don't know."

"You don't *know*? She finds my number, tells me your mouth is all over her and you don't know? Tell me how that happens."

"I can't . . . I don't . . . I have to . . . I—"

"She's the woman you've given your ring to apparently. When were you going to drop that bomb on me? Let me read between the lines. You gave her a ring, but then fell in love with me. It's over and she can't let go. You're letting her down easy, by making love one last time, right?"

"No."

"Didn't you classify her as an acquaintance? Why did you bother hiding the truth? No wonder Dana asked you where she was. And by the way, when were you going to tell me your casual relationships get engagement rings?"

"I wasn't. Wouldn't. I didn't. Please, I'll . . . Listen, I'll get to the bottom of this."

"I bet you will. Just ask her. Isn't she's in your room lying right next to you?"

"She's not with me." He was firm and clipped with his responses. I wasn't used to him responding this way. I was agitated. I wanted emotion. I wanted to here the fight from him. Instead, calm laced his voice.

"It all makes sense," I concluded. "Now I know why you told me to forget about coming."

"Jesse has nothing to do with you being at home. I wanted your parents—"

"Wanted my parents to . . . what? Be fooled like me?"

"Yes. That's it exactly. We wanted your mom and dad to approve of our relationship. I thought it was best. No. Wait. I don't mean fooled, you're—"

"*You* thought it best? Well, thanks for that. Let me see if I've got this right. I'm not supposed to be friends with the opposite sex. Have I understood that correctly? And yet, you're able to have Jesse with you?"

Silence.

"You said all you needed to be done with other women was a commitment from me. Wasn't it you who promised the past you enjoyed would be over when I said I loved you?" I was at my breaking point. "I begged you not to play me."

"I'm not."

"Listen, Ryan. I'm giving you an out right now. If you admit that you're still sex friends with Jesse, I'll understand and back away. Tell me the truth. Let's at least save that part of us so we can remember what we had with a smile."

"We're not sex friends."

"Right."

"After her text, I guarantee you we're not even friends."

His statement made me pause. I wanted to believe him. I was on the edge of believing him and then the doubts crept in. All I'd ever experienced with my family were broken promises. I didn't have enough faith in Ryan—or myself—to take a chance.

"Your move, Ryan."

"I'll get to the bottom of it."

"Sure, take your time. I'll just take your word for all this and wait here for your return call."

"I'll handle it," he said with a voice that held no tell.

"I bet. Handle *her,* you mean." I threw all the sarcasm at him I could. "While I sit here with blind faith you'll swoop me up and we'll ride away on your white horse as soon as you tuck Jesse away somewhere? I'm not one of the women you're used to being with who sits and waits for your call. You suggested I stay home—no. Wait. Actually you *told* me to stay home—and I'm supposed to wait on you? Go play a game with someone else, buddy."

"Be reasonable."

"Oh . . ." I took a breath to keep from exploding. "I'm being quite reasonable under the circumstances. If you're not with her, then how did she get my number?"

"I don't know. I'm not with her, Nicky. I'm asking you to believe me."

"Sorry, but after her text it's not reasonable to ask me that. She got a hold of your phone to get my number. You're not innocent in this. Why was she that close to you?"

"We were—"

"Let me save you the trouble. I'll tell you how it happened. She grabbed your phone from your nightstand and looked through it while you were in the shower, right?"

"No, no, we—"

"We what? You couldn't reach me the last few days, so you strayed. You were worried I drifted again and you reached for comfort. Isn't that about it, Ryan? Can't handle that I have a full life and won't drop everything to be with you?"

"I wouldn't discourage anything you want for your life," he stated. "You know that."

"Well . . . except giving me the room to make my own decisions about coming on the road trip with you, and that bugaboo you have with me and male friends. Yet, you continue full speed ahead with your lady, Jesse. All your sweet words—promising you wouldn't abandon me. I didn't understand that meant when you came back and were in town. Different when you're away, right? How could I have been so stupid?"

Cut him off first. Hurry . . . he's about to tell you he needed his long time sex friend because you're too much trouble.

"Nicky, I wouldn't do that. Just let me—"

I was certain the end was right in my face and another person I loved was lost to his addiction—this time it was sex.

"Don't bother, Ryan. I understand. This is the second time you've dropped me because of sex. Jesse's name has circulated ever since I've known you. Don't deny it like you did at The Waterfront.

I get your history with her, but you said I shouldn't be worried." My voice started to break. "Were you afraid I'd see the sparkle in your eyes—the sparkle that's reserved just for her? I'm glad I found out early on about the two of you. Just leave me alone. Please leave me alone."

"Don't cut me off." His response finally contained some emotion. "Hold tight for an hour and let me find out . . ."

True to form, I couldn't chance hearing the hurtful words—those words that would end as lies and broken promises—slice another piece from me.

I had taken down my armor for him. Angry I'd done so and unable to bear the pain and bruising of what was happening, I prepared to raise it once more. Mom and Dad had abandoned me so many times that I should have been used to it but I never could stand the empty feeling.

Being abandoned by someone in whom I'd had complete faith and allowed myself to be vulnerable with made me feel as if every future relationship would be the same, ending in devastation.

After my journey with Ryan, would I ever look at another man—or woman—without casting my suspicious net over them?

"Why did you make such a big deal about seeing only me, like I was the one?" What I wanted was for him to convince me and keep talking. I couldn't stand to listen any longer. I knew the inevitable had come for me, the way it always did for my family.

"I haven't, I mean I have—" Ryan stumbled. Perhaps his perfect plan had unraveled. He was pulling together the bits and pieces he could salvage, hoping to hear me say I would agree to wait for an explanation.

I didn't stop.

I couldn't.

I knew in only a matter of minutes he'd give up. I'd hear, *you're right. It's too hard to be with you. I'm sorry*. I'd started counting down the seconds. I knew if I pressed him and didn't keep the peace, it would be over. I was ready to cut him down before he did the same to me.

"You asked me to try on this relationship. Guess what? It's not my size. I expect you to keep helping my father and sister like you promised. Don't wag your golden tongue and give me any excuses. I didn't blow this, you did. Besides that, just fuck off. Or . . ." my Evil Twin rose up viciously and sarcastically. "Go fuck Jesse, your acquaintance. You're dead to me."

If I had been on a landline, I would have slammed down the phone. I wanted to smash something. *Anything*. I wished I could have taken all the plates in our kitchen and thrown them against the walls, leaving the broken pieces everywhere.

Maybe if I numbed myself like my father had, I wouldn't hurt so badly. Was that why he self-medicated? Maybe his emotions were too severe and he couldn't control them. Maybe getting drunk was the only way he could cope with pain and disappointment. Alcohol was a depressant that kept him subdued until the raging beast inside of him, no longer able to be contained, took him over.

I ran into Jenise's room.

She wasn't home.

I tried to call her.

Reached voicemail.

Should I try Ethan? No, I couldn't call and tell him I was at odds with Ryan—not again. I'd lose his friendship for sure.

Frantic, I called Patty, Lorraine, Marilyn, and Kathie. Not one of them answered their phone.

Where is everyone? I need to calm down. I've got to get out of here! Run, Nicky, run away! The only way you'll be happy is to study. Grab your books. No, better yet, ice cream!

Crashing through the house in every way, I fought my rage, hurt, and tears by doing the simplest of things—washing the dishes, dusting, and vacuuming the living room carpet—as if in doing them, I'd feel better.

My phone rang with messages and texts from Ryan.

I wouldn't answer.

I finally turned it off and took a bath. Periodically I poured in more bubble bath, drained the cool water and replaced it with hot. I did this for over an hour. I got out. My mood hadn't changed.

As night began to fall, I became more nervous and unsettled. It was then a feeling of hopelessness sunk in.

I tore apart my room. Rearranged my furniture; sorted old magazines and journals; wrote some poetry; organized my hope chest.

Down our basement stairs. I ran into the back yard. Played with the garden hose. Made waterfalls and water snakes in the air. Watered the lawn and flowers under a crying moon.

I guess I went a little crazy.

I realized how bizarre the scene was.

I stopped.

Stopped to let the hurt in.

Stopped to feel the crush of my heart.

Stopped to let the images of Ryan having sex with Jesse—a woman he'd assured me was a part of his sex-filled past, with him this very minute—burn inside of me.

Oh God . . . I'm so sick. I miss him. I hate him. I hate her. I hate that I gave in.

The words of Jesse's text played repeatedly in my mind. "*His mouth all over me.*"

Maybe they couldn't let go of each other.

Maybe their sex was so incredible they needed to physically connect every so often because no one else could satisfy them.

Maybe Ryan was desperate to be rid of her and he'd used me to convince Jesse he was in love with someone else so she'd leave him.

Maybe it was the reverse—*she* had left *him*. I was the ploy to make her jealous. Was he in love with her?

Or was it that he'd taken a change to reach back for the innocence of his childhood with someone that understood abandonment? Once he'd gained some new perspective, he'd reach back to the woman who knew how to handle him?

Even though it hurt, I understood.

I had only wanted him to admit it.

Was she part of his past, present, *and* future?

I could visualize their naked bodies touching. Ryan's mouth must have been all over her as she typed in her text, both of them laughing as she pushed send.

For adults only.

My body ripped apart.

She has a ring to show me.

The revelation was clear—I wasn't ready for a relationship with *anyone*. Obviously that was why I chose not to have sex. It complicated everything. Those sexual dynamics between boys and girls and men and women, were too confusing for me.

That kind of intimacy meant pain.

That world was wicked and cruel.

My kisses weren't so special after all.

I was only one of the many giving them away.

Somewhere deep down, I'd always known that dating would no longer be fun when sex was on the table. I guessed reaching any sort of intimacy wouldn't be possible for me.

How dare *he ask me to give up Jerry, when he can't even give up Jesse!*

I tried to block out Jesse's words and her cutesy text symbols, but she'd made the picture way too clear—and it wouldn't stop repeating in my mind.

The two of them glued together.

His mouth on her.

His *cock* inside of her.

His lips on her breasts.

His hands on her thighs.

The sexy words he whispered in her ear.

Furious that I had shared my orgasm with him, my hands tightened into fists. I was nothing more to Ryan than hundreds of similar experiences. How could I have been such a fool?

I felt out of control and became obsessed rereading her text. I should have erased it; instead I reviewed each word, each symbol, and imagined various inflections dozens of times.

I should have called Ryan.

Instead, I was determined not to talk with him.

I should have held back my judgments. I didn't.

I couldn't relax, sleep, or eat. Instead, I gave myself over to the despair infecting my body. I'd given my heart just as my mother had. Her heart had been trampled. Now, mine was, too.

I knew his reputation. Stupid! How could I be so stupid?

One by one my family came home. I heard doors open and close. Muffled voices chatted for a while. Slowly the activity settled down. No one knocked on my door to see if I was all right. Why would they? I was always fine—at least, that's the way I appeared. In our family of dysfunction, if we seemed okay, it never crossed the minds of our parents that we might not be. I bounced from one TV channel to the next.

Turned that off.

Listened to music.

Played every sad song I had in my playlists.

Nothing calmed me.

Sometime around one a.m., I called Alex. She'd just gotten back from her photo shoot and I knew she'd be awake. She immediately invited me to her house.

Imaginary scenarios played in my mind.

"*I told you she was immature.*" I envisioned Alex saying to Tara. "*We should have known she was too young to have as a friend.*" Tara would respond.

I left a note on the kitchen table for my parents, letting them know I'd taken the car and where I was going.

Hoping she wouldn't turn her back on me for ignoring her warning about Ryan, I drove to Alex's house.

Chapter 15

A Witch

*A*lex stood at her door waiting for me. I threw myself in her arms and shared my story in between the sobs.

"Oh, girlfriend." She offered her embrace and then let me cry it out. A teakettle whistled. "I made us some chamomile tea. It'll help you sleep."

She put her arm around my shoulder. We headed to her kitchen. Pouring the hot bliss into beautiful china teacups, she placed them on delicate matching saucers. It reminded me of a fantasy I'd had as a little girl—of wanting to serve my imaginary friends with my beautiful tea set. My set of cups and saucers was tucked in a basket, quilted inside to protect the fragile porcelain. I'd sit in my basement at an old table and have conversations with all of them, creating fantasies and an imaginary life that seemed out of reach.

"You take cream, don't you?"

"A teaspoon, please." Her voice jerked me into the moment. I watched as she stirred and lightened the hot liquid, circling and mixing, creating the look of an entirely different drink when she was through. I felt as if I were that drink—no matter how I appeared outwardly, inside, I was dark.

"Let's sit on the sofa." She'd positioned her tea set on a tray and placed it on the coffee table. We sat down. "From all you've said and what Darrell told me, it seems that Ryan loves you. The problem," she sighed and stirred her tea. "Babe, you're playing in a world in which you shouldn't dabble. First love is tender, Nick. It's like being on a high where everything is blue sky and roses as you dance in the clouds. It's also deep and full of earthquakes."

"You're right," I sipped my tea. "I've experienced so many of them and we've only dated for a month or so."

"You doubt yourself constantly and overanalyze everything he says and does. Those emotions and vulnerable feelings should be out of the public eye. At your age, to be exclusive with anyone?" She shook her head. "It just isn't right. Those doubts of, *is he really seeing her* and *are the rumors true*, they aren't meant for an inexperienced woman. Not when it involves a man like Ryan."

"I told him I wasn't ready." I reached for my tea again but my hand shook so badly I couldn't hold the cup. Alex took it from me and steadied it on the table.

"You're not the average Suzie Q who's going to any college—this is Stanford. Your guy isn't Joe Smith—he's a professional athlete who's in the limelight because he excels in a way that few do. What do you really know except that your heart is aching?"

"I know a lot about him." I assured her. "You'd be surprised at the things he's shared with me."

"Yeah and that could be strategic. He knows what gets to you."

"I didn't think about it that way."

"What you need and deserve is to discover life with people your age, not with a twenty-five-year-old man." She winced a little as if wanting to withdraw from the conversation. "I understand why he's attracted to you. Shit, who wouldn't be with your big innocent eyes and brilliant ideas?"

"I haven't done anything brilliant, Alex. Why do you say that?"

"You're a witch!" she laughed.

"What?" I chuckled a little in between my sniffling. Was I entering into the first moments of clarity after my heartbreak and perhaps beginning the baby steps of recovery?

"You're an enchantress! The way you love us and immerse us in your life, the hope you have—you're a magnet, Nick. Your sweet innocence and loyalty, the way you put your friends first . . . don't you see who you are by now?"

All I see is that I can't make relationships last. I'm an expert at causing misery.

"No." I'd always doubted my strengths. Trusted the weaknesses. "I can't see it. My sister asked me the same thing. All I recognize is how much trouble I am."

"Your glorious radiance is what put Tara and me under your spell. It comes from your body. Through your eyes, smile, and embrace . . . do you know I've never been hugged the way you hug me? It's full. Complete. You pull me in and won't let me go. The way you hold onto me? It tells me I have a friend who loves me. Ryan sees you that way, too. He's reaching back to when he was a boy. He's using you to regain his innocence. And who can blame him? Shit, you make me feel like *I'm* new, Nick. You make a person feel like they're in a daydream sometimes."

"I don't get it, Alex."

"It's like you have fairy dust." She rubbed her fingers together as if sprinkling magic powder all around us. "You're fuckin' Tinkerbelle or something."

I blew out a nervous laugh. "I don't know what to say."

"There's nothing *to* say. It's the way you are." She put her hand on my shoulder. "Listen. There's nothing is wrong with sex. If it's between two consenting adults, everything is fair game. My only hesitation . . ."

"Is?" I poked.

"The first serious relationship you dare yourself to have is with Ryan? It doesn't fit." She picked up her delicate teacup and saucer. "You're such a private person and you're throwing yourself into a social realm that isn't easy. Not easy at all." Her cell phone rang. "Hang on. It's Darrell. Sorry, I won't be long."

I took the opportunity to freshen up. When I returned to the living room they talking sexy and saying goodbye.

"Kissy poo?" I teased.

"A little sexy nighty night," she giggled. "You okay?"

"Yeah, just put some water on my face. Continue where you left off—if you remember."

"Let's see . . . oh yeah. The public stuff."

"You mean *pubic* stuff?" I teased.

"Nicole Lynette Young!" she exclaimed pretending to be embarrassed.

"Well, don't tell me what you guys just said was innocent."

"Anyway," she slapped her cheek. "If only you had some experience or you were a little older, I'd say go for it. Even then it's tough to be with an athlete. Sometimes it's not easy for me, honey. And I get hit on all the time. Women are everywhere for these guys. I mean e-v-e-r-y-w-h-e-r-e."

That's what I've been telling him—he needs someone his age.

"Oh Fuckin' A. I sound just like your mother, I'll bet." Alex took a sip of the tea and set it down again. "Why does that happen? I never wanted to sound like that. Drink your tea, Nick."

She had me. I laughed because of the way she ordered me to drink my tea while making a point to say she didn't want to sound like a bossy parent. For a moment it was as if we were buddies getting together rather than she consoling her Sad Sack friend.

"I'm such a hypocrite," she mused. "Here I told you I had an experience with a guy eighteen years older than me when I was your age. The thing is, he wasn't my first—or second, or third!"

"God, Alex." I laughed and wiped my eyes with my shirt, half in despair, half amused.

"I'm so sorry." She pushed my hair over my shoulder. "I know it doesn't seem like it, but you'll get over him. Your heart hurts. Your stomach is in a knot. It's so big you don't think you'll ever recover." She patted my leg. "But you will."

"Do you know if he still sees Jesse?" I asked between sobs.

"I . . . um," she paused, perhaps considering if she should go any further. "I don't know if I should say this." Five beats. "Crap. Here goes. Sometimes she traveled with him."

"So, yes, then?" She'd confirmed what I'd hoped to hear so I could begin letting him go.

"I'm not sure, Nick. I haven't seen her with him this year. Well, I take that back. I haven't seen her since May. He wasn't ever exclusive with her, though. Honestly? I never pay that much attention. Darrell and Matt don't hang with Ryan. He's usually with the single guys or the ones . . . well, you know."

"The ones that play around?" I asked the obvious question.

She nodded.

"Look at this." I showed her Jesse's text.

"Oh, that's disgusting," Alex's face scrunched as she read it. "Obviously, she has no self-respect. I'm sorry you had to see something like that."

"Apparently, she has *plenty* of respect for herself, or at least a pair of very big balls to write all that. Who does this at her age?"

"I don't know, she's a little—"

"What?" I was frantic and needed to hear something positive.

"I don't believe her," she revealed. "Something's weird. It doesn't make sense. Before you, Ryan was with multiple women. Jesus, Nick—I never saw him with the same woman twice, except—"

"Jesse."

"There were a few others he saw repeatedly, but mostly it was Jesse."

"Doesn't that say it all? He was finding himself. I helped him get there."

"Although I'd love to push you away from him, I'm not convinced what happened with his ex is real. Did he commit to you like you did to him?"

"He begged me to commit. He told me he's waited for me since last year. One day after I turned eighteen he made a point to tell me that he'd stop seeing other women and he'd made good on his promise from the end-of-the-year party."

"What happened at that party?" she looked suspicious.

"He took my hands in his and said he'd see me on my birthday and lay everything out. He told me to save my heart for him and not to let a high school boy fool me into thinking they loved me. We volunteered several times together at the Veteran's Hospital in Yountville, I told you that, and he stopped because he supposedly couldn't take it any longer because it was too much temptation."

"Oh shit."

"Yeah. Why do all that just to end up cheating with her?"

"Not sure I . . . I just haven't seen athletes—well, any man his age, who can do that, quite frankly." She looked at the ceiling and back at me. "Guess he might be one in a million, but in my mind? He can't hold back all that testosterone. He's playing a man's sport and he's with men all day. What do you think they talk about?"

Oh yuck, this is just what Mom said.

"Sports." I knew better. I didn't want to face the reality. I wanted Alex to sympathize and tell me everything I wanted to hear—even if it wasn't true. "I know what it is."

"Pussy." She wouldn't let it remain unsaid.

I turned away. Like Ryan had done many times, she turned my face so I looked at her.

"They're men. Physical, bulging, pulsing, oversexed men playing sports. In their off time they work out and have sex with their wife, girlfriend, boyfriend . . . anyone they find attractive. Their bodies are on sexual overload. As a man moves through his twenties, his hormones pump continuously. They're alpha males. A part of that—a big part—is being physical and that means competition and sex. Lots of sex. You know how women wait for those guys, and . . . oh fuck; I'll just say it. Guys your age are still masturbating if they're not having the real thing. They're just as happy to jack off and get their orgasm because they're not experienced yet."

"I'm not stupid but I don't get your point."

"I can just about guarantee Ryan doesn't need to jerk off. A man like him, like Darrell and Matt, too, they're not satisfied with masturbation. Ryan can snap his finger and get a buffet of options, one for a blow job and two for pussy."

"God, do you have to—"

"I'm saying point blank, he's got plenty of options, doll."

"Oh."

She means Ryan can't wait for me. No matter how much his mind wants him to, his body won't let him.

Were men really that weak?

Or was it only because they didn't try?

Was there too much temptation to even consider being faithful?

"Do you think Jesse is one of those options?" I asked quietly.

"Oh, Sweetheart. You're looking at me with your sad eyes and I don't want to let you down, but . . ."

"You go on your modeling assignments and Darrell is on the road. Do you mean he can't hold out, either? You seem to trust him, he seems to trusts you . . . you're both in your twenties. So how do you guys make it work?"

"Darrell and I have sex when we're together. You're not having sex with Ryan even when he's home."

"Yeah." Just that quickly I felt like Ryan faded from my life. I'd pushed him away. It was as if he disappeared in front of me.

"Can't you let him go?" She took my hand in hers.

"I never told you this, but . . ." I shared what he was trying to do for my sister and father and told her about Half Moon Bay. Her expression softened.

"I'm sorry. I didn't realize. I shouldn't have said those things."

"No. You're right. I need to face that I've been dreaming about a man who exists only in books. What happened is contrary to the Ryan I know. We opened up to each other in so many ways. The things he shared with me were so intimate. I still can't believe he'd cheat on me when I'd just told him I loved him. And I can't believe he's with her. He *promised* me." Tears launched into a downpour. "I know that's juvenile. I was so sure he was a man of his word."

I felt like one of her delicate teacups, but instead of beautiful, I was chipped and ready to break apart.

Alex held me until I finally wound down. It was a little before dawn when we started up the stairs to go to sleep. We cuddled together. My arm was draped over her shoulder. Her foot touched mine. My body tucked into her back and legs.

She brought me to her photo shoot the next afternoon. The location was an hour away at a winery outside of the little town of Healdsburg. It was the perfect example of the Sonoma County Wine Country, with beautiful vineyards and a creek that meandered through the valley. Ben, Alex's photographer, asked me to run errands for him. It helped take my mind off Ryan. After the shoot we were treated to a catered dinner, where I collected several business cards.

Next morning I woke up alone. I opened my eyes slowly, lying in the thick blankets and comforter. I imagined having a future that included the luxurious conditions of my friend's home. Once my eyes adjusted to the light, I noticed the note on the side table. Alex had written that she'd been called for an assignment in Las Vegas and invited me to relax at her place as long as I wanted.

That wasn't a problem. I sat up slowly. Hugged the covers to my neck. Swung my legs over the side of the bed and finally padded into the bathroom. I drew a bath in their sunken tub. Once filled to the brim, I slipped in and relaxed in the warm water, hoping it would help to take away everything that existed in the outside world.

My phone beeped with messages and calls from Ryan. I ignored them, hoping to stay in a make believe place a little longer before facing the real one that waited for me.

When my sister called, I couldn't ignore it. Half-drunk from the soothing water, I picked up the phone. "Jenise?"

I really didn't want to leave Alex's apartment. I'd planed to sit at her make up table, try on all the colors and shades in her eye shadow palette, spray on her perfumes, use all her brushes, check out her closet, and cook in her kitchen.

Jenise wanted to have lunch with me at *The Cliff House*.

I couldn't say no.

Chapter 16

Reconnecting

𝒯he minute I saw my sister, I started crying. With each new person the details of Ryan and Jesse took a new turn. Some previously undiscovered sadness rose to the surface. She embraced me as tightly as she ever had, almost holding me up while letting me sob as I sunk into her body.

"Okay, Sis," she petted. "Tell me all about it."

"Two?" the host approached us with a smile.

My sister nodded. We were quickly ushered to one of the window tables, probably to remove the spectacle of a brokenhearted crybaby. As soon as we were seated, I spilled every detail. Jenise offered logical, soothing responses as I stabbed hopelessly at my salad. I couldn't eat.

He's even tainted my special place—the Cliff House. Is there no escape? No, Nick. You're doing this. You're choosing this.

"Well," Jenise rested a finger on her cheek. "What I keep going back to? Hard for me to believe Ryan would go straight to Jesse immediately after you proclaimed your love out loud. He's been waiting for weeks to hear the words. Wouldn't he look like an idiot to his teammates? Matt and Darrell would have told Tara and Alex, wouldn't they?"

"Who knows."

"Well, talk it over when he gets back," she suggested. "You'll find out the entire story then."

"Yeah . . ." I played with my napkin.

"Oh no." She glared at me. I could tell she knew I'd let fear control my decision. "What did you do?"

"I told him that he was dead to me." Saying the words out loud with sadness rather than anger made the severity of what I'd done even worse. "I hung up on him."

"Fuck me, Nick. *Why* do you keep doing that shit?"

"It just came out." I dipped a crouton in some blue cheese dressing. "I couldn't stop myself. All I feared was the possibility hearing how sex with Jesse meant nothing."

"At this point you don't know what's true. He asked you to wait an hour and he'd get back to you after he talked with her, right?" She pointed a finger at me. "Quit cutting people off until you've talked it through."

"I know." I looked out to the churning waves just beyond the thick floor-to-ceiling window then flattened my palm on it as if to steady myself. "My mind plays out all these horrible scenarios, my anxiety shoots through the roof . . . her text was terrible, Jenise. Here. Let me show you." I watched her face contort with disgust.

"Yeah. That's . . . well, fuck it." She handed me my phone. "Screw all these needy guys. Let's dress up and go out. We can pretend we're roomies looking for a new apartment. Let's prowl around and take down this city."

"What about Sean?" I admired the way she balanced her life with Sean, allowing for time with friends and also with me.

"My sissy needs me right now," she squeezed my hand. "Let's check out Pinnacle and Avalon luxury apartments. We can walk around the Financial District and . . . hey, I'll show you where City Architecture is! Maybe we can sneak in the lobby and I can get a glimpse at the CEO. We'll dress up—*femme fatale!*"

I've already had a glimpse of the CEO. Trust me, you don't want to be in his office.

"*Femme fatale.* You crack me up." I took her hand and kissed it. "Thanks for rescuing me. I could put on that St. John's business suit I got from LA. Ooh! I think Caden Blockley designed Pinnacle. Maybe you'll run into him and you can make a quick pitch for your project."

"How do *you* know what Caden Blockley designed?"

"I saw his projects at City Architecture." I was so happy to share the day with Jenise that I'd forgotten about keeping my visit with him a secret. A few weeks earlier I was checking on Ryan's contacts that were in a position to help my family. Caden Blockley was one of them. My sister wanted to work at his company when she graduated and was working on being awarded their internship.

"*What* were you doing there?" She crossed her arms.

Oh crap. She's not supposed to know.

"He's," I cleared my throat. "Oh shit. I might as well be honest. Ryan knows him."

"When did you meet him?"

"That day I went to see Dad's supervisor, Mr. Freeman. Right after my appointment at Municipality I went to City Architecture. After I sung the Anthem last month when Ryan was on our front porch? He told me he knew people who could help my family if I'd give him a try. Remember I told you he was trying to help with Dad's pension?"

"I wonder if that's what he means . . . God, I don't even want to hope," she chewed a nail.

"Hope?" I pressed.

"Ryan told me he'd try and put a word for me with someone he knew when we were at the Waterfront. *Now* you tell me he knows Caden Blockley? Don't you think that's it? They're talking? Oh, God, I—"

"Shh." I put my hand on her forearm.

"You're right. I'm overreacting and analyzing too much, but wow! My mind is spinning."

"I hope I didn't blow it for you."

"We'll see," her body deflated. "Let's go home and change."

We dressed up and began our adventure.

We window-shopped and she browsed jewelry stores, chatting excitedly about the wedding ring she'd love to have. We went in a wedding gown shop filled with designer gowns. Charming the sales person, they allowed her to try on a few dresses. I could picture her coming down the aisle and felt a bit of remorse as I realized that day was probably closer than any of us knew.

Because my sister's ability to talk business lingo and drop names, we easily got into the two buildings in which she was interested. She even used Ryan to get her way. We were even escorted to the tops floors by the on-site realtor. After showing us two residences, each three thousand square feet with killer views and a price tag to match, the woman asked if we'd mind showing ourselves to the lobby. She explained she'd just gotten a text that a couple interested in the same apartment were on their way up. We thanked her, took her card and then waited at the elevator.

The doors opened.

Two striking men stood inside the car in expensive three-piece suits. They stepped to the back to give us room.

"Ladies," one greeted.

The other stared attentively.

"Gentlemen," Jenise smiled, her eyes twinkling.

My sister is flirting! I wonder if Sean knows she flirts?

Both men were in their late twenties to early thirties, taller than six feet, dark haired with chiseled features, brown eyes, fit to an elevated degree, and gave a scent that invoked carnal invitations.

"That's him," I mouthed to my sister.

"What?" she mouthed back.

"That's him," I mouthed again.

"I can't understand you," she said aloud. "What are you saying?"

"I believe Ms. Young is trying to tell you that I'm Caden Blockley." He stepped forward and extended his hand. "Pleased to meet you . . . Jenise?"

"Yes, how did you—"

"Your sister and I had an interesting meeting a few weeks ago," he smirked. "Isn't that right, Ms. Young?"

"Yes." My answer was clipped.

"I hoped I'd run into you again. What a treat this is."

"Like our meeting." I shot out sarcastically.

He threw his head back in a laugh.

"Exactly like that," he purred. "Tell me you're looking to lease an apartment here." It was as if his voice was a snake slithering at our feet. "I'll make sure you get the one you want. In fact, if you're going to be a resident here, Ms. Young, I might even co-sign the contract if you promise to let me visit."

"You designed the building and you live here?" Jenise asked, ignoring his pompous offer. "Nice."

"Ah, a woman who studies her future," he commented. "Well done. Will you and your sister share the apartment?"

"We're not serious." I stated the obvious. "Just bowsing for the future." I cleared my throat, correcting my error. "Browsing, I mean." I quickly glanced at him. It was as if his eyes saw through my clothes. His gaze was unwavering and held me inside of it.

"Speaking of the future, your sister tells me you're quite a brilliant woman, Jenise. First impression, I'd say she's spot on."

"Oh, she did? Thanks, sis!" She nudged my shoulder.

"You're all we talked about," I informed her.

"Well," he looked me up and down. "It wasn't the only thing. Jenise, I look forward to reviewing your project. You're graduating next year which is exactly when we give out the award . . . I presume you're submitting an idea for us? I seem to remember your sister asked me if I'd taken a look at your work."

"Yes! I've been working on it for two years."

"Tell him," I whispered.

She shook her head and mouthed a firm *no*.

"Don't worry, Ms. Young." He smiled and then turned to Jenise. "Your sister will have plenty of time to discuss her project with me." His eyes darted back and forth as if looking over my whole face. "You look quite sophisticated today, Nicky. Even lovelier than I remember. Ryan shouldn't let you out on your own, someone's liable to snatch you up."

"Snatch me up? I don't let that kind of thing happen." I wasn't amused and used a dull tone to convey my lack of interest.

He laughed a one-syllable deep laugh like Ryan's. Suddenly I was reminded of how much I loved it. Just like that, I missed the stir I felt in my belly when my lost love released the sexiest voice I'd ever heard. I missed him.

"Mitch, it's my pleasure to introduce you to Nicky Young and her sister, Jenise." Caden made the introduction for his friend.

"Nice to meet you both." Mitch shook our hands.

"May we offer you ladies a ride to your next destination?"

"No," I looked straight ahead.

"Join us for dinner, then?" he lifted my hand and kissed it. I pulled it away. "Mitch is single. New to our fair city, in fact. I think I speak for both of us that we'd enjoy your company."

"My sister has a fiancé and I have a boyfriend as you know." *Well, not anymore but he doesn't know that. Or maybe he does?* "No thanks."

"And the problem is . . . I assume your sister would enjoy the opportunity." He turned to her. "Wouldn't you, Jenise?"

"Love to!" she gave me the evil eye, daring me to disagree.

"The three of you can enjoy dinner together," I answered. "Better yet, Sis, why don't you call Sean and he can join you?"

"Just what do you think our intentions are? I mean really, Ms. Young." From his grin it was obvious—he was toying with me. I was taking him much too seriously. Still, I couldn't relax and had a hard time being around men. "I'm only inviting you for dinner, not a date in my bedroom."

Oh, damn. I can't believe he said that.

Jenise looked at me, waiting for my move.

"I'm not dressed for dinner," I stalled.

"I'd be proud to escort you," he said boldly. "In fact, the restaurant I'm thinking of encourages their guests to come dressed as they are."

"Do you want to, Sis?" *Please don't say yes. This was supposed to be about us. Okay, well, it could mean your career . . . still, please find another time even though there probably won't be another time, but . . . oh, damn. There's no way she can turn down an opportunity like this.*

"Like I said before," she rolled her eyes at me, "I'd love to." Her determination was evident.

"It's settled, then." The elevator door opened. Caden held is open. "After you ladies. My driver is out front. I know just the place."

Please don't say Gary Danko's. I'd like to think it was special and not the regular place for you and Ryan to tease and torment your dates.

I got into the limousine. Jenise purposefully sat on the other side, knowing Caden Blockley would take the seat next to me. The conversation flowed easily, and the sexual aura seemed to evaporate as we got to know one another a little better.

The driver took us to Saison. It was an upscale, Michelin three-star restaurant on Townsend Street in SoMa. The exterior and interior was brick. It had an open floor plan. Exposed ceilings, distressed wooden piers, grey and walnut themes, concrete floors mixed with wooden tables and chairs and a very large open kitchen had fabulous copper pots hanging everywhere.

"Caden. Welcome." A gorgeous hostess greeted him. "Four?"

"Yes, please," he loosened his tie. "Mitch, Nicky, Jenise, this is Heather."

We shook hands.

"This way," she beckoned. "Joshua would love to say hello. I'll let him know you're here."

I half expected her to ask about Ryan. To my amazement, she kept it professional. I wondered if this was normal or were the women I'd seen so far the usual when it came to good looking, powerful men.

"Who's Joshua?" I asked.

"The chef. Expect a delicious surprise now that he knows we're here. May I take your jacket?" Caden offered me while Mitch tended to Jenise.

"Yes. Thank you," I forced myself to participate. He draped it on the back of my chair.

"St. John," he looked at the label after giving me a once over. "You have expensive taste."

"Not really," I corrected. "It was a gift. I'm more of a jeans and T-shirt woman."

"You'd do anything justice." He opened the cocktail menu and quickly announced, "The wine list is extensive here. Mitch, you have to—"

Just then his friend's cell phone rang. Mitch reached in his pocket. Looked at the screen. "Sorry, I have to take this. Please order drinks. This shouldn't take long. I'll have whatever you're drinking, Caden." He excused himself and stepped outside.

We were given menus and water. Caden ordered two glasses of Smirnoff on the rocks. Jenise went with the Sommelier's suggestion of a Preston Vineyards Syrah after he'd made her promise to accompany it with a melted Brie and chopped olive plate. I ordered an iced tea feeling like the ugly stepchild. At the encouragement of our host, Jenise began talking about her project. He seemed interested until Mitch returned with a serious look.

"I apologize. That was the hospital. I have to go."

"They've made a decision?" Caden asked.

"It seems I have the job and a surgery on my first night." The way Mitch sighed seemed to indicate he was in for quite a challenge. "I've applied for the chief surgeon of the neurology department at UCSF and have been notified of my acceptance earlier than expected. I'm sorry Jenise. Nicky. I'd love to have another evening where we can all get together with . . . Sean was it?" He then turned to me. "Of course Caden has told me who *your* special man is. I love baseball. Maybe we can all catch a game together and enjoy a hot dog instead of caviar."

I like him.

We stood to shake his hand.

"Unfortunately," Caden grabbed his jacket and shrugged it on. "I'm his ride and that means I'll need to cut my evening short as well. What a shame." His hooded eyes conveyed all that I didn't want to know. "Dinner is on me, of course. Order what you like. Ms. Young, I look forward to our next rendezvous. Don't be a stranger. Nice to meet you Jenise. When you're both ready, call this number. He handed me a card. My driver will take you home."

"This is too much," I protested. "We can—"

"It's been brought to my attention that you're not a woman who accepts gifts lightly or easily." He knew too much. Obviously Ryan had filled him in. "Please don't worry. Enjoy yourself. I mean nothing by it."

I hesitated.

"I'll call Ryan for you and let him know." He took out his phone. "Put your mind at ease."

"No!" I jumped. "No, it's okay."

"All right, then," he tilted his head, knowing from my response that something wasn't right. "Have a good evening."

"God, Nicky!" Jenise said after they left. "You and your damn surprises!"

"What do you mean?"

"The people you've met through Ryan," she said. "Who's next? The fuckin' President?"

"I'm not even hungry," I laughed half-heartedly.

"We have to get *something*," she interjected. "First, it would be rude, but second . . . I mean this is Saison! We'll never be back here."

"Yes you will. You'll be working for him, after all."

"Yeah," she blushed, perhaps imagining her future.

"Look at this menu . . . caviar, pigeon, fish, words I've never heard of . . ." I wrinkled my nose. "Have you ever had any of this?"

"Have one of their salads, then," she suggested. "Personally, I'm trying some caviar and one of these items we'll never taste again. Think of it as a networking opportunity for some future client so you're not talking out your ass when they order it." She cracked up and proceeded to flirt with the waiter, asking him to interpret everything for her. By the time we were done, she had her caviar and duck. I had a few spoonsful of soup.

"We're not really going to call his driver, right?" I begged.

"I think we can get home on our own. Besides, he might be in the car and invite you up to his place for a nightcap."

"He's awful," I told her. "I hope you were able to at least talk a little bit about your work."

"I did. And Caden Blockley is into you . . . *Ms. Young.*"

"No, he's an ego on legs. He's like the jocks. They go with models. They flirt with big girls like me because they think it makes us feel good. His type? Size zero. Underwear, bikinis . . . that's the world I'm battling, Sis."

"You and your damn self-esteem. Your body rocks. Stop that negative self-talk. Yes, Nicky, he is definitely into you. He never stopped looking at you. As soon as we stepped into the elevator he spotted you and knew who you were. You couldn't see him looking at your body. I did and I'm telling you, he couldn't wait to catch your attention. Did you know it was him?"

"What the hell do you think I was trying to tell you?"

"Yeah," she laughed. "That's right. Sorry. I couldn't understand you. He's a sexy beast. I'll bet women all over him. Well, there's your rebound man. He's yours to try if you ask, I'd say."

"No thanks. When I went to talk with him last month? He turned heads everywhere. He was trying to flirt and he knows I'm with Ryan? That's disgusting. I'm done with that crap. I want a nerd." My eyes teared again as I realized I wouldn't tell Ryan anything about our afternoon. We were over.

"God, I wonder if Sean would let me . . . just one last time, you know?"

"Jenise! Shut up!" I slapped her arm.

"Just kidding. Kind of."

We continued the evening at Nordstrom's. Spritzed our bodies with Jadoire and Eternity. Went into Sak's to try on the outfit in the window that Jenise had drooled over a few days earlier. We even had a personal shopper create an entire wardrobe for us. Ending the evening with some of her college friends for coffee, we got home after 2 a.m.

While the Goliaths and Ryan were on the road, my days were filled with women. I'd even made excuses to politely turn down Ethan's invitation to drive to Mendocino when he was in town. I was sick of guys. Their fragile egos and constant hunger for sex suffocated me. I had no intention of being the one to soothe them. I spent time going back and forth between a few of my high school friends, Jenise, Tara, and Alex. They helped to redirect my sadness and I understood more about the subtle and not-so-subtle differences between men and women.

Being with loving, confident, assertive, and beautiful women on the inside as well as outside, taught me the life lessons of always making room in my schedule to spend time with my girlfriends. No matter what happened with Ryan, cheering for the Goliaths had brought me Tara and Alex.

Five days had passed from the moment I'd read Jesse's text.

I'd found out from Tara her tests had been inconclusive. They'd rescheduled her for another round and her mother agreed to stay over—at least until Matt returned.

Overall, I was recovering. My head was better, I didn't cry at the drop of a hat, and I had refocused. The problem? My appetite still hadn't returned. I'd only been able to stomach a few crackers each day. It was stupid to take it so hard. But I knew I'd made a mistake I could never take back. I'd not only ruined a chance for love, I'd cut off a friend.

I wished it had been different between us.

His spirit seemed to reside deep inside my body.

His echo was getting louder every day.

Chapter 17

Revelations

*C*olleen finally called me with less than forty-eight hours until our next game. It was the first time we'd spoken since we'd received our plaque of appreciation from management and the players two weeks earlier.

"Hey stranger, what have you been up to?" she sounded overly perky as if there was a catch to her phone call.

"You're actually calling *me*? I thought you guys had everything handled."

We'd had a falling out. She'd taken charge of the cheer team and took for herself an award that was supposed to be shared among all of us. That same night she'd purposefully excluded me from a team get together to posture and position herself as the team leader.

On the other hand, you let her. Weren't you sulking about Ryan then, too?

"I deserve that," she said with a guarded tone. "I admit I got carried away. Who knows what came over me. I saw the chance to shine and I took it. I'm sorry."

"Uh-huh," I replied. "I never did have a problem with you taking the lead. It was being excluded that hurt."

"Sorry. It wasn't right. Can we put it behind us?"

"Yes." *That's what I'm doing with everyone these days.*

"I'd like to hold a practice, can you come?"

"I was thinking of dropping out," I revealed. "I didn't come to the last game and you guys didn't call or seem to care. I figured it was no big deal."

"Please don't leave us," her voice was spiked with panic. "We're all friends and I want to finish the year together. Let's go out with some great memories, okay?"

"I was hoping so, too, but—"

Don't make her beg. Cheering was your idea. You're letting Ryan ruin it for you and you promised yourself you wouldn't let boys get in the way.

"We'll never be together again like this and I want to do it right." She sounded as if she was down. "Please come. I'm planning a new move and I need you on the bottom so I can finish with a trampoline jump."

"A *trampoline*?" I couldn't help but laugh. Designing a tough routine was her obvious attempt to stand out and get the attention she craved. I couldn't deny her the opportunity. "When do you want to practice?"

"How about four? We need you for this strength move, Nick."

"Oh, thanks. My big old body needs to stabilize the group, right?" I was only half joking. I tried to bring levity as a stepping-stone to our conversation.

"Well, you *are* the strongest," she laughed meekly. "Your boobs and ass will give us all a cushion if we fall."

"Ha-*ha,* Colleen."

"Just kidding," she snickered. "*Sort of.*"

"I wouldn't wish my body on my worst enemy. It's trouble, trouble, trouble."

"Oh sure, because then someone *else* would get Ethan or Jerry."

"No, I'm done with boys," I replied sternly. "Where do you want me to meet you?"

"The high school gym. We can go out for a bite to eat after practice and talk about you being done with boys. But, come on. No woman can *really* be done with them, can they?"

I couldn't resist her giggle. Our fragile relationship rebooted— just like the stop and start of others I'd made during my life and the ones I'd observed in my family. The bonds that seemed unbreakable when we were little girls were now delicately held together with bits of compromise and kindness.

Sometimes, just moving on rather than talking through a tough issue was the best option.

I decided to do exactly that.

Our practice brought back some feelings of "normalcy." Afterwards, Colleen and I took off for a nearby diner to grab a bite to eat. It was nice to hang out with her as a friend. What was it about high school friends that were unlike others? We knew each other. Didn't have to put on. It was the best feeling.

Even after dousing myself in the blessings of friendships, I still couldn't bring myself to eat the hamburger I'd ordered for dinner. It sat in front of me, untouched, as I talked through some of what had been going on in my life.

"I knew it!" For a change Colleen had listened intently. The look on her face was obvious—shock. "I knew even last year

Tilton was infatuated with you. I told you, didn't I? I told you! How's the sex?"

"We haven't had sex." I was embarrassed that once again I had to admit I still hadn't entered the same world my friend had fallen into several years earlier.

God, everybody assumes that I've had intercourse with Ryan. Did all my friends have sex as soon as they had boyfriends? Am I the only one who hasn't? What's wrong with me?

"What *have* you done then?" Her eyes investigated mine.

"Things," I said.

"Not very exciting." She scrunched her face.

"Well, he's a gentleman." I defended him as if trying to reassure my friend and myself.

"A gentleman who had sex with another woman as soon as he went on the road," she scoffed.

"Yeah." I put my hand on my forehead. "If it weren't for us being in two different places, it might be different. Right now, all I want is to be free from anything heavy. I mean, we've got all this seriousness coming with college, right?"

"Right! It's hang loose and party time, not serious time!" She pumped her arms.

"You know, I would've thought about going further if it weren't for that fucking text from his former girlfriend."

"What?" she asked excitedly. "Not like you to use the F word. Are you pissed off?"

"Hell *yeah*, I'm pissed off." I affirmed. "How could they—he— do that?" I still hadn't deleted Jesse's text and I showed it to her.

"That's just bullshit stuff, don't you think?" All of a sudden she went into hysterics. "I'm sorry, Nick."

"What's funny about any of this?" My anger needle drifted into the red zone.

"How old is this Jesse woman, anyway? It's so high school."

"Ryan's age, I think. They went to college together."

"God, what a loser." She sipped her water.

"Apparently she's rich, but—"

"Yeah, well, rich or not—she's got a screw loose to send that," she stated firmly.

She's coming to my defense! Hooray!

"Thanks, Colleen."

"You still care for him?" Before I could speak, whatever look I had on my face gave her the answer. "Yep. You do."

"And that shit, Jerry? He only wanted the same thing. After all these years, we barely begin talking about intimacy? Suddenly I'm the bad guy because I'm not ready. Stupid boys."

"I probably should shut up." She stirred her milkshake with a straw. "But . . . I heard he's been seeing Terrie. We all know she's lusted after Jerry for, well, forever, right?"

"Oh, duh," I agreed. "Jerry and Terrie sittin' in a tree . . ."

"K-i-s-s-i-n-g," she cracked up. "I saw the both of 'em at Mel's and they looked pretty chummy. She was draped all over him. So don't get bent about anything he says."

"I *knew* something was up with her. I thought I saw her picture on his cell phone when we went out. Fucking guys. Why can't they stay away from women, Colleen? What's so difficult about giving me some time to figure it out? Am I *that* backward?"

"Well shit!" Her eyes widened. "I'm a *woman* and can't stay away from sex. It's spectacular! I whole-heartedly recommend it!" She cracked up.

"I don't know." Just getting out my inner dialogue helped my appetite a little. I ate a tomato slice and a small piece of the hamburger. "It's all tied to my spiritual beliefs. I hear the logical side. For me, it's hard to let that part go. Ryan made such a big deal telling me he wasn't with any woman and he'd wait for me. I relaxed, thinking I had some time. Why bother saying all that? And if he can't stay away from other women when we're at the beginning of our relationship, won't it be only a matter of time until the next comes along? I thought he was true."

"*True*?" she mocked. "Nicky, women are all over him trying to get his attention. I'll just say this . . ." She left the end of her sentence dangling. I couldn't wait for her to finish.

I waved my hand like a wheel, encouraging her to continue.

"Well, you're not having sex with him. What's he supposed to do?" she challenged. "Aren't you giving him mixed signals?"

"I didn't give him mixed signals, Colleen. I was very clear that I wasn't ready."

"That's my point. He has sex in his face every day." Colleen affirmed the things Alex said. "How can you expect a man his age to hold out? Hard bodies offering him their pussy? I mean . . . come on."

"Oh damn, Colleen, do you have to say it like that?" *Yuck.*

"It's disgusting but he's gonna get blue balls waiting for you. From what Brett tells me, that hurts."

"Blue balls, poo balls. I think that's bullshit." I shifted in my seat. "I think most men have it more together than people give them credit for. They're not Neanderthals."

"Oh no?" Her eyes widened. "Yet, Ryan *and* Jerry just failed in that category, right? That's two of two!"

"No, my friend Ethan . . ."

"You weren't thinking of more with Ethan. I stand by what I said. Men want sex first, relationships second. If they can't get sex, there's no chance for a healthy relationship. And frankly, I'm with them. I need to know the sex is good."

"I'm not sure I agree," I hesitated. "Anyway, I can't wait to finish out the summer and be done with all the old stuff. Tell me . . . are you finally together with Sy?"

Once I asked her to talk about her life, she didn't stop until she had to leave.

When I arrived back at home, I shut myself in my room and pulled out my journal. I wanted to yell and shake Ryan. All I could do was retell the steps of my anger in writing.

The remorse settled on me.

How many times do you expect him to keep calling without getting a response from you? How often should he reach out only to be denied, pushed away, and beaten down? He tried for an entire week to reach you, but you wouldn't answer him.

When all was said and done, I realized I'd reacted like a girl instead of a woman. I should have given Ryan a chance to explain himself. As usual, I didn't.

When Friday's game arrived, just the thought of seeing him made me shake. When it came down to it, I wasn't certain I should even attempt to cheer. Watching him flirt with another woman—or worse yet—seeing Jesse flaunt her victory in my face, made my stomach sick.

I was uneasy.

Missed him terribly.

This time, I had to let him go.

My cell phone had stopped ringing and beeping with Ryan's messages. By now I knew he'd moved on. I'd known since our beginning we weren't right for each other and told him so—often. During our breakup, he must have determined I was right. Our timing was completely wrong.

I arrived at the Bay Gate at five o'clock. My nerves were shot. I still hadn't eaten much. I was putting back together my focus toward my future in small steps.

My teammates and Tara were already in the bleachers. Whenever we had a new routine, Tara and Alex often came to give us input, constructive criticism, and of course, encouragement in-between our dances.

"Tara!" I gave her a big hug. "I didn't expect to see you."

"I needed to get out." She smacked her lips after taking a sip of lemonade.

"What about—"

"I don't know yet," she whispered. "I promise I'll tell you as soon as I know. Nicky," her voice returned to a normal volume. "This is my mom, Elaine Wheaton. Mom, my girlfriend, Nicky."

"Wonderful to meet you, Mrs. Wheaton," I shook her hand.

"Just Elaine. You as well, Nicky."

"I sure love your daughter," I praised.

"She's a quite a woman, isn't she?" The way her mother's eyes twinkled and her posture straightened, it was obvious she was proud of her Tara. When I turned to look at her, she seemed to glow. It was clear that her mother's love was what she needed.

"Hey ladies." Alex came up behind us and draped an arm on each of our shoulders.

"Hey!" We gave each other a kiss.

"Feeling better?" Alex whispered.

"Much," I confided. "Thanks for the downtime at your place. It really helped."

"Anytime, doll." With another squeeze she let me go and turned to greet Tara's mother. "Elaine! So nice to see you."

The night was unseasonably hot.

A different kind of electricity hung in the air.

It seemed alive and crackled with danger.

The ballpark flags hung limply as if the game was to be played in the middle of the Sonoran desert. It was one of the few night games when breezes refused to blow. The heat from the day radiated off the concrete and metal benches.

"It feels like earthquake weather, doesn't it?" I joked. None of us who lived in the city were used to nights like this one. Generally when it got warm in San Francisco, we waited a few hours and the fog would roll down the coastal hills. By the late afternoon we were blessed with nature's cool blanket, relieving us from a rare day of heat.

That night at the ballpark, at seven o' clock it was still hot.

The players took their positions on the field.

I was dripping with sweat underneath the thick, black shirt I wore with my jersey.

"Earthquake weather?" Elaine's voice was woven in panic. "What do you mean?"

"It's way too hot," I pulled the neck of my shirt away. "When there's no wind at night and it's warm like this, the superstition around here is that an earthquake is coming."

"Oh, holy Moses!" Elaine turned to Tara. "What would we do? How do we protect ourselves? Do you and Matt have an evacuation plan? Is there one at the ballpark?"

I almost laughed, but was able to hold in my amusement.

"Mom, that's just an old fable," Tara put her hand on her mother's shoulder. "Nicky, don't you know people who aren't used to earthquakes are scared to death of them?"

"I'm sorry, Elaine. I didn't mean to scare you. It's only a superstition. Like Tara said."

I joined my team while trying to hide my grin. Making Tara's mom worry about an earthquake gave me a strange and satisfied sensation. For reasons I didn't quite understand, I enjoyed planting the little seed of fear in her. Perhaps it was because my usual instincts were to keep people calm and reassure them. For once, stirring up a little trouble felt mighty fine.

Is this how Jesse felt when she sent her text to me? Was it her chance, being a lady of society, to show her rebellion and stake her claim for the man she loves?

I surveyed the field for Ryan, but didn't see him.

"God, it's hot," Kathie, my friend and teammate, blurted. "I think an earthquake is coming."

"I know." I smiled a mischievous smile.

Chapter 18

Earthquake

*W*arm nights in San Francisco brought restlessness.

Natives weren't used to it.

It made us feel like crawling out of our skin.

As kids, those were the nights we'd stay out later than usual, playing tag and hide-and-go-seek. When we were older, it meant doing the things that made our parents go crazy—partying—which also resulted in weeks of being grounded.

Now, my games had transitioned to cheering for a professional baseball team in order to build a resume to Stanford, and pointed to an uncertain future when it came to making relationships that lasted. I wondered what would be worse . . . not to have my college education at Stanford or living a life that was lacking an intimate connection?

Even after an entire week of talking it through with my friends—even Colleen, I couldn't escape the image of Ryan's mouth all over Jesse's body.

Their sex was for adults, Jesse texted. What kind of sex was it that would rip my body apart the way she'd described? I'd never heard any of my friends describe sex with their boyfriend that way.

Apparently the man I was interested in wanted it rough and the woman who could accommodate him had gone to meet him in Denver, joining him on his road trip because I couldn't.

Facing a fact I couldn't deny any longer—that I was better off staying away from the man I had fallen in love with—was gut wrenching. It was the right thing to do; I knew that, but on top of everything, I was still upset over Jerry's obnoxious behavior. Losing the friendship of both men at the same time was at the very core of my fears—being alone and abandoned.

It was why I had taken so long to take a risk in the first place and hadn't yet told Jerry about falling in love.

What kind of man chose to trade his history with a woman because of sex? Most? Some? All?

Were Ryan and Jerry really that shallow?

On top of everything, I should have taken better care of myself over the last week. I took a big chance with the safety of my teammates by not eating. I knew it was possible I wasn't in the shape I needed to be. A gnawing fear turned in my gut. Agreeing to such a demanding routine . . . maybe it was it a mistake.

"Let us know what you think of our new moves, okay, you guys?" Colleen asked Tara and Alex.

"We will," both said at the same time. They scooted to the edge of their seats.

"Jinx," they said together.

"Personal jinx," they yelled.

I cracked up at two sophisticated ladies acting like girls.

"Be sure and watch them when they're on the field, Mom," Tara directed. "They're so good." Suddenly she reached out and put her hand on my forehead. "Nick, are you feeling all right?"

"Fine, why?"

"You look a little pale." She turned her hand over so the back of it rested on my cheek.

"I'm fine." At that point, the truth wouldn't have done anyone any good.

Bottom of the first inning and we were on. Our routine went well. Tara and Alex agreed we looked great. Second performance, I was into it. We stepped it up to another level. The shaky feelings had left me and I was happy I'd decided to cheer again. My nerves had finally settled down. I was having fun. Eight-thirty at night and I was still perspiring. Without realizing it, I'd lost precious water from my body—and it was too much.

By our third routine, I was severely dehydrated.

Water and other clear drinks had made me nauseous all week and I hadn't given myself the nutrients I'd needed for the demands of what my team was about to do.

"Here you go," Tommy announced, carrying a tray of six bottles of ice water. Tommy was the ten-year-old batboy and we danced at the end-of-the-year party together the prior November. He let my friends take theirs and handed me the last bottle. His crush was sweet and obvious.

"Thanks, Tommy." I wiped my forehead with the cool bottle and then took several long swigs. "Just what we need. You're so thoughtful." I gulped it down. "Playing summer league baseball?"

"Yeah! I made the team!"

"All the good athletes make summer league," I praised. "Tommy's the man!" We high-fived. He walked away with a bright smile.

Positioned to the right of the Goliaths' dugout, a mini trampoline was set out for Colleen to be the star in our final performance of the night. The first set of jumps and stacking were perfect. The fans clapped furiously. They seemed to appreciate the difficulty. The moment came. People in the area stood, anticipating Colleen's jump. A few seconds remained before she executed her move. I only needed to lift Lorraine on my shoulders.

Lorraine jumped.

I held all of her weight.

She reached high and waved her arms.

I felt my strength crumble.

My legs started to shake.

When Colleen made her jump to the top of our pyramid, the final addition of her weight made my knees buckle. I shut down and my energy drained away as if I were an hourglass.

Turned over.

Vision fuzzy.

Acid shot into my legs.

Before collapsing to the ground, my mind filled with racing, random thoughts: *I don't feel good. I really need to sleep. Maybe Lorraine can stand somewhere else while I take a nap. I hope no one gets hurt.*

The team fell down and tumbled on top of me.

Everything went to black.

When I awoke, I knew I was at the stadium's medical station. The cheer team had been given a tour of it before we ever performed at the ballpark, in case we were faced with an emergency. I recognized the pattern of the drapes that surrounded me as I lay on a table with an IV in my arm. A cool towel rested on my forehead. My jersey was off. I had a gown on with several nodes attached to my chest.

"What's going on?" Panic ricocheted through me. "Hello?" I yelled, not bothering to hide my fear. *Ow! My head hurts.*

I didn't see the attending nurse in my room and jumped when her arm came from behind me and rested on my shoulder.

"Stay calm, Ms. Young." Her voice was soothing. "You're all right. You're at the medical station. My name is Graciela. I'm the attending nurse. Do you remember what happened?"

"What are these things on my chest?" I grabbed them. "Are you monitoring my heart?"

"We took an EKG reading," she took my hands away from the nodes and placed them at my sides. "Please keep your head down. We're taking precautions at this point."

She asked me to perform some basic commands. I followed her finger without moving my head and answered easy questions such as my name, the date, and what day of the week it was.

"Do you remember what happened?" she repeated the question.

"I fell down."

"You've been unconscious," she advised. "How do you feel?"

"So-so."

"Noted. Are you sick to your stomach?"

"No."

"How's your head?"

I knew if I confessed my worsening headache, she'd put me through more tests and perhaps transport me to the hospital. I had to get out of there. I just wanted to get home and reset my life.

"Fine," I lied.

"Any soreness in your stomach or back?"

"No."

"When we're done here, I want you to go home and call your doctor. Make sure you see them first thing in the morning." Graciela took the nodes off my chest. "We don't have the equipment to measure head trauma, but you need be aware of the signs. Do you know what they are?"

"Headache, nausea, feeling off, cognitive challenges, vision changes, confusion—yes, I know them." I first thought of the vets in Yountville, but then flashes from a scene in my childhood crept into my present.

Wall.

Cement.

Fall.

Thud.

Stairs.

Drunk.

"That's right. It's also important to have someone watch you. If you manifest any symptoms you've just identified head straight to the emergency room. Don't second guess yourself or try to be brave. Go," she cautioned. "If it turns out to be nothing, so be it. You can't be too careful with a head injury."

"Why did you take an EKG?" I asked. "You keep talking about head injury and yet . . ."

"Because you collapsed. In my experience, that's indicative of exhaustion or circulatory problems. The doctor agreed."

"I see. And where is the doctor?"

"She left, however I may be able to reach her cell phone. Do you want me to try?"

"No, that's okay."

"Any idea why you passed out?"

"No. Well . . . yes." I reconsidered my short response, deciding that she needed to have some input so she could do her job. "I haven't been eating or drinking very well during the week."

"Your blood pressure is high; do you have a history of hypertension?"

"Uh, no, not that I know of." The cobwebs started to clear from my head. I blinked hard a few times. "I think it's because I didn't hydrate properly."

"Except for your blood pressure, your vitals are good. The IV will replenish your electrolytes and minerals. You'll need to take it easy for the next few days. No cheering tomorrow. I want you to relax here for a while. I'll let you know when it's okay to leave."

I nodded in agreement and lay my head down.

"Oh. Tara Summers and Alexandra Flowers are outside the door." Graciela added. "You up for company?"

"Sure."

"I'll give them ten minutes. By the way, did anyone tell you how you got here?" She stopped writing her notes and looked up.

"No, I don't . . . uh . . . no, I can't remember." I was still a little dazed. "Did I walk?"

"You weren't in any shape to walk on your own. You were unconscious."

"Right," I confirmed. "You said that."

"Ryan Tilton carried you."

What?

"Are you related?" she asked with a raised eyebrow.

"We're not related." I imagined being carried in Ryan's big arms in front of forty thousand people.

What is he trying to prove? He cheats on the road and now he tries to show his fans he's my savior?

"Everyone is buzzing about it," she informed as if a gossip reporter. "*Someone* sure made an impression."

"We're just friends," I said dully. *Well, we were.*

"Whatever you say, Ms. Young." Graciela eyeballed me doubtfully.

Big deal, he's the cause of all this because he couldn't keep it in his pants. Maybe his date canceled tonight and he has nothing better to do than look good to the fans.

I heard Graciela tell Tara and Alex what my room number was. They rushed in and hugged me immediately.

"Oh honey, are you okay?" Tara stroked my hand.

"My blood pressure is high. Other than that, I just feel stupid."

"We feared the worst," Alex smoothed my hair. "It looked terrible. Everyone was on top of you and you were all twisted in a pile . . . oh, poor girlfriend."

"Nicky," Tara held onto my hand as if her life depended on it. She had tears in her eyes. "I was so afraid for you. We all were. Your body was just . . . awkward."

All this worry—Guess it looked serious.

"Your girlfriends wanted to stay. We told them to go home," Alex informed. "You don't need to hear all of them going on and on with their high-pitched voices."

"Ah," I gagged. "I'm . . . sick. Can you hand me—"

"Here," Tara handed me a plastic barf container and both women turned away while I filled it.

"Guess she needs a little more rest, ladies," Graciela came back in the room to check my IV. Her eyes glanced at the container on my belly. "I'll get something for your nausea," she lowered her voice. "Say your goodbyes. Back in a minute."

"Sorry you guys. I don't want you to go, but . . ." I winced as I looked at them. "Can one of you call my mom to tell her I'm okay? I'll call her when I'm ready to be picked up."

"Do you want us to stay and give you a ride home?" Tara volunteered.

"No, I'm sure someone in my family is already coming. Thanks for offering, though."

"You *sure*?" Tara tested. I could see the doubt on her face.

"Yes."

When I'm ready, I'll call home. Right now it feels good just to lay here. I don't want to be rushed or an inconvenience for anyone. Besides, who knows what's going on at home? I'm better off staying away from there.

"We'll talk tomorrow," Alex gave me a hug. Tara did the same. "When you get home, tell those girlfriends to leave you alone."

"I will." I giggled softly at their insistence. "I love you guys."

"Love you, too," both chimed in at the same time and started to leave the room.

"Jinx," I said weakly.

"Personal jinx," they retorted and then blew me a kiss.

"You should feel better soon." Graciela came back and injected anti-nausea medication into the clear, plastic IV tube. "Only a few more minutes and we'll discharge you."

"You just said nausea . . ."

"You don't have any of the other symptoms, do you?" she double-checked my responses. "Don't hide anything."

"I'm not. No other signs."

Just this headache, but no one in my family goes to the hospital and I'm not about to be the trendsetter. I wonder why neither of my friends mentioned Ryan carrying me up here? Maybe Graciela was pulling my leg. But why would she?

When she left the room, I could tell the baseball game was over. The fans were leaving the stadium. Echoes of empty rang through the corridor; the upper decks creaked with sighs of relief. Loud speakers quieted. Voices that had been alive with thunderous cheers and the footsteps and stomped in excitement, quieted.

The memory of my father's fall pushed forward: *Do I call the police? Dad? Are you alive?* I wasn't sure how much time had passed when the door opened.

"Is it okay if I go now?" I didn't raise my head.

No response.

"Does everything check out?"

I lifted my head.

Ryan.

Chapter 19

An Agreement

An orange janitor's uniform and hoodie disguised him well. It covered his head and most of his face. From the click I heard, I assumed he'd locked the door.

"What do you want?" I tried to sit up. Between the IV in my arm and my light-headedness I decided to lay flat on the bed. "I told you to stay away from me. You played your game and toyed with my heart. You got me. Please go."

He took the cloth off my forehead. Slid his arms underneath my gown and around my back. Held me. The moment seemed frozen. His eyes were fixed on mine.

Damn it. His hands . . . I love them . . . miss them.

My heart raced. I was fragile. Vulnerable. Had to be strong.

"Can you sit up for a minute?" His voice was quiet and calm.

"I'm not supposed to." I kept my tone as cold as my heart felt.

"Then I'll continue to hold you until you listen to me." His voice had the bite of authority.

Like hell; I'll support myself even if I barf all over you.

"Please leave me alone," I begged, changing tactics. "I'm throwing up and feel like crap. It would serve you right if . . . what do you want?"

He put his hands on my cheeks. I closed my eyes so I wouldn't have to see his warm expression and have a false assurance of security.

"Open your eyes and look at me," he commanded.

"I'm done with all that." My lip curled in a sneer. "Your false promises damn near destroyed what little faith I have left in meeting people."

"I'm asking you to look at me," his voice softened. His masculine hands gently squeezed my back. "I deserve that at least."

"Why should I?" I opened my eyes. Immediately looked away. "You're not the man I thought I knew."

He pulled his hood down. Turned my face toward his.

When I saw how distraught he looked it saddened me at first but almost immediately, I was glad about it. I wanted him to hurt the same way I'd been.

"There's more to what happened." His darkened eyes raised the hairs on my neck. I knew I was in for a battle. "Search yourself. I wouldn't do what you accused me of doing."

"I heard this same crap at Java House, Ryan." Not wanting to be taken down by his charm, I continued lashing out. "I thought you were an honest man. Now I know better. Try your broken record on someone else."

"Why are you doing this to me?" His stare was unwavering.

"Look in the mirror." Ice hung on my words.

"You keep cutting me out of your life."

"Your girlfriend's text told me everything I need to know." I tried to wipe my tears. "I begged you not to use me. I don't care about your explanation. It's too late for us and I'm done with you." My bottom lip quivered. "I lost you on the road. I knew I would."

"I'm right here."

"Go build up your ego with Jesse and all the others you need. I don't care." I could feel my body tighten like it was cramping from head to toe. "I'm sick. You made me sick."

My sobs began to crest.

I completely unraveled in front of him.

As much as I tried to remain callous, it was clear.

I cared.

"I know you're angry. You're wrong about what happened." His voice quavered, however his focus remained absolute. "You *will* see me tonight and listen to what I have to say. I've waited all week for you to return my call. I've phoned and texted you dozens of times. I left message after message. Even after our long discussions addressing the need to talk through our challenges, you're still unwilling to listen to anyone's explanation except for the one you decide is true. You say you love me. Whether or not you believe me, we're finished with this dance of advance and retreat. It ends tonight."

"Listen to me and listen to me good." I lifted my chin with defiance. "I. Don't. Want. Us." It was as if I moved in and out of reality. "Please leave me alone so I can recover." Ryan caressed my head without speaking. "You can't be serious," I tried pulling away from him. "Ow." I put my hand to my forehead.

"Your head hurts?" His face flushed. "What . . ." He read the chart Graciela left hanging over the edge of my bed. Anger washed through his eyes. His cheeks reddened. Worry followed. "Why didn't they—" he refocused. His stare was firm. "When you're done here I want you to come to my apartment."

"I'm supposed to melt in your arms when I get there? I won't get weak. No more. No more."

"Shh, sweet Nicky, shh. I never lied to you."

"You did," I insisted. "You said no other woman mattered. If you commit to someone, you don't relieve yourself with a past girlfriend because you can't get the current one to sleep with you."

"Oh, yeah?" There was a new tone of challenge in his voice. "*You* committed to *me*?"

"You know I did," I replied confidently.

"You told Jerry it was over? I don't think that's what happened, was it? In fact, didn't you walk away to hug him, leaving me standing in the parking lot waiting for you? Didn't I see him pull you close?"

"*I didn't let him!*" Pain radiated through my head. "Ow." I squeezed my eyes shut. The ache throbbed. "When I could, I pulled away. He gave me a friendship ring and pledged his loyalty. I wouldn't even wear it when I went out with him. Can you imagine the hurt he felt?"

"So you *did* go out with him after I left. You—"

"I did what I needed so I could get to *you!* All I wanted was you." I gasped. My body jerked in my despair. "I told my mother I loved you and that I was coming on your road trip and I meant it. I would have. I fought my Mom harder than I ever had, standing for what I wanted—you. I only needed two days. Before those two days ended, you texted me and told me to stay home. You didn't want me." *Oh, my head. I shouldn't have raised my voice.* "Until the parking lot, I hadn't committed to you, and—"

His fingers rubbed my temples.

"Where does it hurt?" he asked softly.

"There." I closed my eyes. "You're on it." *Keep going. I could lie here all night.*

I thought about that word—commitment. I had wanted more with Ryan from the first time he'd taken me to Yountville to volunteer. Although I had been fearful to declare it out loud, I'd done it in my heart. What did my words, *until the parking lot*, mean? Did Ryan have a right to be as frustrated with me as I was with him?

"*You* said you weren't seeing *anyone*," I reminded. "How many times did I hear you say you'd cut off your relationships? Should I have followed your lead and taken on *both* Jerry *and* Ethan?" Each word was loaded with sarcasm. "You'd have dropped me like a hot potato. I can hear it now. Wouldn't you tell me goodbye because then I'd be used goods?"

"When the nurse releases you tonight," Ryan ignored my jabs, "Manny will walk you to the security lot and escort you to my apartment. I'll be there as soon as I can. Afterward, if you don't believe what I say and don't want me, I'll stay away and I'll fuck off like you asked."

I didn't know what to do with the ache I felt from him. I was confused about my own suffering.

"No, my mother will—"

"I've already called your mom," he informed.

"She only told you what you wanted to hear. Jenise or Mom will be here any minute. They don't believe your lies, either."

We both know they won't come. He told Mom he's taking care of me and that's enough. Jenise would have backed off, hoping I'd let Ryan take care of me and begin our relationship again. For my parents? As long as someone else handled the trauma, it was enough. For them, if I seemed okay, I was. Our mantra? Don't involve too many outsiders or family secrets might spill.

"You'll hear me out," he demanded. "You can make your decision about the man you think I am after you listen to me. If you want us to turn to ashes, I'll let us go." He closed his eyes and shook his head. "How could you think I wouldn't come to you, Nicky? My heart almost stopped when you passed out. I can't let you fade from my life. I won't. You told me you wanted someone to fight for you and I am. Just like you wanted." He massaged my temples again and I closed my eyes. "I planned to come to your house tomorrow. When you fell, I knew I couldn't wait. Hear me out and then if you want it, I'll be dead to you forever." He dropped his head. Lowered his voice. "Like you asked."

"Just take me in your car, Ryan. I don't feel well enough to argue. I won't run." As I looked at him, I saw complete surrender in his eyes. I couldn't be cruel or harsh any longer. Even though I didn't trust him, the hurt he wore on his face was real.

They always feel bad when they're caught in the act. You can't believe his story.

"I need to do something first," he announced. "I'll see you in a little while."

And just like he'd come in, undetected and invisible in his disguise, he slipped out of the medical office the same way. Judging by the remaining quiet, no one recognized him. My hands shook. Raw anxiety possessed my body.

* * * * *

His eyes were fixed.
Open stare.
Is he breathing?
Dad?
Are you alive?

* * * * *

The more I thought about going to Ryan's apartment, the more nervous I became. I wasn't interested in listening to his explanation of why he slept with Jesse. The stress from having to talk with him made my neck and shoulders tighten as if under the clench of invisible fists.

Once again, I'd have to go up in the elevator women's sighs.

This time, instead of heaven, I was certain I would enter hell.

Chapter 20

The Final Stages of Release

*D*uring an unusually hot night in San Francisco, I'd tormented

Tara's mother, Elaine, with a myth that told how warm weather brought earthquakes.

When all was said and done, the fairy tale had come true.

I was shaken.

When it came to trusting others, the smooth path to my future was cracked and jagged.

I couldn't understand the changes that came so suddenly there was no way to control them.

God, I desperately wanted to.

The entire interaction between Ryan and me seemed slow and drawn out like a preacher's sermon at Sunday mass. In reality it had lasted only a few minutes.

"How are you feeling now?" Graciela asked her final questions while taking my vitals once again. "Still dizzy or nauseous?"

Didn't you hear voices in here? I want to tell you I feel like hell. I need to get out of here so I can get on with my life.

"I haven't thrown up since you put that stuff in my IV." I did my best to sound upbeat and happy. "Can I use my phone?"

Just let me push the reset button so I can go to college boyfriend free.

"Looks like your IV drip finished. Let's take care of that and then you can make your call." She took the needle out of my arm, put some cotton over the entry point and covered it with a bandage. "Are you calling someone for a ride?"

"It's all taken care of," I reassured.

"I'll need you to sign the release forms on your way out. Your uniform is on a hanger over there." She nodded to the area where my jersey and shirt were hanging.

"Thanks for everything, Graciela."

Her smile was an acknowledgment of a job well done. She left the room.

I considered leaving my uniform in the room and walking out of the stadium in only the medical gown. Doing so would have been my symbolic gesture of closing the door on my cheer team idea. Dirty—it was if my dream had been dragged through dull colors. I hadn't envisioned this gloom on my original pallet and didn't want it on my life's canvas.

"Mom, did you talk to Ryan?" I phoned home to double-check the two of them had spoken.

"Yes and I'm not at all happy with that man," she huffed.

That makes two of us.

"Why didn't one of your friends stay with you? What's wrong with them, leaving you there by yourself?"

Can you finally see how injured I am on the inside?

"I'm not alone. I told my friends to leave because I'm going to Ryan's apartment."

"Let me speak with him," she ordered me as if having me in the room with him would change the conversation they'd already had.

"He was just here, but had to go to a meeting." So many lies rolled off my tongue I wondered what number of rosaries I'd have to say for my penance to forgiveness. "His friend, Manny will drive me."

"Manny?"

"Handles security at the ballpark," I said calmly. "He a good guy. So, I'll see you in a few hours. I won't be long at Ryan's."

All I could think about was Mom. When she got involved, that meant something serious had happened. Such as Dad passed out on the front lawn, lying there for all the neighbors to see as she helped him walk inside the house. Or when he'd wandered the streets in a hospital gown not knowing why he'd been admitted. Or a night like the one when Jenise was raped and instead of being at the hospital with his wife and daughter he was passed out in the bedroom.

I didn't want to become a part of that memory book.

I only wanted to bring lightness to my mother's heavy life—to my family's heavy life—and I was failing with that goal.

You're not their savior, Nick.

"I didn't want to bother you," I admitted. "I was going to call Jenise, but Ryan said he'd already talked with you. I wanted you to hear it from me that I'm all right."

Silence.

What are you thinking, Mom?

"Are you still at the ballpark?"

"Yes, in their medical office, but—"

"I'm coming to get you," she demanded.

"I'm all right," I sighed, trying to ease the pressure in my head. "I appreciate you want to come and get me. I'm dehydrated, that's all. There's no reason to be upset."

Well, except for this heartbreak.

Even though my emotional wound was open and bleeding, I continued to act the part I'd played my entire life—the reliable, secure, invincible daughter. No matter what happened, my parents seemed to think the bullets bounced off of me. I had only myself to blame for their thinking. I hated to ask for anyone's help, especially Mom and Dad. I wanted to be in control of my own life and choices and do everything I could to prevent it from spiraling out of control like my parents had.

As long as I seemed to be doing well—getting A's in school, volunteering, participating in after-school committees, or staying with friends—no questions were asked of me. That was all a façade. Mom and Dad never understood how desperate I was for their love—be it a warm smile, full embrace, or a shoulder that could comfort me. A fleeting thought rushed in and out of my mind as I wondered if their distance with showing affection was exactly why I had the same trouble.

Would there ever come a day when they'd finally realize how fragile I was? Could they understand, although they covered up their vulnerability by drinking to excess and hiding under codependency, even they were fragile? Didn't the child in all of us need to be held forever?

"Ryan doesn't know you well enough to understand if you're okay," Mom argued. "What's his number again?"

"No. Mom, I told you, I'm all right."

"If he had any sense . . . God, how selfish of him. Even if he has to drive you himself, he should make you come home."

Did her voice just crack a little?

"Ryan wanted to take me home," I lied for the third time since I'd fallen. I felt like Peter denying Jesus in the garden. I had become a detriment to those around me and also myself. "*I'm* the one who insisted I go to his place."

Even you *don't know how good of a liar I can be, Mom. I've had plenty of practice holding back our family's dark secrets.*

"I should have called you sooner. Don't worry, I'm fine."

I wanted her to insist she'd get me no matter what Ryan had told her. I was ready to give in. In the end, however, it was Mom who gave in.

My family always gave in.

We were tired of the storms that had blown through our lives. Surrendering to the temptation and seduction of sweet darkness was a tempting promise of peace.

Trauma—when it was upon us we denied it was happening. That way we could stay numb and stuff our feelings way down inside us. We'd carried so much pain on our heart that learning techniques to avoid and move around it became normal.

"Your fall was on the news," she gave an uneasy laugh.

Thank God. She's finally at ease.

"God, I'm a klutz, Mom. Always falling in front of people."

"You've always had a dramatic flare," Mom resigned to my wishes using humor. Deflection was a way to maintaining distance from each other. "Call me later. Let me know when you're ready to come home. I should give you an hour with him and pick you—"

"I'll handle it." I had to admit I was happy she had made one last offer of help. "I promise I won't take the streetcar. I'll call you if I need a ride. I'm sure he's enough of a gentleman to bring me home." After reassuring her we said goodbye.

I dressed. Signed a release form and given health care instructions for the next few days. Number one on the list read: *Relax. Avoid exercise and stress until blood pressure normal*.

Looks like I'll break the first directive the moment I see Ryan.

"Don't take the symptoms of a head injury for granted," Graciela said as I handed over the release. "Folks think everything is fine and the next day they land in the hospital."

"I won't." *But did you ignore them? I was throwing up, after all. That's one of the signs.* I got a cup of water from the water cooler. "Thank you."

"You were lucky, Ms. Young," another nurse added as I signed the papers. "Very lucky."

As I heard those words, the shock and fear of my father's fall from eight years earlier came full speed ahead. I'd tucked the images of that afternoon into my box of dark memories.

Unexpectedly, the heavy lid on it had finally lifted off.

"Thank you. I know I was lucky." *I know I was.* Somehow I knew luck for our family—and for me—would run out.

Chapter 21

Walls

$\mathcal{M}$anny, the security guard seemed to appear from nowhere when I walked out of the medical station to the elevator.

"Where did *you* come from?" I asked coolly.

"I'm accompanying you to Mr. Tilton's apartment." His voice was steady.

"I know where I'm going." I stared straight ahead. "I don't need you to go with me, Manny."

"I'm only here to make sure you're all right." He held my arm. "You shouldn't be alone. You're smart enough to understand that."

* * * * *

Dad.
Genius.
Numbed.

Mabel.

Cement wall.

His head.

Dented.

The scenes of my father's accident were like flashes within my midnight. I was drawn back to that day—a day like so many before—average for our household.

I was ten-years-old and home alone. Mom was sure I could take care of myself. I could under normal circumstance. She took Jenise shopping. I had my piano to practice and she'd planned to be back before Dad woke up—actually, before he'd *passed out* from drinking too much. We called it *napping*.

Although we lived together, my family carried on with separate lives. We moved steadily and unemotionally, the same way I descended in the elevator.

* * * * *

"I'm not that smart, Manny. If I were, I wouldn't have gotten involved with your Mr. Tilton and I'd be heading home right now."

Bony fingers lifted the lid from the coffin of hidden memories. They rolled out like the fog that crept over the coastal hills—thick, covering me, and demanding that I reexamine the past now circling in my head.

I'd fallen.

Like dad.

Pointing.

Pounding.

He was numb.

I was numb.

"I'll make sure you're all right," Manny held my arm.

"I'll be all right. I always land on my feet."

Shame.

Family secrets.

They were rising from the grave in which we had buried them. Family secrets that never *really* stayed buried—or quiet—were clawing, demanding their recognition.

Never. Staying. A secret.

Need.

Attention.

Greedy.

Screaming.

Look. At. Me!

As the elevator lowered to street level, it seemed we were descending faster and faster. Memories flooded. I was skidding through blinking lights.

Bright.

Too bright.

Close my eyes.

We all closed our eyes.

Slowing down. Stopping. Dark now. The demons are here. Forcing me. Making me look at them.

Remember, Nicky. You're there with him—with them.

Mabel.

Ambulance.

Piano.

What were you doing then?

What are you doing now?

Pushing down. Hoping the problem will disappear. Not dealing with it. Avoiding. Three floors from the elevator to the street.

It was enough time to travel back to my basement.

* * * * *

I played my Arabesque—one of the many pieces of piano music I loved. It was loud. Fortissimo and dramatic. Ragged and purposeful I struck the piano keys. The composition gave me permission to pound on the old upright player piano that sat in our basement.

It was mine.

All mine.

A friend of my father's had gotten the player piano from one of the saloons in Virginia City. No longer wanted, its mechanical guts were removed and replaced with actual hammers and steel strings. She was weathered and out of tune.

When she landed in our basement, I loved her instantly. She gave me the escape I needed as well as another outlet to create.

The keys were real ivory and the flats and sharps, ebony wood. The carriage that once held the old brass music spools was walnut. Thick legs held her keyboard and were adorned with hand-carved waterfall and leaf designs. At the bottom and in the middle of the heavy floorboard were three brass foot pedals, to soften, make louder, or sustain musical notes.

One of them was broken.

She was broken and it was what made her special.

With loving care I oiled her, kept her dusted, and made certain she didn't fall useless into our shadows. She was a forgotten star. I made sure she got to be in the limelight once more. Every day my fingers danced over her.

Pounding with all the fury I had I tried to empty out the frustration of my home life.

The day my father fell down the stairs, I stopped abruptly. He hadn't slept the usual number of hours after passing out. Why couldn't he wait five minutes to focus before heading downstairs?

It wasn't the first time he'd fallen. Several months earlier and in the middle of the night while still drunk, he opened the basement door, thought it was the bathroom, and sat on an invisible toilet.

If it weren't so tragic it would have been comical.

He tumbled down all thirteen steps.

Going downstairs to get a drink from the bottle he'd hidden was probably so much of a routine his comatose mind couldn't differentiate between awake and asleep.

Was he taken to the emergency room, or at least a doctor when he fell? No, of course not. It wasn't serious enough. Everything *seemed* okay. And if it seemed okay? Well, it *was* okay.

Dark secrets were held close.

That time, my mother and sister helped him up the stairs and back to bed—that is, after Mom cleaned the piss and shit off of him. We never talked about that night.

* * * * *

"It's always good to talk things through," Manny offered me his wisdom, perhaps trying to soften me at the same time.

"What?" I jerked my head. The pain radiated through my neck and the pain I felt was obvious.

"I have something in the car for your head. Does the pain radiate, throb, or is it dull?"

"All of the above," I answered. "No not dull. Do you have some aspirin?"

"I have a neck pillow." He seemed to sense my uneasiness. "It will hold your head still. You can rest against it on the way to Mr. Tilton's apartment."

"Thanks."

"Our conversation earlier . . . sometimes, we think we have all the answers but it ends up entirely different, Ms. Young. You might find that very thing once you talk it through."

"Sometimes."

Talk things through? How can I do that with Ryan? Will I ever bring a new friend or love in my life? How could I ever open the conversation about Jesse in a calm way? All I want to do is kill our memories.

* * * * *

Memories.

Sounds of his footsteps.

Clunky steps.

Dragging feet.

The clanking of his bottle; its cap twisting; the swig, the gulp, another swig, the sloshing of the whiskey rocking back and forth in the bottle . . . it made me sick.

* * * * *

The elevator doors opened.

I took a step forward.

"One more floor." Manny tugged on my arm. "Are you all right?"

"Sort of."

"Do you need to sit down?" he turned to face me.

* * * * *

I'm sitting, playing. Playing my piano. I was safe playing my piano, like I'd been safe hiding within my cheer team. Surrounded by better looking friends, more popular, more gifted—no, not gifted, just . . . different.

As I hid in my music, enveloped, taken and surrounded in its power, I thought I was invisible.

I tried to be invisible and indifferent.

Then.

Now.

Never could.

Cared about people too much.

Too sensitive.

Paid attention.

Didn't know why.

Let down.

Didn't trust.

Even Dad.

Thought I was alone.

All the time, I had an inner strength. She was my subconscious, gut feeling, intuition, perhaps even my guardian angel that waited to make her move. Her name was Mabel.

Now? She had morphed into my Evil Twin, pushing me in every direction for independence. Back then? I felt as if she'd been a grandmother—a soft-spoken, gentle woman who had seen things and knew what to do.

* * * * *

"No, Manny. Let's keep going so I can get this over with."

My mind couldn't stay focused.

It kept reverting back to that day—the day I lost all hope of being a child. Even then, I knew I had to toughen up, survive, and protect myself. My focus included getting out of my house as soon as I could—in any way possible.

* * * * *

The typical places Dad hid his bottle was behind his workbench, in his truck, or underneath the stairs in a box of Christmas decorations. Once in a while he'd get creative and find a new spot—the clothes box by the washing machine, his tool chest, or mixed in with the oil rags he used to work on our vehicles. Half the time, I knew where his bottle was before my mother. I'd practice my piano for hours—too long for him to go without a swig of his medicine.

It was how I found out he'd fallen off the wagon.

Again. Again. Again . . .

It was how I knew I'd lost him for another night.

Week.

A few months . . . sometimes years.

* * * * *

The elevator dinged.

The doors opened.

"Here we go, Ms. Young. Do you want to hold onto my arm?"

"No." I tried to make sure I was steady. "Yes."

"When we get to Mr. Tilton's apartment you'll see why he couldn't ride with you."

Yeah, because he's lining up all of his women for sex later.

I started to open the back door to Manny's car.

"No, Ms. Young. I need you to sit up front. I want to be sure you don't fall asleep. Let me get that pillow for you."

"Okay." I sat in the front, buckled the seatbelt and closed my eyes. I heard Manny rustling in the back. Soon he lifted my head and secured the pillow around my neck.

"Better?"

"Mm-hmm."

Manny drove and eight years melted away.

* * * * *

I am ten, only a child.

Always wanted to be a child.

Missed the innocent living of those years.

Never had them.

Continued to pound out my emotions on my piano.

Dad takes a step.

My shoulders rise. My body stiffens. I prepare to see his vacant eyes and feel his sloppy affection around my shoulders. The slurred, drunken talk is about to begin when all I want to do is practice on my piano.

The next second took away those worries.

The awful sounds of wood, metal and cement had taken the place of my piano music. His inebriated body repeatedly thudded down the stairs and crashed through the metal gate at the bottom. His head hit the remaining cement wall with a dull thud. Finally his tumble stopped.

For a few seconds, I am afraid to move.

* * * * *

"Ms. Young?" Manny shook my arm.

"Yeah?" The jolt of being in a trance-like state was taken away suddenly; my calm disrupted.

A streetcar clanged.

"You shouldn't go to sleep yet," Manny reminded. "If you're having trouble staying awake, I'll roll down your window to let the cold air hit your face."

"What cold air?"

"It *is* warm, isn't it? I'll put the air conditioning on, then." He reached for the dashboard.

"No, I'll um . . ." I yawned. "It's okay."

Taking his suggestion, I rolled down the window. The heavy wheels of the streetcars were grinding alongside of us, down the steel tracks of the Embarcadero. Taxis and busses honked their horns. The glare of the streetlights flashed through the windows as we drove underneath them, blinking on my face and eyelids every few seconds. I felt as if they were lightning, striking against the desert sky of my mother's childhood.

Was time folding back onto itself? Were these lights the pulses that counted down the minutes until we arrived at Ryan's apartment?

As soon as I closed my eyes, I could smell the dust of my basement.

* * * * *

My fingers arched over the piano keys. They felt like bones. All the softness and control of my body—gone. Everything grinded together as if moving in gears that were rusted and worn.

I was frozen.

194

Knew I had to get up.

The piano bench moaned as I rose from it.

No other sound in the basement.

Everything had been shaken apart.

I carefully approached him.

Hesitating, I finally reached out and lightly touched my father.

Oh God, is he dead?

His eyes were fixed. They stared straight ahead.

"Dad?" I was fearful if I spoke too loud, I'd disturb some delicate balance of life and death.

I tapped his arm, confused and unsure of what to do.

Pacing back and forth.

Tried to find a clear answer.

Thousands of impulses fired in my head. I struggled to remember where my mom said she'd be. Ran upstairs and called the local supermarket. The dry cleaner. The bank. Ran outside to our neighbors' houses.

No one home.

Back in the house.

Down the basement stairs.

Shouted at my father.

Leaned over his body and looked at . . . an empty shell. Was that really my father lying there or had his soul flown away? Physically, I was at his side, but my mind was separating from my ten-year-old self.

I detached.

The smallest of details filled my mind.

There was an old picture of a desert scene hanging on one of the 2 x 4 studs above the cement wall. A smattering of red seemed fresh on the gray concrete.

My father's blood?

Sheetrock had broken to the left of where the picture hung; the cobwebs around it were broken and drooped lifelessly from the force of the crash.

I looked out to the backyard. The roses were in bloom.

Our long-forgotten Ping-Pong table had sat on the patio for who knows how long. Puddles of water soaked the top of it. The middle sagged. A tattered net stretched across the chipped and peeled green paint.

Suddenly, Princess, our collie dog, cowered at my side and nuzzled my hand to pet her.

The horror of the situation finally engulfed me.

"Are you okay?" I screamed. "Dad!"

No response.

* * * * *

"Ms. Young?" Manny grabbed my wrist and shook my hand gently. "Stay awake."

"I'm okay," I mumbled.

* * * * *

"An ambulance." Only in my head, but as if she were at my side, Mabel whispered, *Call 9-1-1. They'll send an ambulance to take him away for you.*

I moved through trauma one-step, one tear, and one breath at a time. The little girl in me was scared to death, but even at ten, my inner adult handled it.

The way my father's head was against the cement—I couldn't tell if it was his head or the wall that was damaged. His eyes— open and fixed in his stare, showed no emotion.

He wouldn't answer me.

His breathing was rapid and shallow.

I was afraid to touch him too much. In my family, we were *all* afraid to touch. Touch was intimate and too personal. Touching meant love, opening up, being vulnerable—the possibility of being hurt, falling, and being bruised. Touch meant taking a risk.

We couldn't dare open our hearts that way.

The slightest caress or glance of a hand, carried risk.

That's why we took care of our own needs. It was better not to depend on anyone for happiness or dare to hope for love. We knew if we hoped for too much, the inevitable would happen—the next bad thing would come to smash us all down again.

I broke protocol.

Contrary to the way my family handled things, I called the ambulance. They drove him away to the hospital.

When mom came home, I told her what happened.

She went there while Jenise and I remained, each of us separating mentally and physically as we went to our rooms. Everything would be okay. Nothing could really faze us.

We were used to walking in numbness.

We took care of ourselves.

Mom and Dad came home that night with his head bandaged. They never told us anything about his condition.

We never talked about any of it.

He was lucky that day and a hundred days like it. He always seemed to live on an edge of life and death, sober and drunk, addicted and free from the pull of his liquid seduction.

Was I on that same edge in these moments of hurt?

Chapter 22

Harem of Sighs

"*Y*es, Mr. Tilton, I've got her," Manny spoke into his phone. "She's sitting next to me." Pause. "I won't let her sleep."

Minutes later, the car stopped. My door opened.

"Can you make it? Are you all right?"

"Give me a minute." I wasn't ready to get up. I sat as still as I could be. The pillow felt so good surrounding my head and neck. "Can I take this with me?"

"Sure you can. Take your time." He stood at the curb holding the car door open. "When you're ready, I'll get it for you."

After a few minutes had passed, I stepped out of the car.

"I've been here before, Manny. You don't need to follow me. I'm . . ." I stretched as deeply as I could, " . . . tired. I want to lie down."

"I know." He closed the car door and then held open the one to the lobby. I walked in ahead of him, shuffling to the elevator with my hand on my forehead. Manny was alongside me before I knew it. I was too exhausted to protest and walked with him. We rode steadily to the top floor where the king's harem came and went. As the elevator passed each floor, I could almost hear the sighs and whispers, *he'll use you and leave you like he did to us.* Now, I was among those same voices fading away.

My heart pounded. A whooshing sound filled my ears. My head buzzed and throbbed. Dizziness hit immediately upon reaching the top floor. "I need to sit down."

He held onto me until the doors opened. We walked to a bench in the hallway. I sat there while he unlocked the apartment door.

"I feel like crap." I massaged my shoulders. The vertigo had dissipated.

"Take your time," his voice was low and comforting.

"You must think the world of Ryan, right?"

"I do admire him," he answered. "He's a fair man."

"Why didn't your wonderful Mr. Tilton make sure I went to see a doctor?" Once again, I thought back to the day my father fell. "Guess it's the usual. It's no different in my family. I'm used to it." *We're all used to it.* "I'll be in the guest bedroom," I moaned and walked through Ryan's apartment doors.

"Ms. Young, I'm trained in CPR and I'm a licensed EMT. I won't bother you. But I can't let you wait in the bedroom where you might—"

"I'm going to lie down in his guest bedroom and I wouldn't care if you were the president. I appreciate you're doing your job, but I'm tired and sick and need a bed."

"Yes, all right," he gave in.

"If I don't answer when you knock, break it down. Ryan can afford a new lock. I need to close my eyes. It's too bright out here."

"I'd rather you rested on the sofa. I should keep an eye on you."

"Yeah. We just talked about this." I walked into Ryan's guest bedroom, locked the door and lay down in darkness.

My brain felt like it was banging against my skull. My eyes were sensitive to the light, so I left it off and tried to relax. I didn't mean to fall asleep, but I did. A knock on the door pulled me out of a misty dream. Suddenly, I was awake.

"Okay, okay." I was still groggy. Muffled voices and footsteps were outside the door. *Oh, no . . . now what?* "I'm awake," I said as loud as I could, not certain if anyone heard or if I really had said the words aloud.

A woman said *bathwater, robe, and soup.* A man's voice I didn't recognize said something. Manny and Ryan exchanged words and then said goodnight. Ryan and the stranger remained.

A teakettle whistled and then subsided.

Silence.

Footsteps.

Louder.

More pronounced.

Stopping at the bedroom door.

Oh, damn, here we go. I know that's you, Ryan. Go away.

The doorknob turned back and forth.

"Nicky." Ryan knocked on the door. "Let me in."

"I'm not coming out," I said stubbornly. "I'll stay in here all night until you go to bed and then I'll leave. Say whatever you need to say so I can go to sleep."

"Shit. She's not coming out." Ryan's response seemed panicked. I heard him take a deep breath before he turned and walked away.

Good, I've finally said enough to make him understand.

The sound of a key slipped into the lock, letting me know that my time alone had ended. The door clicked open.

"Please come out with me." Wearing a timid smile, Ryan stood in the doorway. He tossed a key in the air and caught it.

"I'm sick," I said faintly.

"I know." Ryan snapped on the lamp. Light flooded the room.

"Ooh . . ." I covered my eyes. "Can you leave that light off?"

He sat down next to me and put his hand on my shoulder.

"Do you have any aspirin?" I groaned. "I didn't feel this bad until I got in the car with Manny. God, my head hurts. Can I just lie down for a little while longer?"

"Not yet. I brought—"

"You can talk about whatever you want after I get a little more rest, okay?" I turned to my side and closed my eyes. "Just let me sleep a little bit."

What are you going to do now? Drag me out?

"No!" He raised his voice. "There's someone—"

I jumped at the way he spoke, but sat up. I used all the strength I had to cross my arms in defiance.

"This should be good. I can't wait." I cut him off, certain he was only trying to unburden his conscience. It never occurred to me he was attempting to help. "Aren't you going to bat your blue eyes and try to excuse yourself from what happened? If *only* it weren't for the friend who joined you I could have come. Oh, I mean someone *you had your mouth on.* Oh, God what a friend. Don't worry about anything, Ryan. I told you from our start I wouldn't get in your way and . . ." I massaged my head. "Let me rest. I feel terrible."

"I know." Ryan's voice was hushed. "I brought the team doctor with me to make sure you're all right. Once he's done with his exam, if he gives the okay, you can sleep."

Sliding off the bed from the other side and away from Ryan, I gradually stood up. I wanted to keep my distance physically and mentally.

He moved to the door.

I couldn't get by him.

"I'll go out there by myself," I put my hands up. "It's too bright, though. Can't you *please* turn the lights down?"

"Dr. Welluck needs the lights to examine you." Ryan put his arm around me for support. "He's a good doctor; one of the best in the city. Will you let him take a look at you?"

I knew seeing a doctor was important. I hated to admit it, but he was right and I let him take care of what I needed. I walked into the kitchen where the doctor waited.

"Ms. Young, I'm Dr. Welluck." He extended his hand. "Ryan said you fell?"

"Yes." I returned the handshake. "I'm okay now."

"You're squinting." He was a gray-haired man somewhere in his mid-fifties. His rounded and baldhead matched his portly body. "Do your eyes hurt from the lights?"

"I've been lying in a dark room for . . . I don't know how long. What time is it? Can't you turn down—"

"I need to check your vitals," he interrupted.

"They already did that at the ballpark," I said obstinately. "My blood pressure was high. Everything else was okay."

"I heard," he acknowledged. "I'd like to see for myself. With your permission, I'll also look at your head, neck, spine, and take some blood. Those medical stations at the stadium are designed to attend to your essential needs and get you stable so you can move on. Do you understand what I've just explained?"

I nodded.

"Do you agree to let me examine you?" With my affirmation, he pushed several papers in front of me. "Please sign here." His voice and mannerisms were comforting.

"What are you looking for?" I signed and then handed him back the papers.

"You're inquisitive." He tucked the forms into a file and took out several checklists. "That's good, Ms. Young. We need to be advocates for our health. I have a series of markers I'll go through to establish a baseline of your health."

"And those are?"

"First, I'll check for signs of internal injuries or head trauma. Let's begin with a basic eye exam to see how your pupils respond. I know your eyes are sensitive." Dr. Welluck turned on his light. "I won't leave it on your eyes longer than necessary. What do you remember about collapsing tonight?"

"I lifted my teammate and my legs got weak . . . I had random thoughts right along with serious ones. The last thing that went through my head was I hoped no one would get hurt." I put my head down; embarrassed I'd brought this trauma to my teammates, family, and me. "I've been so upset, Doctor. I found out my boyfriend cheated on me." I glared at Ryan. "He's the whole reason I got sick."

"Oh?" Dr. Welluck asked suspiciously. "Did he have something contagious?"

"Well, no." *Crap. Why did I tell him that?* "I'm sure it was the warm night. I haven't eaten or hydrated properly, just . . . some crackers. You know, I couldn't even eat at my favorite place, The Cliff House. My sister took me there. Have you been?"

"Yes, it's delicious." He turned off his small flashlight.

"My boyfriend ruined it. He wrecked the whole week."

"How so?" He wrote down some notes.

"I don't know," I suddenly reversed my conversation.

"Should I have a talk with your boyfriend?" He put down his pen and looked at me.

Did he just chuckle under his breath?

"He won't listen. No one listens to me."

"Seems like he did. I'm here, after all."

"Yeah, well . . . I didn't ask for a doctor."

"But here I am," he quipped. "How are you feeling right now?"

"My head's pounding."

"That's a concern," he observed. "Can you tell me—"

"You know what, Dr. Welluck?" I interrupted. "I would've gone to *my* doctor if I hadn't come here." I shot a hard look at Ryan.

"Let me make a note of your doctor's name. What is it?"

"Well, I . . . I haven't been in a long time and I'm too exhausted to think about it. You know what else?" I felt like spilling everything to his sympathetic ear.

"Yes, Ms. Young, what else?"

"I've had it with boys. They're why I'm in this mess," I ranted. "And I knew better. Can you give me something to make them go away? What's the deal with you guys?"

"The deal?" his smile was endearing.

"Why can't you be friends and that's all? Why does it always go to sex and commitment?"

"We can be a handful when someone takes our heart." He glanced at Ryan.

"You're all so pesky," I scowled. "I get rid of one, here comes another. It's like all or nothing with guys. You know what I mean, Doctor? I don't wear shorts or low cut tops or tight clothes, but they keep coming. They're like magnets."

Both Ryan and the doctor smiled as if trying not to laugh. Within the fogginess of my mind, I was completely serious and made perfect sense.

"Ryan, she needs a mug of Jeanne's delicious soup." He turned back to me. "I don't want you escalating. Let's try and get your system to calm down."

"I'll get it. I need you to let go of my waist," Ryan whispered softly in my ear. "You okay to stand on your own?"

I was startled when I'd realized I was still holding on to him. Reluctantly, I let go and steadied myself on the kitchen island while he walked to the stove.

"Ms. Young, can you sit over here please?" Dr. Welluck pointed to one of the dining table chairs. "Take my arm," he offered.

"I can do it." I sat down.

Ryan brought me the soup and set it on the table.

"Thank you." I glanced at Ryan and quickly looked away before he could see my nervous smile. A little light glowed faintly for the man taking care of me . . . deep inside . . . just a little light.

I drank the soup.

It tasted delicious and I wanted more . . . more of *everything*.

Chapter 23

Disarmed

"*M*mm, Jeanne's a good cook," I took several long sips and finished the entire serving. "Can I have another?"

"Let's make sure that first cup stays down first," Dr. Welluck cautioned. "For now, we'll continue the examination, all right?"

"No more lights in my eyes, please." I closed them just in case.

"We're all done with that." His hand rested softly on my shoulder. "I'm going to check your heart and quickly examine your neck." He went through a series of brief tests, measuring my responses and listening to my heart and lungs. "All good," he informed while he wrote a few more notes.

"What are you writing?" I leaned over to peek at what he wrote.

"Your lungs sound clear, your heart rhythm and pupils are normal, you follow my finger appropriately and your reflexes respond the way they should," he grinned.

"Why are you smiling?"

"You're a bright woman."

"How do you know?"

"You'll see what I mean when you're my age. I've examined enough people over the years. Now, your ears, please."

"You mean I'm not brain dead?" I turned left and right so he could look in them. "Maybe that would keep all these damn boys away from me." I laughed sarcastically. "On second thought, they'd probably like me better because then I couldn't respond to all their stupid statements. No one really cares what I have to say."

"Your sense of humor hasn't been affected," he laughed softly. "Did you know sarcasm is a sign of high intelligence?" He put the blood pressure cuff around my arm.

"In that case, my entire family are geniuses," I rubbed my arm.

"Hmm . . . this reading is high—230 over 120," he frowned. After taking it again, I knew by his expression he'd gotten the same reading. "You're not going anywhere tonight."

"Oh, but—"

"Do you have a history of hypertension?"

"No. No one in my family does."

"You're the first, then."

"Damn it. After the last few weeks . . . trust me, I know why it's so high. You're very gentle, Doctor. I like you." I witnessed Ryan's smile and I turned my attention to him. "This doesn't change my feelings for *you*." I sent an imaginary arrow his way. "I can't stay here," I almost pleaded to Dr. Welluck. "My blood pressure won't go down."

"I'll give you some medicine that will lower it immediately and I have something for your headache. You're in good hands."

"Yeah, hands, mm-hmm," I muttered. "That's what got me here."

"Here's our last step," he swabbed a vein in my right arm. "I'm going to get five vials." He prepared the area and set the vials on the table. "This won't take long."

"What are you looking for?"

"I'm running a complete blood panel to look at your electrolytes, your white and red blood cell counts, your glucose, iron, vitamins B and D and some other indicators."

"Indicators of what?"

"Of a body that's depleted because its owner didn't take care of herself."

"I know." I looked away ashamed.

"I'd also like to run an STD work-up while we're at it, so we have a starting point moving forward. Is that all right?"

"Go ahead." I watched as he filled the little glass vials with my blood. I looked at Ryan. His head was down.

After capping the last vial and putting a bandage on my arm, Doctor Welluck asked me to walk to the sofa and lie down. I did as he asked. He put his hands on my abdomen and pressed down. Felt along my ribs and my sides. Rotated my ankles. Asked me if anything hurt. After telling him no, he rolled a small device similar to a pizza wheel on the bottom of my feet.

"That tickles." I pulled my foot away.

"Good." He turned to Ryan. "She's sharp."

"She is," Ryan agreed.

"You don't appear to be impaired, Ms. Young. There can be a delayed reaction to internal injuries . . . I don't think you're in danger. Nevertheless, I want you here. Ryan will watch you."

"Well, you can't see it," I began.

"See . . . ?" Dr. Welluck trailed off.

"I *am* impaired. It won't show in any medical tests, but your friend, Mr. Tilton has impaired me for sure."

Ryan shook his head, but was sporting a smile.

"You've got a lot to handle here, son." Dr. Welluck had a twinkle in his eye. "All right, Ms. Young; you can go ahead and sit up. I want to watch you walk a straight line."

I got up and immediately lost my balance. Ryan caught me from behind.

"I can do it. I tripped, that's all." I noticed the doctor's concerned look. "Watch, Doctor." I walked another line without incident. "I'm a klutz. I even tripped at the ballpark a few weeks ago. I can't dance very well, either. I even took dance and gymnastics classes. I have to practice a lot with the cheer routines and stuff. Repetition is the key to success."

Why did I just say all that?

"With a sense of humor like yours, it's hard to tell if you need further attention," Dr. Welluck said with a wink. "We're done here." He gave me the medication, reviewed the instructions with Ryan and me, and closed his leather doctor's bag. "You're going to take it easy tonight, aren't you, Ms. Young?"

"Yes."

"Here's my card. It lists my personal number. Give it two hours and call me immediately if your pressure remains elevated or your headache continues. The machine Ryan has is an upgraded model from the Goliaths' training room. Take readings every few hours."

Ryan brought over a glass of water. I washed down the pills.

I looked up at him uncertain and confused.

"Be sure you take all the blood pressure medicine, even when you start to feel better," Dr. Welluck advised. "Drink another cup of soup and take a long bath. Relax and let your body wind down. If you need anything else, Ryan can get it for you."

The tenderness on Ryan's face poured over me. It was as if I was a sheer, delicate cloth and he, beautiful ink slowly spreading through me.

"Whatever you do, stay calm and don't argue," Dr. Welluck said. "Your system needs to relax. Save the anger for another day, all right? You don't need to add any more stress to your heart or your head. Do I make myself clear?"

"Yes, doctor. Thank you so much." I was beyond grateful. "I won't yell too loudly at him."

"Well, you might even *thank* Ryan. He's the one who made sure I came to see you. He worried that you wouldn't take care of yourself and I'd say from the way you handled your nutrition he has a valid point. Would you agree?"

I didn't respond. Instead, I looked away from both of them.

"You can see by her reaction, it's true," Ryan revealed. "She looks away when she's embarrassed or knows you're right."

Damn, he knows me too well.

"Shows a lot of concern by a pesky boy if you ask me," the doctor patted my back. "Don't you think so, Ms. Young?"

I nodded.

"Call me next week for a follow-up visit."

"I will, Doctor. Thank you again."

Maybe coming here was a good idea. The way my family deals with every trauma . . . it would have been two aspirin for me and then to bed.

"I'll have this blood work back Monday," Dr. Welluck informed. "I'll call you with the results." He and Ryan shook hands and we were left alone in the apartment.

I sat on the sofa deciding what to do next.

Ryan walked toward me.

"I don't want to talk right now." I waved him off.

"Let me help you to the bathroom." He held out his hand, inviting me to take it. "You can take your bath and relax."

"I'm not weak," I said curtly. "I can make it myself." I didn't want to feel his hand or body touch mine in any way. I'd already held onto him too long before my examination.

Be careful, touching gets you too close.

"Nicky, I know you're not weak and you can make it on your own. I want to be sure you don't trip because you're such a klutz."

"You're not funny." I tried to hide my smile. It *was* funny and I couldn't help but laugh. I decided the smart thing to do was let him help me.

He took my right arm and gently placed it around his waist. As he held my hand there, he put his left arm around my back.

Oh, how I've missed him!

"I saw you trip outside Java House, by the way." He held the weight of my entire body as we walked to the bathroom. I knew I was secure in his arms.

"Oh, God. I tore my pants and those teenage boys . . ."

"You were adorable the way you tried to cover up your embarrassment." Before I could debate or protest, he continued. "My housekeeper left a robe and slippers in the bathroom for you. They're brand new." He leaned close and whispered, "I got them just for you. Nothing used by anyone else. Ever."

Oh damn, I'm toast.

"I put another cup of soup on the shelf by the tub. You can sit in the water while you sip it," his voice was like a warm caress. "When you undress, sit on the side first and then get in slowly. If you need help, I can call Jeanne to come back."

"I can do it," I insisted.

"Take your time and let me know if you need anything. I'll check on you in a little while." He had definitely calmed my anxiety. My headache was almost gone. "Do you want me to call your mom and update her?"

"Please."

"I'll leave the door open a crack so I can hear you. I'll be right outside."

That Ryan had *any* control over me was frustrating. Disaster always loomed whenever anyone had a say so in my life. I was too exhausted to debate it. The only way I'd keep from falling for him again was to stay far away from him—mentally and physically. I was reluctant to look at his face and tried my best not to. I had no choice when it came to his sexy voice, however. I knew his smile and his masculine laugh would break down my resolve.

Maybe I'll plug my ears.

I stepped out of my clothes, grabbed the side grips of the sunken tub, and lowered myself into the heated water. There must have been a regulator somewhere because the water temperature was perfect and stayed that way without cooling down even a little. It soothed me and felt fantastic as it inched up my body. Grabbing one of the towels folded neatly on the side of the tub, I pulled it on top of my chest and abdomen. The water soaked through, turning the towel into a warm, comfortable blanket that hugged me.

Gradually, my body calmed. My shoulders loosened their grip on my neck. I reached for the soup on the shelf and ate it one spoonful at a time. When I was done, I returned the empty bowl next to me and then lay still, floating and suspended in my purgatory. My head grew heavy. I could feel myself drifting. I finally succumbed to some much-needed sleep. It seemed like it had been only minutes when I heard Ryan's voice pulling me from the world of misty gray.

"Wake up Nicky." His voice called to my woman's body. "Come on, honey. Sit up."

Chapter 24

Glistening

*S*till trying to shake the fuzziness, I brought my knees to my chest and hugged them. When I did, I squeezed the water-soaked towel against my breasts. My back was exposed.

"I'll rinse the soap bubbles off of you." Ryan's voice was slightly more than a whisper. "Is that okay?"

"Mm-hmm," I felt sated and comfortable. It was as if my whole body had fallen asleep.

Ryan turned the brass faucet handles until water flowed quiet and steady. He soaked a dry sponge under the water. I watched as it doubled in size. Warm water fell down my back; the suds fell from my body along with my pain.

"Your hair is dirty from your fall. I'll wash it and massage your head," he whispered. "You tell me if it doesn't feel good or your headache worsens, all right?"

"Mmm." My tongue wasn't close to saying anything logical.

Kneeling on the thick, furry rug by the side of the bathtub, Ryan shielded my forehead and protected my eyes. When the sponge became swollen again, he crushed it in his hand and the water ran through my hair. The warmth poured over me. He lathered his hands with shampoo and carefully rubbed it in.

Oh damn, his strong hands and thick fingers . . . all over my aching scalp . . . the size of them are . . . I feel like letting my mouth hang open.

My body blushed as chills raced from my head, to my neck, across my back, over my thighs and down my legs. When I heard his sexy laugh I knew he'd witnessed the visual signs of my enjoyment.

Dammit, he never misses anything.

My heart had opened again. I couldn't let it this soon, could I? Wouldn't it be the same scenario? Was he really sincere?

"Keep your eyes closed so I can rinse your hair."

I was relaxed.

I didn't respond.

"Okay, Nicky?" He tapped my shoulder with concern.

"Yeah."

I'm sinking deeply, invisibly, into his arms. I'm like a baby in her first bath . . . warm, secure, cuddled, and loved.

He rinsed my hair. Twisted and gathered it in his hands. Gently pushed it in front of me so that it fell on the wet towel covering my breasts.

"I love your hair."

The quiet in the bathroom magnified each noise—Ryan's breath, the rustle of his clothes, a crack of his knuckle, the water as it poured from the faucet, the trickle of it as it spilled from the sponge onto my body—all of it seemed a composition of sound.

As if dawn had crept into Ryan's apartment, I felt my shadows lifting.

His thumbs felt like little rubber balls, easing the knots from the base of my neck. They moved down my spine and loosened my muscles one at a time. My shoulders tingled in goose bumps. As he rinsed my back, I imagined the droplets of water fell into shining pools of promise.

"Are you all right?" He took off the bandage and cotton Dr. Welluck had placed on my arm.

I nodded.

Ryan looked at my other arm, where my IV had been inserted at the ballpark and then at me. He kissed my palm and cradled it in his hands.

"Oh, Nicky." His eyes became teary.

I couldn't turn away from what seemed to be love. He cupped my elbow, peeled off the dressing and removed the cotton underneath. In an unexpected move, he leaned over and kissed me at the spot where the needle had left its mark.

The moment reminded me of his kiss on my forehead when we were on the beach. His simple gesture told me there was so much more to his feelings than I'd previously understood. His soft, moist lips felt lovely the way they lingered on my arm.

I wanted to reach out to bring him closer to me. There was a fiery sensation beginning to rush through my veins. The heat flowed into my belly and down my legs. Caress and tell him I was his was the very thing I wanted to do but was afraid to share my emotions too soon.

If I embraced him and invited him back into my life, wouldn't he assume he could get away with whatever he wanted?

When his mouth lifted from the needle mark, he rested his chin in the bend of my soft forearm. I cradled his head. His smile mirrored happiness and contentment. Although he was anything but, I thought him as innocent in many ways.

He closed his eyes.

My heart softened.

I heard the steps of baby feet around me, encouraging me to move forward. Whispers fell softly. My Evil Twin knocked: *give in, let go, give in, let go.*

Trust for Ryan had twinkled again.

Shadows dimmed.

Light filtered through my very soul.

I took another little step forward.

A power rose through my body that wouldn't allow me to run . . . or leave anything unsaid.

I could feel it.

I welcomed it.

Wanted it.

"I'll help you out of the tub." Ryan reached for me. "Don't resist me. There's no fight needed tonight."

"I won't." *I don't want to fight anymore.*

So much more than my body gave in to him as he put his arm around me, assisting me from the bathtub. I stepped onto the furry carpet. The water-soaked towel that had previously been my blanket, dropped off. I reached for it. Ryan took my hands in his to stop me.

"Your rug will get soaked," I panicked.

I watched as he bent down to pick up the towel. He tossed it in the bathtub and then stood up with his eyes closed. I wondered if my nakedness bothered him.

"Don't make any sudden movements." He opened his eyes. "Keep your body relaxed. I'll guide you." He reached for an oversized bath towel folded on one of the shelves above the tub and put it around my shoulders. "I'll take the strain from your body if you'll let me." He breathed deeply. "Raise your arms with mine so I can wrap this towel around you. Let your weight fall on me. You've already proven how strong you are. There's no need for that strength tonight." His words were a song composed only for me. "Will you let me take your pain away?"

"Yes." *Take everything I have.*

Listening to him made everything inside me stir. Even as I tried to calm my head, whenever he came near and that deep voice crawled all over me, I became breathless.

He stood behind me, lifting both of my hands. It was glorious. I felt as if we were giving thanks to a higher power, inviting new energy into our life and creating new love.

"My Shakti." His voice was plush velvet.

Chills rose up and spread from my shoulders to my calves.

He held one end of the towel in his mouth and grasped the side that still dangled with his free hand, wrapping it around my body.

My belly pulsed with one beat . . . and then another.

When he leaned forward, he brushed against me. Another wave of chills covered my body. His arousing laugh saturated the room, letting me know he'd noticed. It was hard for me to stay still in the knowledge his eyes took in all of my nakedness.

"I can do it." *I have to say something.*

"I know you can." It was if his words floated on tropical trade winds. An assuredness began to fill the space around us. He fixed the towel so my arms secured it.

As if my body had merged with his, he moved me slowly and gently. His dance was delicate. His fingers knew how to work the small intricate pieces of our story and were adept at positioning all the details of us within the fabric of our hopes and dreams.

That night, we fit together easily.

"I'll use this towel to pat you dry, all right?" His words oozed like golden honey.

"Mmm," I repeated.

When he opened the towel to dry my body, it fell down on one side. I reached for it, not wanting him to see me naked again.

"Don't worry." He grabbed the towel and then fastened it. "I'll catch you, Nicky. I'll always catch you."

Oh, I'm . . . going away. He's soothing, I'm flooding . . . his sweetness is . . . like a field of flowers and he's the breeze that gently bends them in waves. He makes me open . . . I'm opening.

He patted my body dry. Only the towel touched my skin. I tried to keep the hunger inside of me under control. I wondered, was the pulsing I felt from the throbbing ache of sickness or was it my rising desire?

"Keep your arms down while I wrap your hair." He squeezed out the last of the water and then wound it like a turban.

"The bath sheet is still open in the back," I reminded.

"It's open so I can massage you with lotion. It'll help take the tension from your body. Grab my arm and sit down on the side of the tub. I'll hold the towel so it won't fall." He kissed me at the base of my neck.

Ooh I've missed your lips.

Ryan straightened his arm so I could lean on it. I sat down on the side of the tub.

"I'll be such a good man for you." He looked directly into my eyes. "I respect you, Nicky. I'm here. I'm here forever."

Where am I?

What kind of man is he?

I'm floating, circling, tumbling, just from the sound of his loving words.

Sinking now . . .

Sinking into . . .
Him.

Chapter 25

A Gentle Rub

*R*yan tipped a bottle of lotion. The thick, creamy liquid mounded in his palm. He rubbed his hands together. Smoothed the richness on my body in long, firm strokes at my shoulders and then moved to the base of my spine. Fingertips sliding up and down. Applying perfect and direct pressure. Pushing gently into the ridges of my ribs and sides and stopping where my breasts began their soft, warm crease.

He fastened the towel so it closed. I thought it signaled his completion. Then he knelt in front of me. The look on his face softened my resistance and my body. I wanted to embrace him and cover him with kisses of gratitude.

"Now your legs." His voice was quiet and soothing. Slipping down my calf to my ankle, he lifted my right leg and set it on his hip. As he rubbed the front and back of my thigh, I felt as if his fingertips made hot ski runs down my calf. "Your skin is dry. It's absorbing all the lotion. I'm just . . ." He reached for the bottle. "Don't neglect yourself like this again."

"My Shiva," I offered affectionately and caressed his arm. *Ooh those veins standing up on his forearm, his phoenix tattoo, the way his muscles tighten* . . . Dancing lightly up and down his arm, I played with the golden brown hairs that covered it. I pressed my palm down on his bicep and gave it a squeeze. His smile told me he enjoyed his nickname. The strong desire to honor and hold him because of what he'd done filled every part of me. "I love these." I could no longer resist the urge to trace the veins that stood up underneath his skin. "If a woman had these they would be so ugly, but yours . . . mmm, I love them."

"I've seen the veins stand out in your neck," he teased cautiously. "You were so angry."

"Yeah." My fingers naturally wove together with his. Lifting his hand to my mouth, I kissed it. Held him to my lips. Took a deep breath. Let it out. "Thank you for taking care of me tonight."

"My baby." His serene blue eyes compelled me to look into them more deeply. He put his hand on my cheek. "Let me finish your other leg and then we can sit down. I'll turn down the bed if you'd rather go to sleep."

"I don't want to sleep yet." *I might wake up from this moment and find I was only dreaming.* "I'm not tired."

"How's your headache? Should we take a blood pressure reading?"

"I don't have a headache anymore thanks to you and Dr. Welluck."

His hands went back to their task, pressing on my thigh, moving down my entire leg, making it loose and relaxed. Paths of white heat disappeared into my skin, leaving only the memory of his fingers on me. The arch of my foot came to life as his thumb traced its curve. All of the pressure points inside me begged for his body to touch mine. God, I needed his hands on me. When his fingers slid in and out of the spaces between my toes I thought I might slip off the side of the tub and onto the floor. The feel of each toe being spread apart, gliding in the movements of sex . . . in and out . . . in . . . out . . . it was incredibly erotic. I closed my eyes and succumbed to his silent message.

"How was that?" He said too quickly, placing my foot down onto the rug.

"Really nice," I purred. *It was so much more than nice and you know it.*

Ryan pulled the lever to let the bathwater drain.

"There's the robe I bought." He nodded to an incredibly lush robe hanging on a hook at the entrance to his two-person shower. "Will you let me put it on you?"

"Um . . ."

"I'll close my eyes. Just drop your towel and I'll hold it out for you." He seemed as excited as a young boy. "I can't wait to . . . you wearing it—it's like we're really together. You're here. I'm here." He took a few steps toward the shower. Took the robe from its hanger. Walked back to me. Grasped the shoulders and held it up. All I had to do was slip my arms into it.

"Thank you." I dropped the towel from my body and slipped into the luxuriousness of the heavy terry cloth robe. "Mmm." I petted the material. *Oh crap, I just moaned for him.* "This is nice." I giggled silently as I watched him keep his eyes closed. "You can open your eyes now."

"I'm glad you like it. I couldn't wait until you came over so I could show it to you. I'm only sorry this was what brought you back to me." Regret wove through his voice.

"Me, too."

"I made you some warm granola and milk. There's also more soup and some hot tea. I'll put them on the coffee table for you. If none of those sound good I'll go and get you something else. Has your stomach settled?"

"All of those sound good," I considered which treat might be the most soothing. "I'm not nauseous anymore."

"Is your headache completely gone now?" he asked again.

"Gone with the bathwater." I tightened the cloth belt of the robe.

"Thank God." Relief shadowed his words and his mouth slipped into a smile. "I'll leave the door open and wait for you on the couch. Call to me if you need anything."

"Thank you." I shoved my hands into the pockets. As he closed the door behind him, dozens of questions rushed through my mind.

Who *was* Ryan Tilton?

Was he really in control of himself and his sexual urges?

Was he a man who needed women when he was away or the man comforting me now?

Was he both?

Maybe he's your big Papa Bear and your big love.

For whatever reason, putting on the plush, voluptuous robe made me feel like I belonged. At his apartment. As his woman. In his life. The full-length of it made me feel like his princess—corny, but that's exactly how I felt. I was comfortable, relaxed, and enjoyed being taken care of in every way.

Even though I was comfortable for the time being, a tough conversation remained ahead. Could I say what was on my mind after what he'd just done for me? Dare I bring up Jesse? I knew I had to, but how could I without dismissing everything that had just been mended? Had anything really been repaired?

I didn't want to get angry and take the chance of raising my blood pressure to dangerous levels, but then again . . . wasn't it time to stop shoving issues aside? How many years had my family done this very thing? How long would I reinforce the cycle of passivity, keeping peace at all costs, instead of daring to disrupt the sickness that permeated my life?

The time had come.

I needed to stop the circle of dysfunction and pretend.

All my family had ever accomplished with our postponement and delays of talking about a problem was perpetuating the hurt. The dark feeling we tried to avoid would slither from the shadows and turn into a monster because we hadn't dealt with it immediately.

Ryan couldn't be let off the hook this time.

He had to understand how making decisions on my behalf made me feel like an incapable child. Additionally, Jesse seemed to know I had stayed behind, texting me about their glorious sex life. I needed Ryan to see me as a strong woman; one he'd respect and be faithful to, rather than giving in to sex with another who was easier to handle or seduce.

As the fog lifted and the issues for me had become clear, the biggest question remained: was it fair to make Ryan, who was at the prime of his sexual and physical life, wait for my decision about physical intimacy? In trying to convince me that he would, was he trying to make himself believe he could?

Maybe I should tell him he's lovely, spend the night in his guest bedroom, and then go home tomorrow morning. Isn't the smartest thing for each of us to move on? Aren't the differences between us too wide to overcome? If I don't give it my all right now, will I always come an early decision that someone isn't right for me?

I removed the towel from my head and combed my hair. When it was wet, it fell to the middle of my behind. I loved feeling it cascade down my shoulders, arms and back. My long-flowing, wavy hair was one of the only physical attributes in which I had confidence. After taking a deep breath, I turned off the bathroom light. I made sure the robe's belt was tied securely around my waist and padded into the living room with bare feet.

The bowl of warm granola, soup, and a mug of hot tea waited for me on the coffee table. Ryan rested on the sofa. His eyes were closed as he listened to music. When he heard my bare feet on the wooden floor, he opened his eyes and watched me sit down. Once I was next to him, he straightened to reach for the granola and then handed it to me.

"God, you're beautiful." The rasp in his voice was completely disarming. "Every light inside of you seems to be on. You turn on those same lights in me. Your faith in people—and in us—comes right to the surface."

"Thank you." *Take the compliment. Don't talk.* Embarrassed, I looked toward the balcony. The sliding glass door was open. *Did you leave it open because you remembered I like that?*

Had some balance had been restored?

The usual San Francisco weather had returned.

The delicate evening breezes at the ballpark had vanished into the dark night. The cool, foggy air had taken its place. The flames in Ryan's fireplace sent a shadowy glow around the room.

"Mmm this tastes good." I paused. "And feels good." I dipped my spoon in the hot cereal, blew on it, and then sipped the comforting meal. Every part of my body had lost the stress that gripped me earlier in the evening. *God, I'm so comfortable and relaxed. I could sit here . . . forever?* I put my knees up against my stomach, making sure the robe wrapped around my legs. The only skin showing was my bare feet.

Although I was relaxed and completely soothed from Ryan's earlier massage, I felt something was ready to break open in the air.

Suddenly, I knew our destination was a part of a higher power—it was big.

A desire for a different life called to me.

I felt its message tugging, pulling, and coaxing me inside new affirmations, daring me to trust them.

A door had opened.

Transition had extended its hand and invited me to enter.

I took a step.

The voice was tender and sweet.

Its beckoning strong.

Forceful.

The seduction of a unique life seemed promised to us. I wondered if this was our moment of heaven. Were we mist in the air, back from some ancient time, circling and covering each other as our lives changed and connected once more?

I didn't want to fall back to the way I used to live: keeping secrets. Staying quiet about uncomfortable situations. Always keeping my distance from others. Above all making sure no one got close enough to look inside my heart. After all, that was where the darkness lurked and the place where I sliced people out of my life. It was where I had carved away all possibilities for something more. It was where I kept trust locked away. Tight. Buried deep.

"Feel better?" Ryan asked.

"Yes," I whispered a satisfied sigh of relief.

My eyes closed. My mind was serene. Then . . . my unresolved turbulence surrounding Jesse's text surfaced from the dark.

No! Don't let him off that easy! Let him have it.

My mind had cleared. I couldn't have been more at peace. Still, the vision of them together wouldn't let me stay silent. The image of their mouths kissing and their naked bodies sliding together had become hard-stamped in my brain.

Returning now, it crashed into our present.

At the risk of losing him once again, I had to speak up. If I didn't challenge my fears that night, I knew I never would—and neither would Ryan. When it came to being together, this would be our end if we pushed what had happened under the rug of secrets.

Wrapped in the chains of my family's dysfunctional generations, all of us locked together in shadows because we never took a risk to change . . . *something* . . . that had to be over. Now.

Chapter 26

Pushing Jesse Out

of My Head

*T*he hurt child in my psyche burst through.

She needed to be avenged.

I should have discussed my concerns in a calm and rational manner. Previous to that night, I had known only one way when it came to dealing with pain—detach and become numb.

That tactic had passed and was a part of another woman's life.

I wanted Ryan to feel the rejection and abandonment the same way I felt it—clawing and fighting to experience love—I needed him to understand. I had been in pieces and he needed to suffer, too. My only desire in that moment was to paint the picture of another man's mouth on my mouth and sear the vision into his brain, just as Jesse was in mine.

Straightening, my finger pointed, I prepared to confront my demons.

Were they *my* demons?

Whose demons were they?

He was the one who'd cheated.

Yet, *I* was the one who cut him off and wouldn't discuss it.

No longer could I react in fear or be afraid to talk it over.

I had to stay involved until there was a resolution.

He had to see my dark side and I needed to see his.

"*Why* did you cheat on me? I begged you to tell me the truth. You dismissed Jesse to me like she meant nothing and then took her in your arms when you needed her."

My hands clenched into fists. My body had grown in power. Instead of trembling, my voice was strong. My heart pounded with the drums of my cavewomen ancestors.

"Worse of all, you dismissed me. Then right after you told me not to come on your road trip, I got a text from your *sex friend* telling me to stay away. I told you right from the beginning you needed to be with someone your age. Those women understand your physical body in ways that I don't. I only wanted you to be honest. I know I'm difficult and what I'd asked of you wasn't easy. Just say so and I'll step aside." I gripped the ties of the robe. "All you had to do was be honest with me."

I sank back into the couch. Like a ghost that had returned, sadness rose to overtake the power I felt only moments ago.

I knew this demon wouldn't let go easily.

He'll abandon you, Nicky. Shh . . . you'd better settle down. Just keep it all inside you and it will be okay. Haven't you learned this lesson? You have to keep the peace and forge on.

NO!! What are you saying? It's right in front of you. This is the risk you need to take.

I heard the chains rattling—the ones that bound the men and women in my family. They were straining. Had to break. Tonight.

"All I asked was that you please, please, not go with someone else while you were with me." My chin began to lift. "Why couldn't you give me that much?"

"Stop it!" Ryan moved next to me. His hip touched mine. Both of his hands were on my shoulders. His fingers dug into my back.

I gasped in shock. I'd never seen this side of him. When it came right down to it—hadn't it been deliberate and calculated?

Weren't we both responsible for this crash of misunderstanding and the upcoming battle?

It was time for us to uncover the darkness—his and mine—buried under the dozens of layers we'd been such experts in hiding from the rest of the world.

He had gripped the evil deep within me. Had it in his hands. It was the evil that refused me happiness. Doubt pulsed through my body. I wanted him to yank it out of me. Silently I begged him to do it. At the same time I was afraid I had pushed him too far. I wanted to run as fast as I could, escape from his arms and hide away forever so I wouldn't have to hear, *goodbye.*

He's going to end our relationship this very minute. I should never have told him I loved him. I should have let the incident with Jesse go and not backed him into a corner.

My urge to grab a bag of chocolate and devour it pulled at me. Scoops of ice cream piled high in a bowl with hot fudge sauce, a bag of salty potato chips with sour cream and onion dip, a fresh peach with rich cream and sugar all over it . . . I was already detaching in food's delicious escape.

Could I finally focus on this man, this love, this life?

Although his hands trembled, they were filled with enough courage to wrap around my waist and lift me onto his lap. Ryan's gaze was steady. His eyes held mine. He took my hand in his and placed it on his heart.

Something unexpected happened.

His inner hero rose up to possess me.

He took over my fear, hesitation and the shadows inside.

He had my darkness by the throat.

I felt transported to the day he first introduced himself—the day he lifted my hand and kissed it. When he began talking, his voice was subdued. His movements were slow and purposeful.

"You've judged me. Again. Without hearing what I have to say you've made up your mind." His voice was low and even. "Jesse was in my room and we were having sex. Does that about sum up your conclusions?"

I didn't respond.

Focused on his eyes.

"Why won't you let me talk to you when we have a challenge?"

Silence.

"I tried all week to reach you. Instead of answering my calls and listening to what I have to say, you pound me down with insults. You hold yourself so high above me, don't you?"

"What in the world do you mean? I don't—"

"Impossible standards—you set them for yourself and now you've challenged me to live up to them. And yet," his eyes narrowed. "What have *you* been doing? Why can't I ever get a hold of you when I leave? Who are you out with that you can't answer when I call you? Tell me you haven't seen Jerry. Tell me that you told him in no uncertain terms you love me."

I tried. I did. I didn't give in . . . did I? I wanted to tell him. I made every attempt. Why didn't I tell him? Why do I always try to take care of and soothe other people's feelings before my own?

When will I be strong and decisive and stop trying to keep the peace? When will I finally ask for what I want?

A dark anger simmered beneath his surface. I could see it in his eyes. Had his demon come to tear us apart? Did I need to reach inside *him* and grab his fear as he was trying to do for me?

There was no smile or tease on his face.

He was serious. Wouldn't let go of me.

I tried to pull away. He refused to release me. I was held captive within his strength and all that he was.

He took a deep breath.

I suddenly felt merged with his body.

He still loved me.

Even after I'd lost control and hurled my anger and insults at him, he understood it was from fear and was forcing me to talk it through. Confusion swept through me. Then only seconds later it became apparent—my demon was now his and his demon was mine. This was our night to send them back to eternal hell.

I placed my hand against his chest.

"How did Jesse know my number, Ryan?"

"That's all I've been thinking about." His neck was stiff and his body tightened.

"I've been suffocating in visions of the two of you having sex. My mind keeps repeating her what she texted me. Her written words flash through my head once every few minutes. They vibrate inside of me and tug on my heartbreak." I struggled to continue. "I know it's true, Ryan." My voice splintered. "How could it not be?"

"Not anymore. I swore to you. I haven't been with anyone since the beginning of May. I promised you. That hasn't changed, Nicky." He lifted me off his lap. Walked to the kitchen counter. Grabbed his cell phone and sat next to me. "Here's my list of contacts." He showed me his phone. "Tell me the women's names you see."

"I'm not looking through your phone." I remained stubborn. "How would I know who anyone is in there? Besides, you could have covered your tracks already by deleting their names and numbers before you came home. Maybe your babes hidden under some secret category."

"I don't have categories. The only women's numbers I have in my phone are you, our moms, Frances, your sister, my agent and my financial advisor."

"Wait—your agent is a *woman*?" I veered off the subject for a moment. The only agents I'd read about that signed single, highly profiled male athletes were other males. The offer to sign came with women escorts, admittance as V.I.P.'s to well-known clubs and private parties, and dozens of shady benefits. Having a woman agent was no guarantee of anything different; maybe *they'd* even had sex and it was how they'd met. Still, I was impressed with the possibility he'd broken from the mold.

"Yes." From the look in his eyes I knew he understood the reason for my sudden shift. "Is it so hard to believe I'd have an agent who is female?"

"It's just . . . I'm not that naive. I've heard the stories." I paused momentarily. "Okay, since you insist, I'll look at your contacts." I verified the names he'd just revealed. It felt amazing and I didn't want him to see that I was surrendering so easily.

"I tried to call you quite a few times after you told me to fuck off." He put his phone on the coffee table. "Even though I stood waiting for you in the parking lot, you chose to talk with Jerry first. He put his arms around you. Actually—you *let* him put his arms around you. How do you think that made me feel?"

"Bad," I confessed.

"It made me crazy. Still, I remained open and ready for you in case you wanted to see me. And then, you pushed your way through the crowd as we were leaving." His chest lifted as he sighed. "When you told me you loved me? It was like little hearts were beating through my body. I couldn't wait to see you again."

"You saw me with Jerry?" I could hardly believe it. That meant he'd watched everything. The hug, the ring . . . I wanted to dig myself a hole and crawl into it.

"Nicky, I've already told you. I look for you all the time. I saw you immediately. When you turned and walked away with him, I was afraid you didn't know what you wanted. Then you fought to get in the parking lot . . . the hope you gave me . . . I knew we were no longer together because of what I could do for you dad or sister. It was just you and I. Like last time, I called and sent you dozens of texts. You promised to call me back. You never did. I called you for three days." He stared intently into my eyes. "I understand now you were at Tara's and had forgotten your charger. But you went home and discovered Jesse's message and cut me off without giving me a chance to explain. You say you love me, but instead of having a conversation, you abandoned me. Can't you understand how much it hurts to be told I'm dead to you?"

I closed my eyes.

The pain that filled his voice also filled me.

"Can you?" He lifted my chin.

"Yes."

"You cut into me." His thumbs caressed my cheeks.

"I'm sorry."

"I know you're a strong woman afraid of opening your heart. You need your protection and walls. But you scare the hell out of me and I need to be reassured just like you do. Didn't we already talk about our fears? I took the chance and shared my vulnerable side with you. How can you not understand 'm open in every way? I've shared myself with you like I haven't with anyone else."

I listened to him.

Took a deep breath.

Let out a long sigh.

Breathed deeply, perhaps for the first time since Jesse's text.

Chapter 27

Pushing Jerry Out
of Ryan's Head

"*O*kay," I acquiesced. "I agree I made some quick judgments and drew conclusions I shouldn't have. Try to understand Jesse's text from my point of view. I haven't gotten to share your body the way you have with her and while trying to get to that point, I have to read about the way you two had sex? How would you have interpreted it? The person I thought you were . . . to get something like that . . ." I shook my head. "After we shared such an intimate night . . . God, the words were—"

"Lies," Ryan didn't hesitate. "Disgusting words making my love for you seem dirty. I can't imagine the images that went through your mind but I know what I felt listening to you explain them. When you called I didn't know what had happened. You have to give me the chance to listen to you and absorb what you're saying."

"From my point of view—" I put my hand on his shoulder. "You didn't seem all that concerned. I tried to explain."

"I know it looked bad. What Jesse did *was* and *is* bad. Your interaction with Jerry looked bad, too. Yet, I didn't cut you off. I could have turned my back on you and never stepped off the bus if I used your solution to prevent myself from being hurt."

"I stayed as rational as I could," I admitted. "My gut reaction stemmed from all the years Jerry and I have known each other. I didn't think it was fair to blurt out my love for you at the stadium we've gone to since we were little kids. He came home from a week of baseball, ready to be with me. He didn't know I'd fallen for you. Imagine if the situation was reversed—can you?"

"Yes, but—"

"I'm told if you love someone you're supposed to shout it out to the world. I did that. I said the words in front Goliath Management, your teammates, their wives and girlfriends and your fans. I haven't done anything like that. It was a big a move for me and I felt as if an earthquake shook me. I had to talk to Jerry. If I went to your first, the overflowing excitement and joy for you would negate all that I wanted to tell him. Can you try to understand?"

"I understand you kissed him and let him hug you." He remained stubborn and wouldn't let me excuse me way out of it.

"*He* kissed *me*," I countered. "I squirmed out of his embrace as soon as I could. I didn't enjoy it. He's too strong for me to push away. All I wanted was to get to you."

"I'm trying to understand, but—"

"Just like I'm trying to understand *you*. If you can't hold back your desire for sex until I figure things out . . . I can't be open to you while you have sex with someone else." My body felt as if it would fall to pieces. "I won't be able to travel with you like the women you're used to. When I go to college . . . if you can't stay firm in your resolve, I get it. Let's not pretend we have a chance together. We should end this love affair while we're still friends." My eyes flooded with tears. "Don't you think?" I brought my hands to my face. "That's it. It's all I have. I'm tired and just . . . empty." I cried softly.

I felt his body become ready.

He reached for me.

His touch was knowing.

Our fingers interlocked.

It was as if we had merged and pressed our spirits together.

"I didn't have sex with Jesse. I wasn't with her. When I make promises to you, I'm telling the truth. You need to trust me. After all the things I've shared—my father's story and my relationship with my brother—I'm not a liar. Please have faith in me."

"I did. I was. I was filled with it. Then you dismissed me." Tears ran down my face. "You didn't give me the chance to decide about coming on your road trip. I was ready. I had settled it with Mom. Your decision to cut me out . . . I thought it meant you didn't want me. Then, I got Jesse's text after you told me to stay home . . . no one's ever talked to me like that. How does one human being talk like that to another? I realize it was a text . . . is that, I mean, do you think she'd be softer on the phone or is she so full of revenge she doesn't care? You were, are, her friend . . . maybe she doesn't like it that you have another woman in your life."

"I can't answer that," he tried to offer a rational response. "She's never done anything like this to anyone else I've seen."

"I felt cast aside. Like garbage." I paused. "I'm telling you honestly, I'm not strong enough for that kind of bombardment." I looked out the window and back to Ryan. "I don't want those visions in my head of you with her or any other woman. How am I supposed to maneuver through it? It's hard enough not to dwell on your past without your present pressing up on me, too."

I couldn't hold back the hurt any longer. Just as healing seemed ready to begin, I felt torn apart again. My overflowing emotions spilled. I wanted him to be strong enough to wait for sex with me. I knew that wasn't realistic.

Ryan unlocked our hands.

His loving arms surrounded me, cradled me, and carefully brought me to his beautiful chest.

"My text didn't mean I wanted you to stay home—God, Nicky, no. I wanted you with me. It was all I could do to hold back what I really wanted to say."

"What do you mean?" I probed. "What did you want to say?"

"Screw your mom and dad's speeches and their desperate attempts to make you doubt yourself and the way they hold you back. I wanted you to follow your own heart. Stand up and dig in. Own this relationship. Make them understand how much we love each other. Tell them I'm your man and you are my woman." He trembled as if his body was on the edge. "I wanted to beg you. I came close to begging you. I fought with all the strength I had not to take a cab back to your house and carry you away in my arms."

"You . . . I, um . . . damn it." *How can I answer him after all that?* "You can't . . . next time, you can't decide for me, Ryan. I need to make my own choices. I don't need you to interpret what's best for me. That's not the kind of protection I want. I'm a capable and mature woman who will take the consequences of her actions.

"Please try to understand, as a child, decisions were forced on me all the time. Riding in my father's truck while coming home from the bar or with Mom leaving the house near midnight to go and get him. I went with her to the police department a few times to get Dad out of jail. All those things did was force more hurt down my throat. I learned to endure the numbness forced on me as they imprinted their silent demands I hide and stay quiet while our family's secrets darkened in every shade of black."

I don't want us to be a part of that saga.

"I felt as if you'd thrown me away, just like, like . . ." Could I reveal the deeper and even more complex secrets of my family?

"Like what, Nicky? Trust me this time. Tell me your feelings."

"Like I've always felt with my mother and father," I confessed. "They left me on my own. As many twisted decisions that were made for my sister and me—like making me take care of my dad—when it came to advancing in our lives, it was always up to us to figure it out. I'm strong and independent. I'll make it no matter what the challenges. But there are times I need help. For years I wished for someone to notice me. I prayed that help would come for Jenise and me. I don't want to be controlled or forced to agree with a decision. I want support."

My emotions escalated like a Phoenix from our ashes.

"I've taken care of my father too many times. I've been company for Mom, even late at night when I should have been in bed because Dad was out getting drunk. I've stayed out of trouble and kept my nose clean, while my friends experimented with drugs and alcohol. I'm tired of being *on* every day." I breathed slowly, trying to sound rational. "I need to be in control of my own decisions and also taken care of for a while."

"I know, sweetheart, I know. I'm reaching for you right now." His hands caressed my head, my arms, my fears, my insecurities—he was all over me in every way.

"Underneath all this drive and fight for survival, I'm fragile, just like everybody else. When it comes down to it, I'm just a little girl doing the best she can."

"I want to be the one who shelters you." I saw the tenderness in his eyes. His body and voice crested. They saturated me.

"I've been whining, but—"

"No. You're letting out feelings that have been kept silent for too long." He squeezed my hand as if he understood. "Keep going. Tell me more."

"Let me make some tea for us. Want some?"

I started to get up.

"Stay there. Keep talking. I'll get it."

He scooted from the sofa and walked into the kitchen. The water was still hot as he poured it in two mugs readied with tea bags. "Don't stop."

"Need any help?"

"Babe . . . I got it. Continue. Don't stop now."

"Okay, well, I want someone to say, *I'll get that for you, can I help you, may I give you a hand*, and then not hesitate. Just do it. I'm tired of fighting for survival," I sniffed. "Have you ever felt like that?"

"Yes. God, yes. I know what it is to be in survival mode," Ryan confided. "I wanted a mom who'd be there for me and give me the emotional support I needed when I was a teenager. The examples I saw everywhere depicted the perfect single parent who held family life together. I didn't understand why Mom couldn't get her life on track. I needed her to respond to me—somehow—even as I was acting out in anger. None of us knew what to do after Dad died," he grimaced. "We didn't have anyone who cared enough to dig into our problems. I yearned to explain my feelings to someone every moment that I was awake but I didn't know where to begin. I was afraid that if I showed my emotions I'd be made fun of by my friends. What it all came down to? I needed to be held."

"That's it exactly!" I nodded my head. "I can't believe you nailed it like that."

"What I learned was that we need to save ourselves." He said the words as if they marked the end of a long battle. "We have helpers and people who come in and out of our lives; like my mentor, Walter Dixon. I was the one who had to do the work."

He dipped the teabags into the mugs a few times.

"You take cream or sugar?"

"A little cream please."

"Lemon?" He started to open the refrigerator door.

"No thanks."

He returned to and placed the mugs of hot tea on coasters on top of the coffee table. "They're hot. Let 'em cool down a bit."

"Thank you. So, continuing . . . you still want me to?"

"Yes."

"Once in a while I need to lean on someone else. I'm battling and forcing myself to ask for what I need. Still, my composure is a facade in so many ways."

"I totally get it. You ask me, actually—you *tell* me—I need someone my age. Maybe now you'll understand. Observations like yours . . . you're the woman I have everything in common with. It's you. The things you say . . ." he trailed off.

"Finish!" It was as if the madness was finally unwinding.

"At least there was some good that came from your struggle," he concluded.

Chapter 28

Tucking Each Other In

"How can you say it's good I've struggled?" I crossed my arms as if giving myself a hug. "I sure don't see it that way."

"I didn't say that. What I meant was the struggle you've gone through might be the reason for your strength and insights. Your tender heart and the gifts you share . . . you let people experience an incredible combination of hope and love. I told you at the Embarcadero Hotel I was fighting for you," he reminded me. "I'll take care of you, like I am tonight."

"I want that." My voice was scratchy.

"I need you to take care of me, too, Nicky. I have a fragile heart that's been empty a long time."

"I will. We'll do it together."

"All I wanted to accomplish when I suggested you not come was to take the pressure off of you. You said your mother thought we were moving too fast. I figured we could go on a road trip another time. I didn't want you to push it with her."

"That's not the way you said it," I countered. "You said *it's too far for you*. I have it saved in my phone if you want to look. Let me show—" I started to get up.

"You don't need to do that." Ryan held my wrist. "I understand I didn't write it like you needed. If what I did bothered you, you needed to tell me. I thought going another time would make your family feel better about me. I never got the chance to explain."

"I started to. That first night you were away, I started to." I was disgusted with myself. "I changed my mind."

"Why?"

"I didn't want to rock the boat," I confessed.

"Rock the boat?"

"Push you too far so you'd get frustrated enough to seek the company of another woman who wasn't as much trouble." I looked down. "And then I thought you had done exactly that."

"Oh, Nicky." His fingers slipped under my chin. He lifted my gaze to meet his eyes. "Please don't go there. You can say anything to me. I won't leave in frustration and see someone else because of our discussions. Can we talk about Jesse's text?"

"Yes," I wrinkled my nose.

"Are you sure?" Ryan kissed my hand.

"We have to, don't we?" I forced myself to be braver than I'd ever been. I reached for the mug of tea steeping on the coffee table. Took a few sips. "It's ready if you want yours."

He took a few sips from his mug and then tucked his legs underneath him. His thighs bulged.

"I don't know how she got a text off to you. All I've done is try to figure out how and why. The only plausible explanation is she did it when I discussed the practice schedule with Kevin. He'd noticed a meeting that didn't make any sense. I put my phone on one of the end tables in the lobby while trying to balance the information packet management gave us along with my coffee, room key, and wallet. We took ten minutes to review the papers."

"She moves quick." I said with enough disgust for the both of us—me for not trusting enough, and Ryan for trusting too much.

"I swear she wasn't in my hotel room and I wasn't in hers. Kevin is dating her. I haven't seen or been with her in months."

"Kevin? How . . ."

"They started seeing each other." Ryan's comment seemed careless. He didn't see anything wrong with the scenario he'd just revealed to me.

I stared at him.

"What's wrong?"

"*Really*? Your best friend is seeing an ex, who . . ." I shook my head. "I'm sorry, but . . . *your best friend* is seeing the same woman you shared a big part of your life with, the same woman who texted me her crazy message? Isn't that, I don't know . . . weird, crazy, or . . . at the very least, stupid?"

"She's not my ex." His voice was flat. "I've already explained that I never felt anything for her or considered her my girlfriend. I don't think about her that way."

"Isn't the question more like how does she think of you?"

"It's never been like that between us," he stated too confidently.

"You might not think of her that way, but for her to text me a message like that? She considers you more than a friend. That message was about jealousy. She wants you," I sighed.

"No." He put down his tea. Held my hand. "No, it's not like that, Nicky. I promise you it was never that way."

"I don't know if I'll ever get over my phobia. All the women you've been with . . . and one of them does something like that . . ."

"Nicky—"

"I know, I know. Your past is the past. But you're not comfortable with me being around Jerry and he's only one boy. So I know you understand how I feel when I have to listen to you say you stood next to her, right?"

"Yes," he agreed. "I'm sorry. I . . . never mind."

"Say it."

"I want these trust issues to be over."

"I do, too. We have a ways to go if you're going to be around someone who thinks nothing of sending me a text like that. Just her body being near yours . . . I mean, gee, Ryan, she said you gave her a ring and that you were going to marry her."

"I never gave her any piece of jewelry, let alone an engagement ring." Ryan was obviously agitated.

"You did support her art, however, to the tune of thousands of dollars," I reminded. "Isn't that the same thing?"

"Marriage was the furthest thing from my mind with her or any woman," he ignored the crux of my challenge. "Like I told you before, we had fun in college and then a business arrangement when she came to San Francisco when we were at charity and society functions; that's all."

"*Came* to San Francisco? You mean *followed* you."

"I don't think so," he frowned.

"Well I'm positive she doesn't look at it the way you do. I'd bet a million bucks she doesn't see it that way at all."

"Yes, she does," he insisted. "We discussed this. You know, how we used each other to meet the movers and shakers."

"And yet, look what that friend, someone with whom you had a business arrangement, did to me." I tried to keep from crying. "Something's undone with her. You need to close it."

"I *did* close it." His jaw tightened. He leaned forward as if emphasizing his point. "I closed it in every way, even though there was nothing to close. We weren't—"

"Dating. I know. You've said that. Still, I'm afraid she won't stop." I clenched my robe to my chest. "Maybe if I had the sexual experiences you've had I'd understand. I swear something's off. I don't know what it is, but what happened . . . something isn't quite right. That's not a reasonable thing to do."

"I give you my word that in the future I won't be anywhere near Jesse, even when she's with Kevin. I'll ask him to stay away from me when they're together."

"How can you do that?" I appreciated the gesture but didn't believe him. "He's your best friend. That would mean—"

"*You're* my best friend," he squeezed my hand. "Nick, I can't control what other people do. I can only control what I do. The thing is . . ." He paused a few beats as if gathering his thoughts.

"What?" I tried to digest everything as he revealed it. I couldn't rest yet.

"It wouldn't matter if she stood in front of me naked." He gathered me in his arms. "I know you don't believe me, but she's nothing. I feel nothing. I swear I don't give her a second thought. Jesse's not in my mind at all, except now that she hurt you . . ." A flash of red anger crossed his face. "I had a serious talk with her."

"About the text?"

"I told her in no uncertain terms to leave you alone." His voice roughened. "I wasn't easy about it. I also told her to stay away from me. From the beginning of May I've only been with the guys who don't party. Most of the time I've stayed in my room." Ryan looked down for a few seconds. "Please believe me."

"I'll try harder. It's tough for me to believe anyone's promise for all the reasons I've discussed." I started to push up from the sofa.

"What do you need?" He held my arms, obviously wanting to make sure we were settled.

"Well . . . I do have to go to the bathroom," I blushed and then giggled, trying to end the heaviness of our evening for a moment. "I'd love another cup of soup, though."

"It'll only take a minute to warm it," he laughed at my response and offered his hand to help me to my feet. "Take your time."

Heading for his master bathroom, I turned to watch him as he prepared my soup. Ryan was like an easy smile the way his big body filled and became large, turning on the burner, stirring the pot of soup, watching it carefully, just for me. I loved his shoulders. They were luscious to look at as they moved, bulged and flexed.

Washing my face felt as if I cleared the spider webs I'd felt from earlier that evening. The urge to sleep was beginning to take me over. As I turned out the light and stood in the doorway, I wondered: were we sleeping in the same bed, or would I rest alone in his guest room because I wasn't feeling up to par? I started to put on the slippers he left for me, and then changed my mind. *I've got a better idea.*

"Can I borrow a pair of socks?" I peeked out of the bedroom. "My feet are getting cold."

"I've got a great cure for your cold feet," he smiled. I watched as he pulled the sofa closer to the fireplace and piled some blankets and pillows in front of it. "We can sit here."

"Ah, great idea," I praised, secretly delighted that my plan had worked.

As Ryan turned to get the bowl of soup from the kitchen, I wrapped my arms around his waist. We stood together in a silent embrace, our bodies giving in and savoring the moment. When it was time, our spirits made a temporary agreement to separate. I patted his belly and let him go, sitting on the blankets with my back against the sofa.

"Here you go." He handed me my bowl. A handle was attached.

"Thanks." I blew on it to cool it down before taking the first sip. As the fire crackled and danced, I started to yawn. With a stretch I surrendered and leaned into his body.

"Ready for bed?" He put his arm around my shoulder and caressed my hair.

"Almost. I could fall asleep right here," I admitted. "It won't take much. How come you didn't call and ask me to meet you somewhere to talk? Why have Manny take me here? Was it just for medical reasons?"

"I planned to. I was coming to see you at your house tomorrow, but your fall put an end to that. I had to know you were all right. The only way to be sure was to bring Dr. Welluck with me. I needed to capture you." He cleared his throat. "I had to have you under my control."

"God, Ryan."

"Well, you give on at least that point, don't you?" he grinned.

"Yes, I admit I—"

"Secondly," his face lost its tease and hurt replaced it. "You told me to fuck off." He looked me squarely in the eyes. I couldn't stand his directness and when I looked away, he turned my head so I had no choice but to look at him. "You told me not to call you and I was dead as far as you were concerned."

Those words sound terrible now that I hear them bounce back at me.

"We both know there was no way you would have agreed to meet me." He continued caressing my face. "You wouldn't even answer my calls. How could I explain myself unless I escorted here tonight. Believe me?"

"Yes, I do, but—"

"I was so afraid you were injured. I . . . I didn't know and . . ." he stumbled over his words. "I had to know you were okay. Your body . . ." his voice cracked. "It was twisted, and . . . I wouldn't cheat on you when you'd just told me that you loved me. Why would I take a chance, seeing a woman who means nothing and risk the loss of your confidence and trust? I wouldn't."

"I guess . . ." My mind swirled with the new information Ryan shared. "Because of her text I thought you wanted me for love and sex at home and on the road . . . Alex said you and Jesse traveled together. I imagined the worst."

"*Used* to, Nicky, and only on occasion. Your pipeline of information hasn't been very accurate. When are you going to start trusting what *I* say, instead of your friends' gossip?"

"I don't listen to gossip. They were only trying to—"

"Warn you. Those warnings cause you to interpret outcomes from your fear. That fear can make everything dark and bleak." He kissed me lightly on my forehead.

Oh, I love this place. I've missed it here.

"I wouldn't do that to you." He rubbed my shoulders. "I know the difference between getting laid and having the chance for love. I want your love."

"Why would you want me to come on a road trip if you don't travel with your girlfriends?"

"Oh, Nicky." His eyes became hooded. "It's not the same when it comes to having you with me. Going on the road with you? As much as possible, sweetheart; as much as possible."

"Okay."

I interlaced my fingers with his. We bonded together in the stillness of what might be.

Chapter 29

Flooding

$\mathcal{S}$ilence covered us. We both nodded off. I was tucked into his body. Safe. Comfortable and taken care of in every way.

"Baby?" he squeezed my shoulder to wake me. "Do you need something else to soothe your soft belly before we go to bed?" His arms lifted from my body. Our fingers and hands untangled. After a quick kiss, he got up. I gathered the blankets and tucked one of them around me on the sofa. A sense of being from a higher level whispered.

"I'm good actually." I laughed as he started to walk away. Although groggy, I leaned back to better appreciate the view.

"What's so funny?" An arc of electricity seemed to reach from his body to mine as he turned around wearing his wry grin.

"Just now, when you talked about soft bellies, it reminded me of a vision I had of you as a big, fluffy papa bear." I giggled and saw his face fill with love. "Your bear hugs are lovely and you have a small little belly surrounded by all those muscles. The name fits perfectly. Did you know how much I like to give it a poke?"

"Hmm . . . I think I like that." His body seemed to relax completely.

"Me, too," I smiled.

"Poke me any time." He walked into the kitchen wearing a smirk and fixed another warm drink for me. In only a minute or two he returned and handed me another mug. "Just some warm milk with a little honey in case your stomach is feeling acidic. With the tea and soup swishing around, this will help you sleep."

Another unspoken observation . . . he always knows.

"Thanks." I took a long sip. "I love warm milk."

"Lift up, sweetheart." When I stood, he wrapped his big arms around my waist. Gently, he gathered my body on his lap, first taking the warm milk and placing it on the end table.

His muscular chest pressed against my back.

His legs were under mine.

My belly rippled as his hands rested on it.

"If I wanted sex I could've had it. I didn't with Jesse or with anyone else." His cheek rested on mine. "I'm waiting for you, Nicky, only for you."

The desire in Ryan's voice was obvious. He spoke in low, sensual tones. His voice triggered tiny lightning bolts in my chest and sent electric surges straight down my body. His thumbs rubbed my temples. His hands went through my hair, covering my scalp, touching me lightly. I let my head fall forward.

As my shoulders dropped, it was as if I'd relaxed for one of the first times in my life. My defenses were down. I opened in more ways than I understood that night. My body began to release the anxiety and stress from the days we'd been apart.

Worry gave way to the possibility of overwhelming joy. It was time to say good-bye to those powerful fears. I was suddenly swollen with a dyer need to let go. I fell into tears.

"I know," Ryan whispered. He didn't ask what my tears were about. He understood. Hearing those words come from the man who loved me was everything. It felt like a barrier had broken from deep inside of my soul. That he could see me so deeply, know my pain, my loneliness, and my struggle to let someone come close, was overwhelming.

Glistening droplets from the bathwater that perhaps had turned into diamonds seemed to gather on my body. Their warmth showered me with the precious moments exploding for the two of us. The brush stroke across our lives had become soft and was colored with gold.

"It's why I wanted you with me tonight, sweetheart. I didn't trust your parents would take care of you or that *you'd* take care of yourself because of the way you've been forced to put your own safety at risk on behalf of your father."

This person believes in me. I believe in him. It's all right to open my heart. I may get bruised. Maybe we won't work. This is life. These moments—crashing, forgiving and starting again . . . it's what it means to really, really, be alive.

And so, my protective walls fell down.

My body's core became exposed.

I started to unwind in every way.

I was given a glimpse of the fierce and serene pieces of life.

A glow surrounded us.

I closed my eyes and let it cover me.

Beneath the cliff I'd hung onto all my life—my hands sometimes losing their grip, almost giving up—the pebbles, rocks, and boulders fell. They grazed me. Had almost crushed me. Now I was at a place of being safe. Through all of the failed trials and mistakes. The bleeding and rawness from the years of clawing and grasping to stop all the madness around me . . . all of these had finally filled the abyss below.

I stepped down and let the light surround me.

It was radiant.

I was free.

A kiss on the nape of my neck.

A whisper in my ear. His tongue licked its curve. Hands traced my shoulders. He slowly grasped each side of my robe. It fell and rested in the middle of my arms. My breasts were almost exposed.

I didn't resist.

I was his.

His lips covered my neck. He untied the front of my robe and held my hands in his. When he placed them at my sides, the robe dropped, fully exposing my arms, breasts and belly. He caressed my shoulders and moved down my biceps to my wrists. His body suddenly tensed. I knew he was taking me to his bed.

One of his arms slid under my legs.

The other moved to my upper back.

Cradled inside his masculine envelope, I was protected; loved; out of danger; away from pain. He carried my exposed body into his bedroom, glancing away only to make sure our path was clear. When he put me down on the edge of his bed, my robe opened completely. It became soft puddles of fabric surrounding my hips. I was naked. Even though I was completely vulnerable, I didn't reach for the robe. I let Ryan take care of me.

My hair tumbled around my shoulders, back and belly.

Ryan's deep sigh filled his bedroom.

"Don't worry." His voice relaxed me in every way. "It's brand new." He held up a nightgown. "Raise your arms."

I obeyed.

After his second sigh echoed off of my body, perhaps giving him pause to make a memory of the evening, he slipped the nightgown over me. It had long sleeves and the soft cotton flannel felt lovely and fresh against my skin.

When he stood in front of me, he looked like a man who was full. His body reflected his feelings—swollen and excited. His sweat pants didn't hide his erection. He embraced me once more. For a few incredible moments we simply looked into each other's eyes. It was a silent acknowledgment of who we were and what had just happened.

Ryan had taken many risks that night—carrying me to the medical station, disguising himself and coming in the room, bringing me to his apartment, having a doctor check me—all for love. In doing those things, I had softened, was receptive and wanted to be together in new ways.

Anxiety that had previously chanted *he'll abandon you*, dissolved into the night. He told me the truth. I believed him. We'd reached another level of togetherness and respect. He lay me down on the crisp sheets, scented as if they'd hung in fresh air and soft breezes. Once the warm covers enveloped me, he kissed my forehead. Ryan sat next to me on the side of the bed, his hand on my cheek.

Love took me over.

I covered his hand with mine.

"Matt told me what you did for Tara when we were away," he revealed. "Your heart is love. Please don't starve me of that again. You're all I want. Do you believe me? Tell me honestly."

"Yes."

"Go to sleep, my sweetheart. I'll check on you in a bit." He kissed my hands, tucked them under the covers, turned out the light, and left the room.

When I'd first come to his apartment that night, I was certain he'd spin some story of why he was with Jesse. I thought he'd give me a dozen excuses to keep alive the possibility of sex with me while having it on the road as well. Instead, he reassured, cuddled, and put me to bed surrounded by warmth. Someone held me instead of leaving me to take care of myself. Ryan made sure my needs were met. I knew I was important to him. He didn't leave me abandoned in my dark shadows. Engulfed in those thoughts, I drifted off.

Later when Ryan got in bed, I was aware enough to know he was naked. He took me in his arms and turned me on my side so I folded into his body. I lifted my leg over his. He held my head to his chest. His gentle movements were as if a promise was made—one that made me believe we could be the moon and sun, Shiva and Shakti, lovers and friends . . . forever.

"You need to behave." I was still groggy.

"I will." He kissed the side of my face. "I promise."

"I love your chest." I kissed it. "I know. I tell you all the time, but . . . I do."

Making sure he knew that I loved him, I said the three words I'd first said in the players' parking lot. They were the same three words that had pushed me through the deep pain of my fears. I said them for us—a man and a woman, lying quietly, unafraid and together.

"I love you, Ryan."

He me throughout the night.

On this day, the direction of my life changed forever.

Chapter 30

Monitoring My Blood Pressure

*M*orning.

I was in the same position in which I'd fallen asleep. The filtered light splayed out in filmy rays through the bedroom window. My hand rested on Ryan's heart. His hand rested on top of mine. I wondered if we had been that way all night.

"What time is it?" I stretched out my calves. Wiggled my feet and toes.

"Almost ten. Mmm, Nicky."

"What?"

"Your body stretching against mine . . . I told you before how good that feels."

"I thought it was late." I tried to stay away from sexy talk. I was afraid my heart was so open that it might explode through my body and all my blood would be lost.

This morning, this feeling . . . it's too good to be true.

"I feel like I blacked out," I lifted my head a little to look at him. His eyes were closed.

"How come?" He squeezed my hand.

"I don't remember waking up at all. In fact, I haven't slept this late since . . ." I felt his body come to life. "You know . . . the first time you stayed overnight with me in my bedroom." I tried to move off him. He tightened his hold on me. "I went back to sleep after you left for your road trip. You called and woke me up."

"You invited me to kiss you—a lot." He turned on his side to face me.

"I just woke up, Ryan."

"And?"

"Doctor's orders were for me to be calm. Hearing you talk about kissing isn't good for me, so shh."

"How do you feel this morning?" I was weak. More than ever before. "We should get a reading on your blood pressure."

"I feel okay. How's your arm?" I patted and then kissed his chest. "Poor thing having me sleep on it all night."

He lay back on the back again and slowly brought my head down to rest on him. It was a delicate and wonderful move.

Feelings stirred in my belly from that one, simple gesture.

"Nothing in me can sleep when you're close," he replied smoothly. "Every part of me is wide awake, waiting for your touch, kiss, and your body to press against mine. That night we slept in your room when I pulled you close so often? It was because I couldn't sleep without touching you in some way . . . God, woman; you feel wonderful."

The day had barely begun and he'd already pushed the *play* button on my body. I sensed that he'd read a library of books on seduction and had memorized them all.

"When do you have to go to the ballpark?"

"In a few hours. Let's relax a while," he encouraged. "You shouldn't get up too fast, you might get dizzy."

"Just lying here makes me dizzy. Your chest knocks me for a loop." I stretched and brought my leg over his belly. Quite accidentally I brushed his stiff penis. "Sorry." From the way his body flinched, I wondered if I'd hurt him. His laugh soon answered my question. My senses woke in ways I had never experienced and his masculine voice and body stroked every part of me.

"Don't ever apologize for touching me . . . anywhere." He rubbed my back.

We stayed in our heaven a little longer. Our chests rising and falling, our hands loving and silently talking as they played. When he rolled on top of me, his legs surrounded my hips and his arms held me inside them. I wiggled. It was impossible to move. I was *forced* to stare at his deliciously crooked smile.

I know I won't make it out of here alive . . . I wonder if my blood pressure has gone down at all. I don't see how. Guess I should check it to make sure I'm all right.

"Ryan, I can't move." I squirmed beneath him. "You better get the machine so I can . . ."

I felt vulnerable in every way. His power was intimidating— and sexy. My sister told me temporarily giving my power to another was a good thing. I wasn't comfortable with the notion.

"Uh-huh, I know." His body seemed as if it moved everywhere. "You always have control over me. For once it feels good to have it over you."

The contented look in his eyes made me feel as if we were in the middle of cotton clouds, fluffed and prepared for our bodies. I quivered at the tenderness of his kiss. His lips were soft and slow as they caressed my cheek.

"Having you in my arms . . . your innocent face . . ." He took a deep breath. "I'm having trouble holding back my feelings."

"I can't imagine how you'd say that. I must look like hell."

"No, Nicky. You don't understand. Who you are shines through everything. With or without makeup, sleepy or not, at your best or under the weather, having you as my woman . . . you fill a basic need. You ground me. It's an amazing feeling."

"Basic?" My nose wrinkled. "You mean I'm simple?"

"Not simple," he exhaled softly. "I mean in the way you put yourself out there so honestly."

"I feel like I've hidden myself for years," I confessed.

"But that's not how you are," he corrected. "You hide the secrets of your family. You don't hide yourself. People say things they think appeal to an athlete's ego. Not you. Scared as hell, you force yourself to continue forward with your dreams."

"An *athlete's* ego? To *your* ego, you mean."

"I love the way we are with each other." He wore an amused expression. "Don't you think it's because of our conversations last year in Yountville?"

"They were awesome icebreakers." Locked in his love, every part of him saturated and tantalized me. With edgy, sensual movements, his mouth found my face, my lips and my cheeks as if wanting each dimple and crevice to become familiar to his senses. I couldn't help it—I moaned. Something wild within me scratched to get out.

"What was that?" A devastating smile flashed before I could answer. Ryan put his entire mouth on mine while his legs squeezed my hips, stomach, and thighs. "Stay the night with me?" His words sizzled within the breathless question. "Please stay." I hadn't the chance to answer when he asked, "Nicky, will you stay with me?" He kissed my ears with a light touch. The delicate glance of his skin on mine made a deep aching pulse between my legs. "Baby?" he asked coyly.

"Ryan . . ."

While his body lay on top of mine, my throat seemed to close. Long, thick fingers stroked my inner cravings. My muscles tightened. I needed air, but not because of his weight. The excitement of his body stole my breath.

"I think, uh, my mom . . . I think she, she might be worried."

"I'll call her and tell her the team doctor examined you and wants you to stay here. If she's okay with it, will you spend another day with me?"

How could I fight his mischievous smile? I *had* to fight it. Needed to. My individuality was on the line. The man to whom I was giving myself was a succulent sex-devil hiding behind an angel's face—and oh how I wanted to see more of his horns!

"Okay. Our home number is—"

"I know what it is. It's in my phone listed under both you and your mom. Truthfully? I've had it memorized since last year." He kissed my cheek again and lifted the receiver off its base.

That's right. Since last year . . . wow . . . last year!

Still lying on me, his body was an ocean of life and seemed to suggest deeper places to explore. Encouraging me to swim in primal waters, all I wanted was to drift away with him.

My mother answered Ryan's call. I could hear her asking questions. Among his answers: I was resting. Given a thorough exam. Prescribed medication for my headache and elevated blood pressure. While giving me his evil eye, he tattled to Mom that Dr.

Welluck had analyzed what had happened was because of stress and poor nutrition.

"Her blood pressure was elevated when she got here. It was going down when she went to bed," he reported. "She just woke up. No. I haven't yet but I will as soon as we hang up."

I heard her ask him to bring me home.

"I would, Mrs. Young, but the doctor gave orders for her to stay here a few days," he responded with a sinister smile. "Right. The doctor ordered her to stay put and relax."

The snicker of my Evil Twin caught my attention. *Great time to tease that man on top of you don't ya think, Nick?* I gave in. My new mission was to knock him off his game. I tried silly faces. It didn't faze him. *Something more delicious, my Evil Twin hissed. Come on, you can do it.* I kissed the entire length of his forearm. He jerked a little. His eyes couldn't lie. He enjoyed it. Still, he wouldn't flinch. *Raise your head and lick his thick neck.*

"Oh, that little heart that beats in there," I whispered, keeping my voice low so my mother wouldn't hear. Wherever I saw a little heartbeat in his neck, I moaned to tease him and made him suffer. "Mmm, Ryan, my sweet baby. Ooooohhhh, my big man." I moved my hips just slightly, still pinned underneath his body. He turned his head away so my lips couldn't reach his . . . but his earlobe hung close. I wanted to take a taste and I flicked it with my tongue. "Mmm . . ." I kept Mom at the forefront of my mind, her hyper-vigilance on the other end of the phone.

"Hang on a minute, Mrs. Young." He put his phone on mute. "Nicky," his eyes were hooded. "You need to stop teasing me or when I end this call I'll have to take care of you."

"You're already taking care of me." I flirted mercilessly.

"Keep playing and you *will* find out what I mean." The sound that rumbled in his throat was like a warning. He held my head down to keep my tongue and lips under his control, so he could talk without distraction.

That's what you get for all those sexy laughs, Ryan Tilton—pay back.

When he was satisfied I was *captured*, my body pinned below his, he took the phone off mute and told my mother he'd make sure I had everything I needed.

"Two thirty over one twenty," he replied to Mom's question. "Yes." Seconds passed. "Yes." More of Mom. "I know that's high. As I said, Dr. Welluck gave her medicine and last night it was down to one forty over ninety-five." She asked another question. "Not yet." Pause. "I will. I'm going out to get her breakfast in a minute. I promise I'll get a reading and call you if there is any reason for concern. Do you want to talk to her?"

I was amused he didn't tell her he was next to me—actually, on top of me—and wondered what she would have thought if he'd have said something like, *I have your daughter pinned underneath my naked body, do you want to talk with her?*

"Dr. Welluck gave her the okay to sleep." He was all business with Mom. "I made sure she was with—" Interruption. "Yes, Manny's an EMT. He made sure she stayed awake."

Why doesn't Mom ask him to hand me his phone? She knows we've slept in the same bed before. What is she afraid of hearing?

I wanted to grab the phone and talk with her, but then reconsidered. She *was* worried, after all. Hearing from me might have been too much reality, perhaps jolting her back to any number of my father's close calls. Although it was an opportune time to make her understand my transitioning life, I played nice, like the good girl I was.

I was . . .

I was.

"Come over any time, Mrs. Young. I'll leave your name with the front desk." Mom seemed to take his word for everything. Ryan asked her once again if she wanted to talk with me. When she declined, he gave her his address, landline and cell number. I knew he'd reassured her that he had me under control.

Being in control was important to her—control, calm, and unemotional was how she preferred to move through life. I'd witnessed Ryan's keen ability in keeping the people around him comfortable and relaxed multiple times. That morning, he not only made me feel secure, he also comforted Mom—a woman who wasn't often at ease.

After he put the phone down, both of his arms framed my face. His kind expression made me smile as he looked into my eyes.

"Everything's okay with your mom. But *you*," his hand caressed the side of my head. "*You* need to pay dearly for what you just did." The way he squeezed me with his legs and arms—he held my body however he wanted. I hadn't expected his dominance to both excite and frighten me. "You shouldn't tease me like that. You really don't understand the fire you've just lit inside of me." He kissed my lips lightly. "Feeling your mouth on my body and hearing your moans . . . I'd love to be inside you right now."

"But . . ." I warned, " . . . you have to behave yourself. I'll call Dr. Welluck and tell him you're making my blood pressure zoom."

"Uh, no." The vibration of his voice on my body made me tingle. "What the good doctor said was I'd be the one to call him if *you* weren't behaving. I guess I have a *Get Out of Jail Free Card*."

"You just promised my mom." I closed my eyes, imagining those sex-devil horns had sprouted and giggled at my vision. "If you try anything, I might have a stroke. It'll be your fault I'm in the hospital and my sister will take you down for sure."

"I can't be a good boy if you're going to moan like that." He looked in my eyes. I forced myself to stay strong. "Oh, what I could do to you." His constant stare made my body moisten. "I'd better get up, because if I don't . . ."

"Then what?" I provoked him.

"Uh-huh." He kissed me again and got out of bed. His naked body showed what I'd already felt when he lay on top of me—he was undeniably ready for sex. He walked out of the bedroom and returned in only moments. "Here's the blood pressure machine, some water, and your medication. Let's see how you're doing."

He's so comfortable walking around naked . . . of course if I had the body he does I guess I would be, too. I'll bet I could wrap the cuff around his penis as erect as he is. I wonder what kind of reading the machine would give? Ha!

After downing the pills, I slipped my arm inside the cuff.

I laughed out loud.

"What's so funny?"

"Nothing." *I can't tell you.*

"That's not nice," he chastised playfully.

"Continue with what you're doing," I ordered. "Trust me when I say I can't tell you."

Ryan fastened the cuff and turned on the machine. He had a smirk on his face, knowing I'd hid something tantalizing from him. The reading came back quickly.

"Normal. Oh, thank God," he exhaled and then unwrapped my arm. "I'll take my shower and then go to the market and pick up some croissants and fruit. Anything come to mind you'd like me to bring back for you?"

"No thanks. I'll see you in a few hours."

"I won't be gone long."

"Whenever you go out you're surrounded," I reminded.

"I'll wear my disguise," he teased.

"The orange janitor jumpsuit?" I giggled.

"Exactly." He started into the bathroom.

"Cover everything, then. Especially your chest and arms. You'll cause a riot if you go out showing either of them."

"We're certainly comfortable with our teases this morning." He whipped around and walked back to the bed. "Someone obviously feels better." *Oh damn. Just watching him walk back to me makes me squirm.*

"Won't you join me?" He reached for my hand. His body seemed as if it was oiled.

"I don't think so. That might be . . . dangerous." I wondered if I could slide down his chest and thighs, enjoying a ride on his slick, shining skin. The way it looked so moist and smooth . . . *What would I do when his pointed pole stopped me?* I giggled at the thought.

"Giggling again? What kind of nasty thoughts are running through your mind? You're stepping it up rather quickly, don't you think?"

"*Stepping it up*? I haven't a clue of what you mean."

"Uh-huh," his devil's tail whipped back and forth. "As far as showering together? Woman, I *know* it would be dangerous. And don't think by holding those covers to your neck you're safe." After filling me up with his suggestive laugh, he walked into his bathroom.

I watched his legs, beautiful behind, back, and broad shoulders. All of those muscles flexing and retracting—he left me feeling lovely.

Chapter 31

Sex Stuff

*W*hile temptation showered, I should have gotten out of bed and dressed. It felt so good to stay in the warm covers I just couldn't resist reveling in them. Rolling over to his side, I buried my head in his pillow and inhaled his spicy cologne. I gathered his sheets to my face, rubbed them on my body, and pulled his comforter around me.

I was a lioness whose lion had shaken his mane and roared for her. He made me proud to be his and I was filled with love and appreciation. I imagined us rolling together in his den, covering myself in his scent. I found comfort embracing the warmth his body left behind.

I wonder what he keeps in his nightstand? I bet I'll find his sex stuff. I wonder if he reads Playboy or . . . worse.

Reaching all the way to the back of the drawer, the only things I could find were a bottle of aspirin, a pair of nail clippers, and an emery board. Before I could look any further, I felt Ryan's naked body on mine.

"Looking for something in particular?" His legs straddled my hips. He pinned me on the bed face down. His voice poked at every opening in my body.

"Ryan"—sexual tension flooded me—"let me up, you're smothering me."

No rush. It's delicious having your legs surround me, your penis brush against my bottom, and your arms and hands all over my body.

"Give me a moment so I can look at this beautiful feast laid out before me." Ripples of desire rushed to my inner thighs. My cavewoman responded to his growl. It was sensual hell knowing he was raking my body from head to toe. Although I was still in my nightgown, I felt naked and excited. "You're so . . . the lush, curvy body you try to hide . . ."

His hands lightly traced my behind. I felt my nightgown lift up my legs. It seemed little pulses echoed everywhere. I kept still, trying to hide the intense sensual ache in my body.

His thighs tensed.

My thighs tightened.

Silent desire tortured both of us.

His thick penis made me aware of his size; it touched my body when he moved. From his growls and moans I knew he was pleased he had me captured and might be assessing where and how to conquer his lover.

"Relax, sweetheart." Leaning over me, my massive masculine man rubbed my shoulders. "I can see you're struggling. I won't take advantage of you." My muscles clenched. I did my best to relax, but in the end I waited anxiously for him to finish—perhaps finishing me off for good. "How does that feel?" Ryan leaned against my cheek, nuzzled my ear, and lightly kissed me.

"Nice. But I can't relax when you're sitting on me naked."

He pulled my nightgown down and moved off of me. I was no longer pinned and turned on my side to face him. Both of us rested on our elbows looking at each other.

"What did you think you'd find in my nightstand?" he asked coyly.

"Nothing." I knew by the feel of my heated cheeks I'd blushed. "I was just um . . ."

"Uh huh." The tone of his voice seared me. "I know what you were looking for. I don't keep condoms or sex stuff at the side of my bed. Do you want to see what I have?"

"No."

"No?" he asked with a raised eyebrow.

"No." *Sex stuff is exactly what I'm looking for. I want to see what you like in bed.*

"How kinky do you think I am?"

"I have no idea," I replied. "I wouldn't know kinky from normal—well, unless I found a set of handcuffs—that would be obvious, right?" *God, did I just say that?* "But really, is there is such a thing as normal? I tend to think—you know, I . . . um . . . don't know. I guess I was looking for condoms, magazines, and . . . I don't know all the stuff that goes with sex."

Why can't I stop talking?

"Kinky isn't my thing. If you decide it's *yours*, however . . . I'm happy to be your student."

"Yeah." I looked away.

"Come with me." He got up and held out his hand. I took it. We walked to the bathroom together. "Open all of the drawers and look in them."

"I don't need to—"

"Look through everything I have," he insisted. "All of my combs, brushes, hair products, toothpaste, brushes, shampoo, my shaving cream—go through everything."

"No, I—"

"I insist you do it while I'm standing here." My body responded to his command. "I couldn't have had a chance to rush around and put stuff away, right? I was at the game," he continued. "So even though you were in the medical office I wouldn't have known you'd stay the night with me, do you agree?"

"Yes."

"After I left you at the medical station I was with Dr. Welluck. You were already here when I got home. The things I bought for us were after our evening in Half Moon Bay. Now you know that what I've been telling you for weeks is real—I'm committed only to you and I'm not some jock screwing every woman in sight."

"Yes." I looked through all of his drawers and in the bottom one found a box of condoms, some spermicidal foam, and a jar of lubricant—all of them unopened. "These are—"

"Unopened." He finished my sentence. "They're for *you* when you're ready." He put his arms around me. "I'm not trying to hide anything or sneak around. Look through my closet, my office, and every drawer . . . anywhere you want. I'm giving you permission to snoop." He took my hand and we walked back to the bed. "You need to rest, so climb up and I'll tuck you in."

He pulled the covers to my chin and then walked into his bathroom.

Someone is preparing to be my lover.

Canopied with a contentment I'd never felt before, I dozed off until the motion of the bed woke me.

Ryan sat next to me, dressed in a light brown flannel shirt and a pair of faded blue jeans.

"What happened to the orange jumpsuit?" I kidded.

"My cap and hoodie go on when I step into the lobby."

"Damn, Ryan, you look good in anything." I teased. "Isn't that what you said to me when I got out of my dirty sweats after our afternoon of driving on the dunes in Pismo?"

"Your humor is stronger than ever." Excitement filled his voice. "You *are* feeling better. Well that's very good news! Maybe tonight, *I'll* be your doctor. I can um . . . give you a full exam." He kissed me on the forehead.

Is he ready at any moment? Maybe I could be ready, too? He's so fun to tease and I love it when he does the same to me. I wonder how much is too much. Is there such a thing? How do we know when to stop? Do we automatically go to the next step?

"Don't go to any trouble." I rubbed up and down his forearm.

"I'll get some snacks so you'll have a few things to munch on." He put his arms around me. "You'll let me take care of you now?"

"Yes."

We embraced.

I felt as his strong and yet giving body absorb me.

"I'll be back shortly." He kissed me again and left the apartment.

Chapter 32

An Interesting Closet

*W*hile Ryan was out buying breakfast, I decided it was the perfect time to take a shower. After taking off my nightgown I placed it on the bed to pet and stroke the soft flannel. I folded it neatly, smoothing the wrinkles. I hadn't noticed when Ryan put it on me it was patterned with little daisies.

How sweet. I wonder if he picked out the pattern because of the daisy he found for me on my birthday? Probably a coincidence. Still . . . maybe . . .

I touched the material one more time.

Brought it to my nose.

Caressed my cheek with it.

Put it back on the bed.

Lovely.

I cautiously stepped into the shower. Ran my hands along the big squares of grey slate tile on the walls. Followed its crescent curve to a built-in bench. Played with a dozen jets and nozzles on the wall. Changed them from pulsating, soft, and finally a constant flow. All the sensations were pleasurable as the water hit my back.

A big showerhead designed to create the experience of warm rainfall, didn't fail in its promise.

Wow! I love the inside of this oversized shower. It's so masculine—so Ryan. What a spoiled boy. I wonder if he'd mind if I came over just to use it once in a while.

I reluctantly turned off the water and wrapped myself in a big bath sheet. Although I'd have plenty of time to explore after he left for his game, I couldn't resist taking a peek in his closet while he was at the market. To be among his suits, shirts, slacks, shoes and belts, felt sexy. For one of the first times in my life I wanted to indulge in those feelings. I lifted one of his suits from the closet rod and lay it on the bed. I put on each piece—the pants, vest and jacket, fastening the belt as tightly as I could.

I imagined how good Ryan must feel dressing in a beautifully tailored suit fitting his body so exactly. I could envision him entering a room, so handsome, working the event, adored and sought after by fans and prominent people around the city. Thinking about him as he confidently mingled among society, his masculine aura wafting among them, made my body stir. I reached inside the pants to touch myself. I stroked the hair on my vulva, pretending it was Ryan's genital area, and wondered how it would be to pull out a penis and put it into another person.

I thought about his testicles and the way they hung between his legs. Didn't they get in the way? How did the whole contraption fit into a jock strap? Did it cover his tender package completely or did he slide only his penis in some kind of tube? I made a mental note to look it up online and find out.

Stroking my pubic hair a few more times, I felt the little pillows it protected, and then slipped my finger through the moist tissue covering my clitoris. I played in long, slow strokes. *God, wearing his clothes makes me so excited! I better not. My blood pressure and all . . .* I unbuckled his belt and let the pants fall to the floor.

Wrapping my arms around myself, suddenly I wanted to look at myself wearing only his jacket. A full-length mirror sat in the corner of the bathroom. I stood in front of it. Turned from side to side. Looked over my shoulder and noticed that it fell below my behind.

What a plan! To come out in front of Ryan in only his jacket someday, with all the confidence I could muster and no shirt or panties on underneath. I'll have to tuck that thought away for a future play date.

I took off the jacket, prepared to put it back on the hanger, but then nasty feelings drizzled through me. I rubbed the inside of his pants on my vagina, as if I were a female marking her man. His and his clothes were my territory and I'd be the only one to know what that mean. When satisfied, I hung all three pieces neatly in the closet with the others.

I'm browsing in a man's closet. Maybe I'm hallucinating and still in the medical office at the ballpark.

His closet was as big as my bedroom. Built-in shelves and drawers stood floor to ceiling.

Damn he's got a lot of clothes and accessories.

I ran my hands over the wooden and padded hangers. Every item had its place, neatly hung and in perfect order. He seemed to have a theme—the clothes were lighter in color and the fabric less heavy, arranged in a left to right fashion as if matching the seasons.

I wonder if he got rid of those women's clothes.

As I turned the corner, my heart dropped.

There were an entire section of dresses, T-shirts, sweater tops, blouses, and women's jeans.

Oh crap . . . here's the stash. They're hung so neatly . . . well, at least he took them out of the box. I told him to fuck off, so I really have no right to expect anything. Right? Well? Right? Damn, there's tons of stuff in here. How long has it been since Jeanne took care of it?

I pulled the hangers apart. I wanted to look at the clothes he'd asked me to sort through on my last visit. There were no low tops or formfitting dresses. The blouses buttoned to the neck, and the sweaters were loose.

Wait—they're all new, no size zero . . . my size! Oh, God. Are these for me?

The blood whooshed in my head.

I saw the perfect shorts and hiker's shirt for a spontaneous walk at some remote location. A whimsical skirt with a lacy white blouse seemed ideal for a magical evening together. Entranced, I ran my hands on the denim, cashmere, and silk items.

How did a jock figure out what a woman likes to wear? On the other hand, why am I surprised? He's just . . . I'm so impressed.

I ran my hands over a Calvin Klein black dress with a V-neck and flowing skirt. Shiny black beads were sewn around the shoulders and a thin, delicate, black cashmere cardigan was paired with it. An embroidering of small, silver-colored flowers lined the ribbing and curved around the back. The fabric was luxurious.

How would I look in this?

Unable to resist, I lifted the hanger and held the dress against my naked skin. The plush sweater brushed across my breasts.

Well, I simply have to try this on. What other choice do I have?

Once again, I stepped out of the closet to the full-length mirror. I twirled and posed, and wrapped my arms around myself, pretending they were Ryan's arms. I blew kisses to someone in the mirror, even winking at the woman's reflection that had changed overnight. Back to the closet. I took off the beautiful dress and returned it to its hanger. I looked at the brands of jeans—True Religion, Michael Kors, NYDC and others. Boots, flat shoes, and cross trainers were placed in a shoe rack that obviously went with the clothes, as well as a dozen jackets, both formal and informal.

Continuing my exploration through his built-in shelves and drawers, I found of drawer of his crazy socks. They made me laugh out loud. They were pink, striped, checkered, neon colors and the more traditional back and white. I scrunched his briefs in my hands and held a few of his T-shirts to my face.

I found one T-shirt that had *Be Gentle With Me* written on it and rubbed it on my breasts.

Imagined his chest against mine.

Put it on and looked at myself in the mirror.

"Who are you?" my Evil Twin murmured.

I don't know, Evil Twin, I'm morphing. In fact, I don't know if I can even think of you as my rebellious, Evil Twin any longer.

Ah . . . now we're getting somewhere, Nicky.

Posing again, I tossed my hair, stuck out my butt and imagined I was one of Ryan's model girlfriends putting on a show for him. Next, I rolled up the sleeves and tied the extra material around my stomach. Threw my hips to one side.

This is so loose . . . he couldn't possibly have fit into the T-shirt he gave me to wear last time I was here. What a sneaky boyfriend.

I decided to keep the shirt as a memory of Ryan, my first love. I put it aside to tuck into my backpack after he left for his game.

The last item I had to wear was one of his long-sleeved dress shirts. I pulled it from its wooden hanger and slipped it on. Leaving the front open, one final time I looked at myself in the mirror. The material was crisp. The creases in the sleeves were defined and stiff. The shirttail fell just below my bottom. Enjoying the feel of being a powerful, masculine male dominating my sport, I pretended to pitch a ball. I tugged on the cotton fabric and pressed it against my breasts. I held each breast and squeezed them, pulling the shirt as wide open as I could until the nipple area was barely covered. I fastened a button at my belly, rolled up the sleeves and then unrolled them.

"Now *there's* a vision I could get used to." Ryan's sultry voice slid down my chest and between my legs.

I fractured into pieces immediately. Caught in the act, I was completely embarrassed. Going through his belongings. Trying on his clothes . . . posing in front of the mirror, for God's sake.

Oh no. Chest hurting, throat closing . . .

It felt like all the breath flew out of me.

Lust surged and cascaded down to the throbbing in the deep V of my legs.

I spun around in shock.

The vision of Ryan leaning against the doorframe with his wry smile and hungry eyes was unbearable. He rested on one elbow and held my nightgown by a finger, dangling it, waving it back and forth, teasing and taunting me.

How long had he been standing there?

He'd caught me going through his closet, okay, but catching me put on a show as I tossed my body side to side and fondled my breasts? Oh my God! I couldn't look at him.

"Ryan, I . . . I didn't . . . oh, I . . ." I stared at the tile floor. "I didn't hear you come in." My rapid-fire nervous ranting began. "I'm sorry, I was just fooling around. How long have you been standing there? Let me just, I'll take this off . . . just give me a minute. I wasn't trying to snoop. Well yes, I was, but not in a bad way. I mean, well, because you told me to just go ahead and look through"—I cleared my throat—"I saw all your clothes. Damn, you have quite a wardrobe. And all those new things! So I just . . . I mean . . . took a few seconds to . . ."

I spoke in short breaths and choppy sentences.

Tossing my nightgown to the bed, he took long, confident strides toward me.

My vagina clenched.

Ryan lifted my chin, kissed my cheek, and looked me up and down.

I'm whipped butter—soft, melting, churning . . . spreadable . . .

"There's nothing sexier than looking at the woman I love dressed in my shirt. The way you've got it buttoned or . . . mmm, baby . . . now that I look at you . . . unbuttoned." The dangerous look he wore caused my body to hum. "What I want to do to you."

His fingertips touched the base of my neck.

My breasts were barely covered. I felt utterly exposed. I was sure his eyes had lit the tiny flames surging through my body.

"I didn't know you were back," I gasped. His expression was the very definition of desire. "So, you um . . . you promised to behave yourself. Remember?"

He stepped forward.

Closing any pocket of air between us.

His breath scorched me. His tongue touched my ear. I felt slippery wet. Offering me a wicked laugh, he reached around my belly and held my lower back.

"That was last night." His answer moved up my body with each swell rising inside me. His hands lifted my shirt. Rested on my hips, bringing my body to a snug fit against his. We pressed together. "You're not wearing any panties."

Oh God.

A thunderstorm of wanton need moistened my inner thighs.

Please don't put your hands on the back of my legs.

My body howled in protest as if saying out loud, "please *do* touch me . . . anywhere, everywhere!" I physically succumbed to the warmth. Invisible, melting candle wax inched down my body. It felt hot and creamy. Ryan looked in the mirror, staring at my more-than-ample behind. The shirt had ridden up just enough to show each of my plump cheeks.

"Ryan! Don't look there." I lowered my head into his chest, frantically pulling on the shirttails so they'd fall below my butt.

"What are you doing?" His voice burned through me.

"I'm . . . I'm trying to—"

"I'm not letting you hide your beautiful ass." He captured my hands in his. I knew my flesh was slowly being prepared for his lion's feast. I buried my face deeper into his flannel shirt. I knew if I looked into his sensual eyes, they would slay me. "Why shouldn't I look at it? I've seen it before. Just let me admire the view. And what a view it is. Holy God, it's, I could . . . All. Night. Long."

"What about breakfast?" I tried to speak intelligently, still hiding in his chest. "You know I'm weak and need nutrition. You're supposed to keep me calm. Doctor's orders."

"*You* can be breakfast."

Sometimes he brings me to my knees.

He lifted my chin. I didn't want to look in his eyes, but of course, couldn't resist. I was so ready for . . . something. He lovingly brought his lips to mine. He moaned with each kiss. The sound was on the edge of desperate as if he'd been starving. There was no denying it—he was ready for me to open my body to him. His hand lifted my shirt, *his* shirt, and felt along the curve of my back. My skin was hot for his touch. I was sure it might peel off when his burning fingertips made contact with me.

His lips moved to my neck where his tongue flicked back and forth like a snake. At the same time, he massaged my bottom. The chills seemed to be in the millions, rising and rushing up and down the length of my body. He made my vagina ache into her depths, as if hot drums from a tribal rhythm . . . my rhythm—*our* rhythm—played inside me.

It was impossible for me to keep up.

I gave myself over to him even more.

Big bear hugs and squeezes from his muscular arms rocked me from side to side, his chest pressed against mine, making me weaker than I'd ever been.

"Nicky?"

"Mmm." I couldn't talk.

"I'm ready for you. I'm ready to love you and to be loved." His body continued swelling with mine. I felt as if a brilliant light had passed from Ryan to me and back to Ryan. Our new connection was forming. "Baby." His lips were on my ear. "I feel your body pushing out to me. Whenever you're ready . . ."

Then with another squeeze, he suddenly broke our embrace and walked into his closet. He came out with a new pair of women's sweatpants; they were quite feminine, lavender in color and trimmed in lace.

"Your continual need for clothes when you're at my place . . . it's become quite an intriguing problem." He handed them to me. "I'll get our brunch ready. Oh. You can keep that shirt on. I'll take it off later."

Why did he stop? But it was fine that he stopped. That's what I wanted, right? Well, right?

As he turned away, I was afraid I could no longer stand on my own. My body had turned to quivering Jell-O. To make it even more difficult, just as I caught my breath, Ryan walked back in with *that* look.

"By the way, that T-shirt you tried on? The way you tied it so that your belly showed?"

"Yeah?" *Cover your ears, Nick, here it comes.*

"Uh-huh." His voice was laden with spice.

Did he see everything I did in his bathroom? How long had he been watching? My face must be bright red.

My nerve endings were alive and ready to fire. I knew why he stopped his embrace. He wanted me to understand how wonderful it felt to be with each other in a sensual way. All he did was leave me uncertain. I questioned everything about myself. Tried to keep away my wicked thoughts—which I supposed was the purpose.

I finally managed to step into the sweat pants. The material was rich and the fit was loose. Perfect! I buttoned his shirt all the way to my neck, and walked into the kitchen, ready for brunch.

Chapter 33

Brunch

Taking an opportunity to watch the way Ryan's broad back and shoulders flexed as worked in the kitchen, I stood back for a moment to enjoy the show.

Nice.

Each time I thought he might turn to look at me, I quickly looked away and then continued to peek at his body without him noticing. The careful way he prepared our meal, using several seasonings from his spice rack, reaching for the right utensil, and stirring the ingredients carefully was endearing. I smiled and turned to look at his photographs by the TV. Whoa! I noticed the difference in his living room—several art pieces were missing.

Oh God. I'm the cause of it.

"Ryan, I uh . . . I didn't notice last night, um, some of those art pieces . . . where did they go?"

"Gone." His back was turned to me.

"Were they Jesse's pieces?" I almost choked when I asked the question.

"Yes."

I didn't want to discuss it any further, nor did I want to make him any more uncomfortable about the issue. It was bound to open a can of worms. Giving away something he enjoyed and at one time must have been difficult. I made him feel guilty over supporting a friend. I let it go the way he had—with no discussion.

You'll have to get over your paranoia about his past.

"I'm ready for you to feed me." I approached the island/breakfast bar ready to talk about anything—other than removing Jesse's art from his home.

"I'll make sure you're full." He turned around.

Don't look at him.

"I have to say," he hesitated. "I like my shirt better unbuttoned. I can help you adjust that later."

"Do you have any coffee?" I visibly ignored him. Internally I took in every word.

"Absolutely." He reached for a mug. "We don't want a crabby Nicky."

Cute boy. He remembered our first trip to Yountville when I told him I need my coffee in the morning so I don't get crabby.

"Thanks, but I'd never be crabby to someone as kind as you were last night. When I got here, I wanted to kick your ass, though." I sat down on one of the stools. "And I fully intended to do it as soon as I felt better."

"I know." He poured my coffee and placed the mug in front of me. "Even though you were sick, you were steaming when you came out of the guest bedroom. When I put my arm around you to bring you to Dr. Welluck, your whole body tensed."

"Yeah, well, you took all my steam away with the things you did for me." I poured some cream in the mug and stirred it. "In fact, the way you say things, what you do . . . they take, um, took, all of the ager—shit, shoot, I mean, anger away. You know what?"

He shrugged his shoulders.

"When you asked me to let go so you could get me some soup? I hadn't realized I was still holding onto you."

"Guess we fit together pretty well." He put two plates on the island counter for us.

"This is so strange." I blew into my mug.

"What is?" He sat down next to me.

"Weeks ago I visualized sitting here with you and now—"

"Here we are," he smiled.

"Here we are," I repeated. "Breakfast looks delicious."

He poured apple juice in my glass and put a multi-vitamin and mineral tablet on my napkin. "Be sure and take the vitamin after you eat a few bites of food."

Count to three and say it.

"Ryan, I'm sorry to be so touchy about your past. I feel terrible that you gave those art pieces away. They really were beautiful."

"It's done. I told you they didn't mean anything. Don't stress over them; I'm not."

He can't keep doing this for you. You need to understand and trust he loves you. Things, people, places from his past are just that—his past. He's allowed to buy art or any other item from a woman . . . former lover or not.

"You can't know, well obviously you know, because you gave them away, it means a lot to me you did that. I promise I'll try not to freak out so badly in the future. Otherwise, you might have to refurnish your whole place," I laughed nervously. "Anyway, thank you. Hey, Ryan?"

"Hey, Nicky?"

"How did Dr. Welluck have the right medicine for me? Usually you have to go to the pharmacy and get it." I ate a forkful of eggs.

"He checked with Graciela at the ballpark." Ryan's face turned red. "She told him about your headache and blood pressure."

"No, that can't be right. I never told her about my headache." *Caught you, Ryan Tilton!* "I lied about it when Graciela asked me how I felt so I could get out of there."

He slid off the stool and gathered me in his arms. "That's why I had Manny go with you so he could assess your condition. I was so worried."

"Dr. Welluck called in the prescription and you went to the pharmacy, didn't you?" I cupped his cheek. "That's why you couldn't be at the apartment when I got here. Now I get it."

"When I saw you fall, all I wanted to do was take care of you. It was hell knowing there was nothing I could do. Please don't shut me out again. I've never felt more helpless in my life." His eyes moistened as he released his hold. Once again he sat next to me.

"I'm sorry. I didn't handle any of it well." I sat down again. Lifted a strawberry from his plate and ate it. With the assurance of his smile, I relaxed and continued. "Everything was wonderful when you left and then Jesse's text . . . I've never experienced behavior like that." I paused. "And I sure hope I don't ever again."

"You won't," he put his hand on top of mine.

"I have a lot of feelings making me crazy. Everything seems serious and important to me. I end up overanalyzing the meaning behind each word and dissect them a hundred different ways. When it comes right down to it, I'm kind of a mess." I shook my head. "Well, not *kind of,* I definitely *am* a mess when it comes to everything about us."

"I know, sweetheart." He ran his finger around the rim of his coffee mug. "Being committed to a woman is new for me, too. Learning to nurture that love in ways that work for each of us is something we'll figure out together. I don't have all the answers."

"Most of them," I teased.

"Hardly," he replied in clipped tone.

"Hardly anything you don't know when it comes to relationships, you mean." I tried to get the last word.

"No," he countered. "It's all new with you."

I give.

"Thank you for taking care of me." I got up from the table after finishing the food he'd prepared. I kissed his cheek and gave him a gigantic hug. "I know I don't accept help easily. I'll do those dishes after you leave."

"You go ahead and relax." He lifted me to his lap. We held onto our new moments. There was a note of aching in his voice. "I have several hundred TV channels, plenty of CDs, On Demand, Streaming, and lots of books in the library. You've never been in *that* room and you could explore it while I'm gone—especially now that you don't have to worry about my bathroom products."

"Okay," I knew I showed the obvious embarrassment of Ryan catching me going through his nightstand. I started to get off his lap. His arms tightened around my stomach.

"Feeling you shift your butt to get off my lap . . ." He took a deep breath. "What that thing does to me."

"What time do you have to go?" I tried to keep his sex-demon from taking complete possession of him—and of us.

"I should get to the ballpark by two so I can start my workout." We walked to the sofa and sat down. "I'll stay close to you until I have to go. In fact, maybe I'll call in sick."

"I'm sure. Wouldn't that be so naughty of you?" I relished the thought of watching the game together and the announcers reporting, *Ryan Tilton is out sick tonight.*

"Rest your head on my lap." His voice sounded happy and light.

I lay down. My head rested on his thigh as he massaged my scalp, neck, and along my arms and back. Every so often, he took my hands in his and kissed them.

"Did you really carry me all the way to the medical office?"

"Yes."

"I'm sorry for your little arms." I kissed his right forearm. "You're strong to be able to lift me. I'm not petite."

"Yeah, you were pretty heavy. I struggled all the way while trying to hold you. I hope I didn't blow out my pitching arm."

"Sorry about that." I was certain my face had turned cherry red.

"You're always joking about your big, tree trunk of a body but all I felt in my arms was my sick little sweetheart. You have it in all the right places, Nicky. And I mean *all* the right places."

"And then there's that side of you that insists on rising up. Sometimes my chest gets so tight I can hardly breathe." I closed my eyes, making every attempt to hide my smile.

"Well, I do have, uh, something that rises up pretty consistently when I'm around you." All it took was his voice to unlock the secret places in my body.

"How come you have all those women's clothes in your closet?" I tried to shift gears.

"You know they're for you." He continued to play with my hair. "When you're here you don't have to use my clothes anymore— unless you want to."

"I like your clothes. In fact, I put aside one of your T-shirts to have all for myself. Then I can sleep in it and keep you close to me all night even when you're on the road. Can I keep it?"

"Knowing my shirt is against your breasts? Yes. Most definitely, yes."

"You know . . . it's a lot bigger than the one you gave me to wear after Pismo. The other one was so tight," I probed. "It must have shrunk and you didn't realize it."

"Huh . . . wonder how that could be?" His luscious laugh and soft seduction sung me to sleep while he gently rubbed my body. Peaceful dreams fell with his gold dust. Each time I awoke, I was treated to Ryan's hands running through my hair, or rubbing my shoulders. Of course, the time for him to leave came too soon.

"I'll see you after the game tonight. I'll try and hurry home." He had a blanket and pillow to tuck me in.

"Mm-hmm." I kept my eyes closed.

Even in his quiet moments I felt his power gathering.

"Nicky?"

"Yeah?"

"You must know how much I love you."

"Yes," I admitted. "I do."

"You must know I'm serious."

"Yes."

"We go on another road trip tomorrow. Even now I'm having a tough time as I think about not having you with me. I want you to come. Please think about it."

"Thanks for inviting me. I'd love to go with you. You're not the only one who dreads being apart from each other." My heart ached with worry. "I think about it all the time. Do you really think we could make a long-term relationship work?"

He immediately sat down and lifted me to his chest.

His arms surrounded me.

My tears dampened his shirt and the bare skin of his neck was wet. "I'm sorry to be so wimpy. I told you I'm a mess, and—"

"You can say anything," he offered. "I want all of you, whatever that means for us. Each day the longing will be a little less and our intense emotions will even out."

"I hope so." I twisted some of the blanket into a winding peak. "Otherwise I know I'll die from internal combustion before we're together for even a few months."

"I'll see you tonight," he chuckled. "There's more food in the refrigerator if you get hungry."

He was almost out the door.

"Ryan, I hate to see you go. The thing is, I never could have imagined I'd love anyone so quickly. I was afraid of my feelings and confess I still am in some ways. Still, I'm sorry it took me all these weeks to sort it out."

He walked over to me and wrapped my entire body in the blanket, carried me into the bedroom, and put me down on the bed.

"I think we'll find out that it's really not so difficult." His eyes softened. "Don't forget, I'll be home all winter and you'll be available all summer. What I wouldn't give to take you right here and sail through the game with your feminine scent all over me. You'd turn on the TV and when you watched me come in to pitch, it would be our secret you were on my fingers, legs and belly. Mmm, I can't wait for that."

"Guess you better get going." I took a deep breath.

"Bye, Nicky Nick." He looked completely satisfied with himself. After giving me a kiss, he left for the game.

Once he was gone, I considered all that had happened that morning.

I knew I was in luscious trouble.

Important decisions knocked.

Ryan's love stood at the door.

Chapter 34

Christopher Tilton Senior

*I*t was almost four when I opened my eyes again. I smiled immediately as I stretched, Ryan's shirt rubbing against my skin, reminding me of our bathroom scene. I couldn't help but grab his pillow and give it a big squeeze as if I held him in my arms.

Ooh, Ryan—my juicy, juicy man.

Reluctantly, I pushed away my cocoon of blankets. I needed to take it slow and easy but I had to write down the details of the prior night before its vivid colors faded. After taking my blood pressure and getting another normal reading, I walked into Ryan's library, also his office, looking for a pen and some paper.

Dark, hardwood floors laid the foundation of a masculine room. Instead of the blacks and greens of the living area, chocolate browns and velvet reds brushed the room. This was definitely *his* hangout. Wooden bookshelves were built into two of the four walls. I ran my fingers over the rows of bound wisdom.

Filled with mostly memoirs, historical novels, and sports books, I perused them until I came across a small, tattered book with a worn, brown leather cover. Written on the inside page was the name, *Christopher Tilton Senior*. I quickly thumbed through the book and realized this was the journal of Ryan's father.

He said go through everything. Would he want me to read this?

While holding it carefully, I flattened my hand on its cover. Said a prayer for Ryan and his dad. Opened it. Closed it. Ran my hand across its face once again. Weighed my decision for several minutes. Decided to read it.

The journal began with his father describing an assignment he was serving in the Middle East. He admitted that this time, his fear had been sharpened. This tour seemed different than all the ones previous. Only thirty-six years of age and two sons at home, Christopher Junior, eighteen, and Ryan, fourteen, he began describing the surroundings. It was his fourth tour and he had eleven of twelve months left to serve.

His writing focused on the terrain, food, culture, weather and the various exploits of his fellow marines. After the first several weeks, his journal took a different turn. Turning the pages, the words filling them quickly turned dark.

Ryan's father and the other men and women in his unit set up a base nicknamed, *valley of death*. He'd written, *fear can reveal itself as anger and contempt. I'm afraid what we've stepped into here is hatred.*

Immediately thereafter, he speculated how the people in the surrounding villages weren't the same as the ones on his previous assignments. They felt betrayed. Didn't trust the troops. He wrote: *This feels like we need to watch our backs every second.*

Christopher Sr. sought and felt comfort writing about his family. As I continued to read, his love filled the pages of his journal.

Among his last entries were these:

July 9th

Everything scattered. The assault came quickly. Frantic. They move fast. The mountains around us give them the cover they need. We can't seem to hone in on the direction. They echo from all sides. May, Chris, Ryan—I love you.

July 11th

Finally zoned in on the enemy's hiding place. Tonight we flush them out. Frank is such a fucking moron—he sprained his ankle. No sympathy for that. Wrap it up and let's go.

Goodnight family.

July 12th

Good mission last night. Think we pushed them back. They'll regroup, but we cleared the area pretty damn well. No one hurt here. That's success. Love you guys. Stay strong. Only ten months until I see you again.

Feels like forever.

July 15th

Settled down. On patrol. Hot—burning hot. Summer is brutal. One hundred degrees + every day. Humidity makes us feel like we're under water.

Wait—is a fire—burning? No, okay.

I love you May, Chris, Ryan. I've decided not to reenlist. Why didn't I tell you all how much I love you before I left?

When I get back, I promise not to take you for granted. Cliché but true . . . didn't appreciate what I had. Not nearly enough. Promise I'll tell you all every day.

I thought we'd have forever.

July 16th

All of us warned the C.O. The location too narrow, no cover, mountains on all sides. Deadly. Heard the stories from the guys who already served about feeling surrounded. Eyes watching. They all knew—some outfit would be sitting ducks.

God, don't let it be us.

We know they're hiding up there.

Pech Valley. That's what they call this place. We name it Valley of Death. Sam, Ted and Carp—they all told me. Yet here I am. Why did I go again? Why did I go again? Fuck. WHY did I go again?

Your birthday is coming, Ryan, I haven't forgotten. If I can't talk to you, know that I haven't forgotten. I hope you and your friends have a good time. I wonder if there's a girl you like at school yet. I miss those talks. Have mom make one of her legendary cheesecakes. I can taste it now.

July 18th

All day in the middle of hell. Explosions. Screaming. Confusion. Shattered bodies. Fractured confidence, I'm suddenly aware of my own mortality. The bullets make sickening sounds as they whiz by. It's as if they're alive and searching for a kill.

Threatening.

Close.

Barely missed.

My ears feel the diseased air as they go by.
Love you, my family.

July 20th
Silence all day. Are they pressing their bodies to the ground?
Are they struggling to survive like we are? No, not like we are.
Desperate. Brainwashed. No way out. Fear universal.
All of us pieces in a chess game. Suddenly, it doesn't make
any sense.
Thinking of an ice-cold beer and a hot dog at one of your
games, Ryan. You're a damn good pitcher. Should have told you
that more often. When I get back, I'll coach you and your team.
Chris, I hope you pursue your music. Know how you love it.
Can't wait to get your letters and hear about college.
We can't call out yet. Only a few more days and I'll talk to
you guys. Can't be soon enough.
Love you all.

July 21st
Too quiet. The enemy let us take patrol today. I have a
strange feeling. A gut feeling, they're trying to make us feel
secure. They're not fooling us.
We all know they're out there—waiting under a sky of
shadows. The confusion is coming again. I hate the swarming . .
. like bees. Shouting. Horns blaring. Shooting . . . the bullets
ready to penetrate, ticking around our heads; I hate it all.

July 25th
Tough night.
So much gunfire. Couldn't find an opening. Hard to target.
Rockets. Machine gun fire. Didn't think it would end. Awful

sounds—that whistle of death. Fireballs exploded from their launchers. Roared through the mess tent. The camp burned.

Faro's head exploded as a bullet ripped through it. Limbs blown apart. An arm and leg only a few feet away from me. Bodies burned, skin melted off of them like wax—I think Cole's spine was severed. Crawled out to get him but haven't seen him since medics took him away. Couldn't move. Had that vacant stare in his eyes.

That stare . . . that vacant stare that says, "My soul is gone."

July 27th

Wish I were home for your birthday, Ryan. With you in spirit, Son. Have a happy fourteenth. I can only imagine you celebrating, playing baseball. Having a party—that's how I'll remember you and your brother always—my sons—the musician and the baseball player.

Don't give it up—either one of you.

July 30th

Pieces of my life are rushing by these days. Feel death's grip tightening. Should have tried harder. Should have found you and grabbed you and said goodbye to you, Ryan. Should have pulled you close, and said "I understand your anger and it's okay. I love you." The words seem so easy now.

If this gets to you, know how I love you all. Please get this journal to my son, Ryan if anything happens. He needs it to move on. Don't feel guilty, son. I'll always love you. If I make it back, I'll tell you every day, in person.

Those words we say in anger, when all is said and done, mean nothing. I know you were frustrated and didn't know how to tell me. I get it. Don't worry about a thing—my family, my loves, and my life.

Christopher Tilton Senior's last entry was three days after Ryan's birthday. *Three days.* I wondered, when Ryan celebrated, did his thoughts automatically go to his father's death? Was he able to celebrate his own life and achievements? Had Ryan moved on? Would he ever?

Some of the pages had scribbles on them. I assumed they were Ryan's. The words, "I'm sorry, I love you," were written across several. It was as if he had been in hell right along with his father.

The remaining journal entries were writing by Christopher Tilton Senior's youngest son.

I wondered if this was the first journal he'd ever kept, co-written with his father.

Tragic.

Beautiful.

Sad.

Heartbreaking.

Amazing.

August 7th

Your wish may be that I'm free of guilt, but I can't let go the last words I said to you.

How do I get over it? How do I live without the fear of losing another person I love because I argued, got angry, lost control, and then never saw them again?

I feel like I killed you.

Maybe I did.

August 8th

Your funeral was today. I'm fucked. No one's here for me.

August 9th

You left me. Angry, pissed, raging. I loved you. Why didn't you choose us? How could you decide to fight again? Four times!
You knew it was bad there. You knew!

August 10th

What do I do now? Play baseball? Seems meaningless. Go to college? Fuck that. Why? How do I face an empty life? Mom is sad. She can't talk or look at me. Only fourteen and I've lost my father. Big fuckin' deal, I have your journal. So the fuck what?

August 12th

Thanks, Dad. You left me and all I have is a book. Even Chris has left us. He doesn't give a fuck if mom and I rot without you.

August 14th

I'm pissed off at just about everything and everyone—especially you, Dad. You loved your country more than your family. Why did you do it? You're dead and you'll never be back. I can't ever talk to you again. Guess you're happy you died serving your country? Big deal. A hero to none.

August 17ᵗʰ

I'll never forget it. A few weeks ago, I headed off to play baseball at school. One month and two days later, on July 31ˢᵗ at 11:35 a.m., I answered our front door.

Why did I answer?

Maybe if I'd pretended no one was home you'd be alive. Maybe if we never got the news, time would've stopped. Instead, two uniformed Marines stood at attention. They were so big is seemed as if they blocked out the sun that shone behind them.

I didn't know that after that day, the sun would never again rise for me. "Son, we'd like to speak to your mother," one of them said. His voice was somber.

I should've told them mom wasn't home.

I stood out of sight and listened from the hallway as they told her the horrible news. She screamed and fell to the ground. I didn't know what to do. I couldn't help her.

You were one of five to die on the same day I learned.

One of the Marines told us you were a good man. How the fuck did they know anything about you?

Well, that's how I got your journal, Dad.

Hope you don't mind that I'm writing in it.

August 31ˢᵗ

Building my walls high and strong, like my father. You'd be proud of me.

You died young, so I guess that means I will, too? Don't worry, I'll control everything—my friends, family, co-workers, reputation, and when I marry, my wife. No one will ever leave me. I'll leave them before they get the chance.

October 15ᵗʰ

Six weeks has gone by. I'm walking in fog. I close this book in turmoil. I'm in trouble at school. My grades have slipped. I just don't give a shit. Why did you die on me? I have no one and I don't care. I want you back. I'm sorry for what I said. So sorry for what I said. I promise I'll be a good son for you.

Don't know what to do.

I need to close this forever.

Maybe I'll buy a journal for myself. I like writing in this, but I don't want to relive your death and sad words. They're too tough for me. I love you, Dad.

I really love you, Father, Friend, my hero.

He'd written the same mantra I had also believed—to make sure we left people before they could hurt us.

At only fourteen, he took up the same fears and built his defenses—abandoned, scarred, afraid.

Ryan's last entry was heartbreaking. His tender feelings brought to life the conversation I had with Walter Dixon—his high school coach and mentor—all those weeks ago.

I held the book to my chest and mourned for the hurt little boy—and perhaps, the hurt little girl that had been inside me. After putting the brown leather journal back on the wooden shelves, I sat down at his walnut desk.

The big leather chair was on rollers. I imagined Ryan sliding across the hardwood floor from his bookshelves to his desk. I sat reflecting on the sadness I'd just read. When ready, I looked for a pen and some paper. All the drawers in his desk opened except the bottom one. When I found what I needed, I wrote about the journal I'd just read and the man and the boy who had written in it. The tragedy and love was devastatingly majestic.

I wrote about Ryan's golden brown hair and the specks of gold dotted through the blue of his eyes. I described the little creases in his lips that invited mine to kiss them. Noted his chiseled looks. Incredible masculine aura and body and the gentle storm he was for me. Every time I opened the pages of my journal, I wanted to remember the story of my first love and every detail I could think of to make me remember him.

Because nothing this good can last. It's been proven in my family. Something bad is always right around the corner. But for now, he's wonderful.

I pictured how someday, I'd sit in my rocker and run my hands over the timeworn pages, smiling at my memories of the wonderful man I once knew. Deep into the alternate world of written emotions, visions, descriptions, and the taking apart and putting back together of things and events, I jumped when the phone rang.

Already two hours had passed.

Oh God, should I answer it? What if it's some woman looking to come over? Should I let it go? What if it's Ryan? Will it go to message? Certainly he has an answering service or machine or voice mail capability of some kind. Maybe not . . . he's on the road so much. What do I do?

"Ryan Tilton's home." I gave in and answered.

"Hello? Is Ryan there?" It was a woman's voice. She sounded aggressive.

Chapter 35

Message Received

"*No*, I'm sorry," I apologized to someone I didn't know. *Oh crap, now what?* "He's at his baseball game and due back around 11:00." Did I give out too much information? Maybe I just told her how she could hook up with him and now he wouldn't come home tonight. "Can I give him a message?"

Please don't say something like, "this is Candy. Tell him I'll catch him at the game. "

"Who is *this*?" she asked with authority.

"My name is Nicky Young, who's *this*?" I shot back.

"I'm Ryan's mother, Mrs. Tilton."

Oh, damn . . .

"My son's told me quite a lot about you."

"Some good, I hope." *Some good, I hope? Why did I say that? I must sound ridiculous. I don't know what to say. I'm shocked she ever knows who I am.*

"It seems my son is quite smitten with you."

Unease slid down my body.

Smitten? What kind of word is that? Is she being flippant?

"Do you have any response?" Her words were clipped.

Red alert! Be on your guard.

"I'm not sure what to say," I replied. "I don't understand how you just used the word, *smitten*."

"Do you think he's in love with you?" With a thoughtful pause, she waited for my response.

"Yes." *Is this normal for someone's mother to begin a conversation like this?*

"Are you in love with my son?"

"Yes." I could hear her breathing.

"You're at his apartment and he's not there—it appears you have the run of the house. What do you think that means?"

Nothing like being direct.

"It means we're friends and we trust each other. He knows I'm not playing games. I'm very fond of your son. Well, I haven't met a lot of boys. I mean, I've met a lot of boys, I've gone to school with them, but not gone out with them, I mean. Your son is unique."

Oh damn . . . I'm just stumbling all over the place.

"He's *unique*?" she asked.

Wrong answer.

"Yes," I gulped. "Very."

"Have you ever had a serious relationship?" she asked. "Do you think you're in one now?"

Think carefully Nick. Your answers could ruin this possibility before it ever begins.

"No I haven't been serious with anyone before. Yes, I'm in one that's serious now."

"How do you know? You're not too young to understand what you feel for him?"

Well, enough of this. Ryan is my love and I'm going to stand up for the two of us, no matter what she thinks. Okay, Mrs. Tilton, here I go.

"I can understand the concern you have for your son. However, before you form an opinion of me because of my age, let me reassure you, I know about people. No, I haven't had a steady boyfriend, but I know Ryan is an amazing man. I'm here by myself because I was sick. He brought a doctor to see me. His orders were for me to stay here."

"What? Ryan ordered you to stay there?"

"I meant the doctor's orders, not Ryan's." I cleared my throat.

"Oh."

Was that a slight laugh? Does she have a lighter side? Will she share that part of her with me anytime soon?

"And, well, I'm not going to beat around the bush, Mrs. Tilton. I don't know how I'd feel discovering a woman I'd never met at my son's apartment telling me she's in love, but I am." *Uh-oh, I'm on a roll now.* "He's honest and very loving. The things he does and says are . . . he really gives to others and I've never seen anyone in his position volunteer like he does." My damn rambling burst to life. "Did you know he started networking groups out here and my sister might get into a program because of him? I've gone to the veteran's hospital because he shared it with me . . . I'm sure you know . . . I'm just nervous, so I'm just, um, nervous."

"You're also smart from what I understand." Her voice seemed to lose its edge. "You've been accepted to Stanford?"

"Yes. I start in the spring."

"And how do you think a relationship with my son might work while you're going to school?" she asked point blank.

"Honestly, I don't understand how we'll work that out. I guess we'll have to see, Mrs. Tilton. I really want a career before marriage or a family. I apologize if I'm being too forward. I probably shouldn't even say this much, I don't know what Ryan will think that I've been so open, but I feel I owe you the truth since you're his mother."

"I appreciate that," she said more gently. "I hate phony. Obviously you're not. I can hear you're nervous. There's no need. I'm coming out the week after next. I assume we can spend a day or two together?"

"Of course." *Finally! I think we're at the end of our conversation! At least she wants to talk. I guess that's a good sign.*

"Will you let Ryan know I called? His cell phone is off. I know he'll be home late, but I need to let him know I'll be arriving next week at a different time than I'd initially told him. I leave tomorrow for a friend's before I make the trip. She doesn't get reliable cell reception and lives in a remote area. Please make sure Ryan gets my message tonight."

"I'll make sure of it, Mrs. Tilton. Until what time are you available?" *I sound like someone who doesn't speak English. Get it together, Nick.*

"I'm available any time for my son," she snickered.

"Of course." I was overanxious to please her. "I didn't mean it like that." *Damn, she says whatever is on her mind.*

"I'll see you in a week or so, unless . . . are you traveling with him this road trip? You'd certainly get to *know* each other better that way, wouldn't you? Maybe we'll see each other at the airport?"

Oh God! She means having sex! Doesn't she? Who does she think I am . . . a woman using sex to enchant her son? Or does she know we're not having sex and that means I don't love him enough? What's the right answer? What do I do?

"I'm not going on the road trip with Ryan. I have commitments here at home." *When will you ask for what you want, Nicky? Quit trying to please others and live your own life.*

All I understood from her judgmental statement was her disapproval if I went with him. I was in his apartment. She probably assumed we were having sex. The way I'd always related to it? Sex meant marriage and during an evening at Ryan Tilton's, the outdated belief rose up against me. It was stupid and rash. In only a moment, all those years of what it meant to be a virgin—the fear of sin and going to hell—made my decision about traveling on his next road trip.

Why it mattered so much that Mrs. Tilton saw me as someone who wasn't having a physical relationship with her son? I supposed I was still trying to be a good girl—ever the good daughter, the good friend, obeying all the rules, keeping the peace, careful not to make the waters turbulent—although in so many ways all I wanted to do was cause turbulence.

Everything was so clear to me in our conversation. I knew if I told her I was going on the road with him, I'd have to fight like hell to get her back in my corner. She couldn't respect a woman having sex with her son after a few weeks of dating, could she? Instead of rooting for her son to have found love, wouldn't she see me as someone who slept around and used sex to seduce and win the affections of her little boy?

"I see. Well, have a good evening." It seemed as if she almost hung up and then changed her mind. "Ms. Young?"

Chapter 36

Damn, Another Call

"*Y*es, Mrs. Tilton?"

"Please call me May."

"May."

"Please don't break his heart. He's been through so much and deserves someone who's ready for his love. You have years ahead of you. He doesn't. You can imagine how I want him to have the right woman when he's never been in love before. He wants a family right away. Did you know that? Of course you deserve what you want as well. But you want a career . . ." she gave a long sigh. "How can you *really* know what you want at your age? Even when you're twenty, twenty-two, those years are full of turmoil."

Ouch.

"If you're not serious and he's only a stopover until you go to Stanford, please cut it off now. You'll meet so many new friends there . . . the longer you stay with him, the more he'll have to wait for the things he's wanted for so long. Do you know his father died when he was only fourteen?"

"Yes, he told me. I'm sorry for your loss, too," I offered.

"Thank you. Of course, you should be free to explore your feelings, I just . . . please don't mistake his. He's already told me you're made for each other. How did he phrase it?" She waited a beat and then said, "*she's mine, and I'm hers*."

"He's told me that since last year," I admitted proudly.

And if you believe in your son, you must understand that I'm not someone who is here to pluck out what I can from his life while he's in the limelight and give him children like a machine.

"You're a smart woman. I have every confidence you'll both figure out what's important for each of your lives and make the choices that further you along that road."

"Yes, ma'am," I gulped, "I know we will."

"Fine then. Well, good night, Nicky. See you next week."

Taking no chance he'd miss her message, I taped it to the outside of his front door. God forbid he overlooked it or I forgot to tell him and I'd fail with the first thing she asked me to do.

I was in the midst of deciding whether or not to tell Ryan about my conversation with his mother when the phone rang again. I hoped it wasn't May Tilton asking me yet another question. One conversation in a day was more than enough with her.

"Hello, Ryan Tilton's home."

Please don't be her.

"Is it?" Ryan laughed.

"What *should* I say?" I sighed in relief. "Why didn't you call me on my cell?"

"Because I wanted to hear how it sounded when you answered my phone, Ms. Young. I've dreamt many times that one day I'll call and you'll just say *hello* because you'll be living with me. How are you feeling?"

"Good. No dizzies, headache, or upset stomach. I've recovered because you left and I've had a chance to relax," I giggled.

"Is there anything I've done to help you get better?" He sounded amused.

"Oh . . . let's see . . . um, I think so. Yeah, I definitely do think you have done a little something for me."

Your turn.

"There's a lot I can do for you. And so much I can do *to* you." His voice slid all over my belly.

"Resting at your apartment and getting that medication from Dr. Welluck did the trick. Oh, and resting on your chest and the great brunch you fixed did wonders, too."

"So what have you been up to? Checking out more of the drawers in my nightstand?"

"Ha-*ha*, Ryan. No, just resting—basically."

"Basically?"

"Well, I've been writing," I shifted on his chair and put my feet up on his desk. Keeping it to myself, I pretended I was living there and we were talking like this for the hundredth time. "I found some paper in your library and I've been sitting in your manly desk chair catching up on my journal notes."

"My *manly* chair?" he laughed.

"It's huge! Big rollers, heavy wood, thick leather . . . so yeah, big time manly. Anyway, I'm writing about all the nice things you've done for me."

"Oh, Nicky. How sweet you are, baby. Did you put on any underwear?"

"Wow! That's a quick change of topic. Of course I put on underwear, why wouldn't I?"

What a nasty boy you are, Mr. Tilton.

"Did you sit on my big *man* chair and fill it with your big, bare, womanly butt?"

"You just can't help it, can you?" I doodled on the writing tablet, RT + NY = LOVE. "Just tell me, as your girlfriend, will I always have to be ready for your sly comments?"

"I'll *never* stop with you," he threatened, a delicious warning in his voice. "You never told me you like to write so much."

"Yes I did. I told you when I was at the Cliff House, remember?"

"Yeah, but that was the day you explored my contacts. I would expect you to write your notes about that day."

"I journal and write poetry all the time," I shared. "I can't go one day without writing. I love it. I admit I wrote more than usual the day I met Walter Dixon."

"Will you ever let me read some of your journal? Particularly the parts about me?" A wicked laugh practically leapt through the phone and tickled my belly.

"No, Mr. Tilton, a journal is private. You know that. And what makes you think there's anything in there about you other than facts?"

"Have it your way. It'll be fun getting you to surrender and listen as you read some of it to me. Baby, I wasn't thinking earlier. Our game ends late and you're still recovering from your fall . . . my head is all muddy."

"Muddy?" I repeated.

"My head is all foggy. Don't wait up for me. It's important you get your rest. Just relax and get some rest."

"*Relax*?" I teased. "Here with *you*? There's way too much danger here to relax when you're here."

"You've relaxed plenty." The sex laugh seemed to come right through the phone and squeezed my belly.

"Come home as quickly as possible and you'll see what I have planned," I dangled a carrot for him. "Make sure you don't eat."

Silence.

"Ryan?"

"I'm here, Sweetheart. I'll see you tonight."

"Oh! Wait! Ryan! Your mom called! She needs to tell you that her flight has been changed. She's leaving tomorrow to stay at a friend's house for a few days. There's no cell reception there. I have the message taped to the outside of your front door. Turn on your cell phone so she doesn't call me anymore! Do you have her number?"

"You taped Mom's message on the *front door?*" He cracked up. "She intimidated you?"

"Hell, yeah she did," I shot back. "She wasn't out of line, though." *Well, yes, I think she was, but maybe that's typical of how the mother of the boyfriend talks?* "Man, I wouldn't want to cross your mama."

"Thanks for telling me. I'll call her now. See you tonight and I'll um . . . definitely save my appetite. Can't wait."

"Me, too." From the tone of my voice it wasn't hard to tell how anxious I was to see him again.

Initially I'd planned to sit on the beach with Ryan. The phone call from his mother changed my mind. I wanted to talk within the warmth and comfort of his home, the familiarity surrounding him, and explore as much of his past as he'd dare open to me. And there was the issue of his father's journal we needed to discuss. I didn't want to keep it a secret that I'd read it.

When I finished mapping out my plan, I decided to use Ryan's concierge service to order the things I needed for our "Picnic on Tilton Beach."

Chapter 37

Tilton Beach

"*R*oss, this is Nicky Young in Ryan Tilton's apartment. Do you remember me?"

"Of course I do, Ms. Young. We met the day you came to pick up the jerseys Mr. Tilton left or you to take to Yountville. I heard you were sick last night. You're feeling better?"

"Much. Thanks."

"I'm relieved to hear that." He kept it professional.

"I fell while I was cheering at the ballpark."

"Better now that you've relaxed at Mr. Tilton's?"

"Oh, much better, thanks! I saw a doctor last night. Well, Ryan brought one of the team doctors here to see me. His name is Dr. Welluck. I couldn't believe he did that. Isn't it incredible? He's so thoughtful. Ryan, I mean. He must be the ideal resident, right? Have you met the doctor before? Gosh, he was soothing. I could've listened to Dr. Welluck for hours. He has one of those voices that give you the chills. Know what I mean?"

"I do," he chuckled. "And no, I haven't met the good doctor."

"I hope you get to one day. I recommend him. He was really . . . Ryan . . . anyway . . ."

"What can I do for you, Ms. Young?"

"Sorry, I know you're busy. I actually called for a reason, not just to talk with you," I was giddy. "I'd like to order some food. Not a lot. Oh, and I want it to be a surprise. Could I use the concierge service and have it delivered without telling Ryan?"

"Sure, what do you need, Ms. Young?"

"I'm kind of embarrassed to admit that I only have enough for the order and not much for a tip. I think the total will be around twenty-five dollars. I have thirty."

"That's plenty," Ross comforted. "What can we get for you?"

"I'd like some chicken salad, French bread, gourmet olives, fresh fruit salad, S'mores, and pear sparkler—enough for two, please. Ryan raves about some deli around the corner? Maybe you could get it there?"

"I'll place the order with his concierge immediately. Her name is Ms. Drivesdale. Let's see, I'm looking at her schedule . . ." sounds of Ross typing on a computer keyboard echoed in the background. "If she's delivers your order between eight and nine, will that work for you?"

"Yes, that's perfect. Thanks, Ross."

"Ms. Young, before Mr. Tilton left today he authorized you to charge on his account. He didn't tell you?"

"No." *What?*

"Perhaps he wanted to surprise you."

"Until I get the chance to talk with him, I'll pay for my order. If the cost is more than I have, I'll take the credit, all right?"

He agreed with my proposal. As soon as I hung up the phone I visited Ryan's closet once again. I needed panties and didn't have any, so I grabbed a pair of his briefs, a pair of his drawstring shorts, and one of Ryan's T-shirts.

I love wearing his clothes. He has so many . . . maybe I'll keep two of his T-shirts!

I put out a pair of navy blue sweat pants and a T-shirt for Ryan that read, *Hugs=Happiness*. The last item of clothing I selected for him were a pair of thick wool socks to keep his feet warm. I placed all the clothes on his bed so he'd see them as soon as he walked into the room.

I started out of the bedroom, but paused to study what I had laid out for him. I decided on pieces that would take more than a few minutes to take off should we go anywhere near *that* place. He looked sexy in his brown flannel shirt that morning, so I chose one in another color. This time it was dark blue, paired with loose-fitting black jeans. I put the other clothes back in his closet.

Relaxed was how I wanted Ryan to feel when he came home. I played with the dimmer switches to find the right combination of lighting. While searching his pantry for dishes, I found a few candles and put them on the mantle and coffee table. Just as I set out the last candle, the doorbell rang. It was a little after nine.

When I opened the door, I found a woman with blond hair somewhere in her early thirties and a bag of groceries in her arms. She was dressed in a stylish business suit cut a few inches above her knees. Her pink lipstick freshly applied. A pink V-neck blouse was secured with a pin strategically placed where cleavage would show without it. A waist-length white jacket and a strand of pearls finished the look.

"Good evening, I'm Ms. Drivesdale," she announced boldly. "May I come in?"

"Hello," I stepped aside and gestured to the kitchen counter. *Oh damn, another tall, gorgeous woman. The parade never ends. I wonder if he handpicked her from several available choices. Maybe they've slept together.*

"Would you like me to review the items we purchased for you?" she took each one out and set it on the island.

"I can see you have everything," I confirmed.

"For legal reasons, may I ask your name?" She carried the slightest hint of a southern accent in her voice.

"Nicky Young. And yours is?"

"Ms.—"

"I'm sorry, yes, you already told me, Ms. Drivesdale. I'm nervous. Sorry."

"No need to be nervous. Thank you for identifying yourself, Ms. Young. These keys are for you and the attached code in the acrylic holder is Mr. Tilton's key code to his apartment. Please sign here."

"What do the keys go to?" I signed the paper.

"Mr. Tilton's Mustang. May I suggest you take off the key code and put it somewhere safe? It's only my suggestion."

"I will," I assured her.

"If you his car brought around front, just call down to the desk. They generally have it ready for you within fifteen minutes. I apologize that I'm late with your order," she continued. "The weekends are always busy and to top it off, I had an emergency. I hope you weren't inconvenienced."

"Not at all. What uh, what time did Ryan call you and ask that his keys be delivered to me?"

"Let's see." She looked at her watch. "Sometime around six, I think. He thought you might need transportation. I hope not getting them to you until now didn't cause a problem."

"No, it didn't." *Ross, did you phone him when I placed the order with you?*

"Mr. Tilton said he didn't want you riding on the bus when you weren't feeling well. It was one of the dearest things. Actually, if I remember rightly, he said he didn't want *my Nicky* to ride the bus."

"How much for the food items?" I tried not to get emotional.

"It's on Mr. Tilton's account."

"I told Ross if I have enough money I'll pay for them," I insisted. "I need to talk with Ryan before I charge to his account."

"The total is twenty-seven dollars. Please don't worry about it." She put her hand on mine. "I've been an employee at Bayside Residences before Mr. Tilton moved in. I understand the different personalities in this building. May I speak frankly?"

She had an affair with him. I knew it.

I nodded.

"I've been his concierge for two years. In my opinion, for someone in his position to adding you to his account and giving you his keys means he trusts you. He expects you to use them. It would be an insult if you didn't."

"Thank you." I gave in and signed the receipt. "For the food, too." I handed her a ten-dollar bill for her tip. "I'm sorry; I don't know what's correct. Is this appropriate?"

"It's taken care of." She handed the money back to me. "Ms. Young, I think you have much more than you know." She winked and let herself out.

Well that was interesting. Now I have a key to his car and access to his apartment even when he's on the road?

I put his keys on my ring and tucked the tag with the apartment code in a pocket of my backpack. As I did, it occurred to me Ryan was showing me another way of how loving each other could be, helping me to trust him more—so much so that I could pop over at any time and let myself in. A door had opened wider and offered me a glimpse of our possibilities.

Could I have more than I ever dared hope for?

I plated the chicken salad, circled it with the baguette slices and olives, and chilled two glasses and bowls for the pear sparkler and fruit salad. For dessert, I assembled the S'mores ingredients on a separate plate. There were several comforters and extra pillows in the guest bedroom. I spread them in front of the gas fireplace and turned it on.

My final item to complete before I waited for Ryan was to taped my invitation to his front door. It read:

> *Ms. Nicky Young enthusiastically invites Mr. Ryan Tilton to a picnic on Tilton Beach:*
> 1. *If you need to shower, please do so now.*
> 2. *Please dress in the clothes that have been carefully selected and are on your bed.*
> 3. *Come to the fireplace and sit on the blanket where our picnic awaits.*
> 4. *Please share the evening with me. I've missed my love.*

When I dimmed the lights, shadows threw themselves on his walls and ceilings. Satisfied with the ambience, I opened the sliding doors to the balcony. After I lit the last candle, I chose a CD of ocean sounds from his selection. I set it on replay and turned the volume to low. I brought the flatware and paper towels to the blanket, and tossed pillows randomly around the fireplace to watch our "campfire" burn.

Ryan would walk into a sensual sanctuary: a glowing fire, low lighting, and relaxing music. I hoped he might immediately wind down. As I surveyed my picnic site, I realized everything I planned could explode into desire. Romantic scenes of our bodies coming together begged to come to life. Although I wanted that, I was sure when he came home he'd only talk. After all, it was just one evening after my fall. Any physical excitement might be too much for my blood pressure and we were aware of the risk.

While I waited in the library for his arrival, I decided to continue writing. As usual, I lost track of time. It was just after eleven when I heard the front door unlock and open. Papers crunched in his hand. He stopped just as he passed his office/library where I hid inside. I heard him give an appreciative and flirtatious laugh.

"Oh, Nicky," he sighed and walked toward his bedroom and closed the door.

Chapter 38

A Boy of Fourteen

I peeked out of Ryan's office/library and crept into the kitchen to get the pear sparkler, fruit, and chilled glasses.

Everything was in place.

I sat down and nervously waited for Ryan to join me.

He opened his bedroom door.

With long, deliberate strides, he made a path straight for me. Like a towering bear, his big paws seemed ready to take me into his wild nature. Kneeling beside me, he wore sweat pants and a T-shirt instead of the clothes I'd laid out for him. The shirt stretched tight over his chest. I could see the outline of everything I loved.

"Wow, Ryan." My eyes were filled with his body. I handed him a glass of cider trying to stop the force coming at me.

Look at that! He's already filled up the room with his masculine essence. He's going to swallow me in one gulp.

"Lift up, sweetheart." He set both of our glasses down. Placed the pillows a few feet away from us near the edge of the blankets.

I knew what that meant—he wanted to lie down with me.

Was my heart trying to escape from my chest to reach his? It was pounding so hard it felt that way.

"I'm ready to be with my woman." I was held securely in his arms as he lowered us to the pillows. He kissed the pulsing hollow at the base of my throat.

Feeling the perfection of his body on mine . . . was this the same sensation a musician had when writing the final note of a magnificent song, or the emotion of an artist signing their name to their perfect painting?

He took each of my legs in his hands and held them against his hips. Soft lips adored me. His warm tongue tasted me. The roughness of his stubbly cheeks caressed me.

His body revved.

My body responded.

His moans became louder and more dramatic with each movement and kiss. Each tingle let me know—my woman's body was definitely alive. Chills flowed in waves over my neck and shoulders when his tongue lingered in sensitive places. His passion swirled through me like a tornado. The more his belly pushed out the more intense the funnel of desire moved and circled inside me. I wanted to be swept up in his touch, no matter the debris we might leave once our longing subsided.

"I'm hungry." He lifted his head. "So hungry. I want . . ." The weight of him pressed down on me. His mouth touched my lips as if it was the lightest of feathers. "I'm aching for you. The flood in my mind and body . . . I need to be with you in so many ways."

"Ryan." My voice was breathy. The heat blushed up and down my body. Heavy under Ryan's passion, I felt as if hundreds of golden arrows softly teased my warm, moist places. As long as I was in his arms, I knew my logical mind would give way to the craving in my core. "I want to have a romantic evening, too. Can we just talk for a little while? I made this picnic for us."

When he sat up, he lifted my body with his.

"I'm sorry. I just thought—you know, the lighting and uh . . . God, I keep misinterpreting, I wasn't—"

"No, don't." I put my finger on his lips. "Please don't worry or apologize. You didn't misinterpret anything. I just want to talk with you a while, that's all. Once we start kissing . . ."

"All discussions will be over?" Pretending to be bashful, he looked up at me with his eyes hidden under thick eyelashes.

"Is that okay?" I put my hand on his cheek. Turned his head to make him look in my eyes.

"We're here together." He kissed my hand. "This is what I need. Thanks for this."

"Can I ask about your mom?" I breathed deeply, trying to relieve the passion still spinning inside of me. "Are you comfortable talking about her?"

"Not much to say." The way his face knotted, I knew there was plenty to say and more than we'd have time for in only one evening. "We have a strained relationship."

"How so?"

"Ever since my father died, our connection . . . it's awkward. The best way I can explain it to you? She failed me." He shook his head. "I suppose I failed her, too."

"I don't understand." *You're blaming yourself for events and reactions that weren't your fault.* "How could you fail her when you were only fourteen?"

"I couldn't give her what she needed." He turned away and looked at the fire.

"What were you *supposed* to give her?" I pushed for an answer, hoping he'd continue.

The same things you expect of myself, Nicky. You made sure to be dependable, giving every effort to solve your family's problems, providing the stability your think they need even though no one sees what you do. You and Ryan were the fulcrums of your family.

"My ear, my company . . ." His eyebrows knotted the way they did when he was worried or upset. "I don't know. She never understood what was taken from me. The pain I felt from losing my father was overwhelming."

I know how it is when part of your childhood is lost.

"It was so sudden—almost violently so—when I had to take care of my own needs overnight. I didn't know how to move forward. It wasn't fair," his voice trailed off to silence. "I suppose when it comes down to it . . . I haven't forgiven her."

He let out a long sigh as if he'd held in that one breath since he'd been a boy. The room was quiet except for the gentle sounds of the ocean that played on the CD. I sat completely still until Ryan was ready to reveal more.

"Don't misunderstand, I love my mother. Even as she fell apart in her grief she did her best to meet my basic needs. The thing is, I was lost. Why couldn't she see I needed help? She was the adult. How could she not know I was barely hanging on? Walter saw. Wasn't it her duty as my mother to talk to me and find out if I was all right? Wasn't it obvious?" He looked to the balcony; his eyes pooled, fighting the tears. "All I heard was how she suffered. As if I didn't? I was left trying to figure out what my family meant after Dad died. Chris left . . . I lost everyone. Mom should have been stronger." He picked at the pieces of fruit and finally chose one.

How could she know what to do? She was lost. How could she know . . . how could she . . . how could my mother *know what to do?* My mom . . .

His eyes showed a variety of emotions: tears, anger, sadness, regret . . . I could see the little boy in front of me was still hurting.

"When she tries to reach out I can't bring myself to be receptive." He recoiled as if I were she. "All that goes through my mind is it's too late for us."

You hold your mom responsible for not saving you like I do with my mine?

As he paused to take a drink of the pear sparkler, I wondered, was it ever too late to forgive what family had done?

Is there trauma that's too difficult to let go of?

What happens to our bodies if we don't? A broken heart and the emotional vacancies lead to disease, constant illness . . . death?

Do we miss out on the joy life could offer us?

Could Ryan and I have true intimacy—the kind that allowed us to keep our eyes open as we made love, witnessing the sensual beauty of two bodies joining together, or talking about deep emotions without turning away—if we remained within the hurt of our past?

Would we ever escape our self-inflicted prisons?

Was there a point where the hurt and darkness was too much to free us from our shackles, keeping us hostage the rest of our lives and barred from the pure brilliance of life?

Should my sister have withheld forgiveness, when my diseased and addicted father tried to choke her at the dinner table several years earlier? She was within her right to do so, but then what? Would disowning him set her free or torment her? She was raped at fourteen—what if she let the anger and hatred consume her? Would she have gotten as far as she was now in her life?

If I couldn't learn to live and love differently from the twisted way my parents related to each other, should I blame them? How long was it only their fault that I had problems in letting people near me? Should I hold them liable for the rest of my life for all the hurt, grief, and anger they showered on me—wouldn't it ultimately keep me locked down?

Ryan and I wanted to love each other. We committed to it. As we explored the fears we had of opening our hearts to each other, was that really possible if we couldn't stop the dysfunction?

Could we trust *each other* enough?

Could we trust *ourselves* enough?

To reach the depths of intimacy I wanted, I knew I had to be vulnerable. I wondered how I could let myself get there.

Maybe Ryan and I had gone as far as we could and our hearts just too tired and bruised to dig deep for each other.

Maybe all the words and promises in the world wouldn't help us go any further.

"You don't have to continue, Ryan. I completely understand the lack of your family's support and also the way you had to take care of yourself at too young an age."

"I know you do." He gave me a hug. "That's why I'm so comfortable talking with you."

Now I understand—what I suspected from the beginning is true—we are the same.

"One of the worst things about my father's death? Mom depended on me to take care of myself. Okay. I can accept that. But she also expected me to take care of her. It was too much. I was only fourteen—a stupid, rebellious kid who was confused." It seemed as if his strength had returned. He sat up, his back straight, his eyes focused. "I didn't want to be that pillar for her. I needed someone to be a pillar for *me*."

"And yet, you feel guilty." I wanted to give him the confirmation he might still need, even after all these years.

"Yes." He closed his eyes.

"You had every right to feel that way." I took him in my arms. "I wonder if . . . maybe your mom is reaching out to you now."

"Mom and I have had our differences—and our yelling matches. The shouting is over. Now we politely co-exist with each other. It's sad, but we walk on flat ground."

"*Flat ground*?" I needed him to explain.

"I mean we're never emotional with each other. It's like there's no dramatics between us. When the yelling stopped, it's as if the love did, too. The obvious love from parent to child is missing and vice versa. Like the scene you witnessed with Chris and Frances at the hotel—that's my family."

"Your mom is coming to visit you." I traced the tattoo on his chest with my fingertips. "And so soon after her last visit."

"Well, that's . . . I think it's more about *you* rather than me."

"Ryan . . . your mother is coming to make sure the woman you love, loves *you*. That's because *she* loves you. No matter what has happened, *you* are her son. The woman who talked to me on the phone today? She's looking out for you."

"Thank you." He turned his head and quickly wiped his eyes. I put my arms around his neck.

"When I'm with you, I see my life in ways I couldn't have imagined. Everything seems possible when we're together one on one. You are my sweet man." He smiled with a beautiful innocence that seemed new. "Bear with me when I explain how I see it, okay?"

He nodded, picking at his fingernails and wringing his hands.

"Your mom was only thirty-five or so when your dad was killed, right?" I shook my head. "That's so young. My mom was almost the same age when I was *born*, and yours is alone with an adolescent child and another ready for college? Who gives any of us a manual, you know? I understand being resentful. I blame my father *and* mother for leaving Jenise and me to figure out too much. Mom never rescued us. "You know," I swallowed. "My poor sister had to seek out her own therapy? My parents paid for it but were so blind to what she needed they didn't even think to arrange it for her. Poor Jenise, only fourteen." I began to choke up. "Raped, torn apart, and had to fend for herself. Can you imagine?"

Ryan looked down. I could see he felt for her.

"And you know what I did? I condemned her because she didn't take those boys to court. She took the brunt of my dad's bullshit and that's how I thanked her." I folded my hands as if in prayer. "Thank God she forgave me."

"You were too young," Ryan consoled me. "You couldn't understand the effects of what happened to your sister."

"And you were only fourteen." I flattened my hand on his chest.

"Yes," he responded quietly, perhaps forgiving the boy inside himself a little.

Maybe you can forgive yourself, too, Nick.

"Don't you think your mom's visit can mend the hurt between you? I'll bet you could both heal if you approach her right. You could say . . ." I looked at the ceiling, trying to gather my thoughts. "*The way I see it*, or *in my opinion*, or *from my view*. You know what I mean? Those non-confrontational phrases therapists suggest? She's probably afraid to bring up the past in fear of widening the distance between the two of you even more."

His big arms encircled me.

Oh, my big boa constrictor.

"I'm yours." I fell into his embrace. He looked down at me absent of his wry grin. His eyes penetrated my soul.

"You know what I hope for?" he asked.

"Tell me," I pleaded as he so often did to me. "Tell me everything."

"I want to be strong for you so you can play like a little girl." A relaxed easiness fell on his body. "I want you to go into the next part of your life carefree."

"Maybe we could do that for each other." I affectionately squeezed his left pec. "I kind of see us like two little kids." Even in the low lighting, I could see the warm blush that crossed his face. I knew he felt the same way. "On another subject, I, um . . . I found your dad's journal." I looked directly in his eyes, making sure I didn't avoid his stare or the difficult question that came next. "I hope you don't mind I read it. You told me to search everything, but is it okay I did that?"

My anxiety wound inside me.

I wouldn't break eye contact.

He returned the intensity of my gaze, looking into my eyes without wavering. Holding me. Fixed. Strong. Searching.

Chapter 39

Intimacy

"*How* did you feel reading it?" Ryan tapped his fingers on the floor, waiting for my response. "You saw the entries I made, too. Do you think I'm an asshole?"

"No." I twirled the hairs on his forearm. "I thought everything was tragically beautiful. Both of you wrote from your heart. That's why journals are such great tools. And . . . I want to apologize again in case you didn't want me to read it."

"I told you it was all right to look at anything you wanted." His eyes didn't show any upset and I believed he was telling the truth. "How else did you feel about it?"

"Mixed feelings."

"What do you mean?" He put several olives on a paper towel.

"Happy your father wrote he loved and forgave you and you shouldn't feel guilty." I grabbed a pillow and hugged it. "That book is an incredible gift. To see his *actual* thoughts in black and white means you never had to guess what might have been going through his mind. You can read them whenever you want, knowing for certain he forgave you. You have the last pieces of your father in a loving, creative way . . ." I blinked a few times. "He wanted *you* to have it. It's like angels inspired him."

"Yes, it is." His shoulders seemed to drop in relief.

"Most people never get a gift like you did from your dad. They're left with the wish they could have said goodbye and resolved their differences, anger, hurt . . . for the rest of their life. You and your father closed the door in your own way. It was heartbreaking to read about how he sensed the end was near." I paused, dwelling on the horrific emotions his family must have felt. "Still, I'm in awe and feel very blessed you shared it with me. The love you each had for each other were all over those pages."

"I didn't understand everything that book did for me when I was a teenager." Ryan looked toward his office. "I've opened it a lot over the years."

"You're not angry with your dad anymore?"

"No." His voice was shaky. "I still miss him. You know, even now, I sometimes wake up and I can't wait to tell him what's happened. To have been able to introduce you to him . . . he would have loved you instantly."

"I'm sorry I didn't get the chance." I reached for the bottle of pear sparkler and refilled both our glasses. "To your father."

We clinked glasses and each of us took a sip.

"Changing the subject slightly," I placed my glass on the end table. "You know the feelings you shared with me about your brother and how he turned his back on you and your mom? Your dad didn't give *Chris* his journal. As significant and personal as it is, he gave it to *you*. Not even your mother. Just you. So even though you might still resent your brother for leaving, I think your dad understood. In those final days, you were the boy he was thinking of. You made an observation of how the marines could know your father was a hero? People just know, Ryan. He risked his life dragging a friend who was shot and possibly paralyzed back into safety. Those marines knew. And you are his wonderful, sensitive, and heroic son."

He broke down.

I wrapped him in my arms.

Let him sob until the devastation left his body.

I stroked and petted him, knowing he probably hadn't grieved the way he needed to at fourteen. Now at twenty-six, I hoped he could get it out from the depths of his heart.

I played with his hair.

Traced the veins on his forearms.

Massaged his neck.

Kissed his cheeks.

The flames in the fireplace burned softly.

A breeze blew through the screen door.

He lifted his head.

"God, you're . . . I knew you were different. Even last year, I knew. Only seventeen and it was easy to see the brilliance of your spirit. What I didn't realize until recently was your ability to look at my soul. I have a new perspective on so many things because you're the first person who's ever really heard me."

"Thank you," I kissed his lips. "You may not realize it, but even from the beginning, I've heard every word you've ever said to me. Even if it seems I'm not listening, I am. That's my specialty, picking up all the innuendoes, looks, and hidden meanings in someone's words . . . I catch it all because I've stood in the background and watched people for years."

"We're lucky, Nicky."

"I know that now." I sat in his lap and reached for another baguette, topped it with some chicken salad and ate it quickly.

"Chomper," Ryan teased.

"Told you," I put my hand over my mouth as I laughed. Washed it down with another sip of sparkler. "I chomp instead of chew."

"Ah, but you're a spectacular chomper," he toasted me with another sip of sparkler.

"Damn straight!" We clinked glasses once more. He gathered my body against his and my back rested against his luscious volcano. I broke in chills as his hands ran through my hair. "When I spoke to your mother she said you talked about me. I didn't know what to say."

"I told her you were the love of my life and I knew we belonged together," he said confidently. "Have you taken your blood pressure today?"

"A few times." I tilted my head so I could kiss his cheek. " Normal. Ryan, I squiggled from his hold. Wrapped my legs around his hips and hugged him tightly. "I have years before I get my degree and that's such a long time to wait for a child." I cleared my throat. "Do you want marriage and family right away? Your mother said you did."

"I want whatever works for both of us." He avoided my question.

"That's not an answer." I continued looking in his eyes, waiting for a more honest response. In the soft glow from the fireplace, I couldn't miss how the rosiness in his cheeks deepened. It was a telling sign. I didn't know what to do with the information he'd silently revealed. "Let's enjoy the time we have together and not think so far ahead, all right?"

"You're afraid of intimacy," he suddenly shifted the conversation. "You think commitment is the same as sacrificing yourself and being locked down. That's so far from the truth or what I want from you."

"You've said that before, but I've been intimate with you." I was unprepared for his response. "We've been close during our deep discussions; like tonight."

"Maybe so, but you're afraid of it," he pushed on. "If the conversation turns to *you*, it's not very long before you begin to deflect or get anxious. You're so generous listening to others, sharing your views and analysis. You're just as good at pushing away the present so you can dwell on your future. I might know why. At least partially."

"What do you see?"

"Your father." He tightened his embrace.

I pulled back a little.

"Just hear me out," he pleaded. "Try your best to keep an open mind. I can already feel your body tense. Try not to get defensive and shut down."

His request was innocent and genuine. I could see he was afraid to open up any further. Any mention of my father was a contradiction for me. I felt a connection to Dad that made me want to defend him in spite of all the twisted things he'd done.

"I won't get mad or shut down," I promised. "Say whatever you want to me."

"You told me he'd come into your bedroom at night when he was drunk?" His head was down. He had trouble even watching what might be a severe reaction from me.

"Yes."

"When he sat on your bed, he told you not to say anything to your mom about taking you and your sister to the bar so he could drink. You both waited in the truck while he got drunk with his friends, right?"

"Yes."

"You said what you knew he wanted to hear just to get him out of your bedroom as quickly as possible. His breath, the stink of alcohol and the sloppy hugs . . . you wanted them to go away at almost any cost. Is that right?" Ryan's face was twisted.

I nodded in agreement. Tracing his brows with my fingers, I let him know with silent, loving, language, it was okay to continue.

"I think it freaked you out so badly that now, when someone comes close, you want to run. Letting someone get close reminds you of those nights. So when you say, *I don't understand, how things will work*, it's like you're already planning your escape. Maybe down deep you're afraid what we have isn't real. You think a relationship is good only as long as someone needs you for their secrets," Ryan continued courageously. "The minute you're challenged to go deeper, to make yourself vulnerable—especially to me—you start to shut down. Do you see your father's face?"

I looked out the balcony doors.

I tried not to cry.

"I'm suggesting—I'm not attacking your father—I'm just suggesting, he taught you the wrong kind of intimacy. Now you're an adult and ready to go out on your own, but the example of love you've had, what you learned from his actions . . . I think that was a kind of intimacy for you and you know it wasn't right. That's the definition you hide and the feelings you try and keep locked away. I'm showing you a healthy connection. Intimacy with no expectations other than being open and loving. No secrets to keep."

I continued fighting the tears. I didn't want to look at him, but I felt his fingers softly touch my cheek and turn my face to his.

"He took advantage of your innocence. I won't do that. What your father showed you wasn't love. He was an alcoholic doing whatever he could to keep his hopeless addiction a secret. He wanted to cover his shame with the innocence of a little girl. He was sick. You know that. The awful lesson he gave you was lying, covering up, making secret promises . . . all of those. He put his sickness on his daughter."

"I know he did." I finally agreed. "You're exactly right."

"I don't want you to keep secrets. I won't let you go and I won't ask you to stay quiet, Nick."

"I don't mean to react that way," my voice trailed off.

"I know," he paused, waiting for me to wipe my eyes. "Please hear me when I say this."

"I'm . . . I'm ready." I braced for Ryan's truth. "Go on."

"His secrets were twisted. I won't ask you to keep those. I'm right here, standing by you. I promise I'll comfort you whenever you feel like running. If you try to run you'll have to go through me. If you do, you'll feel love, not fear."

I fell into his body and let him put his arms around me. He helped me mend a heart that had been broken since my father hit me on my behind in front of his drunken friend, all those years ago when I wasn't even five-years-old. When I had to stare at my dad's sunken eyes and sagging face, it made me want to escape and run as far as I could. I planned my escape each day.

For so many years, I'd hoped to find the father I knew he could be—the one that used to tinker in our basement and put together a bike for me, or work on his car. Each task was performed with clear, shining eyes and a brilliant mind. I longed for the bright smile I saw years ago—the one without sarcasm laced through it. I'd hoped my father's eyes would light up for me again and he would someday take me under his protection—sober and fully alive in love.

"My heart has ached for you from that first day I saw you last year. I can't find a place in my mind where we're not together. Do you feel that way or am I alone? Be honest."

"I feel it." I was sure I could see little stars in his eyes.

"Whatever path we choose and whatever fears arise, I know we can overcome them." His arms tightened around me.

I felt the comfort I had longed for.

Soothed and secure, I believed the safety he promised was real.

We'd found our connection and could stand together in whatever trauma came. He wasn't afraid to share his hurt. Together we could calm the storms and the frightened child within us.

"Thank you, my sweet Ryan." I kissed him all over his face, one after another. He smiled like an innocent child, his eyes squinting in delight. "I told your mom how much I love you and how she raised an extraordinary son. And . . ." I gulped. Counted to three.

"And what, Nicky?"

Chapter 40

S'mores Were Never So Sexy

"*I* told your mother I'm not going on the road trip with you. I'm so sorry. She made me—well, guess when it came down to it, I made myself feel intimidated."

"Oh, babe." His face showed disappointment. "Why?"

"She was so commanding . . . the questions she asked . . . it was as if I could feel her judgment right through the phone. It's um, if I go with you, she won't take me seriously. The inflection in her voice—there was no mistake in her mind I'd be your mistress or something."

"Even if that's her opinion, that's not—"

"Not what you think," I confirmed. "I know. I'm saying . . . some gut reaction is telling me her opinion of me would lesson. The acceptance from my parents and your mother is crucial. In fact, I think her opinion will matter even more than *my* mom's."

"I don't care. I just want us together."

"My reasoning sounds ridiculous. I agree it does," I interrupted. "I can't shake some of religious stuff, I admit, but still, I don't want her to think I'm using sex to open your heart. We've only really been together a few weeks, and—"

"Nicky, you don't understand that part of intimacy yet, but sex open hearts, encourages communication, sharing, and allows people to drop their defenses. It helps people feel gentler to one another. It's so much more than only physical. We've been—"

"I know," I agreed. "We've been working toward those intimate moments for more than a year. With your mother though, something in the way she asked . . . she's watching my moves. We need her on our side if you're going to mend fences." I put my arm through his. "Whatever happens with us, I know who you are. You're magnificent. Please be patient."

I kissed him.

Adjusted my position to get closer.

My hip touched his.

Took his hand in mine.

"Will you meet my mother when she visits?" He squeezed my hand.

"Of course, I will. A big part of her visit is to check me out."

"Yeah." Ryan smiled and couldn't help but laugh. Was he touched that his mother might care about his life that much?

"She worries that I'll break your heart," I told him. "I'm afraid I will, too. I'm trying to be careful and then something comes up I haven't experienced. I'm still discovering myself and I know I test your patience. There's never been anyone who's touched me and spoken to me like you have." I dipped my finger into the chicken salad and started to lick if off. Ryan lifted it to his lips, gently nibbled, sucked and pulled it in and out of his mouth. *Oh, my God! I'm losing it!* "I . . . I . . ."

"Did I interrupt you?" his voice dipped low.

"God, Ryan. You're . . ."

"Here for you." He licked his lips. "Continue."

"I can feel your love and I want to believe our love is meant to be forever. I hear what you're saying about sex. My sister shared the same things with me about opening a person's soul to the entire universe if the sex is right. We haven't nearly explored everything but even the intimacy we've shared has opened my heart. I see . . . forever—that's what I want with you. I want to gaze at those stars in the sky."

He caressed my hair.

A hunger shone in his eyes and I knew my living room picnic would no longer satisfy him.

"Tell me about your writing." My chest felt too small to contain the joy I felt when he asked me about it. "Tell me how it moves you. Is it your passion?"

Once again he began snacking. It made me feel good that he enjoyed the little parts of my picnic. This time he assembled his S'mores. He picked up a marshmallow and popped it in his mouth. Placed another on a skewer to roast. I giggled as he walked on his knees to the fireplace.

He talks about my *butt—his is pretty damn juicy.*

As he knelt by the fire, I imagined us camping together on some random weekend. I'd watch him carry a stack of wood in his arms, his muscles bulging, make a fire, erect our tent and lay out the sleeping bag. Sparks and embers cracked, popped, and shot into the night sky.

"Do you want one?" He broke my dream bubble, pointing to his roasting marshmallow.

"I'll wait a while longer, thanks. I'm thrilled that you're enjoying what I prepared. What a boyfriend you are!"

"I enjoy *you*, lady. So whatever you prepare is a bonus."

He blew out his flaming marshmallow, put it on top of the chocolate he'd placed on one of the graham crackers, and then squished the entire sandwich with a second cracker. He licked a bit of melting chocolate from the side, walked back on his knees and sat down next to me.

"Well," I swiped my finger across his bottom lip to clean a bit of melted chocolate from his face and put it on my tongue. I could see the delight in his eyes, perhaps because I was growing bolder. "Back to writing, I've always loved it. I've kept journals since I was a little girl. I store them in my hope chest."

"You showed me when I spent the night in your bedroom," he reminded.

"Right. That's . . . yeah, I did. Journaling became a tool that has helped me sort through so much. Even now, when I review what I wrote from years ago? I understand situations differently. Putting it on paper is all the difference when it comes to patterns, meanings and behaviors I may have missed. Through my reviews, I see how I could have changed the outcome by changing my reaction."

"Give me an example." He continued eating his dessert. "I want to know everything."

I know you do. You never give up. Oh, those wonderful, thick, long, fingers of yours, the way they hold your dessert . . . it looks so small in your hands . . . your hands . . . I wish . . .

He took a bite of the melting, chocolaty mess. The marshmallow oozed out and covered his lips and his fingertips. His tongue entranced me. I watched it closely. Licked the sticky dessert from his hands, wanting his tongue inside of my mouth.

Transfixed on his eyes as they focused on his task-at-hand—how best to eat the remaining sweetness without making more of a mess—was a treat of my own.

His brow furled.

His nose wrinkled.

He switched hands.

Cleaned his fingertips on one of them. Switched to the other. Began again as he tried to keep up with the sticky sweetness.

I giggled to myself.

He tried to stay cool while licking and sucking his fingers.

No longer able to resist, I "stood" on my knees and moved in front of him. I wanted the man who was mine in every way, especially witnessing the innocent boy in front of me relishing his S'mores.

I lifted his chin.

The corner of his mouth hinted at the eroticism of eating a hot, melting, sticky, dessert.

Without any explanation, I boldly took control of Ryan.

I leaned into him.

Ran my hands down his muscular arms.

Covered his cheeks in kisses.

Licked both lips slowly.

I knew I had him. I moaned, tasting my irresistible, sexy, baseball player boyfriend.

"Mmm, that tastes so good," I said with a slow, exaggerated tone that purred. "I couldn't resist watching my sexy boyfriend play with my dessert." I laughed a little, considering the suggestive innuendo I'd just presented.

"Are you flirting with me, Ms. Young?" He raised an eyebrow, obviously enjoying my frisky attitude.

"I'm not only flirting," I ran my hands through his hair. "I'm saying it plain and simple . . . I want more."

"More, huh?" He put down the dessert. Pulled me close. My breath escaped me with the force of our bodies coming together. We held on to each other's back, arms, wrists, and waists.

My hair tumbled around my shoulders.

His hair was tossed and ready for me to do whatever I wanted to it. A dozen possibilities rushed through my mind.

"I'm all in, sweet boyfriend." I traced the phoenix tattoo on his big bicep and swayed into him, my body surrendering and softening.

Ryan gathered me inside his masculine envelope. He surrounded me in every way. Nuzzled his nose against my temple. Brushed my lips with a delicate kiss.

It was more than an embrace.

As he lowered my body on the fluffy blankets and lay on top of me . . . it was as if he took me to the stars and back.

End of Part I

Although you may not realize it, authors really need your review. Please leave one at least on Amazon, and if you have time, also on Goodreads on my author site, Pamela Taeuffer.

Here are the links:

Amazon: bit.ly/AmazingHeart

Goodreads: bit.ly/GoodreadsAmazingHeart

I hope you enjoyed the first four novels of The Broken Bottles Series, Part I, and have gained some insight into the difficulties of forming relationships of all sorts when growing up in an alcoholic family.

I invite you to read the preview of Part II where Nicky continues to mature and grow, taking bigger risks and considers major shifts in her life—shifts she is certain she needs to break her family's dysfunctional heritage.

Please sign up for my newsletter and e-mail me to receive a free preview of book five, *Rising Heart, Part II* of the Broken Bottles Series. In your subject within your email be sure to reference: *RISING HEART.*

Broken Bottles Series,
Part II

Hello readers!

With book four, *Amazing Heart,* Part I has ended.

While Nicky continues to fight some of the same battles as in *Shadow Heart, Book 1*, especially with sex and intimacy, she is not at the same place.

She's more aware now of what she doesn't want. She's able to stand up for herself in ways she never had before. She is close again with her sister and has made new friends, Tara, Alex, and Ethan. New friends are major steps for her, and to have made three is a celebration!

As much as her family has let her down, she still wants a respectful and loving relationship with them. Nicky is trying to understand her mother and father differently, perhaps considering how their own pasts has shaped their present.

Full-on sex is still an uncertainty. It's more than sex. For Nicky, it's letting someone into her protection. She's kept her love secret and well shielded, hiding her darkness, insecurity and vulnerability. Letting someone come that close is still too frightening. She is trying to come to terms with her internal battle—spiritual beliefs verses desire. Those religious practices formed during the turbulent years of her father's addiction—and they've entwined with her awakening passions. If they are to be pulled away, it will be a slow, methodical process.

* * * * *

Part II has Nicky exploring love and sex in a deeper and more sensual way. These novels definitely call to the New Adult, College Bound and the Transitioning Woman.

Embracing the vivid, tasteful, details of physical love, while trying to bring the intimacy she never imagined possible to her life should be easy, right? But think about this . . . are you comfortable with your lover coming up behind you in surprise with a sexy whisper in your ear? Can you look into your lover's eyes as you talk through anger, or passionately making love, asking for what you need even when it comes to orgasm or putting yourself first?

Another side of Nicky is maturing. Ethan is now a close friend. She is about to meet Ryan's mother and still needs to confront her childhood friend, Jerry. How will he react to the news? Is he still in denial about his own meanderings or will he admit he's already moved on?

And then, there is Jesse Johnson, the woman from Ryan's past that just doesn't give up easily.

How will love unfold with Ryan? He is sought after by dozens of women. Will she see a man who is different from the sensitive, loving one she's come to know? What will she do with the mature world she feared—one of desire and sex?

If she's really matured, she'll make an informed decision of where she wants her life to go. Will that be an independent woman, free and unencumbered, her whole life ahead of her, at Stanford?

I hope to see you in Part II!

Resources

Books

Dirty Words, Ellen Sussman
How to Please a Woman In & Out of Bed, Daylee Deanna Schwartz
It Will Never Happen to Me, Claudia Black, PhD
Sexy Words for Writers, Stefanie Olsen
The Emotion Thesaurus, Angela Ackerman and Becca Puglisi
Thinking Like A Romance Writer, Dahlia Evans
The Bald-Headed Hermit & The Artichoke, A.D. Peterkin
The Complete Idiot's Guide to Amazing Sex, Sari Lockner, Ph.D.
The Romance Writer's Phrase Book, Jean Kent and Candace Shelton

Organizations/Web sites

Information on rape - www.sexualityresources.com
What to expect reporting rape - www.crimescene.com
Pandora's Project - www.pandys.org
Adult Children of Alcoholics: www.adultchildren.org
Adult Children of Dysfunctional Families –
www.AdultChildrenofDysfunctionalFamilies.com
Al-Anon/Alateen – www.al-anon.org
Alcoholics Anonymous – www.alcoholics-anonymous.org
Co-Anon Family Groups – www.co-anon.org
Co-dependents Anonymous – www.codependents.org
Eating Addictions Anonymous –
www.dcregistry.com/users/eatingaddictions

National Association for Children of Alcoholics – www.nacoa.org
Overeaters Anonymous – www.overeatersanonymous.org
Women for Sobriety – www.womenforsobriety.org
Helping Family Members of Friends – www.ncadd.org
Ten Ways Families Can Help – www.thecounselingcenter.org
Adults & Drug Abuse Affects Everyone in the Family –
www.adultchildren.org

Non-profit organization that provides information

Survivors of sexual assault: The Joyful Heart Foundation: Provides information of all sorts, writers, actors, programs, news releases, and more on sexual assault and domestic violence: www.joyfulheartfoundation.org

Acknowledgements

*A*s with any life project, there are many people who influenced my journey. From friends who exist only in my memories, to people who have crossed my path in sweet or dramatic ways, I hold all of you to my heart, even if you're not mentioned below.

For my beautiful sister, whose life ended much too early—I understand you more now than I ever did.

For my father, I wish I had the maturity back then to have understood. I couldn't have stopped you, but I would've spoken differently. You gave me so many twisted gifts, and I thank you in spite of everything.

Claude, my husband, and Aaron, my son, I love you guys so much that sometimes I think I'm sick because the hurt is so deep and the joy is so mountainous.

Louise—I couldn't have done this without you.

My sweet girlfriends from childhood—Colleen, Patty, Lorraine, Kathie, Marilyn

TS Babes—(Santo, Spanky, Uno, GG, Wiseone, BL, Nine, Catnip xxoo) you know who you are, thanks for so much fun during my research.

My editors, Catharine Bramkamp, Robbi Sommers Bryant, and Crissi Langwell, you are awesome and have gone above and beyond!

Mom, you still have problems saying I love you. I get it now.

Special Offer for Readers of Amazing Heart:

For live chats, advance chapters, exclusive announcements, pre-publication dates of future books, and free giveaways, visit:

Website: www.PamelaTaeuffer.com

Newsletter: www.PamelaTaeuffer.com/newsletter

Blog: www.pamelataeuffer.com/dare-to-be-vulnerable

E-mail: PamelaTaeuffer@gmail.com

Facebook: www.facebook.com/pamela.taeuffer.9

Twitter: @PamelaTaeuffer

Pinterest: www.pinterest.com/ptaeuffer/broken-bottles

About the Author

Pamela Taeuffer, Biography

My passion is writing books that tell a story and family saga of leaving old fears behind through a love story. My first series, Broken Bottles, details those fears of growing up in a family battling alcoholism. Along with the struggle and pain of a parent's rage, I hope to reveal strength, intelligence, and survival. The challenge is to love intimately in all relationships. For children of trauma, it can take years to let another person come close. When they do? It's like rainbows cover their heart.

You'll read how my characters slowly become vulnerable, reach for the intimacy that has eluded them all of their life, and how they let go of their fears. They struggle and risk everything to trust others—and themselves. My stories are about daring to take the baby steps that let them really come alive and in every way, experience and give love.

MAKING MONEY TO CREATE: The property management and vacation rental company I run with my husband and son in Sonoma County, California allows me to have my creative life. I love where I live and work, and wouldn't trade being born and raised in San Francisco. My father introduced me to baseball when I was six. I've rung a cable car bell, driven a streetcar and saw the old rock legends like Jimmy Hendrix, The Doors, and Jefferson Airplane.

WHAT I'VE DONE/AM DOING – IT'S A JOURNEY OF DREAMS: Broken Bottles is a four part series. Three books, *Shadow Heart, Fire Heart,* and *Jagged Heart* are ready. Soon to follow is *Amazing Heart.* I'm honored to have three poems in an anthology called *The Beats Go On,* a story in *Sisters Born, Sisters Found,* and a story in the anthology, *Untold Stories.* I have released the first book in a series for introverts called, *The Introverts Guide to the Galaxy: Attending Conferences.*

My dream? To create beautifully decorate and custom journals with gorgeous paper that accompany with each book series: *The Introvert's Journal, A Family Saga Journal, My Body's Journal,* and *Trauma: You Can't Stop Me Journal.* Journaling was a lifesaver for me. I was in shock. You may be in shock. Don't let that keep your heart frozen!

Also Available by Pamela Taeuffer

Shadow Heart

What if you were afraid to even turn the doorknob to your front door because of the family dysfunction that waited inside: rage, mental and physical abuse, the fear of sharing love, or waiting for the embrace of your mother. What would it take to bring you out of the shadows, breaking out of the numbness you've used to protect your heart? Could you take a risk that might change everything? A sexy, professional baseball player wants my mind, body and heart. All my life I've controlled who's gotten close. Risk means terror. This is the slow, intimate reveal of how I learned to

trust myself, let go of my fears and transitioned into joy.

Fire Heart

My heart is on fire. For the first time in my life I am awake and the desires I've pushed down are smoldering. The shadows of my youth dare me to step away from them. I've just come of age and there is one thing I know—I want to live differently than my parents—an alcoholic father and co-dependent mother. I know I need to forgive them. I must learn to trust myself and take a risk. That means being vulnerable and letting another close. But when we did that in our house, rage and abandonment followed. I have to open my heart and learn to trust myself so I can trust another. I dream of letting go of old fears, daring to be loved, and transitioning into joy.

Jagged Heart

I walked quietly so I didn't disturb the fragile web that stretched throughout our home. Nothing good would last; I would ultimately be abandoned; my feelings didn't matter; as long as I looked okay, I was okay. My name is Nicky Young. I stay away from hurt by not risking too much. Ryan Tilton, a professional baseball player, has swept me off my feet and I can't let go. I refuse to be intimate, but then I'm desperate to fall into his arms. Adding to my fears, I've learned about Jesse, a beautiful and successful artist and socialite from his past, may have moved to San Francisco to follow him. My boundaries are softening, melting, being redefined, becoming *jagged*.

Rising Heart
Coming 2017

I am in his arms, a fire is burning both in the fireplace and in my body as I am slowly undressed and feel his lips move down my belly. Our spirits, our rapture, are finally coming together. The only way I feel on this evening . . . is open. The gentle hands that caress me, the soothing words I hear that speak about love make my heart rise like I've come from deep water and can finally see the surface. After battling my fears of abandonment and of Ryan's past seems to have all faded to this—slow, sensual, intimacy that has been waiting to reveal itself to me.

Our time is short. Even as we've come back together, he is leaving to play baseball far away from me. The empty sadness doesn't take long to well up as I watch him leave. And there's his past. There is a woman who won't let go. I feel her circling, waiting for an attack. And finally, it comes. I don't know if I can survive this love. The fears and doubts of growing up in family dysfunction and addiction won't let me go. Do I continue to believe our love can overcome the hurt from our childhood?

www.ingramcontent.com/pod-product-compliance
Lightning Source LLC
Chambersburg PA
CBHW050908250626
47155CB00001B/152